The Murdered Wife

VICTOR MOSS

ISBN: 978-1-961472-68-6

Disclaimer

This book is strictly a fictional account of the police officers and detectives of the Denver Police Department including descriptions of physical settings and the Department's rules and procedures. This book is strictly for entertainment. All characters are imaginary, and any similarity to actual persons is simply a coincidence.

The author is not aware of any criminal or corrupt cops as described in the book. Instead, the author has deep admiration for the hard work and dedication of the men and women who chose to serve and protect society even though their lives may be taken away from them in an instant.

Dedication

To my wife, children and grandchildren who have given me support
and encouragement to keep writing.

Acknowledgments

I thank my daughter, Katherine Stafford and my friend, Melanie Tappen for their advice and suggested corrections. I also thank my sister and her husband, Mary and Duane Janssen for their encouragement and their useful comments and suggestions.

But above all, I have enormous praise for my wife, Rita Moss, for her support and the many hours she spent reading and discussing each segment. Her suggestions and editing were truly invaluable.

Table of Contents

CHAPTER ONE

Present day, Denver, Colorado.

AMANDA ELLIS had an awfully bad day. First, it was with her husband, Steven; then, it escalated to severe conflicts with her employers. The problems piled on early. It was evident to her that her husband was having yet another affair. Because of his roving eye for women, their three-year marriage was once again in jeopardy. Forgiving him on at least two previous occasions, she again knew he was involved in another fling. This time with a sexy assistant in the office, Tina Dionisio. She noticed on a few occasions how the two flirted with each other, just like two high school kids. And she realized that Tina would love to take her place as Steven's wife.

He came home at 11:30 the night before from a supposed urgent business meeting. She smelled the faint odor of perfume on his clothes. She had noticed that same fragrance for the past two weeks as he sheepishly wandered home at all hours of the night. The perfume reminded her of a particular brand that she sampled numerous times at Nordstrom—that of Versace Yellow Diamond, the same brand that Tina wore at an office party and then at a BBQ in their backyard.

Amanda confronted Steven with her suspicion of the affair with Tina. He did not deny it; instead, he belligerently told her to "Mind your own business, you bitch." With that said, he stormed off and bedded for the night in the guest room. She cried, tossed, and turned all night long. The fight that next morning turned out to be a doozy of a shouting match. At first, he denied having an affair, but then he admitted it. "Just live with it. That's the way I am, and you can't change me since I can't change you, it seems."

"It's with Tina, isn't it?" His cheeks puffed out, and his face turned red. "Well, isn't it?" He remained silent for a few minutes. He took a deep breath and calmed himself. Finally, he admitted it and apologized but seemed to lack sincerity. "You bastard, you no good SOB. I've had it with you. I'm finally filing for divorce," she screamed in rage, "I'm going to ruin you. I'll take everything you got, you bastard. You won't have a pot to pee in after I'm through with you." Steven's eyes blazed with anger as he took two steps toward her. His fingers were balled into a fist. He raised his arm as if to strike her, but then, quickly thinking better of it, he lowered his fist.

For a minute, he stared at Amanda with his blazing blue eyes, then turned and stomped out of the kitchen. The spring door to the backyard slammed shut. He strode to the detached garages in the back, raised the garage door, and out of anger, struck the hood of the Lexus LX SUV with his fist, hurting his hand and leaving a slight dent in his car. The tires squealed as he hit the accelerator pedal, almost striking the curb on the other side of the street. Luckily, there were no other cars or pedestrians walking to the adjacent park at the time.

Later as Amanda walked to the garage, she saw the open garage door left unattended by Steven. She shut it and then opened the door to her Mercedes S-Class convertible. Still trembling from the fight, she headed for work in the Cherry Creek area of Denver. Deeply regretting what came out of her mouth when she yelled at her husband, she knew she had made a huge mistake. That was the first time she ever threatened him with a divorce. She knew Steven's faults, bit the bullet and lived with them. She did not want a divorce. As an investment banker, Steven averaged a million dollars a year in income, and she, herself, did not do too badly as an architect in a large international construction firm with a salary of a quarter of a million. They lived a good lifestyle, traveled extensively, stayed at the best hotels, ate at the most prestigious restaurants, had three homes, and belonged to two country clubs. She really did not want to give all of that up. She would have to make it all right again with her husband when she got home. *If, of course, he'll be there.* She thought. *I'll have to make it work.* Not waiting for later, she touched his name on the phone, but after several rings, it went to voicemail.

With a massive pit in her stomach, Amanda exited the elevator on the ninth floor and walked into the architectural department of Jonas, Wentworth, and Briggs International Contractors, better known as JWB Contractors. Too riled up to work, she dragged herself to her cubicle, sat down at her desk, and stuffed her brown Gucci leather bag in the desk drawer. Leaning with her elbows on the highly polished wooden desk, she cupped her face in her hands. She sat there like that for at least five minutes before she decided that she needed to work. The deadline for her part of the project in Dubai was only a few days away.

Standing up at her drafting table, she noticed a sheet of new material requirements for her project. Amanda felt the veins in her temples throb as she reviewed the new specifications. *Oh my God!* She thought. *They want me to replace the material in the project. Less rebar, inferior grade steel panels, and they'll probably mix more sand than cement in the mortar. That's just blatant fraud. I suspected they did this for years, but now I'm involved with it, and I'm the one that'll have to sign off on it.* She searched her desk, looking for the original specs she was given, but they were no longer there. *They took them off my desk! Wow! I must do something, or I'll be in trouble when the hot weather and winds in Dubai deteriorate the breezeway affecting the floors above.* She understood immediately that with just that adjustment to the project of lesser and inferior materials, the company would make a bigger profit. *And that's just my project. What about the rest of the building?* At that moment, she was determined that she had to protect herself and somehow let the Dubai people know about it. *I never thought I'd ever become a whistle-blower.*

The file room was on the eighth floor. Amanda scampered there using the stairs, hoping to find a copy of the original plans and specifications of the project. Being an employee of five years, they trusted her enough with the key. She entered the large room stacked with five-drawer filing cabinets along the walls and in the center, turned on the humming fluorescent lights, and shut the door behind her. Fortunately, the projects were well-indexed. Finding the thick file, she quickly gazed through it, looking for her assignment within the numerous plans and papers. She noticed the cost estimate of the entire project was more than two billion dollars and running her index finger down to the breezeway that she worked on, it showed a figure of three and a quarter million. She whistled to herself out of surprise at what they were charging. At the end of the quote, she saw the signatures of the developers executing the agreement. She quickly pulled out her iPhone and shot a photo of the names. Then she went back and took another photo of the cost of her project. Thumbing further, she found the specifications that she had originally received for the breezeway and quickly took a photo and placed her phone into the back pocket of her tan pants.

Suddenly, the door opened. A security guard entered. The gaze in his eyes advised her that he was not pleased finding her there and that she would be in trouble. She noticed for the first time that above the door was a video camera that must have caught her. "You scared me, Jason," she said to the unpleasant guard whom she had known since she began working at the place.

"Mrs. Ellis, you shouldn't be in here without authorization." His voice was gruff and grating. "You have to leave now, and this will be reported to Mr. Briggs."

"Jason, I have every right to be here. I needed to clarify the specifications of my project."

"Tell that to the big boss, then."

"Of course, no problem."

On the way to her cubicle, her heart beat a mile a minute, her breathing shallow.

Approaching her workstation, Roger Benton, the chief architect and her immediate boss, wearing one of his bespoke silk suits, a custom shirt with embroidered initials, and a red power tie, walked over to Amanda. She had worked with him for the past two years and hated the man. *Surely, he doesn't know I was in the file room this fast, does he?* With his sleazy smile and bright teeth standing out on his olive skin, he greeted her and immediately placed his arm around the back of her neck, his right hand falling off her shoulder, his long fingers touching the top of her breast. Amanda quickly pulled away from him, giving him a disapproving look. *I'm so sick and tired of this crap from him. One more time and I'm going to sue him and this company for sexual harassment. What do I have to lose now? I'll probably be fired anyway.*

"We're kind of behind on the project you're working on," Roger said, not at all happy with the hard look she had given him. He considered himself to be a real ladies' man and thought that Amanda should have been pleased that he embraced her. "The developers in Dubai want to see drawings of the breezeway."

"I stayed late and finished them last night. But you threw a curveball at me. You changed the specs and I can't sign off on the inferior material."

"We analyzed it, and they're fine. Just amend your design a little, if necessary, but those are the specs we want you to use.

Amanda's anger rose within her. "I can't do that. I believe it would make it structurally unsafe."

"Look, Amanda, you're being unreasonable. I've never seen you gun-shy before. Just do it, okay. I'll sign off on it if you're afraid." He started to walk away, but as he did, he slapped Amanda on her butt, laughing.

Amanda lost it. She screamed out loud enough that the other four male architects could hear, "I'm not going to put up with your sexual harassment any longer, you bastard. I'm going right now to the president's office. Expect a huge lawsuit against you personally and this company for millions. Do you understand? That's it. I can't take it anymore. Every day you touch me, and I hate it. This morning was the last straw."

Roger turned white as a sheet. "Amanda, don't do anything rash. I'm so sorry. I'll never touch you again. You should've said something before. Please, I'll make it up to you. But don't file a complaint. It'll ruin me. I'll be fired and no one will ever hire me."

"You should've thought of that before. Sorry, just doesn't cut it. I let it slide these two years because I didn't want to get fired. No one ever believes the woman. But this was a bad day for you to harass me. I'm going to get you. I hope you'll never work at any corporation ever again. I'm going straight to the Civil Rights Commission, and I'll call the TV stations and the Denver Post." Amanda snatched her purse from her desk drawer and left for the tenth floor.

Roger sat down in an empty chair near him. His breathing was labored, and he felt as though he'd have a stroke. He thought he had better go up to the President's office as well and see if he could mitigate the damage. When he got there, he heard Amanda's shouting voice in Simon Briggs' office. The door was open, and he heard the woman unleashing anger on the man. He heard her complain about the sexual harassment and then she switched subjects and began accusing Briggs and the company of fraud by removing and substituting inferior materials. She added that they were committing further fraud by inflating labor and material cost. "I can prove it all," she said. "I'm sure the developers in Dubai would like to have this information. I know their names and they'll know all about it soon, as well as the public through the news media."

"That's why you were snooping without authorization in the file room," Briggs said, his voice deep. Under these circumstances, Amanda was surprised at how cool he looked. She knew she was red with anger, ready to explode. Her body was tied up in knots, and her throat parched. "So, you think you have adequate information just by taking a few photos, do you? Nothing you're screaming at me bothers me. You have nothing, and I don't appreciate your threats. Do what you have to. We, as a company, did nothing wrong."

"We'll see about that. Tomorrow when I blow the proverbial whistle, you'll change your tune."

"Mrs. Ellis, please calm down, go home early and think this matter through. Before you try to contact anyone, come to my office at nine tomorrow morning and we'll work everything out. We will solve your problem with Roger to your satisfaction and we'll go over the issues that you have uncovered. It's not too late. We can take care of it. If we made a mistake in the calculations, we can remedy that."

"What about the entire project, not just my part of it? And I bet if someone inspects all your projects, they'll find more fraud."

"I'll let you go over all our projects for the past year and you can decide if there was any fraud, okay?"

Amanda took a few deep breaths. Even with a pounding head, she managed to cool off a bit. "All right, then. If you give me assurances that the immediate problems will be resolved, I'll wait until after tomorrow's meeting to decide whether I'll go public or not."

At home, Amanda ran into Nellie, their cleaning lady who came in daily for four hours to clean the big mansion. "Oh, you're home early. Are you all right? You look so tired and upset. Not quite as upset as Mr. Ellis was this morning. I just drove up, and I heard the shouting."

"Yes, thank you, we had a small argument, that's all. I'm quite fine. I'll know better tomorrow how fine I am." Nellie looked puzzled but didn't say anything. "But why are you still here?"

"Oh, I decided to wash the insides of the windows on the third floor."

Annoyed with the maid always trying to work extra hours for more pay, whether it was necessary or not, Amanda said in a rather nasty voice, "Nellie, from now one, don't do anything extra than what you're hired to do unless I ask you to. I'll pay you this time, but don't count on it in the future."

"Oh, I'm sorry, Mrs. Ellis. I just wanted to surprise you with clean windows, that's all. I won't charge you anything extra."

"No, I'll pay you. You did the work and should get paid. But please check with me before doing anything special."

"Yes, yes. Of course. Thank you very much." Nellie shuddered at Amanda's cold glare. She quickly gathered her things, said "Goodbye," and left.

Amanda collapsed into the nearest chair in the parlor, leaned back against the soft down cushion, and stretched out her legs. She felt bad at the words she had with Nellie, but it seemed she constantly had to reprimand her for one thing or another. She had threatened to fire her, but her performance did not improve much. She could have handled it better with the poor woman, but she was so sick and tired of everyone. She sat in the chair for almost two hours. Her brain was drained, but she had enough energy to review the photos that she had taken from the file. On a whim, she sent the pictures of the documents to a friend without any explanation. Afterward, she felt so fatigued with no strength left in her limbs. It was now past dinner time and Steven had not returned, which left her wondering if he would return tonight at all.

She finally forced herself into the kitchen and made herself a turkey and avocado sandwich, washing it down with a glass of chardonnay left over from the bottle opened yesterday. After stacking the dishes in the sink, she walked aimlessly around the house, glancing at the various bronze and marble statues in their collection while not paying any particular attention to them. Her mental fatigue was beginning to overcome her as she walked up the staircase to her bedroom and collapsed on the bed. She slept until seven the next morning.

There was no evidence that her husband had come home. Crying, she showered and dressed in her size two blue business suit. Not hungry, Amanda skipped breakfast, set the security alarm and walked to the detached garages that were built adjacent to Cheesman Park. She was nervous about the meeting with Simon Briggs. She knew it would be extremely unpleasant and she would certainly be fired. With her mind so focused on the upcoming meeting and wondering where her husband spent the night, she sat down behind the steering wheel of her convertible. Shutting the car door and right before starting the car to back it out onto the street, out of the corner of her eye, she suddenly noticed a person in dark clothing and a black hoodie speed in from the direction of the park into the garage. Before she could react to the intruder, she felt pain in the muscle of her upper arm. She saw who it was behind her and tried to scream, but the intruder with a gloved hand covered her mouth and nose. She almost passed out from the lack of oxygen. When the hand was lifted, she sucked in the air and tried to scream again, and the hand flew to her mouth and nose again. When the hand was released, she felt another sharp, stabbing pain in the muscle of her arm. The intense, excruciating pain and the near suffocation caused her to pass out. When Amanda came to, she felt her strength dissipate. She struggled to reach out for her Gucci purse to grab her phone to call for help, but the phone was gone. In anguish, she threw the purse onto the passenger side floor.

Mustering whatever energy she could, she forced herself out of the car and fell to the floor. Amanda's mind was fuzzy, unable to think straight, but somehow reasoned that she had to make it to her house. She moved the door of the car out of the way and crawled toward the door that would take her to the covered walk leading into the house. She made it to the door, rose up on her knees, and attempted to reach the doorknob. With extreme taxing effort, she forced her hand to grab hold of the knob. However, she lacked the strength, no matter how hard she tried, to twist the round knob enough to open the door. Total confusion and overwhelming fatigue took over her body and forced her to drop her arm. She began to sweat profusely as the inside of her head swayed and spun. Now the desire for deep sleep overtook her, not caring where she was. Trying at a feeble attempt to cry out, her jaw locked up. She collapsed onto the cement floor. A few minutes later, her brain and body shut down. Amanda lost consciousness.

CHAPTER TWO

THE BLAZING sun began to heat up the city after a cool night, typical for July in Colorado. However, steel gray clouds gathering over the Rocky Mountain peaks began their encroachment into the brilliant blue sky of the Denver metro area. Needed rain was predicted as part of the yearly monsoon season, and it looked as if it would be a drencher by late afternoon. Detectives Clint Hawk and Nora Ricci were en route to investigate the death of a woman on Humboldt Street in the Cheesman Park area of Denver. The detectives didn't have far to go from their Sixth District station on Colfax and Washington Streets. Except for seemingly hitting every red traffic light on the route, it would not have taken them long at all to arrive at the scene.

Neither said a word to the other for a minute or so. That was about as long as Nora could remain quiet. "You know, Clint, those mountains are calling me. They say, 'come to me, come to me. It's cool here; come to me.' Wouldn't it be great right now to turn this car around and head out there? We could stroll along the quaint shops of Breckenridge, get coffee and pastry, and then drive over to Vail. I know of a great German restaurant there that I have to absolutely visit when I'm there. What do you think about that?"

"Nora, not in this bucket of bolts that we're driving. This old Crown Victoria had seen better days years ago," Hawk turned toward Nora. Now she displayed a mischievous smile and batted her long dark eyelashes at Hawk. Hawk could not help but smile back. Actually, his smile turned into a laugh. "You know what I think, Nora? I think that you need a vacation, that's for sure."

"The advantage of living along the front range is that we could have mini-vacations every weekend. Just a short trip to the mountains, and I feel like I'm in another world." Nora hesitated for a moment. "Actually, you're the one that needs the vacation. After all, just two or three days as a new detective, and you almost got killed four times. If you were a cat, you would only have five lives left."

"I guess it's all part of the job, and you're exaggerating the danger."

"What do you mean, 'exaggerating the danger?" Look. The first time was when you were shot at by one of the corrupt cops. Luckily, you spotted him and ducked down in time. The second time another bad cop threatened you with his gun, and fortunately, you saved yourself by crashing the car into an embankment at a high rate of speed. I betcha you're still stiff and sore from that, aren't you?" Before Hawk could reply, Nora rattled on. In reality, that collision was very severe, and his neck, shoulders and back were killing him. "The third time, I stopped the killer before he could get to you in the hospital. And the fourth time was when we were both awfully close to being killed in my house. I still haven't fixed the ceiling from the hole left by the bullet."

"I guess we were more than lucky," Hawk said. "Hopefully, we won't get ourselves into a jam like that again. I never experienced anything like that in my six years as a cop on patrol. And you'd think that's a more dangerous job than a detective."

"I just have to continue as your bodyguard, that's all." Nora laughed infectiously. Hawk returned the laugh. He loved her laugh; it always lifted his spirts.

"Well, I must admit that you are a good bodyguard with your quick Taekwondo that saved me twice."

"Well, finally, you admit it." She laughed again and reached over to stroke the back of his head.

"Nora, I love when you do that, but while working together as partners, we have to act as professionals."

"Oh, sure. But that'll be hard to do. I can't seem to keep my hands off you," she laughed teasingly. "Ooh, looks like we're here judging by all the emergency vehicles. Maybe I should give you a kiss before we go." She giggled at her joke. *She really believes we're officially dating,* Hawk thought; *otherwise, she knows darn well that was totally inappropriate to say while on the job.*

"Nora!" Hawk grinned, giving her a playful toothy smile.

They parked in front of a magnificent three-story mansion with its second-floor porch held up by six white columns gracing the entrance below. A second entrance faced the side street. A wide walkway with two sets of steps led up to the side portico. Nora noticed an amazing stained-glass window that embellished that side of the house, which she assumed was the location of the staircase. She could just imagine a grand staircase where the mistress of the house would descend gracefully to meet her guests. Longingly she said, "I'd love to have something like that someday, wouldn't you?"

"Not on my salary," Hawk said as both walked closer to the garages. "It probably wouldn't be enough even for the maintenance that a place like this would take."

"Well, a girl can dream, can't she?" Nora chuckled.

The detached two-car garage, with an entry from the backyard, was positioned a few yards from the mansion. A curious crowd, which Hawk assumed came mostly from the adjacent park, had gathered and stood behind the yellow police tape. Several held their phones up to take photos hoping they would see something exciting. Being an extremely attractive woman with her long lustrous black hair and dark blue eyes, Nora seemed to be the center of attention. Her curvaceous figure was accented nicely by her light gray suit and pink blouse. Hawk saw several cameras pointed at her. He did not blame them for taking her photos as she had an important presence about her. People often mistook her for some celebrity, especially when wearing sunglasses.

At six feet tall, Hawk was nearly a head taller than Nora. Already earning a reputation around the station as a sharp dresser, today he was wearing his dark blue pin-striped suit with a light blue shirt accented by a solid dark green tie. His brown eyes peered out from a handsome square face. His slim, athletic build, dark brown hair, high cheekbones and jaw thrust slightly forward caused a few of the women in the crowd to take a photo of him as well.

They approached Hawk's old rival while he was on patrol, Corporal Hopkins. "Well, De-tec-tive Clint Hawk, you again?" Nora noticed the officer's blatant sneer and the manner in that he accented the word "detective" with obvious deep scorn. *Those two certainly have a history together that is not pleasant,* she thought.

"Yup. It's me again. I know how excited you are about it."

Hopkins rolled his eyes, his contempt for Hawk more obvious. "Don't push it, Hawk."

Hawk paid no attention to this now familiar disdain. "By the way, this is my new partner, Detective Nora Ricci. Nora, this is David Hopkins. We were at the police academy, and both worked patrol."

Hopkins smiled warmly at Nora, his demeanor in stark contrast to how he dealt with Hawk. "How did you get stuck with this guy, anyway?"

"I guess I'm just lucky." Hopkins didn't know whether she really meant it or she was just being flippant. "So, what do we have here, Corporal Hopkins?"

"I don't think it's anything for a hotshot detective like Hawk or you to worry about. It looks like the woman, Amanda Ellis, probably had a heart attack."

"Who found her?" Hawk asked.

"Her husband. His name is Steven Ellis. He's some kind of highflier in the financial world. He came home for an early lunch and found his wife, Amanda Ellis, lying on the floor by the door to the yard."

"What time was that?" Nora asked.

"He said he got home about eleven this morning. That's when he called 911."

"Is he in the garage with his wife's body now?" Hawk asked. "No, he said he just couldn't take seeing the dead body of his wife on the floor any longer. He said that he was nauseous and had to go sit down. So, a few minutes ago, he went into the house. I told him that the detectives would want to talk to him."

"Thanks, Corporal Hopkins," Nora said. "We'll take it from here."

"Oh, I'm sure you and Hawk will," Hopkins said, glaring coldly at Hawk.

As they made it over to the body, Nora said, "Hopkins doesn't like you much, does he?"

"No, the feeling's mutual. We were friends at the academy. But I passed some exams and rose in the ranks. He kept failing. You can't stay friends if there is too much envy or jealousy by one of the friends. He resented my advancements and did everything he could think of to hinder my career."

Both put on their nitrile gloves as they walked into the garage. "So, it's you again, Detective Hawk," Janeel, the medical examiner, said as she gave Hawk and Nora a toothy smile. "I haven't seen you lately, Detective Ricci. Are you two partnering up now? If so, that's a good match."

Both Hawk and Nora greeted Janeel. She looked at Hawk and said, "For being a rookie, you seem to be busy these days with dead bodies."

"Not as busy as you, Janeel," Hawk said, chuckling. "What do we have here? Officer Hopkins thinks it's probably a heart attack."

"Well, I didn't know he got his MD degree. Even with one, how'd he know it was a heart attack by just looking at the corpse? She looks young, probably in her mid-thirties and a heart attack is unlikely. Her husband is much older. He's the one that should have had a heart attack with a young wife like that." She laughed, then said, "Of course, you both know that was a bad joke. But I've got to have some levity in my life once in a while as a ME; otherwise, I'd go crazy."

"I understand," Hawk said. But Nora was not pleased with the chuckling and the laughing. *This is a solemn situation. Come on, people, there's a dead body here on the floor.* Hawk noticed her displeasure after she gave him a disapproving glare.

Hawk's face immediately took on a more somber appearance, and he asked the next question, "So, Janeel, what is your assessment so far? I understand that her name was Amanda Ellis."

"There's not much to go on here at the scene. I'll have to do a complete autopsy before I know. I did observe, though, that her skin looks unusually pale. I just need to check her out thoroughly. Hopkins may be right. It could be a heart attack."

"And if so, would you know what caused it? Some kind of medicine, perhaps?"

As Hawk and Janeel talked, Nora went over to the body. She squatted down and sniffed the air. She turned to Janeel and Hawk. "Would you two take a good sniff here? I want to know if you can smell anything unusual such as maybe band-aids or electronics fresh out of a box, something like that?" Nora brought her nose closer to Mrs. Ellis's arm. Here the odor was more pronounced.

Hawk joined her and sniffed the area around the arm and heart as well. "I smell something familiar, but I can't place it."

Nora stood up and said, "I think I know what that odor is." Both Hawk and Janeel focused on Nora. "My grandmother is diabetic. Been one ever since I can remember. That smell is sort of the odor I've smelled ever since I was a little girl. To me, it's very distinctive. I've been told by many that I have a very sensitive sense of smell."

"Well, what is it?" Hawk asked. "Don't leave us in suspense."

"It smells like insulin."

"I didn't know that insulin had a particular smell to it. What makes it smell, anyway?"

"It's the phenol that they use with it to stabilize the protein and act as a disinfectant so that you can reuse the bottle for several injections."

Hawk immediately began to carefully examine the victim's arms for any sign that insulin might have been injected. In the muscle part of the left arm, he found what appeared to be possibly a couple of needle marks. The marks seemed to be in the center of what looked like round, very pale burn marks. There were also additional slightly scorched pale marks that trailed off the arm. He stood up and asked Janeel, "Could you look at these round spots on her arm? Could it be that some of the material that was injected spilled after the needle was pulled out?"

Janeel bent down and examined the arm more carefully. It did not seem easy for her to do so as she was overweight and had complained to Nora before about her bad knees. Nora thought that she was in her late sixties and probably close to retirement. She seemed to be out of breath as she touched the skin and pinched it at the spots as much as it would give.

"I was saving a thorough exam until I returned to the morgue. Nora, I believe you're right, though, that it might be insulin. I don't particularly smell it, but the insulin does leave a sort of skin burn if the person is careless or in a hurry and spills some of it on the skin." She placed her hand on the front of the hood of the car as a prop to help her stand up. Hawk saw her struggle and helped her.

"Oh, I'm so embarrassed. I usually don't have this problem, but my knee doesn't want to work this morning. I think I have a torn meniscus along with a flare-up of my arthritis. You know, the older you get, you never know what part of your body wants to work from day to day."

"I know, we're all so vulnerable," Hawk said, sympathetically. "Janeel, tell me, you can die from an overdose of insulin, right?"

"Well, yes. That's especially true if insulin is injected into someone that had never used it. Even if they are a user, a double or triple portion would certainly knock them out and would cause death if not treated right away. I see that the injections were in the muscle and not in the fatty or fleshy part of the upper arm. That means that the insulin would get into the bloodstream faster and cause a quicker death. And because the injections were in the muscle indicates to me that this woman was not a user. A diabetic would know that you need to inject the insulin into a fatty area of the body."

"I guess the autopsy would show if it was the insulin that killed her," Hawk said, facing Janeel.

"Not necessarily. That's a tough one to get results from. The findings may be unremarkable due to the lack of tests. There are certain tests that are very expensive to run and you have to have certain equipment which we don't have. Actually, there is a test that might be able to determine the phenol in the blood, which would give us some indication. So, it may be difficult, but I'll see what I can do. And maybe because it appears to be a very severe overdose with two injections, it might be easier to determine."

"Well, Janeel, we have all the confidence in you," Nora said.

"You're too kind. I'll do what I can. But it'll take a while."

While Janeel and Nora talked, Hawk listened to their conversation and studied the Mercedes convertible. The door to it was not shut all the way. He examined the red leather seat and the leather strip under the driver's window to see if he could find evidence of insulin spill. There were a few spots that looked suspicious. He focused on the boot into which the convertible top was tucked away. He smelled the leather but could not smell anything unusual. He focused on a purse lying on the passenger floor with some of its contents spilled. Next, he carefully inspected the concrete floor. The entire floor was generally clean, but some dust and dried leaves had blown in. The floor adjacent to the car seemed to have been wiped cleaner than the rest of the floor. This same pattern continued to the door that led to the yard. He took photos of the car seat, door, and the floor.

Hawk then walked out of the garage. Most of the gawkers had gone, but some remained, probably waiting to see the body bag leave the garage. As he approached the yellow tape and asked a few of the people to move aside, he noticed how close the garage was to the park. There were several bushes on the side of the garage and trees in the park that were planted close by. A gravel pathway was only a few feet from the property, and a wide cement walkway was a little further away. A pedestrian was walking a few yards ahead of him on the gravel while several joggers and bicyclists used the cement walk. He took a quick thread to the end of the property that bordered the park, glanced over the portion that had a wooden fence, and marveled at how huge the house of the victim was. It was larger than most older hotels, he thought. Nora came up to him.

"Are you hoping to find cigarette butts that were tied to the killer just like you found in the Bowman cases?"

He smiled at her. "You never know. One can hope. But I don't see any right off. It's so easy here to commit a crime. For example, one could use a bike or run in from the park, go around the corner of the garage, inject someone twice and run out, or get on a bike and ride away with the others."

"Do you think that's what happened?" Nora asked.

"It's a good possibility."

"By the way, Mrs. Ellis's purse was on the floor of the passenger side of the car. I placed it in a large evidence bag that I happened to have in my purse. Before I did, I searched for the cell phone. Every woman carries one with her, you know. But there was none in the purse, nor was there one anywhere in the car or on her body. I think the killer took it."

Hawk answered, "Yeah, I noticed the purse. We'll need to give it to Forensics. I wonder why they'd take only the phone. Surely the killing wasn't because of the phone. Maybe the husband took it after he discovered the body?"

"It is interesting, isn't it?"

"Well, let's go back in. There's just too many people milling around here to do a thorough search of the area. We'll have to come back later."

"Nora, do you agree with me that this was a murder. What do you say?"

"I tend to agree. We better get the crime lab people here right away, shouldn't we?"

"Definitely," Hawk agreed. "My gut tells me that Mrs. Ellis was injected with something that killed her while she sat in the car. The killer ran in from the park and hurriedly left that way. Mrs. Ellis then dragged herself to the door, but before she could open it, she probably lost consciousness and died shortly thereafter."

Hawk turned his attention to the ME. "Janeel, how long does it take for a person to die after an overdose?"

"That's hard to answer. It all depends on the size of the person, the dosage and whether the insulin is a fast-acting type. I assume that here the dosage was tremendously high and the insulin was the fast-acting variety. Whoever did this knew what they were doing."

"Could she have passed out immediately while still in the car?" Nora asked.

"It's highly unlikely, but she would be confused and weak fairly soon afterward. I would think that the killer would have held her back in the car seat for a few moments for the hypoglycemia to start doing its damage. Now if you're through with me, can we start loading up the body. My assistants have arrived."

"Sure," Nora said.

At that moment, Hopkins walked in, looking irritated. "How long are you going to take just for a heart attack or stroke? Isn't it cut and dry? My sergeant called and said I'm needed somewhere else."

"No problem," Hawk said. "You can go. Thanks for your help."

"Sure, sure, De-tec-tive Hawk. Want me to take the tape down?"

"Good idea. I don't think we'll need it up anymore."

Nora looked at Hawk and smiled. "Well, are you ready to go talk to the husband?"

CHAPTER THREE

HAWK AND Nora walked up the first sets of steps onto the wide red stamped sidewalk that split the perfectly manicured landscaping in half. Another set of steps led them to the semi-circular covered portico with its terracotta tiled floor. An extravagant ornamental Tiffany-style pendant chandelier descended from the portico ceiling. The multi-colored floral stained-glass door, that Nora first noticed from the car, looked even more spectacular when she stood inches away.

"This is the most beautiful entrance to a house that I've ever seen," Nora said, twisting her neck about, admiring everything that came into view.

Hawk was also looking around. But, now, he was more interested in the multiple cameras that hung around the front of the house, including a Ring doorbell with its built-in camera. "I see all these cameras around here, but interestingly, I didn't notice any by the garage. We should go back and take a closer look if one may be hidden out of sight or maybe was knocked off by the killer."

Nora nodded in agreement and proceeded to ring the doorbell. The door was opened quickly by a handsome, tall, slender man who appeared to be in his early fifties. His tanned oblong face was set in a somber expression as he asked them in. Nora and Hawk introduced themselves as Denver detectives and expressed their deepest condolences. "I know who you are. I saw you arrive and walk over to the garage. I should have joined you, but I just couldn't handle seeing my beautiful wife lying there on the floor." With an agonized expression on his face, he said, "Please come into the sitting room."

Both detectives couldn't help but notice the wealth in the large, wide foyer. In the center was a round table with a tall porcelain statue of an eighteenth-century lady of nobility. "That's a Lladro statue worth big bucks," Hawk whispered to Nora. Nora looked surprised that Hawk would know that. Several oil art pieces hung on the walls of the room. Hawk recognized one of them as *The Green Violinist* by Marc Chagall. *That can't be the original,* he thought; *it must be a print because I remember the original is at the Guggenheim Museum. Maybe the others are also all prints. Even the Lladro might be a knockoff.* Three large statues of knights in armor stood guard in the corners of the rectangular room. Up on the ceiling, there were two large murals of royal court scenes set in gold medallions at each side of the room. Nora felt a little overwhelmed and intimidated by the sheer magnificence of the place, although she was disappointed that she did not see a lavish grand staircase that the mistress would gracefully descend to greet her guests. Then she spotted the beautiful mahogany staircase tucked away in the corner of the foyer but realized that the staircase would stand out if one entered through the front door. She had a great view of the stained-glass windows that graced the first landing of the stairs. To the right of the staircase was another spectacular stained-glass door, the true front door of the house.

Steven Ellis led them into a very pleasant square-shaped sunny room with large arched windows adorned with white airy silk drapes that matched the white color of the walls. The décor of the room was in stark contrast to the large foyer with its renaissance look. Here, everything seemed ultra-contemporary, with its abstract art depicting bright-colored geometric designs matched by two abstract red statues. The room, itself, was not gigantic, but large enough to hold two regular-sized white silk sofas across from each other and both accented with several identical red and blue pillows. Between the sofas was a rectangular glass-topped coffee table held up with a solid piece of geometric white marble. A white marble fireplace stood on the wall between the sofas.

The detectives sat across from the bereaved husband. They studied him. To Nora, he did not seem to be outwardly overwhelmed with grief. *Of course, I always heard that everyone grieves differently. But come on, man, show me more emotion.* Mr. Ellis must have read her mind, because he suddenly closed his eyes, took in a deep breath, and slowly exhaled. He raised his head and pinched the bridge of his nose as though he was struggling. He opened his eyes looking at them and in a low, trembling voice said, "I just can't believe it. Who would have guessed? One day she's here and the next day she's gone."

"How long had you been married, Mr. Ellis?" Hawk asked.

Ellis blew out a deep breath. "We were married for about three years."

Nora asked, "How would you characterize your marriage?"

Ellis seemed startled by the question. "I guess normal. We had an argument occasionally, just like any couple, but overall, we were happy."

"What were your arguments about?"

"Now wait. That's pretty personal, don't you think?" He glared at Nora. Nora glared back. "But I guess if you must know, the arguments were mostly about me working too much and too late. I imagine she thought that I didn't pay that much attention to her at times."

"Were you married before?" Nora asked.

"Yes. My first wife died in a horrible auto accident. She went off a cliff in the mountains. They said that she had a high dose of opiates, painkillers, in her system. She suffered from fibromyalgia."

"Oh, that's tragic," Nora said. "How long ago was that?"

"About four years ago, I suppose."

Hawk asked, "How did you and Mrs. Ellis meet?"

With that question, Ellis seemed to become more alert. "Why does any of this matter here?"

"We just want to get a background of the victim for us to do our job thoroughly. Why is there a problem with the question?"

"No, no. I'm sorry. I'm just so distraught and my nerves are on edge." Ellis leaned forward, placed his elbows on his knees and cupped his face in his hands. He took two sporadic breaths and wiped his eyes, although neither Hawk nor Nora saw any tears. "To answer your question, we met at a fundraiser shortly after my first wife died."

"I'm so sorry to put you through this, Mr. Ellis," Nora said. "What was the name of your first wife?"

Ellis hesitated for several seconds. He stared hard at Nora. "Why are you asking me about my first wife? What in the hell would anything about my first marriage have to do with the fact that Amanda is dead? Corporal Hopkins said he thought it might be a heart attack. So why all these questions?"

Nora said, "I know this is exceedingly difficult for you, losing two wives like that. I see your pain, but as Detective Hawk said, we need to make a thorough report of this incident. It's a simple question, one that we can very easily look up. But since you don't want to tell us, we'll just move on."

"All right, all right. I don't know why that question bothers me so much at the time that Amanda is dead. Her name was Susan Lynn. And if your next question is whether we had any children, the answer is no. I have no children. No one to inherit what I've built up over the years. I was hoping that Amanda and I would have an heir, but evidently, that was not the case." The detectives noticed the extreme bitterness in his voice.

"We won't keep you long, Mr. Ellis," Hawk said. "But we do have a few more questions." Ellis nodded to indicate that he understood. "It is our understanding that you found the body?"

"Yes, I came home early for lunch at around eleven. I was surprised to see that the garage door was open, and Amanda's Mercedes was in its spot. Amanda should've been at work. I parked my SUV next to it and as I walked around the car, I saw…" Ellis stopped talking, sniffled, and grabbed his head in his hands. "Oh God! My God!" He removed his hands and looked at Hawk and Nora with sadness. "She was just lying there. I rushed over to her to try to help her up. She was lifeless. Oh God!"

Nora said, "That must have been so awful. I can't imagine what you went through."

"Yes, it was a tragedy." He deeply inhaled; his chest rose. "I don't want to go through anything like that ever again." He grabbed his head again, swaying from side to side.

Hawk asked, "How did you know that she was dead?"

"I tried to feel her pulse on the side of her neck. She had none, so I called 911."

"Was Mrs. Ellis, by any chance, a diabetic?"

"No, why?"

"Do you have diabetes?"

"No. What's this all about? What's diabetes have anything to do with anything?"

"Oh, it may have nothing to do with it," Hawk said. "But we suspect that your wife died from an overdose of insulin," Hawk observed Ellis closely to see his reaction. Ellis knitted his brow and sat back abruptly.

"What! That's crazy. She never used insulin in her life. Surely, you're greatly mistaken. Why would you even come up with that? Isn't something like that hard to prove?"

"Oh," Nora said. "Why do you say that?"

"Well, over my fifty-four years, I've heard a thing or two. I can't remember where I heard it, though. I suppose now, with that bizarre theory of yours, you'll have to do an autopsy. But my understanding is that an overdose of insulin doesn't show up in any autopsy. What you'll most likely find is a heart attack or a massive stroke."

Nora asked, "Did Mrs. Ellis have heart troubles or high blood pressure?"

"Not that I know of, but she was always rather secretive about her health. Maybe she was sick and didn't tell me. I guess at thirty-three, you don't expect it, but things like that do happen."

Now Hawk asked, "How did she appear this morning to you?"

"Oh, I left early for work and didn't see her." He had a slight twitch in the corner of his mouth. That was the first time Hawk noticed it.

"What about last evening or last night?"

"Unfortunately, I came home late last night, and she was already asleep." He had another twitch.

Nora asked, "Where were you so late?"

"I was behind on so many reports that I determined to finish before my big meeting this afternoon. Which, by the way, I need to get to. Is there anything else?" He squeezed his nostrils together with his hand. Another mannerism that Hawk noticed for the first time.

"Yes," Hawk said. "Did you, by any chance, pick up your wife's phone from the garage this morning?"

"No. She always keeps it in her purse if she's in the car. It must still be there."

"I noticed several cameras around your front entrance. Do you have any camera surveillance around the garages, particularly from the direction of the park?"

"Sure. Let me look on my phone and see what that camera shows." He checked his phone and said, "That's strange; the garage camera doesn't show anything, just a blank screen. I better call my security people to check it out."

"Nora asked, "Who is your security company?"

"It's AYZ Home Systems. Anything else?"

Hawk asked, "Are you still going to that meeting this afternoon? I mean, considering what happened."

Ellis shook his head back and forth and deeply inhaled. "I really shouldn't because I'll be nothing but a basket case, but several people are counting on me to give my report. I have to be there." The detectives could see that he resented the question by the cold stare that he gave Hawk.

Nora said, "Mr. Ellis, I think we have everything we need for the report except a couple of employment questions?"

"Okay, but please hurry."

"Where did Mrs. Ellis work?"

"She is...oh God, I mean, she was an architect at a large international construction firm of JWB Contractors."

"Was everything okay with her employment?"

"Yeah, she liked it well enough. Had, though, a boss that was a jerk by the name of Roger, that sexually harassed her. I felt like going down there and beating him up, but she said that she'd handle it herself. I think, though, that she was getting really fed up with it and said she'd go to the head honcho about it."

"Who would that be?" Nora asked.

"I think she called the president or CEO of the company, Simon something or other."

"Do you know of anyone who would want to hurt or kill Mrs. Ellis?" Hawk asked.

"No, I really don't have a clue. That is, you're assuming it was murder, then?"

"We're just looking at all possibilities at this time."

"Mr. Ellis," Nora asked. "I assume with this large house, you must have a housekeeper?"

"We do have a cleaning lady who comes in regularly, maybe every day, but I'm not sure. Why?"

"Just to cover all bases, that's all. What's her name?"

"I only met her once or twice. Amanda dealt with her. I think her name is Nellie, but darned if I know her last name."

"Here's my card. Would you please call me with that name?" He nodded.

"And what is your occupation, Mr. Ellis," Hawk asked.

"I was an investment banker for many years, but now I manage individual client stock and fund accounts."

"And where is your office?"

"It's at the Wells Fargo Center downtown, forty-fourth floor."

At that moment, the doorbell rang. Ellis, looked at Nora, again avoiding much eye contact with Hawk. "I need to get that door. Would you follow me to the door as I really need to go to that meeting?"

All three got up and Hawk and Nora followed Ellis to the fancy side door. As he opened the door, an attractive, extremely shapely woman in her mid-thirties rushed in and squeezed Ellis to her in a remarkably close embrace, kissing him on his cheek. "Oh my God, Stevie, how are you holding up? I'm glad you called me. This is awful. Who would have thought that Amanda would die, just like that?"

After releasing Steven from her tight grip, she suddenly seemed to notice Hawk and Nora, who stood back in the foyer. "Oh, I'm sorry. I didn't know you had company."

Ellis blushed, feeling embarrassed. "Tina, these two people are detectives with the police department. They're investigating Amanda's death. Nora Ricci and Clint Hawk, am I correct?"

Tina gave a cursory look at Nora but allowed her eyes to linger on Hawk. Nora could swear that she saw a sparkle in Clint's eyes when he gazed at Tina. She elbowed him on his arm out of sheer jealousy. She could not blame Hawk for goggling her as Tina reminded Nora of one of the Barbie Dolls she used to play with. Her figure seemed perfect, and she knew that to men, that deep cleavage showing on her white tank top would be hard to resist a peek.

Nora turned toward Tina, "I'm sorry I didn't get your full name."

Tina looked suspiciously at her. Hesitated for a second, then answered, "Tina Dionisio. I'm Mr. Ellis's assistant." Hawk noticed that her boss appeared uncomfortable by Tina's presence. *There is more to their relationship than employer-employee, that's for sure. How convenient for her now that Amanda is gone.*

"Well, we'll be going," Hawk said. "Mr. Ellis, again, we're so sorry for your loss. Thank you for your time." Then before they left the house, Hawk looked at the woman, "Pleased to meet you, Tina." *I bet he was pleased to meet that tramp,* Nora thought bitterly.

CHAPTER FOUR

BLACK CLOUDS had made their way over Denver as the detectives walked down the steps to the street. Rain threatened to pour at any minute. The typical sunny Colorado had to wait a little while for the rain to pass through. "How about lunch before we head back to the station?" Hawk asked.

Nora smiled and replied, "I thought you'd never ask. Of course, maybe you'd rather have lunch with that Tina woman?" She laughed, trying to make a joke of it. But, in reality, she didn't like the way Tina looked at Hawk. *And he didn't mind it at all!*

"Why should I want that? I want to have lunch with the most beautiful woman that I've ever met. Think her name is Nora or something like that."

Nora laughed again. "Okay, okay. Since you put it that way, I guess I'll go with you."

"First, let's walk over to the garage and see where that camera that was supposed to be there is that I missed."

Under the eaves of the garage, Hawk found a couple of thin wires protruding from a bracket that had been painted and matched the beige shade of the eaves. "Look, Nora, there was a camera there, but someone knocked it off." Looking up, Nora agreed and took a picture of the bracket and the short hanging wires.

"That just bolsters our case that this was a murder," Hawk said. "Nora, why do you keep staring at the park? Do you see something?"

Nora laughed again. "I was checking to see if I see ghosts wandering about?"

"What?! What are you talking about?"

"Haven't you heard about the haunted Cheesman Park?"

"No. Haunted? In this tranquil residential area?"

"Yes. I'm not kidding, Clint. Back in 1858, this land, where the park and the Denver Botanical Gardens exist now, was a cemetery. They called it Mount Prospect Cemetery. It was originally designed for the rich and prominent in the community and was close to the mansions of Capitol Hill. So, they began to bury the wealthy using the north side of the cemetery first. But Denver was a wild town in those days with an abundance of criminals and, unfortunately, a large share of paupers. With the hangings, the killings and all the poor that died, they began burying them in the cemetery as well, contrary to the original plan of a graveyard for the rich and prominent. It is believed that over two thousand bodies of criminals and poor were buried along the outer edges of the cemetery, mostly on the south side. They eventually allowed the middle-class burials in the center areas. You never heard that story? Even in all the years that you were a beat cop?"

"No, Nora. Go on, this is interesting, but don't make it too scary otherwise, I tend to get goosebumps when talking about supernatural things."

Nora laughed, "You baby. Anyway, the wealthy citizens of Denver didn't like being buried among the riffraff. They no longer felt it was their special place and had to find another location for their family members to be buried. In the meantime, the Mount Prospect cemetery fell into disrepair and parts of it reverted to prairie land. It became a blight on the growing town and was being called by such names as the 'Old Boneyard' or 'Boot Hill.' Eventually, the politicians wanted this cemetery gone and made it into a park. So, they hired a man by the name of McGovern to remove all the bodies and contracted with him to pay three dollars for each box. Well, he decided that the fee wasn't enough and being conning and corrupt as he was, he cut up the bodies and placed different parts into separate boxes so he could be paid more. Eventually, he decided that it just wasn't worth it and quit, leaving countless bodies still buried, some in pieces that he didn't finish hauling away. The mucky-mucks at the time in the 1880's decided that they couldn't wait any longer for the corpses to be removed, so they went ahead with the park anyway and left them there. Even today, workmen excavating in the park bring up bones that were buried way back then."

"Gads, that's a gruesome story," Hawk said.

"Okay, to make a long story short, and you really should read up on it, this place is haunted. Spirits make sure people know they're there one way or another, not only within the confines of the park, but also in the houses and apartments that surround the park. There are moans, whispering voices coming from the park, and tales of people resting on the ground, not being able to get up without effort as though something is holding them down. Also, there is this story of two men seeing what appeared to be a zombie with seventeen stab wounds asking them if they had seen the man that stabbed him."

"Okay, Nora," Hawk said as he took off his jacket and rolled up his sleeve. "You did it. Look at the goosebumps on my arm and my hair stand up."

"You have got to be kidding."

"I told you supernatural stories freak me out. Next, you'll tell me that it was a ghost that killed Mrs. Ellis."

Nora laughed, "Who knows? Maybe?"

As they began their return to the car, Hawk asked, "Okay, so where shall we eat?"

At that moment, it started to sprinkle. Nora and Hawk sprinted for the car as the sprinkle turned into a light rain. Once in the car, the rain came down in buckets. "We made it in just in the nick of time," Nora said. "We were lucky. It's really coming down now. What'd you say if we went to Park Tavern? I really liked that waitress, Janice. She was so friendly and helped us out with our case against the corrupt Bradford and his gang. What'd you say?" Hawk readily agreed.

Most of the lunch crowd had dissipated by the time the two detectives arrived. As soon as they walked in, Janice rushed over to them, giving both Hawk and Nora a heartfelt hug as though they were long-lost relatives. "Ooh, the good-looking couple is back," she gushed and laughed in merriment, her ample bosom shaking. Her hair didn't change a bit since they saw her last, with a red French braid crowning her round head. "You sure look like you belong to each other. Are you still only working partners or is there something more to the relationship?" She laughed again and Nora returned her infectious laugh. Of course, Nora did not need much prodding for her to laugh. "Come on, Clint, what is it? I need to know if you're seeing each other now?" Hawk felt the eyes of everyone in the restaurant and became embarrassed. "Oh, I get it. There is something between you two."

"You're very perceptive," Nora said. "May we just sit at the bar?"

As they sat down on bar stools with backs, Nora paid more attention to the restaurant than when she was there on official business. It was a wide but narrow space. The focal point of the place was the large semi-circular metal bar on the east end, with plenty of space for the staff to work behind. In the center area of the counters stood a stainless-steel table with three glass shelves on top containing an assortment of liquor bottles. On each side of the bar was beer dispenser taps. Overhead, inset lighting within a wooden drop-down ceiling mimicked the counters and gave the place a very updated look.

They ordered a salad, each with an order of nachos. Both had water only. Hawk asked Nora if she wanted to talk about the murder or wait until they will have to fill in the other detectives of the homicide unit. "Let's just enjoy a quiet half hour or so without thinking about work," she said.

Hawk sat quietly, mulling over how this relationship with Nora started. They only met a short time ago, the day that he began his new job as a detective. He was placed in the homicide unit under the supervision of Lieutenant Bradford and, as a rookie, did not know what to expect. His first case was the murder of a man in a carjacking and the next day, his second case was of the murder of the same man's wife during a botched burglary.

Hawk got off on the wrong foot the first day when he blatantly disagreed with his supervisor regarding what the evidence showed. To Hawk, it was clear, and he knew that Bradford was totally wrong. Bradford did not like his analysis and ordered him off the cases with specific instructions to stay out of it. But in his gut, Hawk knew he was right and that he smelled a coverup. He disregarded his superior's specific orders, realizing that would probably be the end of his new career.

But to him, justice was more important than his job and he continued with the investigation, nevertheless. It turned out that Bradford was part of a gang of dirty cops that dealt in blackmail, extortion, murder, and money laundering. Hawk was getting too close to discovering them and they attempted to kill him. He shuddered when he thought how lucky he was that he escaped the attempts on his life. Nora was there to help him and together, they brought down a corrupt group of cops. She also helped save him twice from being killed and, in so doing, put her life at risk as well. Those incidents brought them closer together.

Nora took an immediate liking to Hawk from the start, it seemed. He saw how much she wanted him. She was pushy and obvious about it, maybe too pushy and that bothered him. In many ways, she was perfect: smart, kind, caring, beautiful, and exciting to be with. He enjoyed her company and certainly, that pulled him to her. He liked her. He liked her a lot. He knew that in her mind, she thought that they were in a relationship. After all, she admitted as much to Janice. But Hawk was not sure he wanted a steady relationship with her just yet. *Maybe I do. Oh, I just don't know what to do. She'll expect a firm commitment soon. I know she will.* He realized that he had a problem with commitment. He lost two wonderful women that he dated for that very reason. He realized that most women, once they are in their thirties, begin thinking seriously of settling down, having children and living the life their parents lived. Even, Marcie, the computer tech, in the unit that he met, the one that he thought he was head over heels over, sized him up right away and accused him of a commitment problem.

Hawk still thought of Marcie. He could still smell the lingering scent of her shampoo on her blond hair as she bent over his desk a few times to help him with the computer, her hair falling over the front of her shoulders. He could still see that glowing smile and those sparkling blue eyes. The few times that they had together brought him many pleasant memories. Both women, Nora and Marcie, working in the same office would certainly complicate his life since both women seemed to pay much attention to him. And he, liking them both, would have a problem deciding who to date. In a way, it was a relief to him when Marcie told him she decided to move back to California and pursue a career as an electrical engineer. Yet, he was sad about it. Sad that he lost maybe something wonderful in his life.

He snapped out of deep thoughts and glanced at Nora. He even jerked back and widened his eyes as he saw Nora's jeweled eyes staring hard at him. *Did she read my mind? She seems upset.* "Boy, you were really concentrating on something hard. What were you thinking about?"

"Oh, Nora, so much has happened since I walked into the homicide unit that I feel I've been there for a decade. I thought of the Bowman murders, Bradford, and his cohorts. Then I thought of you. Of how lucky I am that I met you."

"Oh, Clint. You're so sweet. I might be falling a little in love with you."

"Nora, that sounds wonderful, but we really don't know each other very well. I've got my idiosyncrasies that you have no idea about. So, we need to take it easy."

"Well, I'm not worried. Unless you're a serial killer, I don't care what's in your baggage. By the way, my parents would like to meet you over dinner next week. It'll be a great Italian meal. Real comfort food to make you relax. Would you come?" *Oh God. This is just too fast.* Hawk thought. *Meeting her parents already? What should I tell her?* "Okay, by the way, you hesitated. I think that maybe you're right. We should take it easy. Let's do it the week after next." Nora laughed, but her laugh was not long-lived.

Hawk did not know what to say, but he didn't have to because he was saved by a tune. His cell rang out his ring tone, *Bad to the Bone* by George Thorogood and the Destroyers. Nora chuckled every time she heard the phone go off. The call was from Stanley Orlinski at the unit. "Clint, is Nora with you?"

"Yes, why?"

"Captain MacGregor wants a meeting with all homicide detectives at two. You better be here."

Nora asked, "What was that all about?"

"That was Orlinski. Said that Captain MacGregor wants a meeting. I have never met her yet. She was on vacation. What's she like?"

"She's a tough lady. Pretty busy overseeing both the Homicide and Robbery units. All business-like. Too bad, though, that she didn't have a clue as to how corrupt her Lieutenant Bradford had become."

Hawk paid the tab for both, and they headed to the station. Hawk had no idea what to expect from the captain.

CHAPTER FIVE

THE HOMICIDE unit was quiet when Hawk and Nora walked in ten minutes before the meeting. Hawk glanced at the empty desk by the door that Marcie had used previously. He missed her bubbly greeting accompanied by a brilliant smile. Senior Detective Orlinski no longer occupied the lieutenant's office as his short stint as acting boss of the unit, after Bradford was arrested, came to an end. He sat at his regular desk. Through the glass, Hawk noticed their new Lieutenant assigned to the unit was sitting in his office. Orlinski nodded to them and then stuck his head back into a file he was reading.

At a desk, across from Orlinski sat the new detective, Mortimer Holliday, that transferred from Tampa. His elongated face looked serious and somber, his head topped by a tall crew-cut hairstyle. As Nora and Hawk walked past him, he did not nod or say "hello," just followed them with his eyes. Hawk and Nora briefly met him after Orlinski had introduced him earlier in the morning. He came up to them to talk, but they had to excuse themselves as they were in a hurry to investigate the death of Mrs. Ellis. The other two detectives in the room, Nancy Salazar and Harry Ling were as friendly as usual and asked them about the case. Nancy also informed Hawk and Nora that detectives Withers and Higgins were transferred to other Districts, and she did not think that they would be replaced.

"That means we'll have to pick up the slack," she said with disgust in her voice.

Nora and Hawk sat down across from each other at their respective desks. Both began to review whatever notes they took from their observations at the crime scene and the interview with Mr. Ellis. Nora rolled her chair closer to Hawk. "You know, Clint, they always say that if a wife is murdered, chances are that the husband is the one that killed her. Do you have that feeling here? I mean, he didn't seem to be overly shocked when we told him that we thought it could've been an insulin overdose."

"My first impression also," Hawk said. "And he knew that an insulin overdose doesn't show up in an autopsy."

"Yes, how would he know that, unless he researched it."

At that moment, Captain MacGregor and Lieutenant Perez walked into the detective area. Hawk and Nora turned silent, waiting for them to speak. The captain wore a beige shirt tucked into coffee-colored pants. The tall, big-boned athletic woman appeared to be in her fifties. Nora thought that, at one time, she must have been good-looking, but the years did not seem kind to her. She looked like a lifelong smoker, her face almost leather-like with deep creases in her cheeks. But she had a kind oval face with caring hazel eyes. Her short, medium-brown thick hair was combed with a part in the center. Nora decided that the style did not become her at all. *I need to send her to my cousin, Annette, to do something with her hair. Actually, Mortimer needs to go see her also; that hairstyle of his makes his head seem a mile long.*

MacGregor had a rather large diamond wedding ring on her solid hand. As was her usual pastime, Nora began to imagine what the captain's husband looked like. She imagined him to be a rough, husky, broad-shouldered man. *But I'm so often mistaken. He might be a small mousy-looking man who likes big women.* At the thought of a perfect match, she glanced at Hawk, who still studied his notes and appeared deep in thought. *Now, that man would be a good fit for me. My mama would approve and get off my back about getting married and giving her grandchildren. But is he the marrying kind?*

Nora next turned her attention to the new lieutenant. Perez was about the same height as MacGregor, but at least ten years younger.

He had a ruggedly handsome face; his jaw thrust forward. His black hair looked dyed to Nora, as was his meticulously trimmed mustache. *He must work out a lot,* Nora thought. She noticed his gold wedding band and pictured his wife as a beautiful Latina whom he probably dominated.

Iona MacGregor spoke first. "We've had quite a shake-up in this unit because of what our previous Lieutenant Bradford had done together with Detective Jeffries. Bad cops engaged in blackmail, extortion, and coverup will not be tolerated, and this behavior will not be tolerated and should never happen again." She turned her attention to Hawk. "Detective Hawk, I haven't met you yet since I've been on vacation, but I want to commend you on pursuing justice even though you were specifically ordered not to by Lieutenant Bradford. You certainly jeopardized your career and I'm sure you'd not be here if you were wrong. We appreciate your efforts."

Addressing Nora, she said, "And Detective Nora Ricci, I want to thank you as well for your brave and conscientious contribution in bringing down the corrupt cops. You and Detective Hawk seem to make a good team." Nora smiled widely at that comment. "And now I want to introduce you to your new lieutenant. Standing next to me is Lieutenant Ernest Perez. He had been transferred from District Three, Homicide unit. He's been with the Department for over twenty years. He's very experienced and I believe he'll be a good leader for you." She turned to Perez. "I'm sure you'd like to say a word or two to your detectives, Lieutenant."

Perez forced a wry smile as he glanced about the room again. "It's an honor to work with you. I want you to know that my door is always open for questions or problems. I'll meet with each one of you later this afternoon and discuss the cases you're working on. I don't know how Bradford handled each case, but I expect a team approach. We all work together, helping each other out. I have nothing further at this time."

"A man of few words," Nora whispered to Hawk.

"Seems that way. Orlinski told us that he is a no-nonsense type of guy."

"Those are the ones you have to watch out for," Nora whispered back. "They may be hiding a lot of nonsense."

"What in the heck do you mean by that?"

"Never mind. I'm just being silly."

The captain spoke again, "Thank you, Lieutenant. Now, I want you, Detectives Ricci, Hawk and Holliday in my office. Please follow me there."

The four of them went down a long hallway to the captain's office. The office, with its pale green walls, looked well-used. MacGregor went around her large walnut desk and plopped down into the high-backed black leather chair. She pointed to the four cops to sit. Perez and Holliday sat in the short-backed black chair across the desk from the captain. Hawk and Ricci sat down on the light-brown vinyl couch that sat off to the side.

"I called you four in so that we could get to know each other better since all four of you are new to the unit." She looked at Nora. "Detective Ricci, I've met you before, but since you were in the unit just a week before I left on vacation, I really didn't get to know you very well. Tell us briefly about your background."

Nora looked somewhat surprised at being singled out first. "Well, I was born and raised in Pueblo, Colorado."

"Oh, Pueblo," MacGregor interrupted, "My husband, Albert, and I go down there every year for the Chile and Frijole Festival. I just love the smell of those roasted chiles. We buy a big bag, freeze it and eat the wonderful chiles all year long. I can't believe how popular the festival is. The crowd must be over one hundred thousand from all over."

"Yes," Nora said. "I have an uncle and cousin that roast the chiles right there in their big fire roasters."

"Well, I can hardly wait for September to come. We're already out of the chiles. I'm sorry, Nora, I interrupted you. Go on, where did you go to for your education?"

"After I graduated from Pueblo County High School, I wanted to be a science teacher. University of Northern Colorado in Greeley has a good reputation for training teachers, so I went there. But, in my senior year, the thought of becoming a policewoman kept festering in my mind. So, after graduation, I enrolled in the academy and here I am."

"Good for you. Are you married, any children?"

"No, not married and no children."

"Now, Clint Hawk. Tell us briefly about yourself."

"Nothing much to say. I don't have anything as exciting as chiles to talk about." He immediately regretted his lame attempt at a joke. He noticed that the captain's smiling expression had lost some of its luster. *Geez, when will I learn to keep my mouth shut at times? I must've made her conversation about chiles seem trivial.* "I came up from Tyler, Texas, and go to school at Colorado State University in Fort Collins for my bachelor's and the University of Colorado for my master's in psychology. I guess that deep down inside me, I really wanted to be a cop and make a difference in the world at the street level. So, like Nora, I went through the police academy and became a patrol officer. After six years, I was appointed detective. And here I am. And no, I'm not married either or have any children."

MacGregor thumbed through, what Hawk assumed, was his personnel file. She lifted her head and once again cracked a smile. "Very good, detective, I see that you passed the sergeant's exam and received several commendations for your excellent work. Please keep it up. We're lucky to have you." Hawk thanked the captain, but as his eyes met those of Perez, Hawk's smile faded. Perez seemed to glare at Hawk. *Oh, God! Here we go again. I know that look of jealousy or envy, whatever it is. I've seen it with every promotion or commendation that I've received. I better treat Perez with kid's gloves and never gloat over anything that I accomplish.*

Next, MacGregor took a good look at the new detective and squeezed her full pink lips together in what Nora thought was a disapproving look. He wore red-rimmed glasses on his clean-shaven, wrinkled face. He was tall, slim as a rail and stooped. He sported dark brown pants whose cuffs were at his ankles, a light-green coat that hung loosely on him, a white shirt with a navy blue and gray striped bow tie, and matching suspenders. "Now, detective Mortimer Holliday, you transferred in from the Tampa Police Department?"

"Yes. I applied here and once I was accepted, I resigned in Tampa. I must say it was a difficult decision for me to make after fifteen years to make this change."

"Oh, why did you apply to Denver?"

"Captain, I never thought that I would ever say this, but I met a lady from Denver on a cruise. She seemed to be a good fit for me. We hit it off and corresponded by email on a regular basis at ten o'clock in the evening, Florida time and that would be eight Colorado time. Anyway, she asked me to come out. I lost five days of vacation coming here, so you see, it cost me a pretty penny. And after seeing her every day, she asked me to marry her. I had never been married before and so I thought I'd give it a try." Everyone expected that he made an attempt at humor, but his face remained perfectly serious. "She refused to move to the Tampa Bay area because of the heat and humidity. So, if I wanted to marry her, it seemed best at the time to make the arrangements to move to Denver."

Both MacGregor's and Perez' eyes were fixed on Holliday, but neither spoke up. The captain seemed to be apprising him carefully. Hawk could see that she was not overly impressed by him and probably wondered how soon she could transfer him off to another District. Nora felt the awkwardness of the moment. Her gaze went from the Captain to Holliday, but when her gaze shifted to Perez, she suddenly felt uncomfortable as she caught him subtly eyeing her body. When their eyes locked, he quickly turned his attention to Holliday. Nora crossed her arms over her chest.

As Holliday waited for another question from MacGregor, he took his pinky and picked his tooth. Then he took a deep nasal intake of air, exhaled through his mouth, then studied his lapel. After seeing a piece of lint on it, he flicked it away. After a minute of silence, MacGregor asked him, "Detective, how do you like Denver?"

He took another deep breath through his nose, making a whistling sound. "You know, Captain MacGregor, it's a beautiful city, all right. But, my fiancé, Josephine, says that there are many things I must get used to. For instance, it's awfully dry here and my nostrils whistle. I've had a light headache since I got here. Josephine says it's the high altitude and I'll be all right in a week or two. I sure hope so. My skin seems dehydrated and itch." Just then, Mortimer scratched his thigh with the suggestion of an itch.

"I guess it's all right here and I'll get used to it. The mountains are magnificent, even though I understand there are ticks that carry Lyme disease, so I don't think I'll be spending much time in them. And Josephine told me about the dangerous curvy roads on steep cliffs and the tall passes. The idea of driving on them quite frankly scares me." The four other persons in the room sat silently and stared at the incredulous man. Nora tried her best to suppress a laugh, but a small snicker broke through. She put her hand over her mouth and pretended to clear her throat. Mortimer continued, unfazed.

"I lived in St. Petersburg and will miss the long strolls on the beach. Of course, I got bitten by sand bugs and I didn't like that. You know, I commuted to Tampa, and I miss the Howard Franklin Bridge. It's seven miles over water and I miss seeing the water." He scratched the top of his head, disheveling more of his graying dark hair.

"I've relatives in the Tampa Bay area, Detective," Perez said, "And visit with them often. I can't see how you could possibly miss the constant backup on that bridge or on the Gandy Bridge during rush hours."

"Well, I guess I was used to it. I admit I had to come in late a few times because of an accident on the bridge."

"I'm curious, Detective Holliday, as to why you chose to be a police officer and detective?"

"Oh, I was bullied throughout school. I was short, really skinny, sickly, and clumsy and everyone made fun of me. I wanted to study karate or something like that to fight them off, but my parents couldn't afford it. Besides, they didn't believe that violence of any kind was the answer. One day I and a friend of mine from St. Petersburg College, where we both got degrees in business, talked about different occupations. He told me that he'd considered becoming a cop because of how he admired the men and women who were brave enough to go through all the training and put up with all the crap that's out there. That got me thinking that I wanted to do that. I needed some discipline and training to handle people and, in the process, make a difference in their lives."

"But, why a detective?" Perez asked.

"I'm usually very perceptive and actually able to read people pretty well. After I was on patrol and there was a death, I seemed to be able to visualize what happened and, sometimes, could even feel that a certain person was the murderer, if, of course, the death was due to foul play."

MacGregor said, "Based on your file sent down from Tampa, I did see that you had some success with closing cases. By the way, Detective Holliday, please do not wear sandals to work anymore."

Holliday said, "I guess that includes shorts. I almost wore them today but wasn't sure of the policy. I'll need to get some more pants, I guess. In Tampa, sometimes I got away with wearing shorts."

"This isn't Tampa and no shorts. Furthermore, I suggest you wear a well-fitting suit or a sports jacket to work." MacGregor hesitated, then said. "And make sure your pants are long enough to cover your ankles."

"Yes. I'll get that done. I have some suits already, but I'll need to get another. Is there a Goodwill around here that you'd recommend?"

Irritated, MacGregor said, "No, Detective, I don't know of any. Please make sure that your clothing is decent enough to represent the Police Department, okay? As a matter of fact, I want you to read the Denver Police Department Manuel to see what is expected of you."

"I already tried and will work on finishing it before long. But don't worry, I'll have Josephine pick a new pair of pants and maybe another suit for me. Thank you, Captain."

Captain MacGregor had an exasperated look on her face. She took in a deep breath and exhaled it with force. Then smiling, she turned to Perez and asked if he would tell them a little about himself.

"Not much to tell. Had a normal childhood growing up in Los Angeles. My father was a carpenter and my mother cleaned houses. We weren't rich, nor were we poor. Went to Catholic school, then to LA City College, a degree in criminal justice, then two more years at UCLA. Started out as a cop in LA, then found my love, just like Mortimer here, who lived in Denver. So, I transferred over. We have four children that keep my wife, Connie, mighty busy. Worked myself up to lieutenant and now I'm lucky to work with you, Captain."

He's a real brown noser, that's for sure, Nora thought. On the first appearance, she did not like him but hoped that their work relationship would be okay. MacGregor's faked a smile and said, "All right, detectives, you're excused. Lieutenant Perez will go over your assignments." With that same smile, she picked up her office phone and Hawk could hear her call in the lieutenant from the Robbery unit.

CHAPTER SIX

CLINT HAWK anxiously began work on the interesting case of Amanda Ellis. He knew that proving who killed her would be a difficult task and he wanted to get to it. The introductions to his new bosses and that "get acquainted meeting" in MacGregor's office, in his opinion, were a total waste of time. He realized, though, that he was not quite the same today. His normally athletic body hurt all over and sitting on the soft couch in the captain's office listening to Mortimer ramble on didn't help his miserably aching back, stiff neck and shoulders that he now endured.

A sharp stab of a spasm suddenly attacked him as he bent over to retrieve a sheet of paper from his desk. The lack of solid sleep did not help much, either. Horrible nightmares kept him from a peaceful sleep. In one, he relived the collision and the huge chance he took to save his own skin. The only way he thought to escape certain death out on a secluded country road was to cause a forceful head-on collision into an embankment and take a chance of surviving it.

His life depended on the airbags. The recurring vision in his head caused him to jerk up in bed, covered with sweat. He saw the passenger, Jeffries, passed out but still holding a gun in his hand. He, himself, was not much in better shape and barely got out of the crumpled vehicle. He finally fell asleep. Towards the morning, Hawk then had another nightmare of the main boss of the murderous cops holding a gun on him and Nora. Both feared for their lives. They were so close to not making it, as close as anyone could get. *I wonder if Nora had similar nightmares as well.*

Hawk saw Nora return from the break room carrying a cup of coffee. As she walked past Orlinski's desk, the man stopped her to talk. Hawk watched her as she listened to what the man said, nodding and smiling. Then came over to Hawk.

"What did Orlinski tell you?"

"Oh, I see you watch my every move. I guess I like it."

"Nora, get serious. Was it anything important? It looked like it was extremely urgent."

"He always looks that way." Nora chuckled, but Hawk was not in a chuckling mood with another sharp stab to his back. He grimaced.

"Oh, you poor baby. Please come by my place after work. I'll give you a terrific massage guaranteed to cure you. And I'll make some pasta with my grandmother's marinara sauce. That'll help you as well." Hawk thought that would be great and readily agreed. "As to Orlinski, he's insisting that you and I get some therapy from the police psychiatrist. He said that what we went through, especially you, Clint, a few sessions would be good."

"Maybe you should go, but I'm not going to any shrink. Just another day or two and I'll be back to normal both physically and mentally. Body needs time to heal, that's all." Hawk was becoming irritated at the thought. He hated the idea that someone else thought he had a problem.

"Okay, okay. But I betcha that we'll hear something about seeing a counselor from either Perez or MacGregor."

"Well, we'll see. It's usually when we do the shooting and kill someone."

At that moment, Perez walked up to them. He sat down on the edge of Nora's desk, one leg on the floor, the other swinging. "Tell me about the death you're investigating."

Nora told him about Mrs. Ellis and that they were sure she was murdered by a double injection of insulin into the muscle and not the usual soft tissue. "She was not a diabetic and obviously didn't use the stuff."

"What's the difference if the injection is in the muscle and not the soft tissue?"

"Lieutenant, injection into the muscle gets the insulin into the bloodstream faster."

Perez turned his attention to Hawk, "You sure it was murder, then?"

"Yes, sir."

"No possibility of a heart attack or suicide, then?"

"No," said Nora.

"Well, you better be sure because Mr. Ellis seems to have some pull with some councilwoman. His position is that it was a heart attack because she was stressed out too much at her job. He accused you two of drumming up something that isn't there. This councilwoman got ahold of the Division Chief, and it went down the line to me and now to you. The pressure is on us and I want this wrapped up within a week. What does the medical examiner or forensics say about it?"

"Janeel agreed with us at the scene that it was murder," Nora said. "We both smelled a very faint odor of the insulin injection and saw two needle holes in her left arm. She's running tests to make sure."

"Well, that's just the point that Ellis is making to the councilwoman. He is adamant that insulin can't be detected. He says that we'll find no real evidence of murder."

"Insulin, itself, may not be detected, but there are tests that can detect an ingredient used in the insulin," Hawk spoke up after clearing his throat. "That ingredient is phenol."

"Well, I'll give you a week. If you can't find me the murderer, the coroner better classify it as a natural death. Got that!" Perez had a smug expression, evidently pleased with his command. Both Ricci and Hawk nodded that they understood. "Oh, by the way," Perez portrayed a devious smile, "Holliday is going to help you with this case, at least for now, until I find something else for him to do. He should be a great help to you since he can read people and solve cases," Perez tried to look serious, but his wily smile broadened, his capped teeth showing. Nora and Clint exchanged dismayed glances. Perez yelled out to Mortimer. "Holliday, would you please come here."

Holliday quickly complied, his black socks with tan sandals moving toward them. Perez asked him to ride with Hawk and Ricci and help where he can. "You bet, chief. Your wish is my command. Oh wait, I have to sneeze. AHH CHOO!"

"Bless you," Nora said.

Mortimer wiped the back of his hand over his mouth; then he pinched his long nose with his fingers. A second or two later, he said, "Ah, that's much better. Sorry about that. I'm not sure of this dry climate."

"Just go to work," Perez said. "Oh, Holliday, I'm not a chief, so don't call me that."

"I know that it's just an expression I use."

"Well, don't use it in the station."

"Okay, boss." Perez walked back to his office, shaking his head back and forth. Nora was sure he was rolling his eyes as well.

The three detectives piled into the Crown Victoria that was assigned to Hawk to use on official business. Hawk drove while Nora sat in the passenger seat. Holliday squeezed into the back. Nora could see that he didn't have enough room for his long legs and large feet, so she moved her seat forward. "Ah, thanks a bunch, Nora. How many miles are on this heap?"

"Hawk glanced at the odometer, "172,780 miles. It's been around. It was a patrol cruiser before they let rookie detectives drive it."

"In Tampa, this vehicle would've been sold to a cab company long ago. I've seen some Ford Explorers and newer Ford sedans around; why are we stuck with this car?"

"We're lucky to have it, Mort; there's always a budget crunch for the police."

"Please, don't call me 'Mort.' I prefer Mortimer."

"Sure, anything, Mortimer."

"So, what is this case about? I guess the case needs my help." *Like I need another hole in my head,* Hawk thought.

Hawk did not feel much like talking, especially to Mortimer, at the moment. He glanced over to Nora and their eyes connected. He rolled his eyes toward the backseat passenger. Nora took the hint. "Mortimer why don't we hold off until we're at the scene of the crime? If you don't know too much about it, maybe you can give us a new perspective on the case."

Mortimer seemed disappointed and sat silent for a few minutes. Hawk appreciated the quietness, at least for a short time. But the silence did not last long. Mortimer sneezed again and blew his nose. Nora once again said, "Bless you." Then both Nora and Clint heard his stomach growl. "Are you hungry, Mortimer?"

"Well yes, I expected that there'd be donuts and rolls available for breakfast. Looks like no one brought any in."

"No, no one does that at Homicide," Nora said.

"Well, I'm used to someone bringing in something. In Tampa, there were a couple of detectives and techs that always did. Come to think of it, lately, I think that they started to hide the donuts from me. Maybe I should've brought some in once in a while." Hawk and Ricci weren't able to suppress their laughter.

"What's so funny about that?" Mortimer asked.

"Oh, nothing," Nora said. "Tell us about your fiancé?"

"Oh gosh, let's see. What is there to say? She's clever, almost as tall as me and also very thin. She became a vegan a couple of years ago. I, myself, like a little meat once in a while, but she won't hear of it. She's very frugal and believes meat is too expensive these days. I like that in her because I consider myself frugal as well."

"Well, what do you do for entertainment with her?" Nora asked. "Obviously, you go on cruises."

"Yeah, that's the only cruise either one of us had taken. Costed a lot of money. No, we sit at home mostly and watch PBS or the Discover Network. Can't stand much anything else on TV." Mortimer thought a moment. "Oh yeah, we both like to read and play board games."

Hawk listened to the conversation and decided that Mortimer and his fiancé were definitely on the boring side. He turned onto Humboldt Street, past the sign that read, "Humboldt Historic District" and soon turned left and parked on the same side as the crime scene. When Mortimer exited the car, he noticed the magnificent mansions on both sides of the street.

"What a waste of money these places are. They were built as trophies for whoever occupied them. Josephine inherited a lot of money, and she could buy either one of these mansions for cash if she wanted to, but she's smart enough to live in a small bungalow in the area that she calls Washington Park."

Nora and Clint exchanged glances, equally surprised that Josephine was so well off. "Well, Wash Park is a pricey area as well," Nora said.

"Really? Her house sure doesn't look like it. I think it was built in the 1920's judging by the kitchen and bathrooms. The bedrooms are pretty small. Hers is a little bigger than mine, though."

Nora had to suppress a laugh. Mortimer just cracked her up. Everything he said was said with such seriousness, never a bit of humor. *Come to think of it, I haven't seen him smile or laugh since I met him.* Hawk's head and neck were killing him, and Mortimer's dry conversation became too irritating for him to take. He wished that Nora would stop asking him questions. He just wanted some peace and quiet.

As Mortimer and Nora were still engaged in some conversation, this time over Mortimer's fear of mosquitos, Hawk walked up to the house, hoping to find someone home to open up the garages. Ricci and Holliday followed him to the door.

CHAPTER SEVEN

THE DOOR was answered by a physically fit woman in her late thirties with a freckled, weather-beaten complexion. She wore black pants, a light gray shirt, and black sneakers. Her thick light brown hair was tied back into a bun. From the open doorway, she stared at the three detectives with her large gray eyes noticing the shields on Hawk's and Nora's belts. Holliday wasn't wearing one because it hadn't been issued to him yet. "Yes, may I help you?"

"Are you Nellie, by chance?" Nora asked, her tone serious.

"Yes, what can I do for you?"

"We're detectives with the Denver Police Department investigating the death of Mrs. Ellis, Nora said. "You're the cleaning lady here, is that correct?"

"Well, I like to consider myself more than just the cleaning lady. I'm the housekeeper."

"Sorry. We got the wrong information."

"Yes, you did because I not only clean the house, I make up two beds on account of the Ellises don't sleep together for at least a year now. I also put away their clothes that they just dump on the floor and leave there, expecting me to pick them up. And I wash the dirty dishes and pans and put them away. Even do their laundry. So, you betcha, I'm not just a cleaning lady." Hawk noticed how sensitive she became by being called the cleaning lady. "Oh Jesus, just remembered that I won't be doing anything for Mrs. Ellis anymore. It's sad even though she was a rather nasty lady, always tight with her money, wouldn't spend an extra dime. It made me feel like crap most of the time. But nobody should die like that."

Nora asked, "Do you think you'll still have a job?"

"Well, I think so. I'm thinkin' that mister couldn't run this place without me." *She's pretty sure of herself,* Nora and Hawk both had similar thoughts.

"You mentioned that Mr. and Mrs. Ellis slept in separate beds," Hawk said. "In separate bedrooms?"

"Well, yeah. What'cha thinking? That's a strange question."

"I have another question for you. Why didn't they sleep together?"

"It's because they always fought, but lately, the fights seemed worse. Yesterday, they were so loud yelling at each other that I could hear 'em as I walked up the steps to go to work."

"Do you know what the fight was about?" Nora asked, pleased that they were able to talk to the loquacious woman.

"No. But it was sure a doozy. They were fixin' on burning the barn down; they were so furious. Saw Mr. Ellis storm out of the house and back his fancy car out of the garage onto the street, still lookin' mighty mad and kinda red in the face. The Missus was so upset with him that morning and even more so when she came home early after work." She hesitated, then said. "As I said, it's so terrible what happened to her."

Do you think that the mister had something to do with it?" Hawk thought her eyes shifted slightly. Her eyebrows fluttered. *She's hiding something,* he thought.

"Well, do you?" Hawk asked.

"Oh Jesus, I sure hope not. I need this job and hope that he didn't."

Nora said, "We didn't get your last name and where is your home?"

"Pyle. I live with my grandma and my three kids in a little three-bedroom house that I rent on Decatur and Kentucky. It's the cheapest place that I could find at the time because rents in Denver are too unaffordable for us poor folks."

"Thank you, Mrs. Pyle," Hawk said. "Could you open the garage doors for us so that we can continue our investigation?"

"Sure, no problem. If you need to know anything else about the Ellises, just ask."

"I do have a question, Nellie," Nora said. "Do you know Tina Dionisio?"

"Nope."

"She is Mr. Ellis' assistant."

"Nope, never met her. Oh, wait. There was a woman who brought some papers for Mr. Ellis the other day. That might have been her. A real pretty, sexy looking woman."

"Thank you, Nellie. Now if you'd open the doors."

"I have to open them from the inside of the garage. Meet you there."

The three detectives walked over to the garage and waited. Holliday said, "She's certainly talkative, isn't she? I think that it's so unusual for a person to come right out and talk down your employers. Don't you think?"

"You're right about that, Mortimer," Nora said. "But I'm glad she did. Those are the questions I would've asked so it saved us some time. Interesting how bad the Ellises marriage seemed to be, isn't it?"

The garage doors opened, and Nellie started to walk toward them. "Please hold off," Hawk said. "We'd like to examine the garage now that it's empty before too many people walk around inside."

"Oh, sorry." Nellie stood at the threshold. "Yeah, your CSI people towed Mrs. Ellis's Mercedes to the crime lab; at least, that's what they said. And while I was walking out here, I remembered that I think I saw Mr. Ellis' assistant about a week ago. The same girl that delivered the papers to him. She must've been running in the park as she came around the garage there and then ran down the street." She pointed to the edge of the garage as it stood adjacent to the park. "I watched her run to the corner to Humboldt and get into a car and leave."

"When did you say that was?" Nora asked, again pleased to hear the scoop on Tina.

"Can't remember the day, but 'bout a week ago."

"Did you see her since?" Holliday asked and for some reason, glanced at both Hawk and Nora as though seeking their approval of his question. Nellie answered in the negative and since no more questions were thrown at her, she left. But first, she advised them to press "enter" on the keypad to close the doors when they are done.

The three entered the garage. "What are we looking for?" Holliday asked as his head seemed to pivot from one corner of the garage to the other, then at the ceiling.

"Anything that possibly would be helpful," Nora said. Holliday did not respond. While Hawk moved about checking things out, Holliday stood in one spot, his head rotating about on his skinny neck.

"I feel evil in this garage," he said.

"Well, yes. For sure, a woman was murdered here," Hawk said.

"No, more than that. I feel a presence, an eerie presence. Don't you feel the sudden coldness? I've had this feeling before in haunted houses. My heart races and I become really anxious."

"See, Clint," Nora said. "I told you about all the spirits in the park and beyond."

"Well, maybe we can ask them who killed Mrs. Ellis, then," Hawk snickered.

Mortimer said, "Oh, it's not funny. There is something here. I'm very sensitive to it. I think there's also a presence in Josephine's house. But she laughs it off. Maybe, I'm just crazy."

Hawk said, "Well, Nora told me about the history of this park and so I googled it. I saw a story that in one of these houses, there is a woman ghost that sits on the edge of the dining table sobbing and moaning. She complains that she can't find her head anywhere."

"See," Nora said. "That's because that guy, McGovern, cut the bodies up in the cemetery and put their parts in different boxes."

"What is that? What about a cemetery?" Holliday said, still not moving from his spot in the garage.

Nora said, "Mortimer, it's a long story. I'll tell you all about it later. We better get on with our investigation."

Hawk walked around the perimeter of the garage, not sure what he was looking for or what he could possibly see. Next to the wall of the garage, he squatted and studied some spilled potting soil from a bag. "Well, look what I see," Hawk said, pointing out to the others an open bag located on the victim's side of the garage. "Look here, some of the soil is spilled and I can barely make out part of a heel from a shoe. It looks like a men's sneaker." Nora came over to Clint and studied the imprint. "I wonder if anyone from CSI spotted it?"

"No wonder your name is Hawk," Nora laughed. "You seem to have a hawk's eye. I don't think I would have spotted it."

"Oh, I don't know. It's mostly luck. But I'll call Chet Watkins from the crime lab and ask him about it and also find out when we'll get a report of what their technicians found as far as fingerprints and that kind of stuff. As a matter of fact, I think I'll call him to know. If they hadn't noticed it, he needed to come right over and get an impression of the heel. It looks like whoever it was backed up into that loose dirt from the Mercedes."

Hawk gave Chet a call and he answered on the second ring. Explaining why he called, Hawk was told that no one from the lab noticed it, although they saw the bag of potting soil. Watkins told Hawk that he's just a few minutes away and he'll come by and take a mold of it. Hawk filled the other two detectives in on the conversation. By this time, Holliday had come out of his trance-like state. He walked over and looked at the bag and the spilled dirt. He again seemed to scan the garage and said, "It could very well be that there might have been two people in this garage and not necessarily together."

Hawk and Nora turned to him. "Why did you say that?"

"That's the feeling I have."

"A feeling?" Hawk asked. "Is that all it is?"

"Yes, for now."

"It's certainly a possibility," Nora said. "But we have no evidence of anything like that at all."

"I know, but sometimes my feelings work out. I'm trying to be helpful."

Hawk said, "We'll keep it in mind. Let's see what other evidence we can find, if any. With that, though, I'm through in here. Let's go into the park, at least along the fence line. Let's examine the area more closely."

Nora cocked her head, "Are you thinking that the killer could've discarded a syringe in the park?"

"Yes, I think it's a distinct possibility. I assume that the killer probably was dressed in jogging clothes so that he or she could fit in with the other runners and wouldn't want to be seen holding a syringe or two in his or her hand or needles sticking out of a pocket."

"Nor be caught with the syringes if stopped for any reason," Nora said. "Yeah, I think it's a good idea. Let's go into the park as you suggested and check around the fence line."

They asked Mortimer to join them, but he was adamant about not entering the park and asked to stay behind.

"Fine," Hawk said. "If you don't mind, you can wait for Chet to arrive and take a mold of that partial imprint. We should be back before he comes, though."

Nora and Clint went around the short cinderblock retaining wall on the east side of the garage that separated the Ellis property from the public park. Out of hearing range, Nora whispered to Clint, "Can you believe it, he's afraid of ghosts." She laughed and Hawk returned her laugh. They walked very carefully, examining the area next to the fence and around and under every bush. "I guess this is a bust," Nora said. "I doubt the person would've run or walked across the park. He'd want to leave the area as quickly as possible. Maybe we should try the other direction to the north."

"Okay, you go north, and I'll go south."

"Oh gosh, that sounds like we'll never meet again." Nora laughed. "Just like the song."

Hawk smiled at her, "Nora, you're always fun, even in such mundane work as this."

"I aim to please." She giggled and went on her way.

Hawk scanned the area further down the fence. He saw some bigger bushes up ahead and went on following the fence line. By the next street, he stopped at a large lilac bush. He squatted down and began to push aside some of the branches hanging low and scrape some leaves and twigs from underneath. Disappointed not to find anything of evidence, he made his way back to the garage.

As he started walking around the short cinder block wall, he noticed that one of the cap bricks had been damaged, leaving a hole about the size of four inches. *What the hell? Very unlikely, but I better take a look.* Nora also made her way back and walked up to him. She saw him checking out the cavity. "You've got to be kidding. You really think that the murderer threw the syringes in there?"

"Probably not, but why not check?"

Hawk had his small LED penlight attached to his keyring and directed the light down the hole, lowering his head to investigate it. The depth was only as deep as the next row of cinderblocks. He let out a whistle. "Shit! Here they are. There are two syringes in here."

Nora laughed out of merriment. "Your luck is still with you. I remember how you found evidence by fluke in the Bowman cases."

"Well, don't get too excited. We don't know if those were used by the murderer or thrown there by some drug users. But since there were two of them and thrown out evidently together, I'm going to bag them. Wait, I hear Chet and Mortimer talking. Chet needs to see this."

When he returned to the garage, Chet Watkins was making an imprint of the partial heel. "Hello there, Detective," he said. "Yeah,

I don't know how we missed this one. It was awfully hard to see, don't know how you spotted it."

"Just luck, I guess. In the last case, you told me that you're an expert on shoe soles."

"Yeah, I studied them thoroughly and still have to keep up since the manufacturers change the style so often. But this one is pretty distinctive. If I had to guess, I'd say it's a size ten shoe, and it's probably from a Solomon sneaker. Don't see too many of them, that's for sure. But they're great shoes, I've been told. Some can be pricey."

"Thanks, Chet," Hawk said. "We really appreciate you coming out so fast. You met Detective Ricci and Detective Holliday, I take it?"

"Oh yeah. I've known Nora for a while. Detective Holliday is new to me, but we got acquainted. He's from Florida, where I grew up. So, we have something in common." He looked at both Ricci and Holliday and gave them a wide smile.

"Chet, before you go, we think we have more evidence for you to process. Would you follow me?" Hawk showed him the wall with its hole and shinned his light down for Chet to see.

"Those look like hypodermic needles down there. You think they're the murder weapons?"

"I don't know. You'll have to tell us. I'm particularly interested, if the lab can find fingerprints or, better yet, DNA other than that of the victim."

Chet walked back to his truck to get his camera. He took several shots of the wall in relation to the garage, then the hole, both outside and inside, with the syringes lying inside the cavity. Pulling on his nitrile gloves, he reached in and picked the syringes up and placed them carefully in a plastic bag that he pulled out of his pocket. He made sure that the needles didn't penetrate it.

Mortimer watched everything closely but didn't say a word. Although, he nodded his head up and down in approval.

Nora smiled at Clint and squeezed his arm. "Good job. Well done. Do you think we should go interview that Tina now, the one you had googly eyes over?" She laughed.

Hawk shook his head, "You're crazy, Nora. But, sure, let's go before their offices close."

"Did I miss something? What about this woman you're talking about?"

"Oh, it's just a joke, Mortimer. Tina is very pretty and I'm teasing Clint about it."

"A joke? Oh. Okay, let's see how pretty she is then, but you know, I won't care. Stuff like that doesn't interest me that much."

Hawk and Ricci gave each other a quick glance and a smile played at the corners of their mouths. "On to Tina, then!" Nora said enthusiastically and pointed her arm and forefinger toward the downtown area, marching toward the Crown Vic.

CHAPTER EIGHT

THE RAIN that had pounded Nora and Clint before they left for lunch earlier that day had stopped within five minutes and, as typical for Colorado, sunshine returned. Now that they, along with Holliday, were on their way to downtown Denver, the clouds rolled in again from the west and it looked as though it might rain. Travel time to Ellis' office at the Wells Fargo Center was short and hopefully, they would still catch Tina Dionisio before she left for the day.

Nora asked, "Which is the Wells Fargo building? I can't remember."

"It's the cash register building," Hawk replied; his mood greatly improved since the neck and back pain that he experienced in the morning and early afternoon seemed to have abated.

"Oh yeah, that's right."

"The cash register building?" Mortimer asked. "What's that, might I ask?"

Hawk laughed, "You're right, Mortimer. That is confusing. Look over there," pointing to the tall structures of downtown looming on their right. "Do you see the one with the top floors curved together?"

"Yes. Oh yes, I see it. It does look like an antique cash register. That is certainly interesting. Is that the tallest building in Denver?"

"No," Nora interjected, wanting to exhibit that she knows something about the buildings as well. "I remember reading in a book about Denver that the tallest is the Republic Plaza Building with fifty-six floors, while the cash register building is fifty-two floors. Isn't it the third tallest in Denver, Clint?"

"I think so."

"Well, Denver has some impressive high-rises. Tampa doesn't have as many, and I think the tallest is something like forty-five floors. Much easier to get around there, though. Denver sure seems congested to me."

"Have you and Josephine gone downtown and just looked around?" Nora asked, making conversation.

"Oh no. We wouldn't go anyplace like that unless we had to. Josephine would say that it would cost too much money in gas, and then she'd tell me that the parking fees are enormous."

"You mentioned that you never go to restaurants?" Nora asked. "Is it for health reasons?"

"I'd go to a cheap place in the Tampa Bay area, especially if it was during a lunch break. But since I arrived in Denver, we haven't gone anywhere. Josephine tells me that the food in restaurants is too expensive and unhealthy. She says it's too full of salt and fat to her liking."

"That's no fun. I love going out to eat. It's one of the pleasures of life, don't you think, Clint?"

Clint laughed. "The more fat there is, the better it tastes. Mortimer, we'll have to take you out to a restaurant for lunch soon."

"Oh, I don't know. I wonder what Josephine would say about it."

"She doesn't need to know, does she?"

"Oh, I'll have to think about that."

"Does Josephine have any children?" Nora became intrigued with Josephine and wanted to know more about her.

Mortimer cleared his throat and continued to try to clear it a few more times. Then he sneezed and wiped his mouth with his sleeve. "No. She's never been married before. She has cats, though, which I'm allergic to, but she says I'll get used to them. She told me that they are her heirs." Holliday thought a moment. "It's really a shame that all her millions are going to her cats. I've been thinking about that. She probably means that she'll leave her fortune to an animal shelter, don't you think?"

"Most likely," Nora said.

"Oh, I hope so. Although, I'd rather see her money go to humans."

Hawk shook his head at the thought of how much control this Josephine had on Mortimer. He could not believe that any man would want to get into such a relationship voluntarily. *She's leading him by his nose.* He thought someone should tell Mortimer to be a man. *What's with this guy? Is he for real or is he putting us on? Or maybe, Mortimer and Josephine deserve each other.* He turned onto Seventeenth Avenue toward the underground parking garage, but luckily, he found a vacant spot on the side of the building. He parked on a slant since the street was hilly. He and Nora exited, but because of the slope with his long legs, it was difficult for Mortimer to get out of the back seat. Hawk helped him out.

"I tell you; we don't worry about hills in the Tampa Bay area. Another thing I'll have to get used to." *Nothing seems to be quite right in Colorado to this guy,* Nora thought.

They walked into the lobby and Nora immediately rushed over to peek at the directory. She found "Ellis Group" listed and assumed that that was Steven Ellis' office. "We go to the forty-fourth floor," Nora told the men.

In the elevator, Nora glanced at Mortimer. He did not look healthy. He broke out in a sweat, holding his chest with his hand and seemed to struggle for breath. "Mortimer, are you all right?"

"I'll be all right. I just need to get off this damn elevator. Sometimes I get hit with a bout of claustrophobia. I'm fine, don't worry." With a concerned look on his face, Hawk surveyed Holliday to see if he needed immediate help.

Fortunately, they were on an express elevator and their floor came up relatively fast. Mortimer took some deep breaths and waved with his hand that he was all right. They quickly found the office suite and walked in. A cute, pixie-faced woman in her late twenties with a button nose and short straw-blond hair smiled broadly to the detectives. "Hello, may I help y'all?"

"Yes, we're here to see Tina Dionisio," Hawk asked. "Is she in?"

She smiled sweetly at Hawk, brushed her hair back with her thin hand that showed off her expensively manicured fingernails, then said, "She sure is. I'll tell'er that y'all here." She picked up the phone and without taking her eyes off it, Hawk informed Tina that she had visitors. "Why don't y'all just have a seat over there," pointing to two green leather sofas sitting at right angles to each other in the corner of the room. In between was a rug with a modern geometric design topped by a glass and brass coffee table. Above the sofas were paintings of snowy mountain scenes.

After the three sat down, Hawk said to the receptionist across the empty room, "You're from the South, aren't you?"

"Why yes; how did y'all know?"

"Mississippi?"

"Why, are you the smart one? Yes, exactly."

"Where from?" Nora gave Hawk a dirty look. *What's he doing? Is he flirting with her?* Hawk noticed Nora's reaction, but he really wanted to know where she was from for a reason. Her accent was very familiar to him, and he was unusually good at picking up various accents from different parts of the country. "Let me guess. I bet you're from northern Mississippi, southern Tennessee."

"Gads! How would y'all know that?"

"My parents had close friends in Pontotoc. They lived on a lake, and we'd spent almost every summer with them. They showed us everything—Oxford, Tupelo, Memphis."

"I can't believe it. I'm from Pontotoc!" She stood up and rushed over to Hawk. "Let me give y'all a hug. It's like we're related or something." She pulled Hawk close to her and Nora was about ready to either punch her or arrest her for an assault on a police officer. She looked angry and knew it. At that moment, Mortimer stood up and asked to be excused. He asked the receptionist, who had sat back down again, where the men's room was. She told him. On the way out the door, looking over his shoulder, he told his partners, if need be, to start the meeting without him.

Tina soon joined them. She was dressed in a stylish lavender dress and purple high-heeled Prada shoes with a smile on her face. She expected perhaps new clients for her boss or old clients that needed updates. But upon seeing the detectives, her smile faded instantly. "May I help you?" Then she recognized them from the Ellis house; "Oh, yes, I remember you. Police detectives, right?"

"Miss Dionisio," Hawk said, "You're absolutely correct. We're sorry to bother you, but we have a few questions."

She hesitated, trying to decide whether to cooperate or refuse to talk. "Sure. No problem. Let's use this conference room here," pointing to a glass-walled room with a long conference table and ten chairs around it. She sat down on one side of the table as Hawk and Ricci sat on the other. She smiled sweetly at Clint and said, "What can I help you with, Detective," ignoring Nora.

That immediately rubbed Nora the wrong way. She didn't like that woman from the start, now even less so. *I hope she did it. I'd love to put her away.* At that moment, Holliday walked into the room. Tina's eyes widened at the sight of the tall, stooped, comically dressed man.

"Who is this?" She looked at Hawk for an answer.

"Oh, this is our human lie detector."

"Well, thank you for that, Detective Hawk. I've been called that many times before because I can tell when people lie." Continuing to glare at Tina, he introduced himself and sat down at the head of the table. As Tina watched him, she fidgeted in her seat. Nora noticed that she actually looked intimidated by Mortimer. *Perhaps it's because Clint said he was a lie detector.* She chuckled to herself; *good one, Clint.*

"Can we get on with this now?" Nora said aggressively. She reintroduced herself again, because, in her mind, Tina wouldn't have remembered her, only Hawk.

"Oh, Ricci. We're compadres and about the same age. Did you grow up in Northeast Denver like I did? A lot of Italian families did."

"No, I didn't." *I'm not about to discuss my background with this wench.* "Is Tina Dionisio your full name?"

"No, it's Christina Angela Dionisio."

"And your address?"

"I have a loft on Market Street, Number 1599E."

"Marital status?"

"I'm divorced."

Hawk interrupted the line of questioning as he thought that Nora sounded a little too aggressive with these background questions. "Tina. May I call you Tina?"

She again smiled sweetly at Hawk, removing that frown she had on her face when Nora questioned her. "Oh yes, please do. All my friends call me Tina." Nora could not understand what was going on inside her. She was almost always a very even-tempered person that was not prone to an outburst of anger. She felt that a volcano was brewing and was ready to erupt. She took some deep breaths hoping that no one noticed. She knew she had to control that geyser within. *I don't understand why this is happening to me. This is just another witness that may lead us to the murderer. Why does she bug me so much? It can't be that she's flirting with Clint, can it? All women seem to flirt with him. And why am I so upset? As long as he's not serious, let her flirt all she wants. Oh well, let him ask a few more questions and hopefully, I'll calm down.*

"Tina, I can't help but admire your stunning bracelet. Those are some great tourmalines, and the diamonds are not bad either."

"Yes, thank you. It is beautiful, isn't it." *He better not say, "it's as beautiful as she is."* Nora thought. *I'll deck him, I swear.*

"Yes, it's quite impressive. I bet it was a gift from an admirer."

"Yes, it was, as a matter of fact."

"He must love you very much, wouldn't you say?"

"I guess so. I hope so."

"It was from Mr. Ellis, wasn't it?" Tina seemed stunned at that question. She was lost as to how to reply. She decided to deny it, but then she glanced at Holliday. Mortimer sat still, glaring at her.

The human lie detector, she remembered Hawk's words. She glanced back at the strange detective and suddenly got the shivers. Nora noticed her reaction to Mortimer and almost burst out laughing but suppressed herself. That incident left her calm and she thought she could proceed.

"You're right. Steven gave it to me for my birthday." She quickly added, "For my contribution and the many years of service to this company."

Nora cooled off and she was back in the swing of things. "Oh, how many years have you worked for Mr. Ellis?" She forced a fake smile.

"Well, I guess it wasn't all that many. But it seems a lot," she attempted to chuckle and make a joke of it, but the detectives observed how nervous she had become talking about Steven Ellis. "It has been little more than three years."

"You were having an affair with Steven Ellis, weren't you?" Nora said.

Tina felt like she was being cornered. She was going to deny it, but once again, she glanced at Mortimer and felt intimidated. "I don't know if you call it an affair. We got together a few times."

"Had sex?"

She again glanced at Mortimer, who had not moved a millimeter from the time he sat down, his eyes drilling into the poor woman. "Yes."

"And Steven Ellis was married?" Nora asked, pleased that she could stick it to her.

"Yes," she answered in almost a whisper, her head bent slightly down.

"What was that?" Mortimer spoke out for the first time, his voice deep and loud. "I couldn't hear."

"Yes. Yes. Yes." Tina was almost shouting. "He was married. We had sex, but what does that have to do with the death of Mrs. Ellis?"

"Wasn't she in your way and Mr. Ellis didn't want a divorce because he would've lost at least half his fortune, maybe more?" Nora continued. "You wanted to be the grand dame of the castle. You wanted to be Mrs. Ellis with all the social perks that would give you."

"Listen, Ricci. I would never kill anyone. It's not in me. Now, are we through here?" Tina was shaking visibly. "Next time, I'll call a lawyer. Goodbye."

Hawk said, "Before we leave, and thank you for your candid answers, Tina, could you clarify for us why you were at Cheesman Park about a week before Mrs. Ellis' murder?"

Tina was at this point standing up to leave but then sat down again and faced Hawk. "I was there with my friend, Kara Summers. She and I meet every week for a run at different parks around the city. Last week we were in Cheesman. The week before, we were in Washington Park, and before that, at City Park. This week we're going for a run around Sloan's Lake. You know, we try to make it less boring. You can ask her yourself. She'll verify it. Now, I really need to get back to work."

As the three walked out, the receptionist said to Hawk. "It was great talking about Mississippi with y'all. My name is Luanne Sue if you ever want to talk more about it."

"Why, thank you. That's very kind of you. Oh, by the way, was Mr. Ellis in all morning yesterday?"

"Let's see, yesterday morning," She scratched her head with a pen, trying to remember and looked up at the ceiling as though the answer was written there. "I believe he was in early, at about eight and then left around ten. Said he'll be gone the rest of the day. I haven't seen him since."

Hawk reached into his jacket pocket and pulled out a card. "Well, if you can think of anything else, here's my card. My cell number is listed on it."

Hawk smiled at her and she returned a generous grin. Mortimer moaned at the thought of getting back into the elevator. They were alone in the elevator and Nora burst out laughing. "I can't believe how much the 'human lie detector' intimidated her." She looked at the man standing behind her, who was now breathing hard. "Your act was superb, Mortimer."

"What act are you talking about? I didn't do anything out of the ordinary, just sat there." Her laugh was so infectious that Hawk laughed hard as well. As they walked outside, heading for the car, Nora and Clint were still laughing but Holliday never cracked a smile. "I don't understand what you're laughing at. Can we get back to the station now? It's past quitting time and Josephine needs me to pick up some kale and broccoli for dinner."

They parked the Ford in the police lot. Holliday went directly to his car while Hawk and Nora walked back to the unit. Perez was with Orlinski and upon seeing the couple, he asked them to come to his office.

CHAPTER NINE

LIEUTENANT PEREZ wanted a rundown of their investigation so far. Hawk explained how he saw a partial shoe print and where he found the two syringes. "It's a long shot, but both might be related to Mrs. Ellis' murder." He also described the interview with Tina Dionisio, Mr. Ellis' assistant. He explained that she had admitted to having an affair with Ellis. Hawk proceeded to describe the expensive bracelet that Ellis gave her, indicating to him that their relationship was serious.

"So, what do you think of everything so far," Perez asked Nora. "Do you think the husband did it?"

Nora looked up at the lieutenant. "I think there is definitely a strong possibility. He wasn't honest in some of his answers. It was obvious that he was hiding something, most likely the affair with his assistant. But the way the murder was committed, I don't know. I think we need to talk to him again."

"Tell me about your questioning of Tina."

Nora said, "Nothing unusual. We got her to admit to the affair. If I had to bet who did it, I would bet on Tina at this time. There's something dishonest about her. She seems to me to be two-faced and those people are hard to read."

"Would you say that your questioning was a little rough?"

"Why did she complain about it to you?"

"No, but Steven Ellis had a few choice words to say to Captain MacGregor."

"Well, if we're always gentle with our questions, we would never get anywhere."

"True. I'll tell the captain about the affair. I'm sure she'll agree to proceed full steam ahead. And, by the way, I think you did good today."

He stopped and looked at both Hawk and Ricci. "You both had a long day; go home. Oh, yes, how did Holliday do? Was he any help?"

Nora laughed and explained to him the remark that Hawk made describing Mortimer as a human lie detector. "He looked so serious, glaring at Tina with that intimidating stare that I think she would confess to murder, if we were able to push her further." Nora laughed again, joined by the two men.

"Before you leave, tell me of your plans for tomorrow."

Nora said, "I thought we should go to interview Amanda Ellis' supervisor. The one we've been told sexually harassed her. And later we'll interview the president or CEO of the company."

"Good. Come in first and pick up Holliday."

As they were about to leave, the door to the Homicide unit swung open and Marcie, a tall, attractive blond-haired woman, slowly walked in, looking around the room. She was visible through the glass of Perez's office. Surprised to see her, Hawk quickly stood up and rushed toward her. Nora's heart sank. "Who's that?" Perez asks Nora. Both watched as Marcie threw her arms around Hawk, her face in his shoulder. The longer she stayed in his arms, the more Nora's insides trembled.

"That's Marcie Turner. She used to work here."

"Oh, that's the one that Orlinski told me about. Wasn't she suspected by almost everyone except Hawk as being the mysterious boss of the dirty cop gang?"

"Yes, she's the one." *Too bad that she wasn't. I'd love to see her in jail. But nooo, she's that sweet Marcie that I bet Clint is still hung up on.*

They watched as Marcie pulled away from Hawk, wiped her eyes with the back of her hand and ardently explained something to him, her arms waving in the air. A minute later, Hawk escorted her into Perez's office.

Marcie forced a smile, her eyes filled with tears. "Hello, Nora," she said coldly. Nora's response was the same. Hawk introduced her to Lieutenant Perez, and she managed to widen her smile for him.

Hawk said, "Lieutenant Perez, I'd like you to meet Marcie Turner. We know each other because we worked together here. She was our computer tech." Perez nodded, acknowledging the woman. "Marcie just informed me that this morning she found out that her best friend died this morning. It was Amanda Ellis."

"Oh, I'm terribly sorry," Perez said. "It appears to be a great loss to you."

"I'll be all right. It was such a horrible shock when Steven, the husband, informed me that she had died. He thinks it's a heart attack. But I'm not sure that I believe it. Amanda has had it pretty rough lately. She and Steven had grown further apart, and she had problems at work with sexual harassment. She hated her supervisor in the architectural department and was going to raise some stink for the company. Also, she thought that she had uncovered some fraudulent dealings in the office. Perhaps it was a retaliation of some kind."

"We're aware of all that," Nora said. "But I'm also sorry for the loss of your friend. I lost one a few years ago to cancer and it was an exceedingly difficult time for me as well."

"Thank you, Nora. I appreciate that."

"The reason I wanted Marcie to come in to see you," Hawk said, "Is that last night she received a text from Amanda Ellis showing documents."

"Yes," Marcie said, "Let me show them to you. I believe that they are probably from her place of employment."

"Let me see them," Perez said. Marcie handed him the phone and he studied them, enlarging them in places for easier reading. He then handed the phone to Nora. She perused the documents and then passed the phone to Hawk.

"So, what do you think?" Perez asked.

Hawk said, "I think we have more to inquire about when we visit the company tomorrow. It looks to me that they are substituting inferior materials for the contracted materials. I bet they're not reducing the cost to the customer, though."

"That's the way I see it," Nora mumbled, hating the thought of Clint and Marcie standing close to each other at the side of Perez's desk.

"I agree," Perez said. "But if you could tie the homicide to these documents, then I guess we can pursue this case; otherwise, it really should be referred over to the Financial Fraud unit."

Hawk said, looking suddenly concerned, "Marcie, when exactly did you receive the text from Amanda?"

"It was late last night."

"I see that you answered her, asking what the documents mean and why she sent them to you. That was at ten-thirty last night."

"Why, why do you look so worried?"

"I'm thinking that we never found Amanda's cell phone. I also think that if they killed your friend because she discovered the fraud, then with you getting the text with the documents, that...." He hesitated. "They now would know that you also would know about the fraud.

"That now my life is in danger! That's what you're saying, isn't it?" Marcie's face looked petrified with fear.

CHAPTER TEN

THE ROOM fell suddenly silent. Hawk, Ricci, and Perez focused their attention on Marcie. With an unsteady voice, she appealed to Hawk, "Is that what you're saying? You think that they'll come after me now?"

Hawk swallowed hard and didn't say anything for a few seconds, his jaw tight. "Marcie, it's only a slim possibility. You know me, I sometimes make a mountain out of a molehill. But, out of an abundance of caution, we shouldn't discount it altogether." *What does he mean, you know me?"* Nora pondered that statement.

"Oh, God!" Marcie stroked her forehead with her right hand and squeezed it. "What shall I do?" She looked at Hawk with pleading eyes.

"Marcie, I really doubt that you'd be in any danger, but if you are, it would probably be tonight only."

"Why is that?" Nora asked, opening her arms as though in disbelief.

"I'd like an answer to that myself," Lieutenant Perez said.

Hawk cleared his throat. "This is the way I see it. If they, and I would assume that 'they' are the group from Mrs. Ellis' employer, know that Marcie received the text containing the documents, they would try to silence Marcie and take away her phone before she has a chance to show the documents or discuss them with anyone. They would assume that she hadn't had a chance yet to figure out what that's all about...."

"Unless they are convinced that Amanda had told Marcie the details of the scheme," Nora interrupted Hawk.

"In that case, Marcie, they could think that you have damaging information and could use it against them, either by going to the developers or to the police," Perez added.

"Oh God! What did Amanda get me into? She never explained anything to me. She just texted me the documents and I really don't know what they mean."

"Yeah, but they don't know that," Nora said.

Hawk looked at his distressed friend. "Marcie, I really feel that if they're going to do anything, it will be tonight. You need to stay somewhere else tonight."

"Stay somewhere else? How would they even know where I live."

"They have your phone number if they have Amanda's cell. She must have you in the contacts list with your full name and might even have your address. But if not, it's possible to obtain the address and name from the phone number alone."

Perez addressed Marcie. "I agree with Clint that you take precautions and don't stay at your place tonight. Maybe not even tomorrow night. Do you have someone you could stay with for a day or two?"

"No, I really don't. I could've stayed with Amanda, but...." Her eyes welled again.

Hawk wanted to offer his place, but then he thought that Nora would have a coronary over the idea. After a pause, Nora said, "You need to come and stay with me, Marcie. I have an extra bedroom that you can use for a few days." *Why in the hell did I offer her the place to stay when she wants to steal Clint away from me? But I guess I'm too nice of a person and I really don't want anything to happen to her.* Hawk's eyes widened when he heard Nora's offer.

He was surprised. But then, why was he? After all, Nora had always shown her gentle and thoughtful side.

"Nora, thank you so much, but I don't want to bother you. I'll just go to a hotel for tonight."

"I won't hear of it. You're staying with me. I'll prepare dinner for us and we'll have a good time. *Just keep your hands off, Clint.*

Marcie reluctantly agreed and it was decided that Hawk would follow her back to her apartment to grab a few things that she would need. She was to leave her car in the underground garage and he would drive her to Nora's.

As they left the Division Six station, Hawk had his eye on Marcie's Mini Cooper as she made her way to her apartment building in Glendale. Twenty minutes later, Marcie used a key card to unlock the metal mesh to enter the garage. Hawk parked in a visitor's space and waited for Marcie to take the garage elevator and make it up to her apartment. After five minutes, he exited the vehicle. On the way to the front door, he looked back and spotted two short, beefy men approaching behind him. Dressed in black jeans, each had a polo-type shirt of a different color underneath their black suit jackets. One of the men was white with a dark tan and wore dark sunglasses on his pitted face. His hair was cut short. The other man was Asian with long black hair tied into a man bun, also wearing dark sunglasses. With one quick look, he formed an opinion that they were probably up to no good.

Hawk would have liked to ask who they were, what they were up to and frisk them, but he had no probable cause to do so. *Other than being ugly in public,* he thought to himself and chuckled. Besides, he had no jurisdiction in Glendale as it was an incorporated municipality within the confines of Denver. He decided to proceed and see what played out. *They probably have nothing to do with Marcie and I'm just being paranoid again.* He punched in the number of Marcie's apartment, 783, and made sure the men did not see the numbers as they stood just a few feet behind him, waiting to get into the building themselves.

The buzzer sounded and Hawk proceeded through the front door. He tried to quickly close the door behind him, but the men hastily followed him in. Once in the lobby, the men sat down in the lobby as though they were waiting for someone else to join them. Not trusting them, Hawk took the elevator a floor above Marcie's in case the men watched what floor he got off on.

As soon as he exited, he heard the elevator start again and he immediately assumed it went down to pick up the suspicious men. He hurriedly ran down the stairs to the seventh floor and tried to find a spot where he could hide and yet see the hallway and the door to Marcie's apartment, which door was just a few doors down. Looking around earnestly, he spotted a door that had a sign, "Utility Closet," next to the elevator. He turned the handle and miraculously, it was unlocked. As he entered the closet, the light from the hall gave him a chance to spot electrical and telephone boxes and wiring on the walls and a mop with a bucket and a vacuum cleaner positioned on the floor in the room. He left the door slightly ajar so that he could see part of the hallway and more importantly, Marcie's door in the distance.

He heard the elevator stop on the floor. *Oh Jesus, they're here. I was right; they are after Marcie.* He tensed up as he heard the men get off the elevator. His heart felt as though it wanted to jump out of his chest. The elevator doors closed, but the men were not immediately visible. At least he knew whom he was watching for. They slowly walked to the middle of the hall, and he got a good look at them. Standing still, they carefully appraised the surroundings. *Checking for cameras,* he thought, of which he knew there were none. Hawk took photos of the men on his iPhone 11 through the small crack of the door opening. He also focused on the shoes that the men wore. The Asian man wore black leather shoes, while the white man wore dark olive-green sneakers with a large crisscross pattern on the sides of the shoe.

After making sure that the coast was clear, the men made their way toward Marcie's apartment. Suddenly Hawk spotted a gun held down to the side by the Asian man. Just as the other guy was about to ring the doorbell, Hawk popped out of the closet with his Sig pistol pointed at them, yelling, "Police! Move away from the door. Get down on the ground, now!"

A few of the neighbors opened their doors to see what was going on. "Get back inside! Police business!" They complied, but the two men did not. The Asian man instantly raised his gun and knowing what awaited him, Hawk fell flat to the floor in his attempt to make himself a smaller target. A shot whizzed above his head, and he heard it hit the wall behind him. Instantly, after the shot, the men made a dash for the stairwell, the door to it just a few feet from them. Hawk rose from the prone position and took off after them. At the first landing down, he saw the men scamper down the stairs. One of them shot up toward him from several floors below, the slug hitting the ceiling. They were too far gone, and he did not want to take any unnecessary risks running after them and possibly to endanger the lives of the residents. Besides, he needed to get back to Marcie. *She must be going absolutely nuts and I don't blame her.*

Marcie was hysterical. She heard the gunshots and panicked. She realized that killers had come for her. She managed to open the door after Hawk yelled out for her to do so. "It's okay. They're gone."

She rushed into his arms and held him tight as though her life depended on it. With tears rolling down her face, she backed off a little and looked up at Hawk. "God! What did Amanda get me into?" she repeated what she had said at the police station. She kept repeating it over and over. Her body was racked by tremors. "I'm not a strong person, Clint. You know that. I told you that when I said I'd be going back to California. The main reason I decided to leave is that I didn't see a future between the two of us because of your profession. I couldn't stand waiting and worrying to see if you'd come home at night. And now the danger came to my door."

"Marcie, relax if you can. They'll not come back here. Nevertheless, it'll be best to get you out of here for tonight. Who knows? If you venture out, they may be watching." Hawk immediately regretted saying that. It seemed to cause her to stiffen. "But chances are they're long gone. Especially since they know that I can identify them." Marcie had an expression of horror on her face. "Marcie, we'll get through this. I'll make sure you're protected. Try to relax a little, if you can. Take some deep breaths and say to yourself, it's over with. You know, the more I think of it, I identified myself as a police officer and they should figure out that you'd given me the documents by now, told me everything you know, and leave you alone."

Marcie took Hawk's advice and began to take some deep breaths. It seemed to have helped to calm her down a little. "Perhaps you're right. Maybe now they realize that I know nothing or had given the police whatever information I had. Who do you think those men were?"

"To me, they seem to be hired thugs."

"Well, whoever hired them must think that I know more about their fraud than I really do." She hesitated. "But I don't want to stay here another minute, nor do I really want to go to Nora's." She looked up at Hawk with intense eyes. "Unless you stay with me here tonight."

"No, Marcie, that wouldn't work out. Nora would really get pissed off. I have to work with her, after all. She's my partner."

"Nora, Nora, Nora. I can tell she loves you, but do you love her? I mean, truly, do you love her?"

"I like her a lot."

"You didn't answer my question."

"I'm just not sure at this time, Marcie."

"Well, as I told you before, you'll never commit yourself to any long relationship."

"Why are we talking about this now? I think it's best that you stay with Nora, at least for tonight and let's see what tomorrow brings. We'll make it clear to the construction company people that we know about the fraud and that you know nothing about it at all other than receiving a text with no explanation."

Marcie wiped her eyes with her forearm. She walked over to the speckled quartz kitchen counter, reached for a tissue out of a box and blew her nose. "Okay, I'll get my things together."

While Marcie went into the bedroom and before the police arrived, Hawk first called Lieutenant Perez about the incident and then Nora and explained why they'd be late. "Oh my God! Clint, you can't be serious. You could've been killed! What am I supposed to do with you? I need to be around you constantly to protect you. I can't believe it. Again! That's the fifth attempt on your life since I've known you just for this short while." Hawk could hear her deep, hard breathing over the phone. She hesitated a minute, then asked, "So, who were the creeps and weren't they blatant with the attempt to kill Marcie right at her apartment?"

"Listen Nora, I'll give you a rundown when we get there. See you soon."

"Clint, they may follow you to my house. Be careful and if you see anyone suspicious, try to lose them."

"Gads, Nora, maybe we shouldn't go to your house. I don't want to put you in danger now."

"Oh no, you don't. I'm not going to leave you alone with Marcie. You make it here safe and sound. I'm expecting you. I have the room for Marcie set up and I'll have dinner ready to go a few moments after you get here."

"Okay, we'll be there in a few then."

CHAPTER ELEVEN

HER HEART beating erratically, Marcie held onto Hawk's arm as they walked to the elevator. Hawk felt so badly for her. Her face was as white as a sheet of paper, her usual sparkling blue topaz eyes now appeared dull and seemed to be focused on her shoes. Without looking up, she said, "Stay near me, Clint. I won't be able to make it to the car without your help."

"Marcie, we'll be all right. It's all over with. I'll be here with you." Marcie grabbed his hand and squeezed it hard but remained silent. Hawk wanted to tell her to be strong and buck up, but he realized that now, those would have been just empty words. He knew that she would feel better and return to normal once the shock from that attempt on her life wore off. *Maybe, I'm rushing her out. Maybe, she should've had a chance to rest before we left.* But he wanted to get her out of there, so she did not have to explain why they came after her to the Glendale cops. Going through that procedure would have been like rubbing salt in a wound. Perez promised to come right over and deal with the Glendale police.

Hawk, himself, was not yet back to normal. His nerves were jittery, and his breathing was still labored. A pounding headache from stress slowed his thought process. When he abruptly fell to the floor and then rapidly rose again to chase the shooters, he reaggravated his neck and back strain. He, himself had to get out of there, get some fresh air and not put up with the tons of questions that he knew he would face with the Glendale Police.

Once Hawk and Marcie exited the building, Hawk carefully studied their surroundings. His car was not far, parked in the visitor parking. He heard sirens approaching and quickly escorted Marcie to the passenger side of his Jeep Cherokee. He waited for her to settle in and shut the door. When he walked around the car to the driver's side, he spotted a dark blue BMW 5 series sedan parked across the street at a distance. The reason he paid notice to it was that he thought that he detected, for a brief second, a large camera lens directed at him. The lens disappeared when he took a second or so to study the car. He also thought he saw two heads in the car, but he was not sure because, at 7:00 o'clock in July, the sun shone brightly from the west, obstructing a clear image of what he saw. *Those could be just headrests.*

As he pulled out of the lot, he saw Perez pull in followed by two Glendale police cruisers. Relieved that Perez was there to meet the cops, Hawk made a point of driving past the Beamer to get a closer look. As he did so, he could not see anyone inside. *Either they really scrounged down low, or they're hiding behind the fence*—looking at a four-foot-high brick fence that bordered another apartment building across the street from Marcie's—or *I was totally wrong and imagined everything. Should I go and look around behind that fence? If I go looking for them, Marcie will freak out again and actually, I will leave her vulnerable to an attack if they lead me on a wild goose chase and circle back to get her.* Instead, he called Perez and gave him a description of the car and the Texas license plate number.

Perez said, "Thanks a lot, Hawk! Leaving me here to deal with these pissed-off cops. They're pretty hot under the collar for you and that woman taking off like that. I've got a lot of work to do to make this all go away."

"Sorry, Lieutenant. But I had to get Marcie out of there for her mental well-being."

"Okay, okay. I'll deal with it."

Marcie heard the conversation and seemed to take it well. Some color had returned to her face and her eyes had a hint of sparkle. It was her normally sparkling eyes that attracted Hawk to her in the first place. Marcie glanced back at Hawk and smiled tentatively. Hawk felt that she had recovered from her initial shock. "I hope we're not in trouble for leaving, but I had to. I couldn't stay a second longer." She thought for a moment, then said, "You think that car was theirs?"

"Probably not, but I think to be on the safe side, it should be looked into." Suddenly, out of his rearview mirror, he briefly saw the men jump into the car and, a few seconds later, peel out. Marcie looked back and saw the car as it made a U-turn and slowly began following them for a moment, then turned into the next intersection.

"Oh God! It was the killers, wasn't it?"

"Maybe," Hawk said. "I'll call Perez again and inform him. He should put out a BOLO (be on the lookout) for that car." After calling his Lieutenant, he called Nora and asked her to take her car out of the garage so that he could hide in it. That raised all kinds of alarms with her and again, she advised him to take no chances and try to lose whoever would be following them.

As they traveled south on Colorado Boulevard, Marcie sat silently and seemed to dwell on her predicament. Her color receded again and began breathing rapidly, almost hyperventilating. He took her hand and gently squeezed it. Placing his hand on her nape, he gently massaged it, trying to relax her. "I'll be all right, Clint. You're so caring and a great protector. I'm sorry I'm such a pain in the butt. My parents always used to call me 'scaredy-cat.' Unfortunately, I take after my grandmother, who seemed to panic over everything."

"Well, this just isn't over everything. This is dangerous and actually you're handling it rather well. This is so out of the ordinary that, hopefully, you'll never have to experience anything like it again."

"You're sweet, Clint. I wish I could take you with me to California." She touched his arm and then the hand that he had removed from her neck. He glanced at her, and she forced a pleasant smile.

Hawk did not respond, but he again checked out the rearview mirrors as he had done constantly since leaving Marcie's apartment building. *Oh no! I think the bastards are behind us.* This time, he spotted the double grill of a dark BMW 5 series about a block away. He had seen several BMWs since he left, which was not unusual in the part of Denver that they were in. Up to now, the ones he had just seen, luckily, were mostly light-colored and smaller. With this one, he had a gut feeling that now they were being followed. Not taking any chances, Hawk quickly turned right into the next driveway, which happened to be part of the King's Soopers grocery store lot. He twisted the wheel so that he faced back to the north, went around the adjacent shops, then west and drove out onto Exposition Street and headed west. He again turned to the right onto Harrison, parked in front of another parked SUV and waited to see if a dark BMW followed them.

Marcie held her breath while he made those maneuvers. She knew what Hawk was doing. She knew that they were being followed. She sat silently, her eyes straight ahead. Almost afraid to speak as though if she said anything, they, whoever they were, would hear. Hawk looked at her, but she did not show signs of panic or fear. He did notice that she was taking in deep breaths and letting them out slowly.

"Marcie, this is only a precaution. I really don't know if that was the car or not, but I didn't want to take any chances."

"I understand, Clint. Thank you." He took her hand without taking his eyes off the driver's rearview mirror. The traffic was heavy on Exposition, but Hawk was able to follow it well. A dark BMW drove past, but it was a 3 series. Marcie turned her neck to glance at him and actually a faint smile seemed formed on her lips which Hawk caught out of the corner of his eye. "Clint, I trust you. I'm so lucky that I'm with you right now. If it were anyone else, I don't know how I could handle it. Don't worry about me. The shock of it all came at the apartment. I'm over it and ready to cope and survive."

"Good. I knew that you were a trooper. You're tough and we'll get through this. I'll make sure that they won't find us."

Suddenly, along Exposition Street, Clint saw the dark blue BMW drive past very slowly, holding up traffic. He assumed that the passenger of the BMW watched the north side of Harrison Street and must have seen Hawk's Jeep because the car almost came to a standstill, barely past the intersection. Horns from impatient drivers blared and the BMW was forced to drive on. Hawk knew that it was a matter of time before they turned around or went around the block. He quickly made a U-turn and, seeing a gap in the traffic, made a quick turn back onto Exposition. The light at the intersection with Colorado was green and he was able to proceed onto Colorado and drive as rapidly as he could with the traffic, weaving in and out of three lanes and making several lights before one was on red.

He looked back again, it was difficult to spot a car out of three lanes of traffic, but so far it looked as if he lost them. Not taking a chance, he abruptly turned onto Louisiana Street and then on Monroe Street, he turned left and headed down the residential street at the speed limit, checking for any traffic. Nora lived near Florida Street and Madison. His plan was to drive to Florida Street and then turn back onto Madison. At that moment, Nora called, wanting to know where they were and why it was taking them so long. Hawk explained to her that he might have been followed and was taking precautions.

"Good," Nora said. "I left the garage door open for you."

A few minutes later, after making sure that there were no other cars around him, he turned into the garage. Nora was at the door that led from the garage into a small laundry area and as soon as Clint turned off the engine, she closed the garage door.

She had a broad smile on her face as she greeted Marcie and Hawk.

CHAPTER TWELVE

NORA BECKENED them to follow her inside. In reality, Nora was pissed off with the idea that Marcie, of all people, would be her guest. She was competition for Hawk. Likewise, Marcie detested the idea that she will have to stay with Nora. And Hawk was on pins and needles worrying that the two women would go at each other.

But Nora seemed as gracious as she could be, escorting Marcie to her room. She offered her a choice of either a soft or a hard pillow and took Marcie's change of clothes for the morning and hung them up in the closet. "Now, I want you to be as comfortable as you can be. I have a bottle of water and a glass next to your bedside, fresh towels and soap in the hall bathroom. I have a small bathroom off my bedroom, so the hall bathroom is all yours. Please let me know if there's anything I can get for you. You've been through a lot this evening and you need to relax."

"Thank you so much, Nora. I'll be fine. I'm much more relaxed now, thanks to Clint. He had been wonderful." *Oh, yeah! How wonderful was he?* "You have a very lovely house here. I think it's perfect." Marcie pushed aside the sheer on the window and looked out. "That's a huge backyard. And look at your flower garden; it's so lovely. It's a lot of work, isn't it?"

"It certainly is, especially keeping up with the bluegrass in the front and back. I take care of the plants and flowers, but I have a lawn service to mow and fertilize the lawn." Nora suddenly felt pangs of hunger. "Let's go back to the kitchen, I have dinner almost ready. I bet Clint is starved, as usual." Marcie nodded her approval but did not return Nora's smile. She really didn't want to hear her discuss Clint as though they are so close, and she already knows how hungry he becomes.

"As the women walked out of the short hall into the living room with its L-shaped dining area, they saw Clint stretched out on the couch, his arm over his eyes. "Are you okay, baby? You must be exhausted after your ordeal?" *'Baby?' Nora never called me that before and with such a tender soft tone. Is she doing this for Marcie's benefit?*

Marcie swallowed hard and said, "Nora, your kitchen is so cute. You are a good decorator. I love your house. How long have you lived here?"

"About seven years ever since I graduated from the police academy. The down payment was a gift from my parents. I was so lucky that at the time I bought it, the houses in this Corey-Merrill area of Denver were reasonably priced and affordable. Now these houses go for more than six hundred thousand because it became such a hot area. People with money are moving in, paying those kinds of prices, and then tearing the houses down to build their trophy homes. These small houses of about one thousand square feet were built on vacant land right after the Second World War to accommodate returning soldiers. Now there aren't many of them left. This was part of South Denver, a separate city that some settlers formed in the late 1800s to get away from the turbulent Denver of those days. Here, alcohol was not permitted."

"Well, you certainly read up on the history of this area."

"Oh, I love history, especially how cities were formed. For instance, Denver has a fascinating history."

"I know, I read about some of it myself," Hawk said, smiling. "But can we eat? I'm starving."

"Oh, of course. I think the tamales are heated up by now. Hope you both like Mexican food."

"You bet, I love it," Clint said. Marcie just nodded. As they approached the table, they again noticed the table was set up with both wine and water glasses. Nora said to Hawk, "Honey, why don't you sit at the head of the table here and Marcie and I will sit across from each other." *There she goes again. For sure, she's trying to irritate Marcie.* Marcie and Hawk complied, and Nora brought out a heaping platter of tamales followed by bowls of salad, black beans and green chili.

"Wow, that looks great," Hawk said, his stomach sending up signals that it's ready.

"Yes, this is wonderful," Marcie said.

"I hope you like the tamales. When I visit my parents in Pueblo, I sometimes buy a couple dozen from this sweet lady who makes them at her home. I think that they are the best I ever had."

Hawk did not wait for formalities; he snatched the server and placed a couple of tamales on Marcie's plate without asking and did the same for Nora. He then grabbed three more and loaded his plate up, while Marcie poured some of the chili sauce on her tamales and served herself the salad and a spoonful of black beans. "Nora, this does look delicious, don't you think Clint?"

Hawk had his mouth full of food and nodded his approval. After finishing the mouthful, he said, "This are great. Too bad you only put out a dozen. I could eat them all." He smiled at Nora.

Nora laughed. "I don't think you'd handle it, sugar." He took a quick glance at Marcie and just as he expected Marcie wrinkled her small nose and pursed her red lips. *Come on, Nora, lay off. Enough is enough.*

Marcie felt as though she could punch Nora at the moment. She also began to realize what she was doing. *Just like a dog marking her territory. I get it. She needs to understand that no matter how much I would want Clint, as long as he is a policeman, we can never be. I can't go through the anxiety I feel today the rest of my life. Anyway, I don't think that Clint is into Nora as much as she would like.* It suddenly struck her that she may not be around much longer to worry about it. *They're still out there and obviously they want me dead.*

To distract herself from what was waiting for her, she said, "Nora, this is such a lovely platter," pointing to the dish the tamales were on. "Is it porcelain?"

"No, it's pottery, but thank you. I got it from my great-grandmother who brought it over from the old country. She and my great-grandfather came to good ole USA from Italy to work in the steel mill in Pueblo. It was called Colorado Fuel and Iron then. Now it's owned by a Russian company and called Evraz. Anyway, my great-grandmother and great-grandfather both with only a third-grade education were somehow able to save enough money to buy eighty acres of land on the Mesa, east of Pueblo and next to the Arkansas River, and grow vegetables. They made enough money from that to buy another forty acres, then another eighty acres. They did well and raised eight kids and were able to send those, who wanted to go, to college. My mother was one that went and became a teacher."

Hawk said, "That's a great story. You come from good genes."

"Thank you, honey." Hawk smiled politely but was getting ticked off. Marcie agreed that that was an interesting story just to be courteous but didn't smile.

Hawk had just polished off the three tamales laden with the spicy green chili sauce and was ready to take another tamale when the tone on his cell startled everyone. He answered "Hello."

"Hello, detective, y'all remember me? This is Luanne Sue. You know, the receptionist at the Ellis office."

Hawk rose from the table and walked over to the couch and sat down. "Sure, I remember you, Luanne Sue. We're Mississippi buds, after all."

Marcie and Nora looked at each other, Nora's eyes as wide as saucers. "Who's Luanne Sue?" Marcie whispered across the table.

"She's a bimbo at Steven Ellis' office," Nora whispered back. "I think she took a liking to Clint. But I never dreamed she'd be calling him. What nerve!" Hawk heard and looked up at Nora but continued to listen to the girl on the phone.

"Oh, really," Marcie said.

"Yeah, really, Marcie. He has some kind of a magnetism that makes women fall for him. You should've seen Ellis' assistant drool all over him. I don't like it. That worries me to no end."

Marcie laughed. "I know what you mean." *Yes, you do, and I don't like it either,* Nora almost blurted it out, but restrained herself.

"But when you said 'assistant,' you didn't mean Tina Dionisio do you?"

"Yes. Do you know her?"

"I met her a couple of times when I was with Amanda. Don't worry about Clint and her. It's not Clint. She's just that way with all men. She's a big tease and flirt and gets her kicks that way. It's almost as if she wants to see how far she can go with a man before she backs off. To Amanda and me, she was very standoffish, and I don't think she liked either one of us. As a matter of fact, she really resented Amanda. I heard them arguing at a party in their backyard. I was on the patio and couldn't hear but could see the conversation got very heated. I even thought they'd come to blows. When I asked Amanda what that was about, she basically told me that she didn't want to talk about it and that she's going upstairs to cool off."

"Did you ever ask her what it was about?"

"No. This happened just a couple of weeks ago and I really hadn't seen Amanda after that, come to think of it. You don't think that she killed her, do you?"

"What do you think?"

"Well, she looked mad enough, that's for sure. But…"

Hawk came back to the table. "Well, what was that all about?" Nora asked, her face irritated.

"She said that she thought more about the question that I asked her about what time Mr. Ellis came in to work this morning. She thought that she should cover for him and lie, but that her Baptist conscience got in the way, and she had to tell the truth."

"Well, what did she say, honey?"

Hawk threw her a hard look as if to say *cut it out*. "She told me that he came in late that morning, about nine-thirty, stayed only a half hour, then left again."

"So, what does that mean?" Marcie asked, really sounding interested.

"It means that he had no alibi since he was not at work at the time that your friend was killed," Nora said.

"Yes, isn't it interesting."

"Well, if he did it, why would he want to kill me? Those documents have nothing to do with him, do they?"

"Good point," Hawk said. "Maybe we're looking at two different cases."

"That's bizarre," Nora said. "That would really complicate things. Do you remember that out of the blue, after Mortimer went through some kind of a trance, he said that there were two people in the garage?"

"Yes, but how would he know that?" Hawk asked. "Probably just a lucky guess. But we don't know that for sure, do we." The cell tone rang again. "Hello."

"Hi Clint, this is Nancy."

"Now, who is Nancy?" Marcie whispered to Nora again. "It isn't the Nancy from the Homicide Unit, is it?"

"Yes, it is. At least it better be. I don't think I need to worry about her. She's at least ten years older and looks it and is married." Nora said, laughing.

"Let me put you on speaker so that Nora can listen." Hawk did so and placed the phone between him and Nora.

"Hi Nora. How's it going?"

"It's okay, what do you have?"

"Since I'm sort of the detective on duty tonight, Lieutenant Perez wanted me to check on the BMW that a patrol unit found at the Broadway light rail parking lot. They called it in, and Perez ordered it taken to the crime lab. It looked clean, not even a scrap of paper in it. I checked on the Texas plate and found out it belonged to Emperor Car Rentals. I talked to the local clerk, and he looked up the paperwork but couldn't remember the person who rented it. Said that he and the other clerks were swamped that time of day and they tried to run the people through as fast as they could."

Nora asked, "Well, don't they check for ID's?"

"He said they're supposed to and he's sure he checked the ID thoroughly. I asked him to fax me the paperwork and a copy of the driver's license that the man used. But here's the deal. The paperwork and the New York license are in the name of Jimmie

Kim. The credit card used is in that name, but Jimmie Kim, according to the Schenectady Police Department, his wife reported him missing for at least a week. They told me that they noticed the use of the card at the Denver airport yesterday and were planning to have us check it out. Now, here's the kicker. The photo on the license doesn't match the photos that you, Clint, took of the Asian man. Close, but not quite. The clerk at the rental company if he was in a big hurry wouldn't have noticed."

"So that means that they're still out there, but no longer in the BMW," Hawk said. "Were there any reports of any vehicles stolen anywhere along the light rail?"

"I plan to check on that and call you back if there are any, but it may be too early for anyone to notice their car missing."

CHAPTER THIRTEEN

THANKFUL THAT the evening went fairly well, and Nora and Marcie didn't start throwing tamales at each other, Hawk drove envisioning a deep sleep like Rip Van Winkle had in the story, but maybe not as long. To be cautious, as he approached his townhome, he did not drive directly into his garage, which entrance was from the alley, but drove around the area checking it out for anything suspicious.

He did not know why he did it, he realized that the goons would have no idea who he was. Unless they got his name and address through his license plate. They knew which car he was driving. They saw him getting out of it at Marcie's building. But how could they have gotten that information so quickly? *Is it probable that they were able to hack the DMV? And that is highly unlikely unless they had help from whoever hired them.* His paranoia led him to think that they will try anything to prevent him from identifying them or testifying against them. After all, hired hitmen had to stay anonymous to be effective. *Hawk, that's crazy. It's your exhausted, overstressed mind playing tricks.*

Once in his house, he took off his coat jacket, gun and badge and threw them on a chair in his bedroom, preparing for bed. But he felt jittery. His nerves were screwed tight. Needing to unwind before attempting sleep, he decided to go for a quick stroll around the neighborhood. Usually he did not, but this time he made sure that his gun and badge were back on his belt. Once in the living room, walking toward the front door, his cell's melody came on, causing him to jolt. Nora's name came up.

"Hi there, did you make it home all right?" Hawk told her everything was fine, and she continued, "Marcie's building manager called and told her that someone kicked in the door to her apartment. Nothing seemed ransacked and she hopes nothing is missing. She said that she'll stay by the door until her handyman gets there in thirty minutes."

"Oh geez. They're still out there after her. How's Marcie taking it?"

"She ran to her room, and I hear her sobbing. Poor thing. I tried to console her, but she said she wanted some time to herself. I'll try to talk to her later tonight. Listen, Clint, you be extra careful. I have a bad feeling. As your bodyguard, I should be with you."

"I wish you were here too, but I'll be all right. I doubt they know who I am and even if so, why would they come after me. I'm sure they know I gave their description to others already. So, don't worry."

"For revenge, for one, and two because you can personally identify them rather than give a vague description. They don't know that you have photos of them."

"Oh, now I have a call from Nancy coming in. Let me take it. Bye for now." He clicked on the call waiting button.

"Hi Nancy."

"Hi Clint. How's it going?"

"Fine Nancy, what's up?"

"Just wanted to give you an update. We received a report that a smaller silver 2019 Cadillac SUV was stolen from a couple that were having dinner at the Buckhorn Exchange Restaurant. You know, the oldest restaurant in Denver, the one with all the animal heads on the wall. The one that you can see from the light rail station at Osage."

"Nancy, I know the old restaurant well, I live close by. When do they think the car was taken?"

"They don't know. They spent at least two hours in the place. So anytime during those hours. I'll text you the license plate number."

"Thanks for the info. I'll watch out for the car."

"Okay then. Talk to you later. Take care."

After the two phone calls, Hawk was even more frazzled. He really needed to get out and try to clear his mind. It was a good night for a walk as the partly overcast night cooled off nicely from the hot July day. He wished he had his dog, Stella, with him. Since he came late, Stella was still with his neighbor who watched the dog while he was gone.

Across the street from his house was an entire city block that had been cleared for new development. It has been vacant for a few months and weeds had sprouted on the lot in the meantime, enough that they had to be mowed down. As he walked out of the front door of his corner unit, he strode across the street and walked alongside the vacant field. Lipan Street, the next block over, was very visible across the open space. Traffic at 10:00 p.m. seemed non-existent at the time. Suddenly, the headlights of a vehicle slowly approaching on the one-way Lipan Street caught his eye. Then it parked alongside the street, across from the open field. Hawk's heartbeat increased and his breath shallowed as he recognized the silver car by its vertical taillights as a Cadillac SUV, perhaps the xt5 model. *No way! That can't be the stolen vehicle. No way!* By him stood a parked car on his street and he went behind it and crouched down. No one left the Cadillac for a couple of minutes. Hawk continued to wait as the headlights were still on. Then, he saw two short men exit the car, both in dark garb. *That's them! Son of a bitch! And they're looking at my house. Crap! What should I do?*

He had to think fast. He could wait and ambush them, shoot them as they walked by, but that would lead to one inquiry after another, and he could be charged. He could sneak up behind them and tell them to drop their weapons and reach for the sky, but he realized that would be too simple and as two professional hitmen, they would not easily comply. Instead, they could cause a shootout. He could get one of them, but the other could get him. He could run back to his house and wait for them inside, but bullets fly through walls and the neighbors may get hurt plus his place would likely get thrashed. He could run and hide from them; hide in the alley somewhere. Or he can confront them in the field and if there was a gunfight, try to keep the bullets from flying into the adjacent houses.

Hawk stepped from the car he hid behind and moved toward the men. The men had taken only a few steps from the Cadillac. He knew they spotted him because they stopped abruptly, one of them pointing his index finger at Hawk. They discussed something in low voices then he heard one of the men say loudly in agitation, "That's him."

Hawk knew that the width of the entire block, including the alley was about three-hundred feet or one hundred yards. The men were on one end and Hawk stood still at the other end. He was a good shot, but his SIG Sauer was 9mm. pistol was most accurate at fifty yards, although the bullet could travel much further, jeopardizing the surrounding houses. If they still had a 45 caliber as he was told they used in the shooting at Marcie's, it was accurate at seventy-five yards but in both pistols, the bullet would drop at that distance, so each shooter needed to adjust the aim higher to be accurate. With his pistol, the drop is about a foot at one hundred yards, so he needed to aim higher to be accurate. He wondered how good of marksmen those hoods were.

"Police," he yelled out. "Throw down your weapons and get on the ground with your hands over your head." Hawk realized that those were wasted words, but he was required to identify himself as police. Just as he expected, the men drew their weapons and immediately began firing, taking a few steps toward Hawk. The bullets struck the dirt several feet away from him, one flew off to the side and struck the side window of a parked car. Hawk dropped down to the rain-moistened ground, falling onto prickly weeds. Fortunately, the ground at that spot was not level and some of the soil formed a short mound of about five inches immediately in front of his head. Also, some taller weeds surrounding him made it more difficult for them to spot his exact location, at least so he hoped.

The men fired again in his direction. This time the bullets hit closer to Hawk and pieces of mud, dirt and small rocks showered him from the impact of the slugs. He lay as still as possible for at least a minute. The gunfire stopped. *I hope those bastards think they got me. Come on, come on, step closer.* The men took some careful steps toward him, both crouching lower to the ground. In the meantime, Hawk positioned his right hand on the raised mount of soil for support and reinforced the gun with his left hand to keep his aim as steady as possible. He took a shot at one of the men, aiming for his shoulder. He did not want to kill him as he needed both of them for questioning as to who hired them.

He heard a yelp, and some swearing and saw the man hold his right arm. *I hope it's more than just a graze.* He fired a second shot at the other man, trying to disable him in the leg, but he must have missed because he and the wounded man quickly retreated to the Cadillac. In the distance, police sirens were heard. *Somebody must've called the cops.* Hawk jumped up and raced after the fleeing men. The wounded passenger opened the window and began firing at him. Hawk stopped and took a shot at the tire of the escaping vehicle but wasn't sure if he got it or not since it sped off.

All the porch lights were now lit, and neighbors started peeking out of their doors and windows. Two patrol Ford Interceptors stopped as Clint waved them down. He showed them his badge and explained what had happened. Officer Peak wrote everything down on his pocket-sized spiral notebook. Hawk activated the flashlight on his phone and began searching for shell casings and asked the officers to do the same but told them to stay out of the area where the shooters' footprints might be visible. He instructed them to put up flags at the spot if they found any. It did not take long for them to find several casings. Some were from a 45 caliber and others from what appeared to be a 38 special. He also flagged the spot on the ground where he lay. A few minutes later, a third Ford Explorer came to the scene. Hawk was surprised to see Lieutenant Perez and Captain MacGregor step out. "Don't tell me that you've been shot at twice this evening," MacGregor said. "That hasn't happened as far as I know since I was a rookie."

"I'm just lucky, I guess, Captain," Hawk tried to force a laugh, but it sounded weak.

"You're lucky that you're able to laugh about it. I want a full verbal report from you at 10:30 tomorrow morning and a written one the day later. In the meantime, we'll take over this scene. You go get a good night's sleep. You look like hell, Detective. Don't report to work until it's time to see me. That's an order."

"Yes, Captain. Sounds good to me. By the way, you may find their footprints in the soft ground where the shells are flagged."

"I'll get Chet Watkins out of bed tonight to take care of it. Now go home, Detective."

"Thanks. See you tomorrow."

When Hawk dragged himself home, he called Nora and told her that everything was fine that he needed to sleep right now and would talk to her tomorrow. Next, he made it up to his upstairs bedroom, to his bed, collapsed and fell sound asleep. This time he had none of the nightmares that plagued him the night before.

Nora lay on the sofa watching the Denver 7 news channel at 10:00 o'clock when Marcie came out of her room and joined her. She took a recliner and Nora sat up. "Marcie, I'm glad that you joined me. I'm waiting to see if they'll say anything about the murder of your friend."

"Oh. Yes, that would be interesting." She kept her eye on the 48-inch flat screen for a minute, then turned to Nora. "I'm sorry, Nora, that I lost it. I wish I were as strong as you and able to handle stress better. I really admire that you always seem happy, laughing, even under adversity."

"Oh, I'm not sure you know me that well. Sometimes a laugh is just a cover for my insecurity. But yes, I'm usually upbeat. People tell me I laugh too much, but Clint seems to like my laugh. I inherited my optimistic personality from my father. Everyone says that he has great charisma and that I'm just like him."

"I understand what Clint sees in you. Probably when he sees me, he sees a helpless scaredy-cat that falls apart at the first sign of trouble. I really don't try to be that way. I, like you, usually try to be happy and upbeat. But lately, I seem to be going through an emotional state. I can't blame it all on this unbelievable danger that my friend, Amanda, got me into. I just can't decide what to do with my life just now. I'm sure that Clint thinks that I'm an idiot and I'm really embarrassed for it."

Why is she spilling her guts to me like this? Nora asked. "You love him, don't you?" Marcie took a long time to answer. That gave Nora a clue. She felt resentment building in the pit of her stomach. She wrestled to control her emotions, including the big one, anger. Taking a deep breath trying to look sympathetic and awaited Marcie's answer.

"Let's just say, I like him a lot. I'll be honest with you that if circumstances were different, I'd like to get to know him better, but that will never be since it's obvious that you two are an item." *Yes! You got that right. He's mine! I don't believe for a minute that you're not in love with him.*

"Working together as we have, certainly brings us closer," Nora said. "We faced danger, coming as close to dying as is possible yet still breathing. In adversity, we got to know each other very well."

"Well, Nora, you're lucky."

"May I ask, is Clint the reason that you didn't leave for California as you had planned?"

Marcie focused on her bare feet. Moisture welled in her eyes. She looked up at Nora and said quietly, "I don't know, maybe. I see now that I should've left for several reasons. One being that it would've been harder for the gunmen to find me. I think that the same people who are after me were the same ones that killed Amanda, don't you think?"

Nora suddenly felt sorry for Marcie. She could see how devastated she is with her life at this time. "It could very well be. Hope we'll find out more tomorrow." She studied her wretched guest. "Marcie, I think we both need a hug. Come and join me here on the couch." Marcie hesitated a moment, then slid over into the stretched-out arms of the person she wished did not exist in Clint's life. They embraced each other as Marcie sobbed. After half a minute, Nora broke the embrace, went to the hall bathroom, and brought back a box of tissue.

"Marcie, everything will work out. I'm a great believer in fate. What's meant to be, will be. Every day is a new surprise and I'm sure that California will astonish you and your life there will be delightful." She suddenly looked toward the TV as she heard the name of Amanda Ellis come up. "Oh, look, they did cover the story on Amanda. Oh, my gosh, there is Steven Ellis giving an interview!"

Marcie sniffled, wiped her eyes and nose. "He says that he doesn't believe it was a murder, says it's probably a heart attack. How's that? I thought the cause of death is certain."

"Well, the medical examiner believes verbally that it was murder all right, but she still hadn't done all the blood tests or made a final report."

They kept their eyes fixed on the TV, then Nora asked Marcie, "Does he come across sincere to you when he tells everyone how much he loved Amanda? I'm not so sure."

"Oh, I can never tell. You're the detective and if that's what you read from his interview, I guess I agree. Do you think he should look more distraught?"

"I think so," Nora said. "After all, he just lost his wife. Of course, there's Tina in the wings waiting for him."

CHAPTER FOURTEEN

ANOTHER SUNNY morning greeted Marcie as she walked over to the kitchen where Nora hummed *All of Me* by John Legend as she flipped over two fried eggs. "Good morning, Marcie, I hope you slept soundly."

"Yes, good morning, Nora, I did. Of course, I had to take some sleeping pills."

"Well, at least that did the trick. I hope you like ham and eggs."

"Yes, thanks. That's great. One egg is plenty for me."

Nora took a good look at Marcie. "Wow, you're all dressed up with make up on and everything. I still have my robe on and probably look terrible."

"No, as always you look perfect. Again, I'll say it. I don't blame Clint for falling all over you."

Nora laughed. "Thanks, that's a great compliment. Well, make yourself comfortable. I have ham in the oven, orange juice is on the table, and do you drink coffee?"

"Sure, I like it all. I feel badly that I'm giving you so much trouble but appreciate it all. It's great to share breakfast with you."

"No problem at all. Listen, help yourself to the coffee and juice. If you could wait a minute for breakfast, I'd like to quickly get into my suit, ready for work. You look so nice in your green summer dress that I'd feel awkward sitting across from you in my robe."

"You don't need to do that, Nora. I told you; you look great."

"It'll only take a minute. I'll be right back."

Nora was fast and came out wearing her light gray pants suit with a red blouse, a circle pendant hanging off a thin gold chain and a thin gold bracelet encircling her wrist. "My, you look lovely, and I can't believe how quick you were. It seems like it takes me hours to get ready." *Okay, enough with all these compliments. I know she's not sincere, but what I am supposed to do with her. Leave her in my house all day?*

During breakfast, the two women talked about the weather, Denver, the neighborhood, but nothing of any significance. Then Marcie said, "I don't want to be a burden to you any longer. I've booked a place in a hotel as I'm afraid to stay in my apartment. I have a feeling that they'll come back looking for me again. Could you please take me back to it so that I can gather up some clothes, meds, and my car. I'll be out of your hair."

"Are you sure you want to do that? They know what you drive."

"Okay, I'll tell you what. I'll leave my car and take an Uber. If I have to, I'll rent a car."

"You know don't you, that they can trace you through your credit card use. And if they're sophisticated enough, they could trace you through your phone."

"In that case, they know I'm here already."

"Yes, I wish I had warned you not to use it."

"I only made a couple of calls."

Nora decided that perhaps it would be best if she hid somewhere else since now her location at her house might be compromised. "All right, Marcie. I'll do it. I'll take you to your apartment, wait while you gather your things, then take you to the hotel. And I'd like you to make a call from your apartment so that if they're monitoring your phone, they know that you've returned to it. You'll be out of there and don't use you phone after that until we capture the men."

The door to Marcie's apartment smelled with freshly cut wood and varnish where it had been repaired. There was yellow tape crisscrossed over the entrance that said, "Do not Enter." Marcie used her key to unlock the door and both women stooped down to enter below the tape. Nora left the door open, so that no one would be surprised by them being there. "We shouldn't be doing this, they don't want anyone contaminating a crime scene before the tech people do their thing," Nora said. "So, please just go get your clothes and whatever you need without touching anything else."

"I really appreciate this, Nora. I hope I don't get you in trouble."

"Just do what you have to swiftly and let's get out of here."

Nora stood by the kitchen island waiting for Marcie. She looked the place over carefully. She was impressed by the nice furnishings, and what looked to be pieces of original artworks on the walls. *This huge room with its tall ceiling is almost bigger than my whole house. She must really come from money to afford this place. And look at that magnificent view of the Rockies. Wow!* Her mind then shifted to whether she should call Lieutenant Perez and explain what they were doing. After all, she was already a little late coming into work. She was sure he would understand.

He answered on the first ring, and she told him where they were. Explaining that to keep Marcie safe, she needed to get out of the apartment. She also relayed to him that Marcie booked a room at the JW Marriott in Cherry Creek for a few days. Perez didn't seem happy at all for her crossing the yellow tape, but agreed that she should secure Marcie at the hotel before coming in.

While she was on the phone with him, Marcie came out rolling a suitcase behind her. Nora was about to click off the conversation with Perez when two men, one Asian, the other white, tore off the yellow tape and rushed into the apartment. "Oh God! They're here!"

"Whose there, Nora. Who's there?" She could hear Perez yelling into his phone.

"Hang up, you bitch," the white man said, looking somewhat pale and pointing a gun in his left hand at her. His right arm hung to the side as though disabled. Marcie screeched a blood-curdling shriek. "Shut up before I shoot that mouth off," he yelled at her. "Which one of you is Marcie Turner?"

"It's the blond, you idiot," said the Asian in the same New York accent as his partner's. "Let's get down to business and get rid of them. I want to get it over with and get out of here."

"What's your hurry Kwon? Let's have a little fun with them. I'll take the brunette." He laughed callously.

"Are you crazy. That bullet taking a chunk out of your arm took a chunk out of your brain." Kwon pulled his weapon out for the first time and pointed it at Marcie."

Marcie screamed again while Nora moved in between Kwon and Marcie and said, "Yes, what's your hurry. You're going to kill us anyway. We're all alone here so let's have some fun before we die." Marcie's eyes went wide, her mouth flew open. *What in the hell is she doing? She can't be serious.*

The Asian laughed. "I know your game; you're just stalling for time. But time is up missy. I want both of you to lay down flat on the floor, your backs to me. You're going to go execution style. That's our trademark."

Nora's insides twisted, her heart pounded, but she knew that Perez would send help and she had to keep them occupied. "Your trademark? Wow. You don't have a trademark. You guys are just two clowns that think they're something." *Oh my God! What is the matter with her?* Marcie thought, trembling so badly that she could see her hands shake out of control. *She's provoking them. They'll torture us. Shut up, Nora.*

"You bitch." The white man said. "You don't know who you're dealing with. We've executed people all over this country."

"Shut up, Josh." Kwon yelled at him.

"What's the problem with you. We're going to do them in and who cares what they hear. But before they die, I want them to know how important we are and how much money we make. Calling us clowns! They should know who is going to end their beautiful existence on this planet."

Marcie continued to moan, almost hysterically. Knowing that she is going to die, already seemed to take the life out of her. Her face was pale, and she was barely able to take a breath. She felt weak in the knees and thought she will pass out any second. Nora was not in much better shape than Marcie. She was afraid and she knew it. But she had to do something rather than submit to their demands without a fight. She needed to stall and knew that the only way was to continue to push the men's buttons. She was not sure what she would accomplish, but at least they were not executed yet. Trying to control her trembling voice, she badgered them further.

"Make money, huh! What a laugh. You two bozos don't have two quarters to rub together."

She found the dumb one in Josh. "Oh yeah?! You bitch. We already got paid twenty-five grand. And as soon that we show them that you're dead, we'll get another twenty-five thousand. Not bad for a few days' work, is it bitch?"

Nora forced a sarcastic laugh. "Who in the hell in his right mind would pay you fifty-thousand dollars. You're bungling idiots."

Nora suddenly realized that she pushed them too hard, and this would be the end. Kwon yelled out, "Both of you. On the floor with your lips kissing the carpet. Now." Kwon took a step toward Nora.

"Wait! Before you force me to the floor, Kwon, just answer me who would pay you that kind of money just to kill an innocent girl like Marcie?"

Kwon said, "If you really want to take that information to your grave, then you should know that it was some rich guy in Denver, now both of you are on the floor."

Nora saw a ray of hope for more delay. She focused on Josh. "Oh, come on, gentlemen, do you really think that some rich guy would take the chance by contacting you and giving you a check for the money. No way. I don't believe it."

"You sure are a curious one, aren't you?" Kwon said. "If you really must know before you die, we get paid in cash. We don't know who he is. He left us the money and instructions at a business mailbox center in Brooklyn. Now get on the floor. Or maybe we'll just shoot you where you're standing."

Marcie had decided that she needed to do something to save herself. While Nora engaged the men, Marcie faked a moan and fell to the floor hard. It hurt her, but she had to make it look realistic. She pretended to pass buying herself some time hoping that it might help somehow. She managed to fall between the couch and the coffee table. Marcie's fall provided a small distraction, but not long enough for Nora to attempt to do anything to help their situation. She sensed that she had pushed the killers far enough and that she could not stall any longer. The Grim Reaper stared them in their faces.

She sidled a few inches closer to Josh, placing herself in a more strategic spot between the two men hoping that they would not realize her gradual advance. She had to keep them engaged so she asked what she knew would be her final question unless her plan succeeded. She looked directly at Josh and asked, "How would anyone find such incompetent killers to botch a job for them?"

Nora's heart raced; her head felt like it would split open as she saw the anger flare up in the eyes of both men. *This is it. One of them is going to squeeze that trigger. They've lost control,* she knew that it was time to act as Kwon's hand holding the gun shook in rage. Nora studied human behavior and was well acquainted that when a person is in such rage, he loses full control of his faculties and becomes unpredictable. She needed some sort of a good diversion to give her a fighting chance though. She hoped that Marcie would suddenly come to and scream, but that didn't happen. Instead, her prayer for a diversion was answered by the building manager as she knocked on the door and pushed it open. "Hello, anyone there? The tape is down and the door wasn't shut all the way."

Both men turned abruptly at the intrusion giving Nora the opportunity to use her exceptional speed and the Taekwondo skills that she learned since childhood. Going into action, she sprang up and with her right leg kicked the wrist of Kwon's arm, knocking the pistol to the floor. Then in one swift action before Josh knew what happened, she spun around and kicked him in the groin. While Josh cried out and doubled over with pain, Nora spun back to Kwon seconds before he grabbed his gun off the floor and with her left leg struck Kwon behind his knee, causing him to fall backward. Without waiting, Nora spun around from Kwon to Josh and with her leg and foot smashed him across the face with such force that he fell sideways and struck his head on the wall, leaving a crack in the sheetrock. Marcie saw Nora in action, but Nora did not have a chance to see Marcie sit up from her position on the floor, grab a heavy lead crystal vase off the coffee table and bash the head of Kwon as he was falling back from Nora's kick.

Both women were panting hard and fast. Nora doubled over, gasping for air. Marcie looked at her and at the two men lying on her floor, knocked out. "Nora, I can't believe how fast you were," she said in awe. "You were absolutely terrific!"

"Thanks, but it was them or us and I didn't want it to be us."

The graying, full-figured manager who fled when she saw the men with the guns came back, knocked on the door and sheepishly said, "I'm sorry I didn't stick around to help, but I've got a bad back and I wouldn't have been any help whatsoever. But I called the police, and they should be here any minute." I can't believe that you women took care of these scary-looking men."

"It was all Nora," Marcie said. "I can't believe the way she handled them. It was awesome."

Nora recovered her normal breathing and went about her business of securing the men by first removing their guns that lay on the floor and placing them on the back counter by the sink. Then, for the first time, she opened her suit jacket revealing on her belt her badge and a small holster containing a compact Ruger pistol and a leather satchel for the handcuffs. The manager looked surprised. "My goodness, you're a policewoman. Why didn't you tell them that, maybe they would've fled?"

"I decided it was best that they didn't know. The badge wouldn't have scared them since they already tried to kill my partner. I think the result would've been different. They would've killed us instantly without having to show us their bravado as they did." While she conversed with the manager, she pulled out a pair of handcuffs, flipped Kwon over quickly, pulled his arms back and cuffed him. He was still out cold but breathing. "I wish I had another pair for this bozo here," pointing to Josh who she noticed was slowly coming to. "Marcie, do you have any masking or duct tape. Hurry."

Before Marcie could answer, there was a knock on the door and two officers from Glendale Police arrived. "Good thing you're here. Cuff him, he's coming too." The young policeman wasn't sure what he should do, but when he saw her badge, he complied.

The older officer looked puzzlingly at Nora. "I guess you handled them pretty well. Your lieutenant called for help, and we got here as quick as we could, but there was a traffic jam we had to go around. Hey, we still got here within seven minutes or so."

"Is that all it was since these killers got here?" Nora asked. "It felt like hours." Nora gave the officers all the information for their report. They also got whatever they could from Marcie, but it was not much since she seemed frazzled and somewhat incoherent. The officers even asked Marcie if she needed to go to the hospital. She vehemently declined. In the meantime, Kwon came to, realizing that 'his goose was cooked.' The cops lifted him up, Nora took her cuffs off him and the Glendale officer placed his on Kwon.

The two Glendale officers were ready to leave and haul off the prisoners when Lieutenant Perez and Detective Nancy Salazar rushed through the door. "No, no, don't take them," Perez told the officers. "We have a lot of questions for them as they're suspects in a murder investigation and they shot at my detective, all taking place in Denver."

"Oh, I'm not sure," the younger cop said. "We'll need to check with our sergeant."

"Ah, hell, Michael," the older one said. "I don't want to process these two today anyway. Let them take them and if the chief says they're ours, we'll know where they are."

The Glendale policemen left, and Perez had a thousand questions for Nora. She repeated her story to him, as Marcie kept silent. A few minutes later, two Denver cops showed up and hauled away the prisoners. Before they left, glaring at Nora, Kwon threatened, "It's not over with yet. I'm coming back to get you! You're dead meat!"

Josh decided that he needed to add to the threat, "And tell that freaking detective that shot me in the arm to watch his back because he's also dead meat." Josh let out a harsh laugh as he was escorted out the door.

"Yeah, if I had ten dollars for every threat from a punk," Nora yelled out with a smile on her face.

"Shouldn't that be one dollar?" Perez joked.

"Inflation, you know." They both laughed.

But Marcie was not in a laughing mood. "I can't stay here another minute. At least not for a while. I'm going to a hotel now. I'll take my own car. As long as they're locked up, I should be safe enough."

Nora said, "Marcie, you should be safe for now, but remember there's someone out there that hired those men. Be extra careful. Let me drive you to your hotel at least."

Marcie thought about it. "Okay, thanks."

Perez said, "Don't use your credit cards, they can trace your credit card with a purchase."

"I know, I know. I had someone else book the room for me. So, Nora let's go," She seemed to notice for the first time the manager who stood silently by the door taking the drama in. "Linda, please lock up securely after they're gone. Thanks." She quickly pulled her suitcase out the door and Nora ran to catch up with her.

As they headed toward the Cherry Creek area to her expensive hotel, Marcy asked Nora to tell Hawk where she is staying and that she will call him later. Nora could not believe the audacity of that request but realized that Marcie had to vent her adventure to someone. Being in a generous mood, Nora promised that she will. *I hope she realizes that I saved her hide and doesn't make a play for Clint.*

124

CHAPTER FIFTEEN

CLINT HAWK took the opportunity to take it easy in the morning as suggested by his lieutenant. Surprisingly, he slept well, considering that he had a shootout in front of his house just a few hours earlier. He woke up at about seven but refused to get up right away. He lolled around in bed and watched the Today show for a while, then went to take a shower. Disgusted at the news of the morning. While he took it easy this morning, he had no idea that his partner had fought two hired killers and captured them.

As he walked into the unit at 10:15, Orlinski stopped him and said, "Glad you're alive and same goes for Nora." Hawk did not understand what he meant when he referred to Nora. Orlinski saw the puzzled look, "Oh, you're wondering why I mentioned Nora. I guess you hadn't heard. Perez wants to see you right away and you'll hear all about it from him. Nora is there already."

Orlinski's statement bewildered Hawk even more. *What is that about? What happened to Nora?* The anticipation of possibly bad news made his heart beat faster as he hurried to Perez's office. Nora seemed all right, looking a little disheveled, but as beautiful as ever. *Thank God.* Nora gave him a sweet smile and mouthed a kiss to him. He smiled back and Nora softly said, "I heard what happened last night. Why didn't you tell me?"

Hawk looked embarrassed as Perez eyed him. "I didn't want to worry you. It was no big deal. But what happened to you? Orlinski said—"

Nora interrupted, "No big deal? That's not what I hear."

Perez jumped in before he had to witness any more squabbling. "Well, your partner had an incident this morning." Hawk's eyes went wide, and his mouth dropped open as Perez told him what happened to Nora and Marcie. Feeling a great sense of relief, Hawk could not help but admire his partner. He shook his head in awe. Nora filled in the rest of the story for Hawk's benefit and answered a few of his questions.

While they were talking, Mortimer Holliday sauntered in and sat down on a side chair by the wall. He had on a better suit than the one he wore yesterday, at least the pantlegs covered his ankles. His pants were pleated, and the jacket looked like something Hawk's father wore in the 1980's—broad lapels and shoulder pads. Instead of sandals, he wore a pair of black shoes with a narrow toe that made his long feet seem extra long. *He can ski with those,* Hawk chuckled to himself. Mortimer waited until there was a pause in the conversation, then joined in. "Yes, I heard what both of you did and it is unbelievable. In Tampa, I never had to deal with anything like that. But I want to apologize that I just barged in on your meeting. I figured that since I'm working with Nora and Clint I should be here."

"Sure, Detective," Perez said. "I'm glad you're here." He then looked back at Hawk and Ricci and said, "We need to find out from the killers what private mailbox store they used for a drop-off. If we get that info, I'll then assign Orlinski to contact the NYPD and see if they would check it out for us. Hopefully, it'll lead us to who hired them. I doubt if Captain MacGregor would authorize the expenditure of one of you flying to Brooklyn."

"That's a lot of work for them, Lieutenant," Holliday said. "I wouldn't do it for a crime that was committed in Colorado."

"You may be right, so if that's the case, perhaps they would agree to at least try to get us a video feed from the store, assuming they have one, for the last two or three days."

"Now, detectives," Perez began to speak when Captain MacGregor marched through the open door.

"Sorry to interrupt, but I wanted to congratulate both Nora and Clint for their bravery." She turned her attention specifically to Nora and said, "I'm just astonished how a woman your size could take down two husky killers." Then MacGregor eyed Holliday sitting on a side chair and studied him for a few seconds. "Good morning, Detective Holliday. I see that you're trying to bring back the eighties."

"I don't understand, how can I bring back the eighties?" Holliday said appearing totally perplexed by that statement. He knitted his eyebrows and turned his head slightly to the side.

"Never mind, never mind" she mumbled as she shook her head and walked out of the room.

Mortimer looked at the three of them and asked, "Did you understand what she meant?" Nora could not hold her laughter in any longer and burst out in an infectious laugh. Mortimer was so clueless as evidenced by the comical, confused look on his face. The two joined in on the mirth, except for Mortimer. "Oh, I get it," said Mortimer. "It was a joke that she made, correct?"

"Yes," Hawk said, smiling. "It was a joke."

"Well, I simply don't understand jokes. I never could. To me they're silly and a waste of time. My brother, Seymour, always used to tease me about that. Kept calling me an 'egghead.'"

Nora cracked up again. "Mortimer, did anyone ever tell you that you're funny, in a nice way, of course?"

"Yeah, people tell me that all the time, but I really don't understand why they think that. I certainly don't try to be humorous."

"Well, enough of this," Perez said. "What I started to ask is for you to interrogate the suspects. Hawk you take the Asian and Nora and Mortimer take the white guy." He thought for a moment. "On the other hand, I want all three of you to question each one of them separately."

They agreed, then Hawk said, "Lieutenant, I need to call Chet Watkins first to see if he's got anything on the footprint we saw in the Ellis' garage and the ones in the lot where the shootout took place."

"Sure, go ahead. When you get the report, I want to see it first."

The three detectives walked out. Holliday went back to his desk while Nora and Clint made their way back to theirs. In a low voice, Nora said to Hawk, "We're not in the wild west any longer, you know. What were you thinking? Taking on those men as though you were a gunslinger in the middle of the street. You were wide open and could easily been killed if those men weren't such dunces." Hawk didn't say a word as the more he thought about it he agreed with her and chided himself for being so stupid. "And here the captain congratulates you for a job well done. Unbelievable."

"Sorry, Nora. I agree with you but at the time I didn't think I had a good alternative. Even now, I don't think of what I could've done differently other than run away."

"Well, don't do it again," Nora smiled. "I don't want to lose my handsome partner." She patted him on his aching shoulder and laughed.

After they sat down, Hawk placed a call to Watkins and asked him to fax over whatever information he had on the shoe prints as soon as possible. He explained to Watkins that they will be interrogating the men and it would be extremely helpful if he had a photo of the cast of the sole and what type of shoe it was. Chet told him that he had the preliminary results and would fax them right over. Hawk had just hung up the phone when Perez walked out of his office, called Holliday to join him, and came up to Nora's desk where he could address all three detectives. To her dislike, once again, Perez sat on the edge of Nora's desk.

"I guess you'll be interrogating just one of the men." Perez turned toward Hawk. "The one you shot seems to have gotten an infection in the wound, even though it wasn't that serious, we thought. He was taken to Denver Medical Center a few minutes ago." Turning toward all three now, Perez said, "As for Kwon Bak, he lawyered up. The lawyer will be here in twenty minutes, so I'd like you to discuss with Holliday what you have so far and your theories about it. I'd like to join you, but I've a short meeting in my office. I'll be anxiously watching your interrogation of the man over the monitor. So, see ya."

"Damn," Nora commented. "I was hoping to work on Josh Dollin first as I think he'd be the easiest to get a statement from."

"Well, we'll do the best as we can," Mortimer said. "Now tell me everything you can about what happened to you, Clint and to you, Nora." Quickly, they both filled him in on what had occurred last night with Hawk and this morning with Ricci. Mortimer's expression of dead seriousness did not change at all. He just stood there looking at them as though he were in a daze.

They also discussed with Mortimer the victim, Amanda, and her friend, Marcie, including the significance of the documents that Marcie received by text. After that it was time to go as they were informed that the lawyer and her client were waiting for them. But before they rushed off, Hawk filled him in on what they had heard about a sexual harassment lawsuit with which Amanda had threatened the company and her immediate supervisor.

Nora said, "Mortimer, I imagine that there is something that might be even more frightening to the company than a sexual harassment claim. From the photos of the documents that Amanda Ellis took, and later texted to Marcie, it appears that the company was engaged in construction fraud. Something like that, if known, could bring the company down. They had to find a way to stop any evidence of that coming out. That's why, we feel that they hired the killers to get rid of Amanda and Marcie."

As they began their walk toward the number 2 interrogation room, Orlinski stopped them and told them that he got the name of the president of JWB. "His name is Simon Briggs. And the chief architect and probably Ellis's boss is Roger Benton, V.P. of Architecture. Oh yeah, here's the fax from CSI."

Hawk asked, "Do you know who the lawyer is? A public defender, I suppose."

"No. It's one of the best criminal defense lawyers in Colorado and probably the most expensive, Marleen Linkletter."

Nora said, "Ooo, that tells us something,"

"What do you mean?" Mortimer asked.

"Who do we know who is connected to Amanda Ellis, besides her husband, that has that kind of money for Linkletter?"

"I see. You think that's probably Simon Briggs."

"Exactly."

CHAPTER SIXTEEN

LINKLETTER, a stylish, slim, woman in her early fifties dressed in an expensive dark blue summer woolen pants suit, was seated with her client at the table when the three detectives walked in. She did not look pleased or friendly, almost snarling at them. Kwon looked as though he wanted to spit at Nora, "She's a ninja," he whispered to his lawyer. Linkletter did not have a clue what he meant, since she didn't have much time to get all the details about the case.

After they sat down, she addressed them by trying to set the tone for an unpleasant interview. "You kept me waiting. And I don't like to wait!" Her voice was cold and sharp.

Mortimer astonished Hawk and Ricci when he blurted out, "That's surprising. As a lawyer you're used to waiting. Isn't there an expression when it comes to the court system that says, 'hurry up and wait?'

Linkletter kept silent for a moment as she studied him more carefully. "Who is this man?" She asked the other two.

Hawk decided that he will continue to play the game he played with Tina Dionisio. "This is Detective Mortimer Holliday. He's here from Florida because of his talent of being able to read minds. Haven't you heard about him?"

"This is preposterous. I'm not going to put up with such nonsense."

"Counselor, I have a question for you," Mortimer said. "I heard that you're very expensive and obviously this person next to you wouldn't be able to pay you. So, who's paying for your services?"

"I can't believe, you'd ask such a question. Don't you know that's privileged?"

"Thank you. You already gave me the answer through an instant response. Now I know that it is Simon Briggs. And thank you for connecting this defendant to Briggs." Hawk and Ricci were amazed by Mortimer. They, though, tried to act 'cool' and not throw any glances at each other as though Mortimer could do this all the time.

The woman's mouth popped open; her gray eyes widened for a brief second. Then she smiled for the first time at Mortimer. "Oh, you think you're so clever, but let's see how clever you appear when this is all over. Now can we get on with this interrogation which will be noticeably short since I've advised my client not to say a word."

Mortimer did not let go of the attorney yet. "What do you mean by 'when this is all over?'"

"Never mind," Linkletter recovered her mean composure and snarled at Holliday. "I assume we're through here as it appears you have no questions for my client." And she started to throw her file into her burgundy, leather briefcase.

"Just a minute," Nora said. "We haven't even started."

"All right then. But I insist that only one of you do the questioning. I don't want my client attacked by a gang." Hawk noticed for the first time, that her hands trembled. Mortimer had really gotten to her and she was seething. He could see that she wanted out of the room but knew that she had no real excuse to walk out, especially since not even one question was asked of her client.

"That's fine, counselor," Nora said. "I'll do the questioning."

"That's certainly won't take long since I told you I've instructed him not to answer any questions, not even his name."

"All right then, we'll tell him what we have on him to put him away for a very long time." Then she thought that she should throw in, "And detective Holliday will be able to read his mind."

Linkletter blew out a hard breath. "Cut out this bull crap. We all know that's impossible."

Nora continued, ignoring the attorney, and glared with stern eyes at the accused. "You don't have to tell us your name, we know it's Kwon Bak. You grew up in Long Island, New York, then moved to Brooklyn and live in an apartment on Kings Highway. Your rap sheet from New York is a mile long and you served time for assault and got off on a murder charge." Kwon had his head raised, his lips narrowed, his barely open eyes stared at one spot on the wall above the glass window. His attorney sat still, looking bored.

Nora continued, "We know that you and your partner, Josh Dollin, are killers for hire because that's what you told me."

"What do you mean, he told you?" Linkletter blurted out. "Did you advise him of his Miranda rights before he told you anything?" Both Hawk and Nora laughed. The attorney with anger in her voice asked, "What's so funny? My client's life is on the line, and you think it's funny?"

Nora looked at her with a dumbfounded expression. "Evidently, you don't have all your facts, Counselor. Because if you did, you would know that I was not in the position of advising him of anything. I and another woman, Marcie Turner, were this close to taking our last breath because of your client." Nora held her thumb and index finger together leaving barely any space between them. "He and his partner, Josh, threatened us with death, execution style. They forced us to lay down on the floor on our stomachs so that they could kill us with their 'trademark,' a bullet to the back of the head. They were very talkative, bragging how much money they make and how good they are."

"You mean that they just provided information to you without you asking anything?"

"Basically yes, and even if I asked anything, they were not under arrest. It was actually Marcie and me that were under arrest." Linkletter did not say a word, acting as though she was not fazed by any of that. But Hawk could see that she was boiling inside. "Well, to continue the interrogation," Nora again bore her eyes into Kwon, who still stared at the wall. "Because of what you said while we were held hostage, we know that you were hired by a Denver businessman who paid you twenty-five thousand dollars and will pay the same amount on completion of the job. Based on what Detective Holliday said, it was the president of JWB International Contractors."

"That is crazy," Linkletter said. "That is no evidence, but a con job by you. No one would believe that this strange person here could read anyone's mind, especially since that name never entered my mind."

"Oh, we have great confidence in him." Nora said and patted Mortimer on his shoulder for what she thought was dramatic effect. "Now to continue, Kwon, we know that you were hired to kill Amanda Ellis and Marcie Turner. You weren't successful with Ms. Turner, but you did kill Amanda Ellis right in her garage as she was leaving for work. You will be charged by the DA for first degree murder and will never see freedom again."

Kwon became animated. He shook his head vehemently from side to side. His attorney told him to sit still while squeezing his arm. Nora said, "Yes, Kwon, you and your buddy, Josh, killed Amanda Ellis in cold blood." At this point, Hawk slipped the shoeprint report to her. "We know that you were there, at the scene because Josh's shoeprint was found by the passenger side of the car where we believe you took Mrs. Ellis's phone out of her purse."

Kwon continued to shake his head, his lawyer waived her hand up and down for him to stay still and remain silent.

"We know that you were hired by Simon Briggs, the president, because the only one who would have a motive to eliminate both the victim and her friend would be he to keep documents that they acquired hidden. The publicity concerning their fraud could bring down the company. And those documents were on the Ellis phone and a copy on Turner's phone, and you needed to get both phones and eliminate both women."

"How much marijuana had you smoked to come up with this wild conjecture. I don't represent Mr. Briggs, but I'd certainly would recommend that he sues you and this department for slander. My God! Such a cock and bull story." Nora disregarded her comments.

"So, Mr. Bak, you came all the way here from New York to kill Amanda Ellis, which you did, and now you're going to pay for it along with all the other charges that you had accumulated." Nora stated in an aggressive tone of voice.

Kwon was fiery red. He could not remain silent any longer, no matter how much his lawyer tried to keep him quiet. In an outburst, he yelled, "We did not kill that woman in the garage."

"Mr. Bak, Kwon, don't say a word. Keep quiet."

"No, It's my neck on the line. They need to know that we killed no one. So, butt out. You're not here to help me. I know your kind of lawyers. You're hired by some rich dude to make sure that he's kept out of this." The lawyer's face turned crimson.

"This is the end of this interview. I don't want you talking to my client."

Hawk said, "Counselor it looks to us that he's not interested in your counsel. If he wants to talk to save himself, I don't blame him."

"In that case, I'm out of here. Get yourself another lawyer, Mr. Bak." She looked back hard at Holliday. "And I can't stand this strange man constantly glaring at me. He makes me so nervous; I can't think straight." With that, she jammed her file in her fancy briefcase and walked out, breathing hard.

Not fazed by his lawyer's abrupt departure, but with spittle at the side of his mouth, Kwon centered his determined stare on Nora and began to speak. Nora interrupted him. "Your lawyer left. Do you still want to tell us your side of the story?" He nodded and Nora continued, "Do you then waive and retract your request for a lawyer, and do you understand that anything you say may be used against you?"

"Yes, yes, yes. You need to know that we did not kill her. She was already dead when we got there. The garage door was open, we walked in, and she was laying on the floor in front of her fancy car. You're right, we did take the phone as instructed and took off, but we didn't kill her."

"Then who would've killed her?" Mortimer asked.

Kwon looked puzzled at Holliday. "How in the hell would I know that? Maybe no one did. She might have had a heart attack or whoever hired us didn't trust us to get here fast enough from New York and had someone else do the bitch in." He sat silent for a moment as did everyone else. "But really, if I had to guess, I would say it was the husband or a girlfriend of his."

"Oh," Nora said. "Why do you think that?"

"Well, isn't that always the case? It's always the husband. Is he a rich businessman?"

Nora didn't answer, but asked, "How did you get here from New York so soon?"

"We caught the redeye flight out of LaGuardia that same evening that we got the money and instructions, rented a car, and drove straight to the Ellis' house. But we did not kill that woman. You have to believe me."

"But you would've if she wasn't dead already." Kwon hung his head and remained silent.

"You realize," Hawk said, "That you'll still be charged with attempted murder of Ellis and Turner, Detective Ricci and me."

"I want a deal of some kind. I already gave you more information than I should have. That should count for something."

Nora said, "If you help us with details of how you were hired, the mechanics of it, we'll recommend to the District Attorney to go easy on you. Perhaps dismiss a few of the charges."

Breathing hard and fast, his chest rising and falling, Kwon sat quietly for a minute, mulling over what he should do. "Okay, but can I trust you to help me with a deal?"

"Of course, our word is our bond."

He stared at Nora for a minute. "I've never seen a woman fight as you did. You were so fast. I suppose that anyone that can bring down two men with guns can be trusted to do the right thing." He looked at Hawk. "Can I trust you?" Hawk told him he could. He ignored the judgmental gaze of Mortimer's. "Alright, then. We get people from our ad on the dark web."

"You mean, Killers for Hire?" Mortimer asked, bitingly. There was no look of amazement from him, his morbid-looking expression had not changed since he entered the room.

"No, not quite that obvious. We use words like 'We take care of your personal people problems,' etcetera."

"And people can figure out what you mean by that?" Hawk asked.

"Evidently, since they're communicating on the dark web, they know that it's probably not legit."

Nora said, "Okay, Kwon, tell us the mechanics of it all. How do they communicate with you? How do they get you the money?"

Kwon hesitated. "Well, they first express interest over the dark web without any specifics. We send them an address for them to leave instructions and our fee in cash in a large manila envelope marked 'Box 433 Urgent' and drop it into a secure box that Zeb's Mailboxes and Office Concierge Service has on the side of their building. I have a deal with the owner that if an envelope is for us, he'll place the envelope in our mailbox and call us immediately."

Hawk asked, "What were the instructions that you received?"

"We were to catch a plane out to Denver and proceed to the address on Humboldt Street. There was a photo of the woman that they had a problem with, and we had to 'give her an adjustment.'"

"Go on," Hawk said. "Then we were told to obtain her phone."

Nora asked, "How were you supposed to get the phone to them?"

"Ah, yes. They told us what type of car to rent from the rental agency and what restaurant to have a long lunch in at 12:30. Then we were told to park the BMW by the trash container in the back of the restaurant and place the phone under the front passenger seat, leaving the passenger door unlocked."

"Did you do it?"

"Yes. We had a long lunch as instructed. Afterward, we checked to see if the phone was taken. It was and there was a poorly scribbled note that must've been written in a hurry that instructed us to adjust a Marcie Turner at an apartment in Glendale as soon as possible and get her phone. That we'd be paid another $25,000 for that job."

Hawk asked, "What were you supposed to do with Turner's phone once you got it?"

"Ah, yes. We were supposed to come back to the same restaurant for dinner and follow the same instructions."

"Do you have the note?"

"No, we were told to destroy it. So, Josh tore it up and threw it in the dumpster."

"What was the name of the restaurant and what time were you supposed to have dinner?"

"It was some kind of dive on Federal Boulevard, in what looked like an Asian part of town." He hesitated, trying to remember the name. "I think it was called Ginger's or something like that. I have no idea how to get there. Josh drove."

"And the time you were supposed to eat dinner there?"

"Seven o'clock. But we never made it there because of you two," pointing to Hawk and Ricci, venom building in his eyes. He was tired and appeared to have second thoughts about all the information he gave them. "Now, listen here, I gave you everything I know. You are going to keep your word that Josh and I will get a better deal for this. You told me I could trust you."

Hawk said, "We'll do everything in our power to get you a better deal, Kwon. Now, you know New York might be interested in you."

"I'll take it one step at a time. I've got a good lawyer there."

CHAPTER SEVENTEEN

WITH MUCH hesitation and after further coaching by Nora, Kwon signed the statement which was prepared by her. Afterward, she and Hawk agreed that they were starved and needed sustenance. It was shortly past noon and they tried to decide where to go for lunch when Mortimer came up to them. "I thought that went rather well. You both did a good job with Kwon. So, what are we doing next? This case is getting interesting. From what I understand we have several suspects."

"That's right, Mortimer," Hawk said, "But right now we're talking about lunch. Would you like to join us?"

"Oh, no. Josephine would not like it if I spent my money on lunch when we have some beans and rice at the house. She also made some cornbread, which doesn't taste too bad. Thanks anyway."

"Don't worry about the cost. Lunch is on us." Nora looked at Clint to see if he agreed. He nodded and she continued, "Over lunch we can discuss the suspects, although we haven't interviewed anyone from Amanda's place of employment yet."

"I better not. If you buy lunch for me, then sometime down the road I'll have to treat you and Josephine would have a hissy fit."

"No, Mortimer," Hawk said. "We certainly would not expect you to reciprocate. But if that's the way you think is best, we'll be back in an hour and then we'll take off for JWB Contractors."

"Well wait. I'll just tell Josephine that lunch is part of the job today to discuss various suspects. I'm sure she'll understand." Hawk and Nora exchanged quick glances with raised eyebrows.

"Great," Nora said. "Since we'll be in the Cherry Creek area, there are a ton of cool restaurants we could choose from. A few months ago, I ate at True Food Kitchen on Second Avenue. It's really healthy food and I thought it was great. Why don't we go there?"

"Sounds good to me," Hawk said.

"Is it expensive, though?" Mortimer asked, his bushy eyebrows coming together with concern.

"Mortimer, nothing in the Cherry Creek area is inexpensive, but the restaurant prices are fairly reasonable. I mean we couldn't afford to eat out at a nice restaurant every day, but today should be special and we should celebrate with some great food because we're alive. Too bad, though, that we can't have a glass of wine, still on the clock, you know. But iced tea sounds great."

Mortimer stood in place appearing deep in thought. "Look, it's just lunch, my friend," Hawk said.

"Oh, that's very nice of you to call me your friend. You know, I don't have too many. So many people think that I'm strange for some reason. I'll consider you two as my friends as well, but I don't want to interfere in your celebration. And if it's that expensive I don't want you to spend the extra money on me. Like I said, it was a treat to me when I was able to go to a fast-food restaurant of some sort and I'll probably feel uncomfortable in a fancy place."

"Really, don't think about that," Nora said." We'd love to have you join us. And don't worry about the cost, we can certainly afford it and you can help us celebrate with a fun meal. As I said, lunch will be on us, so don't worry." Mortimer still seemed unsure. "If you're still worried as to what Josephine will say, tell her that you were our guest and that it didn't cost you anything." *Boy! I really need to meet this Josephine. Is she really that tight or is it Mortimer using her as an excuse for being cheap and worried that he'll have to repay us someday?*

Mortimer finally said he was willing, but he first had to call his fiancé. A few minutes later, the three detectives headed for the restaurant. Hawk again drove, deciding to take a more scenic route from the station showing Holliday a little more of Denver. They made it to Speer Boulevard and drove easterly partially along Cherry Creek with its rushing waters, tall embankments and bike trails along both banks. Then Speer took them past the Denver Country Club on the right and the pricy large older homes of the Country Club area to the left.

As they approached the business district of Cherry Creek, Mortimer asked with a bit of surprise in his tone, "Are we back downtown?"

Nora said, "No, this is the Cherry Creek area we told you about."

"But it has all these tall, flashy buildings. I get it, this is a very upscale area, isn't it?"

"Yes. But the history is quite fascinating. Would you believe that in the late 1800's the place was an incorporated town call Harmon? And part of that area there," she pointed her index finger to the right in the general direction of the Cherry Creek Shopping Center, "where you see those large stores such as Nordstrom's, Neiman Marcus, Restoration Hardware, Macy's, and others, was, as I understand it, a city dump after Denver annexed the town.

"In the days of the late 1800's and early 1900's, there were just a few houses on both sides of the Creek built by the first black settlers to come to Colorado. They suffered from one flood after another, especially the one in 1933 that wiped out so many homes and businesses. Brutal floods continued until 1950 when the Cherry Creek dam was built to hold the water back. After that, this area became too valuable and so many of the poor blacks were forced out in the name of progress. You can imagine what it looked like before, from poor hovels to these magnificent buildings. There are photos of the area when the black colony was here that are fascinating to see."

As Nora talked, Hawk went around several blocks trying to find an available space along the street to park. He did not want to abuse his status as a policeman to park illegally. Mortimer listened with great interest to Nora and kept stretching his long neck in all directions to gaze at the area.

"Nora, you certainly know a lot about Denver. I never realized how much history there is in this state. I wish I knew more about Florida's history. Maybe when I go back, I'll do some reading."

"You mean that you're thinking of returning?" Hawk asked.

"Oh, well, I don't know. Sometimes Josephine worries me that maybe I'm rushing things with her. She seems to be a little too controlling."

"Oh, don't worry about that. Aren't all women controlling to some degree?" Hawk laughed.

Nora slapped him lightly across his shoulder, "Oh, that's what you think, do you?" She joined him in a chuckle. Mortimer did not see the humor in Hawk's statement, but what Hawk said made sense to him as he remembered how henpecked his father was by his mother.

Hawk finally found a spot to park, about a block away on Clayton Street, and they walked east to Detroit Street. A line waiting to be seated greeted them as they walked through the door. "Doesn't look good," Nora said disappointedly. As Hawk walked up to the desk, a harried, but friendly teenage girl told him that it will take at least twenty minutes if they wanted to be seated on the patio or about five minutes inside. Hawk gave her his name and phone number to be texted when a table inside became available. It was a beautiful, sunny, pleasant day and Nora would rather have sat outside, but she was pleased that they would only have to wait five minutes or so. For some reason that Nora and Hawk could not understand, Mortimer was fidgety, couldn't stand still, had a sneezing and coughing fit and strained his neck to look inside the dining area. He became the center of attention as people standing around them began to move away.

"Is there anything wrong?" Hawk asked.

"Oh, places like these make me nervous for some reason. I told you I'm not used to them. I remember once I was invited to a fancy place by the International Mall in Tampa and I had actually hyperventilated. A bad experience with a waiter who made fun of me. I'll never forget that day. He thought it was funny, but I didn't think so at all."

"Well, this place is not that fancy, Mortimer," Nora said. "It's geared more to health-conscious people. It's just a nice place and I guarantee that you'll have a pleasant experience." Mortimer loudly sucked in his breath, then sneezed three time. A woman next to him jumped from the sudden noise.

A few minutes later, Hawk was notified of an available table that they were escorted to. It was one of the many along an elongated lime green booth that stretched against a long wall in the main rectangular dining area. The tables were separated by a couple of feet from each other. Along the wall above the booth were actual aspen trunks used as an unusual decoration that simulated a grove of aspen trees. On the ceiling three massive copper drum chandeliers. To the left of their table was a bar and serving tables for the staff with another smaller dining area beyond. Nora and Clint were seated in the soft booth, while Mortimer sat across from them in a colorful yellow plastic chair. He seemed to have recovered from what appeared to be a mini anxiety attack.

At the table next to Hawk, across from each other, sat two very well-dressed men in tailored suits, engaged in serious conversation and oblivious to the world. They were in their fifties, both looked fit, thin, and tanned with graying hair. Hawk could not help noticing the emerald cufflinks worn by the man that sat next to him.

"Oh. my God!" Mortimer said. "Can you believe these prices? Josephine and I could eat for a week on just what one appetizer costs. And I don't know where to begin. I mean they have foods I never even heard of. For example, what in the hell is a spaghetti squash casserole?"

"Mortimer, just order something that's familiar to you like a grass-fed hamburger," Nora said.

"Okay, but what's the difference between grass-fed hamburger and a regular hamburger?"

Hawk joked, "Marketing mostly." But then he explained, "One cow was raised in a pasture, the other is fed in a feedlot. It sounds special, but in the long run the result is the same. You get a hamburger." He smiled, hoping that Mortimer would smile back. He really wanted to see what he looks like if he smiled. *He certainly would look more pleasant and less intimidating.* But Mortimer only nodded.

Nora said, "It supposed to be healthier if the cow or steer is in the pasture eating natural grass and able to move around a good distance as opposed eating grain fed from a trough."

"I know that," Hawk said. "But don't you think all ranchers supplement with grain more often than not?"

"Okay, okay. Let's order. Here comes the server." Nora ordered an organic Tuscan kale salad; Hawk took shrimp tacos and

Mortimer agreed on the hamburger. Each had a glass of ice tea to drink.

While they waited for their food to arrive, Nora asked, "So, from all the people we talked to today, what do you think?"

Mortimer said, "They're all a bunch of liars. I didn't meet Amanda's husband, but if I saw him, I bet I'd think he was a liar too."

Hawk said, "I'm sure you would've. I know he lied about how good their marriage was. His assistant, Tina Dionisio, admitted that they had an affair. Who knows who else he might've had an affair with? If Amanda threatened him with a divorce, then he had a great motive to get rid of her to save at least half of his fortune. Or he had an even better motive if he wanted her out of the way so that he could marry Tina or whoever. And we know that he had the opportunity to kill her yesterday morning. He should be our prime suspect."

Nora said, "But why would he hire those killers from New York to kill his wife?"

Hawk answered, "Yes, that's been bothering me, all right. These killers like to use guns. It would've been easier for them to run into the garage, quickly shoot her and get out before anyone knew what happened."

"The noise," Mortimer said.

"What was that Mortimer?" Nora asked as she could not quite hear his muffled response.

"A gunshot would've called attention to them from neighbors and people in the park. They would've looked and would've noticed them run out of the garage."

"That's very reasonable to conclude," Hawk said. "But are they smart enough to figure out to kill someone with the use of an overdose of insulin?"

The food arrived and they quickly turned their attention to it. After a few bites, Nora and Hawk continued to discuss the case. Nora still felt that if the hired killers did not kill Amanda Ellis, then her bet was on Tina. Mortimer was so engrossed in his hamburger and the sweet potato fries that he did not pay much attention to what Hawk and Nora were discussing. Nora had never seen anyone eat as fast and with such gusto as he did. He was almost choking on his food. He ate as though he had not eaten for a week.

"Mortimer, I see you like that hamburger. It's almost gone. Would you like another?"

"Oh, it's best that I don't. It's been a long time since I had such a good meal. As I told you before, Josephine doesn't believe in eating meat. Before I moved in with her, I did eat some chicken or fish, but not much beef. It was always too expensive. I've forgotten how good it tastes. Thank you both for this. I don't think I'll tell Josephine about it because she'll just get angry." Mortimer then took the last bite. He leaned back in his chair, rolling his head back slightly, closed his gray eyes and took in a deep breath. "I must say that was great." Nora and Clint gazed at each other, each with an amused expression. "So, I apologize, I know you were discussing something."

"Oh, Nora was just saying that the death of Amanda really benefited Tina." Mortimer sneezed again, sounding as if a shotgun had gone off, then took a deep breath through his nose, curling his thin lips towards it. "I can see her point."

CHAPTER EIGHTEEN

THE DIRECTORY led the three detectives to the Architectural Division of Briggs, Jones and Wentworth International Contractors. As they zipped to the ninth floor, Mortimer again had a rough time in the elevator. Sweat beaded his brow and his trembling hands were fisted tightly. Hawk glanced at a concerned Nora who also noticed the panic in Holliday and asked, "Are you perhaps claustrophobic, Mortimer?" Mortimer nodded in the affirmative as he swallowed deep breaths. "We'll avoid the elevator on the way down." Mortimer mumbled something that sounded like the word, "good."

The elevator opened directly to the needed office and an elegant reception area greeted their eyes. Instead of the modern can lighting found in most offices, four unusual circular chandeliers in half-moon motif were hung snuggly against the ceiling. A colorful Persian rug covered one section of the floor; several soft beige leather chairs were strewn around. A table laden with donuts, pastries and a Keurig coffee maker stood a few steps away. The wall behind the reception desk was of vertical narrow strips of rich walnut from floor to ceiling while the matching design of the desk had a milk glass countertop bordered by copper corners. A wide hallway was off to the side. No receptionist sat behind the desk. Nora called out, "Hello, anyone here?"

No one came out. She said it again and finally a man shuffled out of the hallway. "Oh, I guess our receptionist stepped out. What can I do for you?"

"We'd like to see Roger Benton," Hawk said. "We believe that he's the chief architect here."

"Yeah, that's right. He's also the vice president of the company." They could hear disgust for his boss in his voice. "But since the receptionist is out, I guess it's all right if you just make your way down to his office. It's the last door on the right. He'll probably be mad for me just sending you there like that, but, hey, with one of our architects dying, the rest of us are swamped."

"Yes, that's very sad about Mrs. Ellis," Nora said.

"You bet it is. But I'm sure the higher-ups are relieved to get rid of her."

"What do you mean?"

"Oh, I shouldn't have said anything." He hesitated a few seconds. "I guess what I mean is that she was a stickler for details."

"For details," Nora said. "You mean she got under their skin?"

"Oh yeah, from what I heard, she was threatening to expose the company—"

At that instant, a security guard walked in. When the architect saw him, he immediately changed the subject and said, "Just go right down the hall, Mr. Benton is in his office."

"Thank you, Mr—"

"Jamison."

"What's this all about?" The tall, thin, black-bearded guard asked in a very gruff voice.

"They're here to see Roger." He turned abruptly and returned to his work area.

"You need an appointment to see Mr. Benton," the unfriendly guard said.

"It's okay," Hawk said, showing his credentials. "We don't need an appointment." As they walked away, the guard was complaining angrily that they had no authority to enter that area. The detectives proceeded to follow the architect's directions and knocked on Roger's door.

"Yes, what do you want?" Roger yelled out in an irritated voice. "It had better be urgent. Come in!" Nora opened the door and the three detectives walked into a large plush office decorated with tennis related posters and a cabinet full of tennis trophies.

Not expecting visitors, Roger's arrogant face portrayed surprise as he stared at the strangers. "I'm sorry. I didn't get a call from the receptionist to greet you. I thought you might be one of my architects. What can I help you with? Do you have a project that requires our outstanding architectural services?" Hawk immediately recognized him as one of the two men that sat next to him in the restaurant.

"Unfortunately, we don't," Hawk said. He introduced himself and the others as Denver police detectives and all three noticed the color drain from his wrinkleless face. His artificial smile faded into a sneer as his lips tightened. Nora thought she noticed a slight tremor in his soft-looking hands. *He has something to hide, that's for sure,* Nora thought.

"What's this all about? Is it about Mrs. Ellis' death?"

"Actually, it is," Nora said. "May we sit down? We need some background information on her for our report."

"All three of you are necessary for that?" His voice quivered.

"Yes, this is a complicated case and we're taking it very seriously."

Roger's eyes floated over to Mortimer who stood still, arms at his sides, head bent, shoulders slouching and his gray eyes boring into the man. "Let's go over to the round table there," pointing at a highly polished walnut table with six brown swivel chairs.

Except for Mortimer, who remained standing across from Roger, they sat down, Roger Benton breathing hard. Nora asked, "Can you tell us a little about Mrs. Ellis such as what kind of a person she was or what kind of an employee?"

Mortimer interrupted, "My two partners always seem to take a kinder approach. I don't believe in that. I get right down to the point." Nora and Hawk threw quick glances at each other. *What the hell is he up to,* Hawk thought. "You see, we know all about you, Mr. Benton. We know that you have been sexually harassing Mrs. Ellis for a long time. But the day before she was murdered, she had all she could take from you and threatened to go to the authorities." Roger's veins at his temples seemed to pop out and the tremor in his hands became quite noticeable. Mortimer did not relent, "That would've ruined you. Your career would be gone. This decadent office of yours would be gone and your money with it." Roger tried to get ahold of himself and act as if Holliday's accusations were simply nonsense. However, the dread he was feeling, could not be hidden. He took some deep breaths and was about to say something, but Mortimer persisted. "That's why you had to get rid of her. That's why you hired the killers to save your neck."

Roger shouted, "No, no, no. That's not correct. I didn't hire anyone to kill Amanda. I admit I have a habit of hugging women, but I didn't kill her." His voice had a high-pitched tone as he shifted his body in his chair from side to side, his face turning crimson.

Hawk thought he should jump in and take over the questioning before Mortimer gives Roger a stroke. "Mr. Benton, it appears that you're the only logical person who would want Amanda Ellis murdered to save your skin. Of course, you deny doing so, although, most guilty people do. If you didn't do it, would her killing have been ordered by your president, Simon Briggs?" Hawk's tone was one of conversation rather than accusation, it seemed to settle Benton down a little.

"I have no idea what the president of this company would do." He folded his legs under his seat and pursed his lips. He then stretched his legs out underneath the table and took a good look at Mortimer who did not move an inch since he walked in, still remaining standing. "Who are you? Are you really a detective?"

"For sure I am and I'm on your case."

He looked at Nora and Hawk, "Well, as long as he's in my office standing over me like a zombie dressed up for a masquerade, I'm not going to cooperate with you. Would you all please leave."

Hawk still had many questions about the documents retrieved from Marcie's phone. "Mr. Benton, we'll ask Detective Holliday to step out of his presence bothers you. We do have a few more questions that are important to our investigation. It won't take long, and it might be helpful in eliminating you from suspicion. Would you agree to that?"

"As long as that person that is boring through me with laser eyes," pointing to Mortimer, "is out of here, I'll give you another five minutes because I do want to convince you that I didn't do anything to Amanda. A lawsuit would not have brought me to that point. Mr. Briggs already told me that he'd support me on that."

Hawk asked the reluctant Mortimer to leave. After the door closed, Hawk quickly pulled out from his coat's breast pocket folded copies of the documents printed off Marcie's phone and placed them in front of Benton. "Do you know what these are?"

He slowly picked up the papers to review, although, it seemed obvious that he recognized what they were immediately. "They look like a partial contract with signatures on one and an architectural drawing with materials that the job requires." A slight tremor returned to his hands.

"What about the third document that has the same drawing with a substitution of cheap materials, or the elimination of materials as shown in the other plan?"

"No, I don't see that." Sweat appeared on his upper lip and around the mouth.

Hawk looked at Nora to continue with the questioning. "Mr. Benton, how can you not know them, these are your documents, aren't they?"

"The partial contract would not have anything to do with the architectural department. You need to ask Mr. Briggs about that one. You know I'm done answering your preposterous questions. If you have any more, ask our corporate counsel. I'm very busy. Would you please leave?" His face still red as a beet, the veins protruded on his forehead even more. Nora thought it was best to leave him alone before they needed to call an ambulance.

Nora said, "Mr. Benton, I really think that you should request our help to put you in a safe house for a few days, considering what happened to Mrs. Ellis. Because of these documents, I'm afraid that now your life may be in danger as well. You must be privy to the fraud that this company was engaged in and we're sure that you know who contacted the hired killers." Roger's mouth flew open, his eyes widened. "You know too much, and someone will try to silence you." Hawk turned his head in surprise toward Nora. *She might have something there,* Hawk thought.

"That's really even more ridiculous than your crazy accusations. What? Do you want me to confess to something I didn't do by scaring me to death? Get out! Get out!"

Hawk thanked him and gave him his card. "Please call anytime if you feel threatened." They swiftly walked out of the room toward the exit. The guard stood by the elevator as they walked toward it. His coal-black eyes shot fire at them, an angry frown on his long rectangular face. Both noticed a tattoo of crossed swords on the right side of his neck which they did not spot before as only the left side of his neck was visible to them initially. Nora smiled at him and said, "Thank you for your help, Mr.—"

"Jason Edwards," he growled, narrowing his eyes. *What's his problem?* Nora thought.

Hawk looked at Mortimer who stood by the elevator. His expression seemed angry, although, at times it was difficult to tell expressions on his face as he almost always had a somewhat grimacing look. Mortimer turned toward the elevator and his chest began to heave by just looking at it. "Are there stairs that we can take down from here?" Hawk asked and Jason pointed to a sign at the other end of the room that read, "Exit." "Let's take those stairs."

"Thank you, Clint," Mortimer said. Once inside the stairwell with its bland concrete steps and painted pipe railings, Mortimer commented, "He did it. He's the one. I have this vibe about Roger Benton. Of course, I expected him to deny that he did it. Wouldn't you? I was going to press harder, but you interrupted me, Clint. And I didn't appreciate being kicked out of the room."

Hawk listened as he made his way down. Nora was on his heels, but Mortimer fell behind several steps, tightly gripping the handrail. Hawk turned around to face Mortimer. "You were hitting him too hard without any proof that he did it. I really feel that one more question from you, he was going to tell us, as he eventually did, to talk to his lawyer. I really wanted to see what he'd say or see his reaction to the documents. You may be right, but we need something more than just a motive."

Mortimer did not say anything. He narrowed his thin lips to the point where they looked like they disappeared and then he fell into a sneezing fit. Hawk and Ricci resumed their trek down and heard Mortimer complain that he cannot stop his nose from running. As Nora turned back to look, she saw him wipe his nose on his sleeve. She reached into her handbag and offered him a pocket-sized pack of tissues. He took two out and placed the rest of the pack into his coat pocket without saying thanks to her. Nora decided not to bother asking him to return the packet.

She said, "It's a good thing that we decided not to see Briggs this afternoon. We'd be wasting our time. Roger must've tipped him off by now. He'll either be too busy to see us or the corporate lawyer would meet us and tell us to get lost."

"Sounds right," Hawk said. "Let's keep working the case and see if we can come up with more facts, then bring him in for questioning. It's getting late anyway so might as well head back. I'm getting really sore from that accident anyway. All these stairs aren't helping."

Returning to the old police cruiser, none of them at first noticed a motorcycle that followed them. They were startled when it zipped past them, its roaring engine breaking up the quietness of the neighborhood. "That punk should get a ticket," Mortimer yelled out, his fist punching the air. *Geez! What got into quiet Mortimer?* Nora could not believe the way he acted after lunch. *Could it be that all that protein in the hamburger got him wound up?* Nora chuckled to herself, anxious to discuss this seemingly out of character with Clint.

Desiring to ride in front, Nora asked Mortimer to sit in the back. Nora regretted her decision after it took a few minutes to get Mortimer to contort himself into the backseat stymied by his pointed-tipped shoes. Finally, they were in, and Hawk pulled the car out a few inches ready to blend into the heavy rush-hour traffic.

Just as he thought it was safe to proceed, the same motorcycle they saw earlier, came out of nowhere at the speed of light. Suddenly, it slowed down as it was parallel to their vehicle. Hawk vigorously slammed on the brakes in order not to knock him down when he saw the helmeted driver throw something at him. The racket from whatever hit the driver's side window reverberated inside the car, causing Mortimer to have another sneezing fit. The unyielding glass saved Hawk from a blow to his head.

The object that struck the window fell to the ground as the helmeted motorcycle rider sped away driving in and out of traffic. A red brick lay by the door with a piece of paper attached by a rubber band. The note read, *"You got your killers so lay off any more digging into the case. Next time it will be more than a brick."*

Mortimer got over his sneezing but remained in the car. "Did you get a look at his face?" Nora asked Hawk.

"No, his visor was tinted. I did, though get a good look at the bike. I believe it was a Kawasaki Ninja like the one I used to own last year before I sold it. The lime green color was even the same. And I bet that if we ask anyone if they saw the driver's face or license plate number, it would be just a waste of time.

Everyone remained silent on the drive back to the station. Hawk's heart pounded and he was sure that Nora's did the same. Suddenly, Mortimer said, "Great. Something else to investigate. And Josephine thinks that I'm in a safe job as a detective in Denver. What's next?"

CHAPTER NINETEEN

SIMON BRIGGS sat behind his custom-built mahogany and leather desk reviewing a bid that his chief engineer sent over for approval. It entailed the construction of a multi-story apartment building in Buenos Aires worth almost half a billion dollars. More than satisfied with the figures, if approved by the developer, it would mean a tidy sum of profit for his company.

Reclining in his alligator leather chair, he smiled with satisfaction. Briggs closed his eyes and, in his mind, counted the cash that this project would bring him personally. He did not need the money. To him, it was all a game as to how much he could accumulate before he died. Since a small boy, he read about the *Forbes* list of richest persons in the world and his ambition was to be included in that category. *I'll do whatever it takes,* he told himself.

With his eyes still closed, his head leaning against the high back of the chair, he reminisced how his empire began. Through his developer father's connections and his MIT degree in civil engineering, he fell into a well-established international construction firm of Jonas and Wentworth. With long hours of hard work and good business sense, he was able to move up quickly in the company, receiving huge bonuses because of his success. Five years later, he was made a full one-third partner and his name was added to the firm name. In the next five years, he was able to buy out Jonas and Wentworth. However, he kept the name of Jonas, Wentworth and Briggs since it was a well-established firm. It was he who added a full-service architectural department and hired Roger Benton.

In business, his strategy was to portray the company's accomplishments to the big-time developers by flaunting trappings of wealth. In the company's offices, he lavishly entertained them by throwing large receptions, especially for the foreign dignitaries, in the huge ballroom that he built on the ninth floor to rival the palace ballrooms of Europe. Appetizers often included such delicacies as truffles, beluga's almas caviar and lobster frittata among others. *Sure, it was expensive, especially the forty thousand-dollar bottles of wine, but it was worth it. That's how I got the Buenos Aires deal. Wine them and dine them. That's the secret.* He paid for prospective clients' transportation to Denver. He put them up in luxurious suites and even provided a limousine with a driver. They could travel anywhere in Colorado they wanted whether it was to see what Denver metro had to offer or trips to the ski resorts—Aspen, Vail, Telluride. The clients' loved the pampering and that led to lucrative deals.

Yet, in his personal life, he lived frugally. If his goal were to accumulate cash, he saved where he could. Frivolous vacations, a mega large trophy house, expensive vehicles, a wife and family all were counterproductive to that accumulation of wealth. That is why he never married, lived in a modest smaller condo in his condominium building that he owned and drove a used Lincoln Navigator as his personal vehicle.

Briggs, now that he was in his mid-fifties, had to admit to himself that, at times, more so now the older he became, his goal changed. Now he had the notion to give up his quest to accumulate riches and start spending money on vacations, multiple homes, and collector cars. Maybe even find a wife and a family so that he could leave his fortune to someone. But marriage scared him because if it did not work out, even with a pre-nuptial agreement with sharp lawyer, the wife could manage to clean him out. *Oh no! I'm not going to fall into that trap. That's why as soon as a woman begins talking about marriage, it's time to find someone else.*

Simon's thoughts came to an abrupt halt when Roger charged into his office, "Simon, we have a problem. And I am nervous."

"Roger, what's this? You never barged into my office like this. Where is Roxanne?"

"Your secretary tried to stop me, but this is too important. We need to talk and now!"

"You look like you're going to have a coronary. Sit down, take a few breaths, and tell me what's this drastic problem. My God, your hands are shaking."

"I think you and I are in big trouble. They know everything!"

"Who knows everything?"

"The police."

"What do they know, Roger?"

"They know that Amanda Ellis was going to bring charges against me for sexual harassment. I had a weird detective accuse me of hiring killers to eliminate her because I had a strong motive for doing so."

"Roger, I feel for you, but what's that got to do with me?"

"I had another detective, a more reasonable one that wanted me to tell him what I know of certain documents that were in Amanda's possession. You know, the ones that show a substitution of cheaper and inferior materials. Simon, they know everything. They know that you were the one that hired hit men to kill Amanda." Roger's face turned crimson, his voice trembling while Simon's was as calm as a cucumber.

"Roger, settle down."

"I can't calm down. You and I are going to jail."

"You will, not me. It was all your doing to eliminate materials or substitute with inferior materials. You're the one that signed off on that. Amanda caught on to you and you had to get rid of her." The air was taken out of Roger at what he heard his boss say. "And you couldn't take the embarrassment of a sexual harassment charge so you must've hired the killers. At least I caught the substitution of materials and sent Dubai the original plans before your amended plans were sent off to them."

Roger fell back against the chair. *What the hell is he up to? He's turning the tables on me.* He sat up and stared eye to eye with Simon whose face revealed a cruel smirk. The smugness of his expression almost made Roger jump over the desk and choke him. Instead, he took a deep breath, heart bouncing in his chest. "Are you insane, Simon? You're pinning this all on me? Why would I come up on my own with fraud and hope a building doesn't collapse?"

"Because, my dear friend, you love those extra bonuses that you get when we make more profit. You must have done it over the years until I caught this one with Dubai. I know nothing of any hired killers. Why would I? Now go home, relax tonight and things will be better in the morning."

"You bet I'll leave! You haven't heard the last of this!"

He sprinted to the door and as he was about to leave, Simon said, "Oh Roger, if I were you, I'd watch my back. Who knows who's out to get you? I hope you paid those hired killers of yours." Simon laughed vengefully as Benton slammed the door behind him.

Roger Benton fumed as he ran back to his office, he heard Simon laugh. There was a file there that only he knew about that he must retrieve before being locked out on Simon's orders. In his office, he opened a credenza drawer and pulled out a non-labeled folder. The binder contained copies of all the memos he received from Simon instructing him to review the material costs of each project and cut the expense one way or another by at least fifteen to twenty percent. At the time when he received the memos, he realized, and Briggs knew it too, that the only way to accomplish that was to substitute with cheaper materials. The file also contained copies of both the original plan and the amended plan that he had to sign off on to keep his high-paying job. Next, he grabbed some of his personal items from his desk drawers, stuffed them in his briefcase with the file and rushed to the elevator down to the parking garage level.

After Roger left, Simon Briggs blew out a hard breath. His head developed a slight headache, and he knew from experience that his blood pressure was sky high. *This is just a slight glitch, that's all.* He tried to calm himself down. But he was worried. Worried that this deal with Amanda Ellis might begin to unravel. This was certainly going to be a big problem that he had to take care of. He was not so much worried about the bozos that he hired from New York. They did not know who hired them. But Roger was a problem. He looked panicked. He never should have told him about the hired killers. *I don't know what came over me. It was that Roger was in a state of panic then and I wanted to assure him that I took care of that bitch.* Roger would sing like a canary if pressed by the police again. He thought about it for a few more minutes, then he called for Jason Edwards, his trusted and loyal employee to come in.

The instructions to Jason were clear. "Eliminate Roger Benton." Jason understood. He would do anything for his boss, the man who saved him from himself. At the time that he met Briggs, Jason had once again lost his job, was homeless, hungry, and extremely despondent to the point that he was ready to take his own life. Briggs came along and noticed him with his cup and little note stating, "Anything would help." He put in a twenty and bent down to where Jason sat against the wall on the Sixteenth Street Mall. He asked him why he was there. Jason told him that he had nothing but bad luck since his single-parent mom died when he was ten, in and out of trouble with first the schools, then the law. Jason explained that he never had a good chance at life. Briggs told Jason to follow him. He put him up in a furnished studio apartment in the building that he owned, told him to take a nice long shower and then they drove to Target. There he filled up a shopping cart with groceries, bought him two pairs of shoes, several pairs of pants, shirts, underwear, and light and winter jackets. He created a new position for him as a security guard, but in reality, he was Briggs' eyes and ears. Jason always appreciated what Briggs did for him. He was the father he never had.

Roger's hands shook as he opened the door to his Range Rover Evoque. Throwing his black briefcase containing the file on the passenger seat, he slid in behind the wheel and leaned his head back. Breathing hard, he knew he had to relax a little before driving out. A moment later, he saw Jason Edwards step out of the elevator. Jason threw Roger a long, hard stare and slowly ambled to his motorcycle parked next to the elevator shaft. Putting on his helmet, he slowly rode away. Jason's appraising glower before he left, sent a shudder down Roger's spine. A few minutes later, Roger left the garage and proceeded onto St. Paul Street.

Driving on University Boulevard toward his house in the Observation Park area, by the University of Denver, Roger's eyes were glued to the rearview and side mirrors as much as possible. He had a creeping feeling of unease, especially after noticing the way Jason looked at him in the garage. Remembering Jason's motorcycle, he felt that he should watch out for it just in case. *Oh, Jesus! I hope I'm just paranoid. I'm reading too much into Jason's look. He was probably just checking the cars in the garage. No! That's not it. He zeroed in on me.*

Taking some deep breaths, Roger tried to relax. His temples still throbbed, and he needed to get home and jump into the hot tub. He glanced at the mirrors again and to his deep dismay he saw a speed motorcycle approaching fast, driving between the two lanes of traffic. When it came closer, he finally noticed that it was green, same as Jason's. *Crap! Oh God! That's got to be Jason. Briggs must've sent him to kill me. Briggs had people killed before, so why not me?* He saw the entry ramp to I-25 not far on his right. He slammed on the accelerator which almost forced the car in the right lane to collide with him. Horns sounded, but he made it onto the interstate ramp and onto the roadway. He hoped against hope that Jason was not able to follow him. But somehow, the motorcyclist was not far behind. Close to the Downing Street exit, he sped up, cut off another vehicle, but was able to exit. He went through a stop sign at the top of the ramp almost causing another accident, then abruptly turned left onto Arkansas Street, then right into the nearest alley. Driving slowly deeper into the alley, he blew out a deep breath concluding that he had escaped Jason.

Jason, however, managed to be close enough to see him turn into the alley. He smiled grimly behind his heavily tinted helmet as he turned into the lane at a fast clip. Roger heard the loud roar of the engine and without looking back, floored the pedal and took off. Jason pursued him and was able to take two shots at him, one flying through the back window and out the windshield, the other coming just a fraction of an inch from Roger's right ear. The two bullets heavily damaged the rear window and the windshield. Roger kept driving with Jason in pursuit. Suddenly, out of a garage along the alley, a black F-250 pickup started to back out, blocking the lane. To avoid the colliding with the truck, Jason had no choice but to brake hard and to save himself and the motorcycle, laid it down causing him to badly skin his left side.

Roger turned left on Louisiana Street and looked for a place to hide. He noticed the Nixon Coffee House and quickly turned toward it and found a place behind the building. He pulled out Hawk's card and quickly dialed the number.

Clint answered. "Hello, Detective Hawk. I need your help. He's trying to kill me."

CHAPTER TWENTY

THE THREE detectives returned to the station and went directly to Perez's office to give him an update. Listening carefully, Perez told them that there was not enough evidence to charge Benton for the murder of Ellis as Mortimer wanted. But as to the fraud by JWB of substituting unsafe, inferior material, he will refer the matter to the Fraud and Financial unit. As to Briggs, he agreed that they needed more evidence before they interview him. "In that case," Mortimer said, "since it's close to the end of the workday and since I'm pretty well beat, I'd like to have permission to go home. Nora and Clint ran me ragged. Besides, Josephine wants me to stop by a store and get her some whole grain pasta. She told me she's concocting some tomato sauce to go along with it. It'll probably taste like catsup." All three chuckled at that last remark.

"Oh, I didn't think I said anything funny."

"With a smile on his face, Perez said, "You're right, nothing funny about catsup. Sure, Mortimer, take off. See you tomorrow."

Mortimer left and Perez shook his head. "He's a character, all right. How's he doing, anyway? Captain MacGregor wants a report next week."

Nora told him about the aggressive tone he took with Benton that surprised Hawk and her. "He really set Roger off to the point that he refused to answer any more questions unless Mortimer left his office."

Perez shook his head again and blew out a slow breath. "Do you think he knows what he's doing?"

Hawk said, "I think so. He just has a different style of intimidation that seems to work and scares people into talking. Didn't work with Benton, though. Maybe it's because he accused him of murder right out of the bat."

Nora said, "I think he was trying too hard to make an impression of how tough he is. I don't think that's his usual character. He wants to be relevant probably because he's still on probation for his job."

At that moment, Hawk's cell rang out *Bad to the Bone*. He looked at the caller ID but didn't recognize the number. "Go ahead and take it," Perez said. "It might be important."

Hawk answered and a desperate voice said, "Hello, Detective Hawk. I need your help. He's trying to kill me."

Placing his phone on speaker, Hawk said, "Calm down, sir. Who is this and who's trying to kill you?"

"This is Roger Benton, and my boss sent the security guard, Jason, to kill me. Listen, I can't talk right now. I'm shaking all over and I can't even think straight. I'm hidden behind the Nixon Coffee House building, under an overhang by the Pearl Street station on Louisiana. I'm afraid to drive away, he may be watching for me. Besides, my windshield is all cracked up from gunshots. Can you come get me? I'll watch for you. Hurry, please."

Perez, hearing the conversation said, "Go, both of you. That may be the break we need. I'll call District Three dispatch and have them send a patrol out there right away."

Hawk and Ricci ran to the old Crown Vic and were soon on the way to meet Roger Benton. Nora yawned. "Oh well, duty calls. I was hoping that I could take you home right after work and we could have a romantic dinner. Afterward, I'd give you a terrific massage. We need to get those knots out of you. I want to see what kind of baby you are when I dig into them." Nora laughed. "You'll probably complain to high heaven."

Clint smiled. "That sounds wonderful. I could use your gentle touch right now. Towards the evening, my body seems to fall apart from that accident, and everything begins to hurt again."

"Gentle touch! Did I say gentle touch?" Nora laughed again.

"You know what I love about you, Nora?"

"What?"

"Here we are going to help a person who's been shot at and in danger and you're laughing, trying to make light of a desperate situation."

"Of course. Most of what we see in our profession is horrible. If we let it dwell inside us, we'd all commit suicide. We must let our minds escape with some levity. Haven't you heard that laughter is the best medicine. And did you say what you 'love' about me? Don't you love everything about me?" Nora laughed again and tapped him on the side of his head.

Oh man! She's making a big deal of me saying 'love.' It's just an expression, but she's pushing me again into a commitment of some sort. Oh well, I might as well play along. Clint laughed, "And I love your laugh too. But getting back to Benton, I hope it won't take too long. Once we get him home, we'd better call for a patrol unit to watch his house around the clock until we catch Jason."

"Okay then. I'm glad you love SOMETHING about me." *I know he loves me; he just doesn't want to admit it. Yet anyway. But he will, sooner than later. Unless that Marcie takes him away from me. Bah!*

When they left the Denver Sixth District headquarters on Colfax and Washington, Hawk made good time the four miles traveling south on Washington Street with his siren and lights. Nixon's coffee house was closed for the day but as they drove around the back of the building, they saw a Range Rover as described by Benton with its back window shot out. Roger jumped out of the car and ran towards them. Without asking, he flung the back door open and hopped in. At that moment, a marked police cruiser turned into the alley and stopped behind Hawk's and Ricci's Crown Vic. Nora went over to talk to them, explained that they were no longer needed and sent them on their way. When she returned to her vehicle, Roger said, "I'm so glad to see you. I was going crazy waiting. I thought that Jason would find me and kill me any minute now."

Hawk said, "You do look mighty distraught. We'll take you home. We'll arrange to have a police patrol guard your house while you're there."

Benton was about to say something when Nora interrupted. "Mr. Benton, since you're a person of interest in the murder of Amanda Ellis, we have to advise you of your rights."

"But I had nothing to do with the death of Amanda."

"That's fine, but I need to let you know that you have the right to remain silent and anything you say can be used against you in a court of law. You have the right to an attorney. If you can't afford to get one, one will be provided for you. Do you understand the rights that I just gave you?"

"Yes, but I didn't do anything."

Nora continued, "Understanding your rights, do you still want to talk to us?"

"You're damn right I do. If that bastard is trying to kill me, I'm going to tell you everything I know."

Hawk turned on the phone recorder and told Benton that he will be recorded. Roger did not object. "Simon Briggs had been defrauding his major developers. He wines and dines them and then he screws them out of a safe product. I had to sign off on several over the years. Always made me nervous, but I made sure that even though the substituted products were not of the best grade, there would not be a great danger to the public. Lately, Simon has been cutting back even more and I saw Amanda's point that what she had to amend rendered her project unsafe. I told her to do what she was assigned, but I didn't feel good about it. After she accused me of harassment, I went to Briggs and told him about the threat. My reputation was at stake. I couldn't have a harassment charge levied against me. Nor could I lose my reputation or maybe my freedom by signing off on unsafe designs. He assured me that he'll take care of everything and not to worry."

Roger swallowed hard, took a couple of deep breaths, and continued. "But when I heard that Amanda was killed, I confronted Roger and he said, 'See I told you not to worry. I, as always, take care of everything.' Over lunch today, I pressed him on how he took care of Amanda and he said, 'Not your concern, Roger.' When he said it, he had that devious smile of his that I learned over the years, portrays some wicked things such as when he was able to defraud someone and make a larger profit."

Nora asked, "How was he able to get away with it? I mean, didn't the developers see the difference?"

"Oh, he is smart enough to know how much to skim. If the materials fail, it will take years of weather abuse and he'd be gone by then."

Hawk asked, "Did Briggs tell you anything about any hired killers, or people he hired from New York?"

Roger thought for a moment. He cupped his forehead with his right hand. Hawk saw him in the rearview mirror and saw he was struggling with an answer. "No."

"You're not sure, are you," Nora said. "You discussed with him the people from New York, didn't you? You knew that was the way he'd take care of things, correct?"

"No, I knew nothing about it. Luckily, he didn't take me into his confidence."

Nora continued. "But you suspected it. Because you knew that he used killers out of New York before?"

Roger fidgeted in the back seat. He glanced out the window and said quietly, "No, I never knew any of that."

Hawk said, "Roger, if you want us to protect you, you need to be upfront with us. For example, why would Briggs send his henchman to kill you tonight unless you know more than you're telling us."

"Well, he's afraid that I'll spill the beans on the fraud that he has perpetrated over the years, that's all."

Hawk said, "I don't think so, Mr. Benton. He wouldn't kill over that."

"You're wrong. Why do you think Amanda is dead?"

"You mean he had someone kill her?"

"Well, I don't know for sure, but I saw that devious expression, that I told you about, when he said, 'See, I told you not to worry, because Amanda is dead.' It was a shock to me, and he only smiled."

Hawk asked, "Roger, you said that Jason Edwards was the one that shot at you. How do you know that?"

"Because I saw him hone in on my car with his devil eyes, then get on that green motorcycle of his and drive out of the garage. Later, that same motorcycle chased me down and the driver took two shots at me. I was saved by someone pulling his truck out of the garage in the alley, blocking Jason's way. I know that Jason thinks Briggs is some kind of god because he'll do anything for him. I've seen him do all kinds of dirty jobs for the man. Briggs seems to have some kind of hold on Jason."

Benton took a good look out of the window, and he suddenly noticed that he wasn't being taken home but to the police station. "Oh my God! Am I under arrest? But I didn't do anything."

"No, not at this time," Hawk said. "Nora needs to transcribe your statement that you gave us in the car so that you can read it and if you agree, sign it for our records. Just standard procedure, that's all."

After they exited the vehicle, Hawk and Ricci escorted Benton into one of the interrogation rooms. Nora Ricci said, "Roger, make yourself comfortable. It'll only take a minute or two to prepare the statement, then we'll take you home."

Hawk handed her his phone and she went to work on the report while Hawk sat down across the table from Roger, hoping to get a little more information out of him regarding Briggs. While Nora had Clint's phone, the music of *Bad to the Bone* startled her. She felt sourness in the pit of her stomach when she saw Marcie's name come up. *What does she want? She wants Clint.* She did not answer the call and let it go into voicemail.

Perez saw them come in and approached Ricci's desk as she listened to the recording. She stopped it and typed what she heard into the computer. Then repeated the task numerous times until it was done. Perez sat down on the edge of her desk and listened.

Afterward, he said, "Good work, Detective." And they both walked toward the interrogation room.

While Hawk sat with Roger, he asked about his black briefcase. Roger took out the file and produced numerous documents that pertained to the fraud that Briggs had engaged in. As Hawk reviewed the papers and Roger's notes, Nora and Perez walked into the room. Hawk introduced his lieutenant to Benton and explained to Perez and Nora what he was studying. He passed the papers to the others. Perez told Benton that he wanted to make a copy of the documents and refer them to the Fraud unit. He walked out to make the copies while Nora went over the typed statement with Benton and asked him to first print his name and then sign it.

Afterward, the two detectives were to take Roger straight home, but he begged them to take him to his car so he could drive it back to his house before someone stole it. What about the windshield?" Hawk asked.

"I was being overdramatic. It's in bad shape, but I'll be able to see out of it well enough for the short distance to the house." Nora nodded to Clint to do it. After they parked next to the Range Rover, Hawk looked over the cracked windshield, thought it was safe enough for a short trip. Then he insisted that he will drive it in case he's stopped by police for a cracked windshield, but more importantly, in case the shooter was watching for the car.

Nora drove the cruiser with Benton in the back seat. "What about your family?"

"Fortunately, they're visiting my wife's parents in Michigan. We're estranged now, I guess. I don't think she's coming back." He remained silent for a minute. "I'm still in danger, aren't I?"

"Let's hope not," Nora said. "I already arranged for a couple of patrol officers to guard your house. You should be safe with them.

A BOLO—be on the lookout—for Jason Edwards had been sent out and I'm sure we'll find him."

"I guess I need to thank you for all your help. I actually feel relieved that all this is out in the open. Simon Briggs is not a good man and I hope you can nail him."

Benton's house was of modern architectural style. The July sun was just setting over the mountains, but its rays were still strong enough to provide a spectacular orange and blue reflection of the sunset off the numerous windows facing west. The staggered flat roof design and the gray stone mixed with white stucco provided a sharp contrast. Adding to the unusual architecture, a glassed tower painted in subdued orange stood out.

"You have a beautiful home, Roger," Nora said as she admired the view. I bet it's even more striking inside."

"Thank you so much. I designed it myself."

As they entered the house, a brown and tan tile floor set in a diamond shape pattern expanded in before them. To the left, a formal glass dining table and eight low-backed chairs sparkled from sun rays. To the right was a small sitting room with retro sixties' style furniture. Nora and Hawk asked Roger to wait in the sitting room while they searched the entire house for intruders. While Hawk looked everywhere a person could hide, including the closets, Nora was totally fascinated by the ultra-modern kitchen, the large, high-ceilinged great room, the breakfast area, and the French doors leading out onto a fully furnished patios sporting an outdoor kitchen. When they met again in the kitchen, Nora said, "Oh Clint, I'd love to have a house like this," She smiled wistfully at him.

Hawk smiled back, "It's not bad. I don't blame you." Nora thought, *you fool, I'd like to have a house like this with you.*

At that instance, Roger yelled out to them, "If you're thirsty, there're some drinks in the fridge. Help yourself." Hawk took him up on the offer, asked if Nora wanted anything to drink. She declined. As he opened the refrigerator door, he spotted off to the side on a shelf a bottle of Lantus Insulin Solution and a couple of insulin autopens. He took out a Perrier for each of them.

Sidling closer to Nora, he whispered, "Roger is a diabetic. He has insulin in the fridge. Also, just in case it becomes useful, I bagged some hair that I saw just lying on the floor by his sink in the master bathroom upstairs. I think Roger is going bald." Nora nodded and held up her right thumb in approval. Since the house checked out clear, with no imminent danger, they rejoined Roger. He thanked them and said that he was pleased that Hawk had found something to drink. It became very noticeable to the detectives that he was nervous about staying by himself in the house as evidenced by his hard breathing and trembling hands. They sat down on the couch to wait for the patrol officers to arrive.

Nora said, "Roger, do you have someone that could come over to keep you company tonight or somewhere we can take you where you'd feel safe?"

"No, I wouldn't want to impose on my friends like that. I have no relatives in Denver. But, detectives, you think that Jason will try to get to me tonight? And what about tomorrow? I don't want to go in and face Simon. I suppose that I still have my job."

Hawk replied, "We really would have no idea what a criminal mind would do. But I don't think that Jason will be fool enough to try to get to you tonight. If he tries, he'll see the patrol car out front and think twice about the risk."

Nora said, "As far as leaving this house tomorrow, that's definitely not an option until we catch Jason. Make sure your alarm is on, the doors and windows are locked securely. Do you have a gun?"

"Yes, but I couldn't think of using it to kill somebody."

Hawk said, "Believe me when it's either you or him, you'll use it."

"Oh, here they are. Your police security is here," Nora exclaimed. "We'll give them some instructions and be off. We'll call you tomorrow morning and give you an update."

As they turned the corner, heading back to the station to pick up their respective cars, Hawk and Nora observed a motorcycle approach at a high rate of speed. In just a matter of seconds, it flew past them. Hawk made an abrupt U-turn, turned on the vehicle's siren and pursuit lights and began chase. The speedy bike did not slow, instead increased its speed, leaving the old Crown Vic far behind. In the meantime, Nora radioed in the motorcycle's location. The dispatcher told her that police units from District Three were in the vicinity and would be dispatched. "Slow down, Clint," Nora said. This is a residential area, and we better not push it."

Hawk listened. "You're right, actually, we're not even sure that was Jason. It was too dark, and the bike zipped by too fast for me to make it out. Besides, I don't think this old lady, and I'm referring to the car, in case you're wondering, is up to it." Hawk chuckled as he threw Nora a glance.

"BETTER be referring to the car or I'll use my moves on you." She laughed.

"I know. You're a dangerous person to be with," Hawk teased, chuckling.

"And the sweetest and the most loving, right?" Nora said as she giggled.

"Oh, of course you are." Both remained silent for a few minutes. Both felt the strain of the day catching up with them as Hawk turned the vehicle and headed to the station.

"Oh, by the way, I forgot to tell you, Clint, that while I had your phone to transcribe the statement, Marcie called you. I think she left a message."

"Well, I can't get to it now."

"Do you want me to play it for you? Or is there something private that's going on between the two of you?" Nora glanced at Hawk as he drove and forced a chuckle.

"Now what secret would there be between us, Nora? Go ahead, let's listen to the message."

Hello, Clint. This is Marcie. Ah, ah, I'm a little lonely here at the hotel all by myself. What about dinner tonight? The treat is on me. Call me when you get a chance.

Nora felt blood rush to her head. "Oh my God! That schemer! I can't believe she has the nerve to call you like that, knowing that you and I are an item. We are an item, aren't we Clint?"

Even though it was getting dark, and Hawk couldn't see Nora's expression, he felt her eyes on him. *Man, this is awkward. I've only known her for a very short time and she thinks we're committed to each other. She's a fast worker, but do I want to be tied to? She's smart, extremely beautiful, fun to be with and I may be lucky to have a girl like her interested in me.* "Yes, Nora, let's give it a try."

"Thank you for that, Clint. I want to feel that we're together." She unbuckled her seat belt and leaned over and began rapidly kissing his right cheek. Hawk turned slightly towards her and she planted her lips on the side of his.

Hawk was too distracted and did not notice the light of a motorcycle bearing down on them from the rear. They heard the growl of the engine, but it was too late. A bullet flew through the rear window, shattering it into pieces. The slug continued through the passenger headrest where Nora would be seated had she not sidled over to Hawk and made its way into the dashboard. Hawk grabbed Nora and held her tight while he slammed on the brakes, both he and Nora wide-eyed and breathing hard. They went for their weapons and as Hawk barely turned his head toward the window, he saw the driver pull up to him, pointing his gun. He barely caught sight of part of a tattoo underneath the helmet as he pushed Nora down and covered her body with his as a bullet went through the driver's window and out the passenger's.

CHAPTER TWENTY-ONE

HAWK AND Ricci sprung up from their position of cover after they heard the roar of the engine fade away. Both were breathing hard. Nora's heart beat so loudly that she thought that Clint could hear it. Hawk blew out his breath and whistled. "That was close. At least the second shot was high over our heads. Maybe he didn't want to kill us, only scare us."

"Oh, such a considerate guy, that Jason is," Nora tried to force a laugh. "And he's even trying to air out the musty old smell of this car." She again tried to laugh, but it turned out to be more of a hiccup.

"You don't have to make the situation seem better, Nora. This is just damn awful. Frankly, I'm getting tired of getting shot at. You never hear of any other detective trying to dodge potshots at him or her. What am I, a magnet for slugs? If my parents hear about this, they'll insist that I quit this minute and pursue my original plan of a PhD in Psychology. Maybe, I should still consider it."

"Clint, honey, calm down. You're not thinking straight. Since you became a detective, you just had a weird, unusual bad streak of luck, but it'll probably not happen again. You're right, detectives usually don't get shot at or attacked, but we were and now are dealing with a crazy man. I mean, why would someone try to kill us, for what? They should understand that we're not the only ones that know about the case. If we're taken out of the picture, someone will step in immediately and continue with what we're doing."

"I know, this whole business doesn't make sense. I think that with Jason, throwing that brick at us and now the gunshots, it must mean that he's taking this personally. I don't think he likes us,

Nora." Hawk laughed. "And we're such nice people." He continued to laugh until finally Nora joined in. They needed the release that the laughter brought. Afterward, Nora called Lieutenant Perez and explained what happened to them.

At the station, Hawk drove toward their usual spot in the lot, but a fairly new Ford Explorer Interceptor sat in the space. "You don't think that's for us?" Nora asked. "That would be great if it were."

Hawk found another spot and parked the damaged Crown Vic. "Nora, I'm so dead tired and my neck and back are killing me. All I want to do is head home and collapse into bed. I'll take a rain check on the dinner and massage."

Now that the adrenaline wore off Nora felt exhausted as well. Fighting those killers that morning and then the shots in the evening took a lot out of her. The bed sounded good. "Sure, I'll see you tomorrow. Call me right away if anyone else starts shooting at you." She giggled, but saw that Hawk was not amused. "I'm sorry, that was insensitive."

"Oh, no worries. Actually, it sounds funny." Out of the vehicle, he moved closer to her. Their eyes met, gazing intently at each other for a long second, then Hawk bent down and kissed her hard. "Sleep tight." He walked to his Jeep while Nora stood there smiling, watching him get in. She then walked over to her Ford Escape.

The next morning, Hawk strode into the Homicide unit. "Hey, lucky guy," Orlinski said. "How do you rate a new vehicle? I've been trying to get a new one for years."

"Really, that one I saw last night was for us?"

"Yeah. I think the captain likes you. Speaking of her, she wants you and Ricci in her office when both of you arrive."

"What's that about, you think?"

"Probably wants to give you an office with your own secretary." Orlinski laughed.

Mortimer overheard the conversation as he just walked in. "What?! Hawk is getting his own office with secretary?"

Orlinski and Hawk both laughed. "No, Mortimer," Orlinski said. "It was a joke."

"Oh. I don't understand. What's funny about that?"

"Never mind," Orlinski said. "Oh, here's Nora. You better both go in now."

"Go where?" Nora asked, smiling, her sparkling eyes on Clint. Clint patted her back and explained. As they started toward the captain's office, Mortimer followed them in. Hawk and Nora gazed at each other, Hawk shrugging his shoulders.

Nora knocked and went in. Perez stood over MacGregor's desk, and it appeared that they were having a heated discussion. *It's probably about us,* Hawk thought.

When Perez saw them, he backed away from the desk and smiled at them. MacGregor gave them a cursory smile, but when she saw Holliday follow them in, her half smile turned into a grimace. She studied his appearance. In contrast to the sharp suits that Hawk and Ricci wore that morning, Holliday looked sloppy, as though he slept in the suit. It was the same one that he wore the day before, except his suspenders were of a different color as was his bowtie.

"Sit down, detectives." She glanced over to Mortimer who sat down on the couch, his arms crossed on his chest, his long legs also crossed, his foot dangling. "Actually, this meeting was to be with Detectives Hawk and Ricci."

"Oh. Do you want me to leave then? I thought that since I was working with them, that I should be present."

"Stay then." MacGregor turned toward Nora and Clint. "It bothers me greatly when one, and here we have two detectives, get shot at."

"Wait. Who got shot?" Mortimer stood up and towered over the sitting captain.

"Sit down, Detective." Mortimer reluctantly complied. "For your information, your fellow detectives were shot at last night by, we think, a Jason Edwards."

Mortimer showed no emotion except for his widened eyes. "That's the security guard we saw yesterday. What happened?"

Perez explained to Mortimer about Roger Benton and why they went to rescue him.

"Well, no one called me. Shouldn't I have been there with them since I work with them?"

"You went home, and the call came in after you left. They handled it well without you."

"Well, I would've been anxious to go with them if only they called me. I could've gotten out of that horrible kale salad that Josephine prepared. As a matter of fact, I think it upset my stomach and I had a really bad night running."

MacGregor was ticked off that Mortimer was there. He irritated her to no end. But when he mentioned the kale salad and image of him dashing to the toilet, she broke out in laughter, as did the others in the room. Except for Mortimer. "Did I just make a joke? I don't know what's so funny here. I was miserable."

Captain said, "Let's change the subject to the one why you're here." She looked at Mortimer, "Detective Holliday, you can leave if you want or you can stay, but this doesn't concern you."

Mortimer cleared his throat and coughed. "I'll stay, these are my partners and I need to be with them."

"All right, suit yourself. Now to continue, I am extremely upset that for some reason, you two detectives, always seem to be in danger." She had her attention on Hawk and Ricci. "In all my years on the Force, I've never run across a detective that has been in such peril as you two, particularly you, Detective Hawk." Hawk chest tightened. *Am I in trouble through no fault of my own?*

MacGregor continued, staring hard at Hawk. "I don't know why people just seem out to get you. Is it revenge? Is it fear that you'll bring them down? Regardless, I think it would be best, over Lieutenant Perez's objection, to take you off the Amanda Ellis case. Detectives Nancy Salazar and Harry Ling will take your part of it." Mortimer loudly grunted his disapproval. Everyone took a quick look at him. MacGregor frowned and narrowed her eyes.

"No, please, Captain," Hawk said. "We're very close to solving this case. Once we capture Jason Edwards, we shouldn't be in any danger. The hired killers are no longer a problem since they've been captured. With Nancy and Harry, we are a team working together on this case. I have this gut feeling that we can solve it in forty-eight hours."

Perez said, "Captain, I think that's reasonable. Give them forty-eight hours."

The captain leaned back in her chair, took a deep breath, and thought about it for a minute. "I'm worried that Edwards is out there watching for you." She turned silent, staring at them. "Okay, I'll give you two forty-eight hours. But be careful. I don't want my best people dead." Hawk felt relief and he was sure Nora felt the same.

"But you and Ricci tell me why you think you're making progress. And why you think you can find enough evidence to put away the killer of Amanda Ellis within two days. I reviewed Kwon's statement, and I really don't think he or his sidekick are her killers. I talked to the DA about an attempted murder charge and assault on police officers for them. Besides the hired killers, who are your suspects, Ricci?"

Perez said, "Captain, I'm sorry to interrupt, but if we're going to discuss who the suspects are, I'd like the rest of the team to hear. They've been working on getting background information and they should be involved."

"All right, Lieutenant, you have a point. Let's all go out to them." She rose and walked out of her office followed by the others in the room. In the detective area, MacGregor sat down on a chair adjacent to Orlinski's desk and faced one of the large whiteboards on the wall. The board had pictures of Kwon Bak, Josh Dollin, Steven Ellis, Tina Dionisio, Roger Benton and Simon Briggs. And a new one was added that morning, a bearded Jason Edwards.

"Okay, Lieutenant, it's your show. Please proceed. I want this case closed. The mayor is on our backs on this one and we need a solid arrest."

Perez looked at Nora and nodded for her to proceed. Nora understood. "Well, the obvious suspects are the hitmen, Bak and Dollin. Kwon Bak admitted that they were hired to kill Amanda Ellis, but they don't know who hired them. We believe that Simon Briggs from the construction company hired them, but we have no proof other than a strong suspicion. He had a strong motive to get rid of Amanda because she threatened his company not only with a sexual harassment suit, but also with fraud. His reputation is at stake. Amanda had evidence of that fraud on his customers. We also know that the new photo up there on the board is of Jason Edwards. We met him at Brigg's business, and we believe that he is the one that threw a brick with a note attached. We're also sure that he attempted to kill Roger Benton, and later that evening, shot at Clint and me."

Hawk added, "The note to the brick is in the evidence room and once we get a sample of Edwards's writing, we'll have our expert compare the two."

Harry Ling who had been intently studying his computer suddenly called out, "Holly cow, everyone, I think we got a break in our case." Every head in the room turned towards him. "Orlinski asked me to help him with some of the videos sent over by NYPD showing individuals dropping off items in the slot outside of the Zeb's Mailboxes and Office Concierge Service. According to Bak, that's how they got their money and instructions. When I saw Jason Edward's photo on the board this morning, he looked familiar to me as someone I remembered seeing in the video. So, I went back and went through the videos again and here he is, clear as day. I'll print it out for all of you to see."

"How is that helpful?" MacGregor specifically looked at Hawk for an answer.

Smiling widely, Hawk said, "Captain, that is truly significant. We know that Jason Edwards works for Simon Briggs. It is obvious that Jason wouldn't have gone off to New York unless Briggs had instructed him to deliver the money and instructions to the hired killers. I think we have enough now to arrest Briggs and obtain a search warrant to seize his personal computers, both at the office and his house. And we need to do it fast before he destroys the computer that we believe he used to search the dark web with."

MacGregor said, "All right, then, let's do it. Lieutenant, please call the DA's office and arrange it. Okay, then. I want to know this from any one of you. If we don't believe that Briggs's hitmen actually caused Amanda Ellis's death, then who did?"

Mortimer Holliday spoke up. "For my money, I believe it was Roger Benton. I have this feeling about him and I'm rarely wrong. He had a powerful motive to do so."

Nora said, "Mortimer may be correct in that. Clint, didn't you tell me that he had insulin bottles in his medicine cabinet? Janeel's preliminary findings officially concluded that Ellis was murdered with an overdose of insulin." Hawk confirmed that he told Nora about the insulin.

MacGregor commented, "Millions of people use insulin to control their diabetes. I use it. Just because he had insulin in the cabinet, doesn't mean that he's the killer. You have to have actual proof here people." She hesitated. "Nora, do you think that Benton is the killer?"

Nora looked at Mortimer and then at her Captain. "I don't. I really don't think he is capable of killing anyone. I think he's a scaredy cat who thinks he's a gift to women. If I had to guess who did it, I'd say it was Tina Dionisio. By her own words, she admitted to an affair with her boss, Steven Ellis. I think she wanted to take Amanda's place and killed her to get rid of her. Plus, she had the opportunity, and she was seen in Cheesman Park a week before the murder, probably scouting and plotting her crime."

Perez said, "Doesn't anyone here believe that it was the husband, Steven Ellis?"

Nancy Salazar spoke up, "I think it was him. Harry and I canvassed the neighborhood and talked to the neighbors. They didn't have much good to say about him. A couple of them mentioned that they heard a lot of yelling and screaming over the last few months between him and his wife. Another told us that he was a true philanderer. While his wife was at work, she saw at least three women, all good looking and sexy, visit him at the house. They stayed for a couple of hours, then left. When we asked to describe them, she told us that one was a dark brunette and the other two were blondes, one tall, the other one short, but couldn't give any more details than that."

"Did they mention what kind of car these women drove?" Hawk asked.

Nancy looked at Harry, "Did we even ask that question?" Harry lowered his chin and shook his head back and forth indicating that they did not.

"That's okay," Hawk said. "I think Nora and I should re-interview them again. Maybe we'll run across someone else that can help us or the people you talked to would remember something else. We also need to talk to Mr. Ellis again and confront him with the many lies he gave us. Also, the housekeeper, Nellie Pyle, may have a wealth of information if we talk to her.

Mortimer said, "Well, I need to be there with them. After all we're in this together, isn't that right Captain? I already told Josephine that I'm working with Hawk and Ricci. She'll be awfully disappointed if I'm not, after all I told her about them." Nora had her hand over her mouth as she glanced at Clint to see his reaction.

Clint raised his eyebrows, then rolled his eyes. As he awaited MacGregor's or Perez's reaction, a notification of a text pinged on his phone. He eyeballed the message and saw it was from Marcie. It read, "Clint, why didn't you call me back? I waited for your call. Are you all right?"

Nora heard the ping and saw Hawk reading the text. She mouthed, "Who's that?"

He mouthed back, "Later."

MacGregor said, "It's up to the Lieutenant, Holliday, who you're partnered with." She stood up, looked at Perez and said, "Lieutenant, you and your team have a lot to do, and you all better get to it." She looked at Hawk and continued, "I'm keeping you to the two-day deadline."

At that moment Orlinski, who had his head close to the computer monitor while the meeting was going on, said, "The patrol officers spotted Jason Edwards going in to work and they picked him up."

CHAPTER TWENTY-TWO

TINA DIONISIO could not sleep a wink after her interview with the three detectives. She said too much. She blamed that tall, shabby, strange detective, if he really was a detective, for intimidating and scaring her into blabbing about her and Steven Ellis. *A human lie detector, that handsome detective said. Ha! And I fell for that. It was creepy how he stared at me, like a zombie. Lifeless, I lost my head.* Not only was she in trouble with the police, but also with her boss and lover, Steven Ellis. She adores the man, but she knows that he will be more than angry for violating their pact to keep their romantic flings secret.

Tossing and turning all night long, she could not turn her brain off with thoughts that she now gave the police a strong motive why she might've killed Amanda Ellis. Tina knew that Steven would deny the affair. With her admission, his denial would portray him as a liar and the detectives would wonder what else was he lying about. She tossed and turned some more, then shouted out, "Oh God! What have I done? I may get arrested, but before that, Stevie will be absolutely livid for admitting to our affair. He'll break off our relationship and fire me."

Tina did not want to lose Steven. Her heart ached just thinking about it. She fell deeply in love with him from the moment he appeared as a guest lecturer in her finance class at the University of Denver. Graduating at the top of her class of the business school, she could have gone on to big things in the world of money, but only a job in Ellis's company would satisfy her. She had to be near him and do what it took to take him away from his wife.

She managed to get an interview for an opening as a financial assistant. As Tina anxiously walked into Ellis's office, she saw the man she wanted. Even though he was much older, to her he looked like Adonis as he presided behind an enormous desk cluttered with stock prospectus folders. She felt her body caressed with his baby-blue deep-set eyes as she strode in. That's the effect on him she wanted. She wore a tight knit dress that emphasized her hourglass figure, and put a little extra sway to her hips when she approached the desk. Steven rose, straightened his tie, and asked her to sit down. His eyes never left her for a second, a toothy smile on his pinkish face. She knew she had him. The initial interview finished with Steven offering her a position as his assistant to work closely with him. He asked her, "Are you able to work late into the night if you have to?" *Yes! I'm in*, she thought. *I'll have him wrapped around my little finger before he knows it.*

Tina thought of all the scheming, flirting, and planning, that she did in the past three years since she began working for Steven to convince him to fall in love with her. All probably would be for naught now because of her blunder. Even though, to her chagrin, she discovered that it was not just the wife she was competing with, but at least two other women, she profoundly believed that he loved her and only her. She convinced herself that with Amanda out of the picture, he would marry her. After all, he promised just that many times. She would make sure that she would satisfy him, please him, keep him busy to the point where he would not need to have roving eyes for other women.

At least, that is what Tina thought until Steven had to replace the receptionist. Against her strong advice, he hired Luanne Sue Adams, a spunky, cute, flirtatious woman who was younger than she. After a few weeks on the job, Luanne Sue was conveniently needed at his home office, just as he asked Tina to do on countless occasions. Tina loved her visits to his home while the wife was at work and after the housekeeper left for the morning. It gave her much pleasure to spend time with him frolicking about in the guest room bed. Tina rationalized that Luanne Sue was just a silly girl and he will tire of her soon enough to devote all his attention to her. When Tina again approached the subject of marriage and asked him about the divorce, she assumed he would get, he answered that he loved her more than anything in this world, but she'd have to be patient. He could not get the divorce because it would cost too much, and he'd most likely lose his house. "We have to figure out another way," he told her. *That detective, Nora something or other, was right on target when she said that I wanted to be his wife and be the lady of that beautiful house. She was correct that I want to walk down those stairs and greet the cream of Denver society.*

All along, Tina suspected that Steven must have had another lover prior to her. And she often wondered if that relationship was totally over or was he two-timing her with this persistent affair. Often, she would notice a faint scent of jasmine perfume when entering Steven's office at work in the morning. It was the same scent that she smelled when he first hired her. She did not think much about it then, but this same elusive scent had cropped up off and on for several weeks. *Can it be that he's seeing someone else?* She thought of the big couch in Steven's office, one on which she is spent time after hours with him. *Oh my God! He is seeing his old flame. Should I confront him about that? No, that will only make him mad. I need to marry him first now that Amanda is out of the way.*

The next morning, a tired and extremely anxious Tina sat in her office when she heard Ellis walk in. Luanne Sue in her bubbly loud southern accent greeted him with an enthusiastic "Good mornin', boss." *She's so phony,* Tina thought, *I just can't stand that woman. I bet he's already tired of that irritating bitch.*

Instead of walking into his office, Ellis made his way directly into Tina's, shut the door and plopped down on a black leather side chair. "I understand that the police interviewed you yesterday. What did you tell them?" Tina saw that he was not smiling as he usually did but looked serious and concerned.

She did not expect such a greeting and even though she expected him to ask, she was not exactly prepared how to answer. "It was awful, Stevie. They wanted to know about your relationship with Amanda," she hesitated, grimaced. "And they accused me of having an affair with you."

"You denied it, didn't you?" Tina looked away from him toward the view of the Rockies through the large glass window, all lit up from the glow of the eastern sun. She cupped her forehead, feeling tears well up. "Shit, you told them about our relationship, didn't you? You fool!"

"I'm sorry, Stevie, I'm so sorry. They knew. They had me cornered and I had no choice but to admit it."

"You foolish, freaking bitch. I want you out of here." Ellis's face turned crimson, his breathing shallow. "You're fired! Accounting office will send you your last check. You have one hour to get your stuff."

"No, please, Steven. I'm so sorry. I made a mistake, please, please forgive me. It'll be all right. Don't worry."

Ellis's chair crashed flew to the floor as he abruptly stood and stormed out of the room. The whole staff could hear him swearing as he walked down the hall to his office. The door slammed behind him. A shaking Tina threw some personal items into her Gucci bag and with tears streaming down her face rushed out of her office, past Luanne Sue, and out of the front door. Then she returned and shouted out to Luanne Sue, "He's all yours, you bitch! Enjoy it while it lasts." Luanne Sue was first shocked by the incident, then wryly smiled.

The next day, Hawk and Ricci met for breakfast at the IHOP on Colorado Boulevard, close to Nora's house. It was the same restaurant where he had pancakes with Marcie a couple of weeks ago. He remembered that evening well. He enjoyed being with Marcie even though the get-together was designed by her to convince him to follow his superior's orders in his first assigned case. He could not do it and disregarded the command to cease his investigation. There was a big coverup and Hawk knew it. He also remembered the call from Nora, who at the time he barely met, warning him that his life was in danger and that they had to meet so she could explain. He could not forget Marcie's disappointed look when he cut the evening short and told her he had to take her home.

Now, he is in the same restaurant, but with Nora this time. It still amazed him how quickly Nora, in a whirlwind, took over his life, and now they supposedly were dating. He knew that Nora was serious about him, but he was not ready to commit to anything more, at least not yet. As he strode in, Nora was already in the booth as he walked up to her. As usual, she greeted him with a disarming smile. He could not resist her red luscious lips as he reached over and kissed them.

"That was sweet," Nora said with a laugh, "but you missed this side," pointing to the right side of her mouth. Clint happily kissed her again, this time lingering a little longer, then sat down across from her. "So how did you sleep last night? Restful I hope."

"Not bad," Hawk said, unenthusiastically.

"You're holding out on me. I can tell that you had another rough night."

"Not really, I was pretty bushed and slept better than the night before." Nora glared at him, expecting the true answer. "Okay, if you must know, I had another one of those nightmares with guns pointing at me. In my dream, I'm running and running and don't know where to, just away. But guns, not people holding them, just guns floated in the air chasing me. The more I ran, the closer they came and suddenly all the guns, and there were many, start blasting. I felt slugs tearing my insides as they strike my torso. I saw myself screaming, and then I woke up in cold sweat."

"Wow, that's scary. Do you think you need to see someone for help?"

"Nah. I'll be all right. Let's change the subject. What are you having?" Hawk picked up the menu and studied it.

"I think I'll just have a fruit bowl and a muffin."

The waitress came and they ordered. Hawk asked for ham and eggs with the multi-grain pancakes. "So, who do we go after today?" Hawk asked. "We have several suspects, but no real evidence. What's your gut say, Nora?"

"I still say, it's Tina and maybe Steven Ellis conspiring together on this. We need to question him again, this time a little more aggressively."

"Like letting Mortimer do it in his style." They both chuckled.

Nora said, "Maybe we should. At least have him there to intimidate with his Grim Reaper appearance."

"Should we give him a scythe?" Hawk threw back his head and let out a great peel of laughter, infecting Nora with his merriment.

Nora stretched out her arms on the table toward Hawk. Hawk took her hands and held them for a minute. "You worry me, Clint. I think you're overdoing it. With all the violence you have had to deal with lately having come so close to death has to create havoc to your psyche. Can't you take some time off? I mean, you're the psychologist, you should know better."

Hawk didn't answer but raised his eyes to the ceiling. "Did you ever notice that one ceiling tile up there is of a slightly different color?"

Nora shook her head in disgust. "Okay, you don't want to answer me. But you need to watch out for yourself. Of course, if you had come home with me last night, I would've massaged you, given you hot milk and honey, tucked you into bed and you would've slept like a baby."

"Do you know that babies only sleep just a few hours before they're hungry again and cry?"

"Oh, Clint. Get serious. Lucky you, you're saved from this conversation by the food arriving. Ooh, those eggs and ham look good. Why did I just order fruit and a muffin?"

"You want to share? I'll give you half of mine."

"Okay, buddy, you're in business. I'm game."

CHAPTER TWENTY-THREE

EVEN THOUGH they came in separate cars, Hawk and Ricci walked into the Homicide unit together. Without any kind of a greeting, Orlinski asked in jest, "Anybody else shoot at you in the middle of the night?" They laughed and walked to their desks. A few minutes later Mortimer Holliday walked in, sporting a nineties-style navy blue checkered suit that had seen better days. But what stood out were the bright orange suspenders and, again, a matching bow tie.

"Look at that," Nora whispered to Hawk through the aisle. "He moved up a whole decade, before we know it, he'll be in the two-thousands." She chuckled softly. "I'm not sure about the orange suspenders, though."

Hawk whispered back, "Nah, he looks great. He'll have all the women chasing him."

"Yeah, chasing him out of town." Nora laughed.

Mortimer sauntered over to them. Nora noticed his penny loafers with an actual penny in the slot of a strip of leather stitched across the saddle of each shoe. "Those are some cool shoes, Mortimer," Nora said.

"Oh, yes. I guess they're fairly cool. My feet aren't sweating in these shoes yet."

Nora held her laugh. "No, I mean they look very good on you."

"Oh. I'll tell Josephine that you like them. She gave them to me last evening saying that she found this suit and these shoes in a consignment shop that she frequents. Said, they weren't very expensive."

Hawk looked down at the loafers and said, "Do you know why they're called penny loafers? Oh look at that, they actually have a penny in each shoe."

"No. Is that what they're called? Josephine said that they're for sailors."

"Actually, she's close. That kind of style was originally used by Norwegian fishermen. But the reason the pennies were in the shoes is because when they first became popular in the 1930's, phones in booths cost two cents. So, if you had to make a call, you would have the two cents in your shoe in case of an emergency."

"Oh, that's interesting. I'll tell Josephine, she'll look it up, though, to make sure you're right. She double-checks everything. Anyway, what are we doing today?"

"We have a couple more interviews to do," Nora said. "Plus, they're going to bring in Jason Edwards later this morning and we'll need to get a confession out of him." When she looked away from Mortimer, and Hawk answered a call, Lieutenant Perez approached.

Mortimer addressed Perez, "Good morning, sir. I assume I'll be working with Nora and Clint today, is that right?"

"I suppose so, Detective, but first, I want to know where we're at as far as solving this case. Captain MacGregor is getting very impatient."

Hawk punched off his phone. He greeted Perez then explained who he was on the phone with. Nora was shocked to hear that Tina Dionisio called him and wanted Hawk to come over right away. Hawk continued, "She told me that she has some very important information to give me, but to only me." He glanced at Nora and sheepishly said, "Tina didn't want anyone else to come along."

"Well, what's that all about?" Nora said with obvious disgust in her voice. "How did she even get your number?"

"I gave her my card as we were leaving, as I usually do with others that I interview, just in case they'll think of anything to add. You and Mortimer walked out of the room first and didn't see me do it."

"Well I don't like it. I don't trust that woman."

Perez said, "I think it's great. She may give us what we want on Ellis. So go for it. When does she want to meet?"

"Now, at her condo in LoDo—Lower Downtown—area of Denver."

"In her condo yet," Nora said, irritated. "Couldn't you at least meet in a neutral place like a coffee shop?"

"I suggested that, but she said that she's too upset to go out anywhere and she needs to talk to me before she changes her mind. I really do think that she'll give us some valuable information."

"Okay, take off and see her," Perez said. "Oh, yes, here's the key to the Ford Explorer that we were able to finagle out of headquarters for your use while at work. It's not new, but a lot newer than any one of the old Crown Vics that the department is slowly getting rid of. I guess it came at the right time for you since you seem to either crash or get your vehicles shot up." Perez laughed. "I wonder how long you'll keep this one in one piece?"

"Not my fault, Lieutenant. But I think Nora wants to interview the Ellis's housekeeper, Nellie Pyle, some more this morning. Perhaps, she should take the Ford. I'll just drive my Jeep to LoDo."

"Gee, thank you so much," Nora said, sarcastically. Switching her gaze to Perez from Hawk, she asked him if Mortimer should accompany her. The Lieutenant told them to get to it and he'd like a team meeting before they interrogate Edwards.

All three detectives walked out together. Before Hawk headed for his vehicle, Nora squeezed his arm and said, "Be careful."

"He smiled and replied, "Always. I'll text you when I'm done." A minute later he was in his Jeep. As he put on the seat belt, a nagging thought entered his head. *I should've insisted on meeting in a public place. She might be crazy or vengeful and accuse me of something inappropriate. Maybe I should call her back and insist on it. But she was specific. It had to be in her condo as she was not up to going anywhere. What's that all about?*

Fifteen minutes later, he turned onto Wynkoop Street and saw Tina's building. It looked like an old factory building of years gone by transformed into pricey condominiums. Tina gave him the code to an underground garage in the next building and within minutes he was on the top floor and knocking on the door. Tina quickly opened it, inviting him in. She appeared to have been crying, her eyes puffy, and a bit of mascara smudged her lower eyelids. Wearing a hot pink summer dress, she looked shorter than he remembered in her bare feet rather than in high heels. Tina appeared tired and deflated.

The condo was a loft with high beamed ceilings and exposed heating and air-conditioning ducts painted black. A circular metal stairway led up to a smaller loft. *A loft within a loft, that's cool.* At the other end of the condo was a hallway with doors on both sides which Hawk assumed were the bedrooms. Tina asked him to sit at the large oval kitchen island that had a stainless-steel sink inserted on the side across from the oven and refrigerator. The countertops were of pure white material, most likely Corian, Hawk thought.

She pulled out two red coffee mugs from the cabinet and without asking whether Hawk wanted coffee, poured them both a cup. Reaching across to the back counter and lifting a cake dome, she took out a plate of sugar-powdered finger-sized cookies and set it down, pushing it closer to Hawk. With a somber face, she sat down next to him in the bar stool and said, "I'm glad you're here. I feel comfortable with you, and I have a lot to tell you."

"Tina, thank you, but before you begin, I need to record this." He wanted to make sure that whatever happened in the condo would be heard. Not giving her a chance to respond, he pressed "Record" on his iPhone. She looked surprised and somewhat apprehensive but didn't object.

"I'm glad that it's just you here," Tina said, her brown eyes studying him intently. "I didn't like the other two detectives, especially the scary tall one who just stood over me." Hawk remained silent expecting her to continue. "Anyway, the reason I wanted to talk to you is that I think that Steven Ellis killed his wife."

"Oh. That's quite an accusation, Tina. What makes you think that?"

"As you already know, we were lovers. Our relationship began shortly after I started working for him. He confided in me and told me many, many times of how much he disliked his wife. He wished that she were gone and out of his life. She was always on his back for one reason or another. Steven felt that he was trapped. A caged man that had to account for every minute of the day to his wife. And all along, he kept telling me that he loved me. I believed him and actually even let myself think of marriage. After all, he promised me that we'd be together.

"When I brought up the subject of a divorce, he never gave me a straight answer over the years that we had this affair. Most of the time, he'd change the subject or told me the timing wasn't right, but 'soon,' he always said. A couple of weeks ago, he began complaining more and more, almost to the point of obsession about his lousy wife and how unhappy she made him. At that point, I again asked him to get the divorce so that we could marry. For some strange reason, he became irritated the last time I discussed marriage. He had a bizarre look in his eyes as he stared at me, not saying anything for a good minute. Then he said, 'Tina, I can't get a divorce because it'll cost me too much,' or maybe he said that he'd lose too much, and then he said, 'I don't want to lose this wonderful house that I love. No, we'll have to think of another way.'"

"When did he say that to you, exactly?"

"It was a week before Amanda was murdered."

Hawk asked, "What did you think he meant by that?"

Tina appeared startled that Hawk would even ask that question. "Isn't it obvious, if he couldn't bring himself to divorcing that woman, what was his alternative? To kill her, of course, and get her out of the way."

"What did you mean when you said that Ellis had a bizarre look?"

"I mean, it was unusual for him. Really out of the ordinary. I mean bizarre. You know what it means. For example, that weird detective you were with has a bizarre look."

"I guess I'm struggling to understand. Did his face have a sinister appearance?"

"Yeah, perhaps that's it, exactly. He did look as if the devil or something evil had entered his brain."

"Tina, now that Amanda is gone, it gives you a great opportunity to become the new Mrs. Ellis."

Tina focused her attention on a modern painting that hung on the far wall, the kind that people buy just for the colors to match their décor. She hesitated. "Yeah, I wanted to be the new Mrs. Ellis so badly. That's all I hoped for while I worked for him. I must admit that I tried everything I could to separate them." She then turned abruptly to Hawk and forcefully said, "But if you think that I would've killed Amanda or did it with Steven, you're totally wrong. I'm not even sure these last few months if he actually loved me or would've married me. I believe now that I was just another woman that he used. There seemed to be several."

"Oh, he had affairs with others?"

"I know that that conniving bitch by the name of Luanne Sue Adams was one. I also suspect that he had someone that he saw before I started working for him three years ago and has resumed seeing lately."

"Any idea who that might be?"

"No, actually. I think she's blonde because I picked off a long blonde hair from his jacket one time. Also, whoever it is, uses some kind of jasmine perfume. I smelled it a week after I started work for him. A faint odor in his office early in the morning. And then I'd smell it periodically again maybe a month ago and actually, when Steven came in this morning, the faint scent of that perfume still lingered on him."

"Could the blond hair have been Luanne's?"

"No, this was before he hired her, and she doesn't use perfume."

"You seem to have a nose for perfume."

"I'm good at it. I can smell faint smells hours after the person leaves. I used to work at a Dillard's perfume department in my last two years of college and everyone there said that I'm amazing at detecting scents."

"Tina, why are you telling me all this today?"

"Because I'm afraid that you think I killed Amanda and I didn't. I wanted to let you know who did."

"Tina, by chance are you diabetic?"

"No, certainly not."

"Is Steven Ellis a diabetic?"

"No. He would've told me if he was."

"Do you or Ellis have any relatives that are diabetic?"

"What's with all these questions?"

"It's just something that may be important in the murder. I mean did you any see any insulin while you were in the Ellis's house?"

"No."

"So, what's your answer regarding any relatives that may use insulin."

"I think my mother is what they call pre-diabetic, but she certainly doesn't use insulin."

"When I walked in, you appeared to have been crying. Did something happen this morning to you that upset you?"

Tina looked hard into Hawk's eyes, and he could see hers begin to well up. "I was fired today and told to get out. Fired all because I told you people that we were having an affair. He didn't like it. It was important for no one to know. I sometimes suspected that he didn't really love me, but now I know for sure that he didn't."

"Was he afraid that it provided us with a motive for the death of his wife?"

"Yes. That must be it exactly."

"But some people might say that you're telling me all this because of sour grapes. That you're so mad at him and making up this story just to get him in trouble. You know, that 'scorned woman' syndrome."

"No, no, Detective. What I told you is all true. I didn't make up anything."

"Is there anything else you want to tell me now?"

Tina sat back in her chair, crossed her arms across her chest and a faint smile lurked on her lips. "You know, Detective, or may I call you Clint?"

"Let's keep this formal, Detective is fine."

She smiled broadly. "At any rate, Detective, I feel better that I told the truth and got it off my chest." She uncrossed her arms and took a deep breath, expanding her ample breasts. "But you haven't even tried the cookies I made. You have to have at least one with your coffee. Here, let me warm up your cup."

"That's so nice of you, but I've got a full day to get through."

"Aw, come on, have at least one cookie. I made them with my—"

"Hawk interrupted, "Grandmother's recipe from the old country."

"Yes, how did you know that?" She said, excitement in her voice.

"Oh, I just knew." *Just like Nora with her grandmother's recipes.*

CHAPTER TWENTY-FOUR

NORA AND Mortimer walked up the steps of the Ellis mansion hoping that the housekeeper, Nellie Pyle, would be there. When Nellie opened the door to them, Nora barely recognized her as she had changed so much for the better, looking much younger and rather beautiful. When they talked to her a couple of days before, she appeared rather nondescript as Nora remembered—her unremarkable brownish hair was combined back into a tight bun. She wore jogging pants and a T-shirt advertising some taco joint. Even though she had good bone structure, her face looked plain and tired with no makeup, looking every bit her age of late thirties.

Now, almost as if in a fairytale or a movie, the ugly duckling became a swan with hair professionally styled, displaying blonde highlights. No longer wearing baggy clothes, her outfit consisted of designer jeans and a light blue blouse that revealed a good amount of cleavage. Her blue eyes were highlighted with makeup as were her cheeks and her lipstick was a subdued reddish tone.

"What can I do for you?"

Nora said, "Nellie, you look great. What's your secret?"

Nellie blushed and smiled, her teeth, though not straight, looked bright. "Why, thank ya. That's what money will do. I'm so grateful to that wonderful mister for giving me a big bonus after Mrs. Ellis died. You know, I never realized how great he is. I hate to talk about the dead in a bad way, but Mrs. Ellis wasn't a nice person. She really made me feel like bullcrap, like I was nothing. Wasn't generous either. I hate to tell ya this, but I'm glad she's gone."

Mortimer said, "So, Mr. Ellis decided to keep you after all. You were worried that you wouldn't have a job."

Nellie looked up at the tall man. "Yeah, and he wants me to keep the same hours from 8:30 to 10:30 and then from 3:00 to 5:00 in the afternoon. Even put me on a salary with benefits." Then she smiled, "Great benefits."

"Like social security, withholding, things like that," Mortimer said.

She giggled. "Yeah, and more."

"I don't understand," Mortimer said.

"Oh, never mind. You're not with it, are you, sport? Let's just say he's an amazing boss to have." With a puzzled look on his face, Mortimer sneezed. "Bless ya, boy."

Nora said, "Before you told us that you thought that he might've killed his wife."

"Oh, surely I was wrong. More I think about it, don't think he would or could do such a thing. That requires conniving and the smarts to pull it off."

Mortimer asked, "Someone like you?"

Nellie's face turned pale. "And what do you mean by that, jackass?

Mortimer's eyebrows shot up. "That's not very respectful of you calling a detective, a public servant, such a name. You have quite a temper, don't you?"

Nora said, "Nellie, he didn't mean anything other than questioning you about what character of a person could kill someone else."

"Oh, that's what he meant."

Mortimer was about to say something, but Nora stepped on his shoe hoping that he will get the hint to stay quiet. He either did not get the hint or he didn't want to get it. "What I meant was that whoever killed Mrs. Ellis had a strong motive to kill her. If her husband didn't do it, then someone with a motive did it. For example, you had a good motive that I can see."

"What motive would I have? What are you talking about?"

"You're just like Josephine who doesn't always understand what I'm getting at. I'm saying that your motive was to get rid of Mrs. Ellis because you were so mad at her for treating you like scum, when you knew you were better than that. Also, you hoped that you would stay on and try to charm Mr. Ellis."

Nellie's face turned crimson. "You bastard, are you saying that I would kill a person just because she treated me badly? She treated me like scum, but I would never even dream of it. You're nuts, man. And who in the hell is Josephine anyway?"

Nora said, "Sorry, Nellie. We're not sure who killed Amanda at the moment. Detective Holliday is just trying to eliminate you as a person of interest."

"Person of interest? You really think I did this?"

"Anyone connected to the Ellis's who might've had the opportunity to commit the crime is automatically a person of interest. It doesn't mean that we suspect you." Nellie was breathing hard, throwing snake eyes at the dull detective. Nora's words seemed to settle her down. Nora was not sure if she was so angry at Mortimer, or did she act so incensed because she, in fact, was the one who killed Amanda.

"Well, I didn't do it and you can't prove that I did. And I want both of you to leave."

Gads, Mortimer, this accusation out of the blue, messed up my plan! "Sorry to upset you like that, Nellie," Nora said. "That was just standard procedure, and we really need to ask you about whether you saw any women come to visit Mr. Ellis."

Still red in the face, Nellie appeared ready to explode. "Why, in the hell, should I help you with anythin'? I want you freaking people out of here now. And no, I didn't see any women visit my boss." She moved back into the foyer and began closing the door. As Nora and Mortimer stepped back, Nellie slammed the door shut.

"Well, that didn't go well, Mortimer."

"What do you mean? She might've very well done it. She just showed us a motive and she had the opportunity. I bet if we dig far enough, we'll find out that she's a diabetic or has access to enough insulin to kill."

"Mortimer, you just can't go around and out of the blue accuse someone of a crime unless you have a strong suspicion. And then only after you get what you need out of the witness. She could've told us some valuable gossip about seeing someone or finding something that would indicate that someone else was in the house besides Ellis."

"Nora, I'm sorry. I guess I fouled up. But in Tampa, a lot of times, I was able to shock a suspect into portraying his guilt by his mannerism and occasionally had someone admit to it. I'm basically a nice man, and to compensate, I have to playact and become aggressive."

"No, you don't. Not with every witness. There is a time and a place like in the interrogation room and not at someone's home or business to accuse them just like that. I don't think aggressive accusations without the proper setting and timing are ever helpful."

"Okay. I won't do it again. I just thought it would be helpful, that's all. I'll just be myself from now on. I guess Josephine is wrong. She's the one that keeps harping that I need to be more assertive and aggressive to be effective. Not to be a nice guy all the time. I'll have to tell her that she led me astray. But she won't like it. Maybe I shouldn't mention it. What do you think, Nora?"

Nora chuckled as they approached their parked vehicle. "Only you can decide that. But if it were me, I think I'd keep my mouth shut." Mortimer suddenly started to sneeze several times, snot running out of his nose. He wiped it with his hand. *Ooo, that's gross.* "Do you have a tissue?"

"No. Do you have one I can borrow?"

Nora quickly looked through her purse and remembered that she gave her whole tissue packet to him the day before. She looked deeper and saw a stray piece of tissue and handed it to him. "I gave you a whole packet yesterday, don't you have it?"

"Oh. No. Josephine went through my pockets when I was changing suits this morning. She gave me everything, but I guess she kept the tissue. Sorry about that." Nora shook her head.

As they headed back to the station, they remained silent for several minutes except that Mortimer kept sniffling, constantly wiping his nose with that one piece of tissue. Nora suddenly felt sorry for this strange man from Tampa. *He's really trying to fit in and be relevant. Unfortunately, may be trying too hard. But that Josephine is quite a character herself. I'd love to meet her.* "Do you have a photo of Josephine?" Nora broke the silence.

"Oh. No. I asked for one, but she told me she didn't like any of her pictures. Promised to get me a good one later."

"Didn't you take any photos of her during your vacation?"

"No. I guess it never occurred to me."

"Let's change the subject. Why did you think that Nellie might be a suspect?"

"To me, it was rather obvious. She didn't like the victim. The victim demeaned her to the point that she was so angry that she could kill. I personally know the feeling of how angry one can become when a person thinks you're trash. But, I, of course I don't have the mentality to kill, let alone hurt someone."

"Mortimer, I'm so sorry that you had that problem in your life."

"Oh, I got over it. I know I'm strange, but I try not to be."

Nora suddenly felt badly for him. He must have had a very hard life fitting in. She decided to change the subject to brighten up their spirits. "Mortimer, what do you say that we stop for coffee and a roll or something?"

"Oh, maybe not right now."

"It'll be my treat. Let's do it."

"Oh, okay then. I agree."

"You know, you shouldn't put yourself down like that. I mean, calling yourself strange. You're an individual that has your own character and believe it or not, you make life interesting. I bet Josephine finds you very fascinating."

"Oh, I'm not so sure she does. Sometimes, I think she gets very upset with me for doing or not doing certain things. But then, I don't think she's perfect either. Maybe we are meant for each other, but—"

Mortimer trailed off and began looking at the houses along Josephine Street. "Oh my, I just noticed that we're talking about Josephine and this street is called Josephine. That's quite a coincidence, don't you think?"

Nora laughed, "Yes, it is."

They stopped at Voodoo Donuts on Colfax. "Do you like that hot pink color the building is painted?"

Mortimer said, "It's bright all right. Just like the colors you see in Florida."

They each ordered coffee. Nora had a cookie while Mortimer ordered two chocolate covered donuts. Before Nora ate even a third of the oatmeal cookie, Mortimer had gobbled down both donuts. "My, you were hungry," Nora said.

"Well, one of the problems of living with Josephine is that she really watches the food supply. Those donuts were so good, but Josephine would never stop and get some."

"Are they too expensive for her?"

"Oh, as I told you she has a lot of money, but she sure doesn't like to spend any of it."

"That's too bad. If you're done, shall we go?"

"What about finishing your cookie, Nora?" She indicated that she is finished. "Well, then, let's not waste it." Mortimer reached across the small table, picked it up and wolfed it down.

With a few blocks remaining to the station, Nora asked, "Why do you think that Nellie Pyle is capable of murder?"

"I think she's a conniver. She'll do anything to get what she wants. Think of it, if she got rid of the wife, she probably knew she could work on the husband. Do you actually think that he would voluntarily offer her a big bonus and put her on a salary with benefits?"

"I wonder if they're sleeping together now," Nora said

CHAPTER TWENTY-FIVE

DRIVING BACK to the station, Hawk mulled over his interview with Tina. Her vengeance for being dumped and fired by Steven Ellis blatantly stood out. If Ellis were charged with murder based solely on her testimony, a good defense attorney would be able to throw the case out even at the pretrial level because of her obvious hatred and attempt to get even. They needed more evidence to back her story up if it's true.

He wanted to trust Tina, she seemed sincere, but there was something about her that he could not put his finger on just yet. Her story was perhaps too self-serving, laying blame on Ellis to take the spotlight off herself. Hawk did not have a gut feeling that she killed Mrs. Ellis, but then he didn't have a gut feeling yet as to who actually was the culprit.

Nora and Mortimer had returned to the station, but Hawk was not back yet. After their interview with Nellie Pyle and after taking time to have coffee and a snack, Nora thought that Clint should have been back already. It would not have bothered her ordinarily, but he was with Tina all this time, and that troubled her. Knowing what Tina looked like and the attention that she bestowed on Clint the first time they met at the Ellis house, and then later at the interview in her office, made Nora feel uncomfortable. *That is so silly of me. Clint is a professional and has a job to do. I've got to get over this. He's going to meet many sexy women and I just have to trust him. But then, is he really mine? He's never given me a strong indication that he loves me. He avoids the subject. Well fine, then. Maybe I should back off pushing him and give him space.*

As these thoughts went through Nora's head, she suddenly realized that she was the one pushing for a relationship. She fell for him from the moment he walked into the homicide unit, so cool and sophisticated, almost a James Bond character. Feeling ashamed of herself for her aggressive, forceful behavior, she had now decided to take a different approach. *I need to simply cool it. Not be as pushy. Let him make the moves. I can't keep him in the long run if he still pines for Marcie or maybe now for Tina or Luanne, whatever her name is, or someone else. He's a chick magnet and it'll be up to him to stay loyal to me. That's, if he wants to.*

A somber Nora sat at her desk, trying to type up a report on the interview with Nellie. She glanced at Hawk's empty desk. He still had not returned. She noticed the Captain and Perez talking at the edge of the hallway, ready to begin the team meeting. A sudden thought flashed through her mind. *What if something bad happened to him? Oh God! Where is Clint?* She could not sit still any longer, she took her phone from her bag and was ready to punch in Hawk's number when he strode in with a big smile on his face.

"Good, Detective, you're here," Lieutenant Perez said. "We can now proceed. The Captain and I want a clear picture of what you folks have been working on."

Both MacGregor and Perez pulled up chairs and sat down, ready for updates from each detective. MacGregor asked, "Detective Salazar, what do you have for us?"

Nancy Salazar faced her colleagues. "Lieutenant Perez asked us to check on flights to New York that Jason Edwards might have taken. Harry and I thought that time was of the essence for Simon Briggs if he had to stop the victim from spilling the beans on his company before morning. We didn't think that a commercial carrier would've made it in time to drop off the money and instructions to the hired killers and then for them to catch a flight to Denver. So we checked and found out that JWB leases a Learjet 75 Liberty housed at Centennial Airport. We were able to access flight plans for the plane and sure enough, a flight was made to New York at twelve o'clock the afternoon before Ellis was murdered."

Harry Ling, said, "Yes, we went to the airport and were able to talk to the pilot, a Hector Pena. He wasn't helpful. Said all questions had to be referred to his boss, Briggs. We then checked the surveillance tapes and were pleased to see Jason Edwards approach the plane."

Nancy added, "And we were able to confirm that the jet returned at two o'clock in the morning on the date of the victim's murder. Tapes confirmed that Edwards exited the plane."

"Okay, Orlinski, have anything new?" Perez asked.

"I've been going over the tapes from New York and I don't see either one of the killers. They must know how to avoid the cameras. But on the twenty-six-year-old, Jason Edwards, I did some research and found out that both of his parents ended up incarcerated and Jason was placed in foster care at the age of ten. He caused so much trouble that he was moved around to at least five different homes until he got his GED and joined the army at age eighteen. But his army record was horrible, spending more time in military jails than out of them, mostly for fighting and theft. Eventually, he was dishonorably discharged a couple of years later. After that, he worked as an instructor at a shooting gallery. Got fired. Then worked at a 7-11, got fired. He was homeless after that, then got arrested for dealing drugs, spend a couple of years at the pen. When he got out, a job was arranged for him at a carwash, but he got fired from that too. There isn't much on him since then. I assume he was homeless until he went to work for Simon Briggs eighteen months ago."

MacGregor said, "Nora and Hawk, I hope you can tie this all in for me. Do we have a suspect at this time for the murder of Mrs. Ellis?"

Nora looked at Hawk to see who would answer. Hawk gave her a signal to go ahead. "Well then, I think it'll be best if I go up to the board and start with all the persons of interest." She walked up and lifted a marker from the tray. She wrote down two columns, one "Office" and the other "Home." Under "Office" column she wrote down the name of Simon Briggs and underlined the name. Underneath she wrote down the names of Kwon Bak, Josh Dollin and Jason Edwards. Leaving a space, she scribbled the name of Roger Benton.

Under the "home" column, she wrote down the names of Steven Ellis, Tina Dionisio. She explained that after she and Mortimer talked with the housekeeper, Nellie Pyle, it was their opinion that she might also be a person of interest. Nora then glanced at Hawk for his report.

Hawk said, "It appears after interviewing Tina Dionisio, that Luanne Sue Adams is also a person of interest. She had a romantic fling with Mr. Ellis. Evidently, Ellis got around. We know he also had a long affair with Tina and who knows who else. There may also be someone else, a longer relationship that he had with yet another woman who we need to find." With that information, Nora wrote down the name of Luanne Sue Adams under the "office" column.

"It appears that Mr. Ellis was unable to keep his zipper shut for too long," MacGregor said with a smirk. "But all I see are a bunch of names up there that you all think could be the killer of Mrs. Ellis. What evidence do you really have against anyone up there?"

Hawk said, "I think we have a strong case right now against Simon Briggs for the attempted murder of Amanda Ellis. We have tapes of his security guard, Jason Edwards dropping a package off in New York as instructed by Bak and Dollin. We know that they flew out within a few hours of receiving the packet with the intent to kill Amanda. But they deny that they had to kill her because she was already dead. Nora and I agree that they probably didn't. That just isn't their MO—modus operandi—as they use guns, not injections of insulin. Instead, they took her phone that had photos of incriminating documents and as instructed delivered it to, we assume, Simon Briggs. So, at this point the most we can pin on them is an attempted murder charge along with all the other charges that Bak and Dollin earned for themselves including trying to kill me, Nora and Marcie Turner. And Simon should be charged with conspiracy of all their actions."

Perez said, "Any possibility that Edwards actually killed the wife?"

"There is that possibility," Nora said. "Clint and I talked about it. He seems crazy enough to do anything his boss wants. Would he use an overdose of insulin to kill Amanda? We really don't think so. I think the killer is someone connected to the house."

MacGregor demanded, "Who?"

Nora said, "Each of us has their own suspect. I, for one, believe it is Tina. Mortimer believes it's the housekeeper, Nellie."

"Detective Holliday," MacGregor said, looking at the man as he sat motionless as though in a trance. "Holliday!"

Mortimer suddenly snapped out of seemingly his deep thoughts. He coughed twice, then said, "Oh, yes. I thought it was Roger Benton who was the one. But after talking to Nellie Pyle, I now believe that it was she. I bet if we dig deep enough, either she uses insulin or maybe her grandmother does, and she took the insulin from her."

"What motive would she have to kill her employer?" MacGregor asked, not letting him off the hook that easily.

"Oh, well." He hesitated then stood up after he sneezed twice in a row. Orlinski was in his line of fire and he, as a joke, put up his arms over his face as a sign of defense.

MacGregor demanded, "Holliday, please sit down. This is not a formal meeting."

After sitting down, Mortimer cleared his throat and said, "Well, I saw her on the day of the murder. She looked ordinary, appearing to be a woman that cleans houses. I noticed that when she talked, she spoke fast, and her eyes really didn't focus on the three of us as though she was hiding something or just overly nervous. Her employer had just died, and she was not a bit concerned about it. I did not point it out to Clint and Nora because I just wasn't sure at the time that it was important. At that first meeting, Nellie complained about Mrs. Ellis of how inconsiderate she was. After Nora and I talked to her this morning, she looked different, for the better. Her hair, clothing, everything about her indicated that she came into money. She said it was a bonus from Mr. Ellis, who now was the sweetest and the best employer a person could have. I can't believe that they would be lovers, but then as Josephine says, 'Beauty is in the eyes of the beholder.'"

Hawk glanced at Nora with lifted eyebrows in surprise. Nora cocked her head to one side and nodded. The rest of the group sat silently for a several seconds gazing at Mortimer. He turned his head toward the ceiling and a second later, sneezed hard, the sound reverberating in the room. "Bless you," MacGregor said, a faint smile breaking through her stern face. "Holliday, I liked that analysis. What do you think about that, Ricci?"

Nora said, "I'm not sure I'm exactly on the same page with Mortimer, but he does have a keen eye and might've seen something that I hadn't noticed during the first interview of Nellie. I agree that she surprised me a couple of days later with her total change of appearance. And what Mortimer says is certainly plausible."

Hawk asked, "Didn't she talk negatively about Steven Ellis when we talked to her the first time? I mean, she seemed to make sure that we knew about the big fight he had with his wife the morning of the murder. She basically accused him of it."

"Yes," Nora said. "And this last time when Mortimer and I talked to her, she had glowing compliments of Ellis."

"Well, all I hear is a bunch of maybes," MacGregor said. "I got a meeting to go to with the Division Chief and he'll want an update. What am I supposed to tell him? Maybe he, maybe she, maybe they. That doesn't sound too good, now does it?" She did not expect an answer and got up from her chair. "I want results, people."

During the entire status meeting with the Captain, Nora's mind was not entirely at that meeting. Her thoughts were about Clint and why had not he said that he loved her after all the time they spent together, even under the stress of death, even after she told him that she loved him. Frustration, disappointment, perhaps anger had seeped in. Then, quickly, she thought, *what is my problem? Give it time, girl. He'll eventually come around, but for now maybe we should not see each other so much. Let him miss me.*

After the Captain and the Lieutenant walked out, Hawk turned to Nora and whispered, "Nora." She ignored him. Hawk raised the tone level asking, "Nora, do you want to go to lunch later?"

Hearing no answer, Hawk again asked her about lunch. *What's going on with her?* Finally, a minute later she twisted her neck to Hawk and said, "No, I think I just want to be alone over lunch. I'll grab a sandwich through a drive through somewhere."

"That's a good idea. I'll go with you."

"What part of 'I want to be alone,' don't you understand?" Her tone was firm, startling him and even herself. She really did not mean to come across that way.

Hawk sat back in his chair and blew out a deep breath. "Nora, what's wrong? Are you mad at me or something?"

"Not at all, Clint, I just want to be alone over lunch. I also have errands to run. Why don't you take Mortimer out to lunch? He's always hungry." Slighted by her response, Hawk felt rejected. He looked forward of having lunch with her as he had the last few days. Nora always made every situation more pleasant and fun. But he decided to leave the matter alone.

A few minutes later, Hawk asked, "How about dinner then? Where would you like to go?"

"Sorry, Clint, but I really feel like taking it easy and curling up in bed and reading a book."

Determined to get to the bottom of why the sudden change in attitude, Hawk was about to prod her about it when his cell's tune sounded. He answered and Nora heard him say, "Hello, Marcie. How are you doing?"

Nora's ears perked up and she stopped typing, pretending instead to read a file. She heard him say, "That's good, I'm glad that you've calmed down considerably." She could not hear what Marcie was saying. "I know. It was very traumatic. It's all over with now though." Hawk listened while Marcie spoke. Then Nora heard, "Oh, I'm sorry, Marcie, but I won't be able to today. I'm pretty busy for lunch and I got dinner plans." Another pause. "Well, let me call you back about tomorrow." Another pause. "If it's that important that you need to see me, then how about coffee? I don't know where I'll be this afternoon, but what if I call you later and let you know my schedule?" Short pause, then Hawk said, "Okay then, till later."

Seething from what she heard, Nora did not say a word to Hawk, although, she was glad that he turned down lunch and dinner with Marcie. But the mere fact that Marcie called him to go out to lunch or dinner made her furious. If he had a seen at that moment, he would see the anger in her eyes. With her breathing thin and rapid, feeling an ache in her chest, she turned towards the wall and tried to calm down. Hawk realized that something was really eating at her. He needed to know but decided to wait and let her tell him later. He got up to stretch, his back ached and burned. The remnants of the accident were still there. Deciding to move around, Hawk walked out of the unit, down the hall and then a couple of minutes later, back again.

Stopping at Nora's desk, he tried to touch her soft hand, but she snatched it away from him. "No, please leave me alone. Go spend time with Marcie."

"Marcie? What's she got to do with anything? What are you mad about anyway? You know how much I like you. I want to be with you and not with anyone else. *She's probably upset that I haven't said that I love her. But that's just too much of a commitment right now.*

Well, that's better than nothing, she decided. *What's wrong with me. I've never had been so jealous before. It's just that I love this guy so much and it'll be too painful to lose him. Maybe not seeing each other all the time would convince him that he can't live without me.* Nora was still deep in thought when Perez came up to her and Hawk and said, "Okay, guys, Edwards is in Interrogation, room Two. I don't think this will take long at all. Guess who his lawyer is?"

"Marlene Linkletter," both said at the same time. Then she glanced at Hawk and laughed.

CHAPTER TWENTY-SIX

MARLENE LINKLETTER, Esquire, and her client, Jason Edwards were seated waiting for the detectives to arrive. When Hawk and Nora walked in, Hawk said, "Hello, Ms. Linkletter. It's nice to see you again."

With a toothy smile on her face, she replied, "Cut the crap, Detective. You're as happy to see me as a scorpion on your belly." She nodded to Nora. "Well, at least that unpleasant detective is not here."

Nora said, "Oh, you mean Detective Holliday? Don't worry, he's behind that mirror analyzing the situation."

"Well, he will analyze nothing as I've instructed my client not to answer any questions."

"You know, counselor," Hawk said. "You have a pretty dumb client, Simon Briggs."

"I told you before, he is not my client and why would he be so dumb?"

Hawk answered, "He sent you here twice to defend three men, all involved in the death of Amanda Ellis. That ties Briggs to all three and points to him as the man that ordered the hit. He could've had some imagination and used another attorney for Jason, don't you think?"

"Listen, you're as bad as that Holliday, trying to rile me up. Well, it didn't work with him nor is it working with you."

"No, I'm not trying to rile you up, far from it. I was just making a comment, that's all. And I'm sure we'll have the pleasure of your company when your client, Briggs, is arrested."

Linkletter's face became flushed as she about to respond with some nasty retort, but controlled herself. "Will you get on with whatever you need to do here so we can leave."

Nora said, "Very well." She addressed Jason and asked him for his name.

He didn't answer. Nora looked at the attorney and asked, "Can't he at least tell us his name and address."

"No, I instructed him not to answer anything. You already know his name and his address. Go on, what's the next question that he won't answer."

Nora said, "All right, we'll do the same thing that we did with your other client, Kwon Bak. We'll tell him what we know. Okay, Jason, this is what we know. We know that you were kicked out of several foster homes and out of the army and out of several jobs."

"What's that got to do with what he's charged with?"

"Just some background, counselor. To continue, Jason, we know that you were homeless and begged Simon Briggs for a job." Hawk studied him carefully and noticed that when Nora mentioned that he begged for a job, Edward's chest tightened as he quickly sat up straight from a slouching position, a smirk on his face. "And, Jason, we know that Briggs sent you by his private jet to New York with the money and instructions for the hired killers. You hurried back here. Then your boss sent you to make sure that Amanda Ellis was dead since he wasn't sure whether the killers from New York would make it in time to do the job. So, you killed Amanda Ellis while she sat in her car."

Jason screwed up his face, scrunching up his black eyebrows. Linkletter noticed and grabbed his arm whispering for him to remain silent. But he couldn't help himself, bursting out, "You bitch, I did not kill that woman, nor did Mr. Briggs tell me to."

The lawyer immediately said, "Jason keep quiet as I instructed you. Don't fall into their trap. They have no evidence that you did anything. They're just fishing, intimidating you to say something you shouldn't. They don't know who did it any more than you do. So shut up and stay that way."

Hawk said, "Good speech, counselor. But I think he wants us to know that he didn't do it. What's wrong with that. If he tells us what he knows, we can then eliminate him as a suspect in the murder."

"Jason, don't fall for that. Keep quiet. Anyway, are we through here?"

"No, not by a long shot," Hawk said. Turning to Jason from his lawyer, he asked, "Why was it necessary to throw a brick at us? Mr. Briggs asked you to do it, is that correct?"

"Jason, don't answer that." Jason remained quiet as he squirmed in his chair.

"We'll assume for now that you did that on your own. But killing Roger Benton was Brigg's idea, wasn't it?" Jason stared back at Hawk with gritted teeth, shards of ice in his dark brown eyes.

"Jason, remain silent," Linkletter said. "They have no evidence of any of that."

"Actually, we do," Nora said. "Mr. Benton, saw Jason take the motorcycle from the office garage. He saw him follow him and shot at him, trying to eliminate him. Then, he followed us," pointing to Hawk and herself, "and tried to kill us."

"That's no evidence. It could have been a different motorcycle with a different rider."

Nora said, "That's impossible. We have the same motorcycle driven by a man wearing the same clothing that Mr. Benton observed on Jason Edwards. The clincher is that unique tattoo that Detective Hawk was able to observe right before the last shot was fired on us. Besides, who else would've had a reason to follow him from his office and try to kill him? Only Simon Briggs could've sent his lapdog to do the dirty deed. Not very smart of him, especially after he threatened Benton in his office." Jason squirmed more in the wooden chair. His breathing was shallow as his chest heaved.

"That's all speculation. You take that theory to court, and I'll make mincemeat out of it."

Hawk noticed Jason's body language indicating his disdain when Nora suggested that his boss was dumb. This gave him the idea that Jason venerated his boss and did not want to hear his boss attacked by them. He then decided to push him further in that direction, "So, your not-so-bright boss ordered you to kill my partner and me? What a smart idea, trying to kill two detectives. You'd think he would have more sense than that. But after all, how clever was he when he hired a loser like you? He is the dumbest jackass out there." Hawk and Nora saw the anger flare up in Jason. They wanted him to explode, to yell out, perhaps hang himself with a statement.

Linkletter noticed it also. Afraid that he'll incriminate himself or his boss, she hurled out of her chair and quickly said in a loud voice, "Detective Hawk, that's enough. You're over the line. You're badgering my client and this interview is over."

Incensed at hearing his boss so maligned, Jason felt that he had to defend him regardless of what the attorney that he just met said.

Like a bull in a rodeo chute raring to get out of the gate, he lunged at Hawk. Only the restrains that were placed on him kept him at bay. In an uncontrolled voice of higher pitch, he shouted out, "You can't talk about Mr. Briggs like that, you freaking bastard. He's the smartest, kindest, generous man. He's like my father. I'll do anything for him, you understand? Even kill for him as he asked me to. And sonofabitch, I did not beg for a job from him. He found me on the streets and took me in. I should've killed you both last night when I had the chance and not just scare you." After that outburst, he leaned back against the chair, his head hanging down, breathing hard.

Marlene Linkletter's eyes were about to fall out of their sockets, her mouth agape. She recovered quickly, though, "You provoked him to the point where he didn't know what he was saying."

Nora said, "Oh, I think he knew very well what he was saying. Too bad that he has such a temper. That's what got him into trouble all his life."

Hawk added, "His outburst leads us to more questions. Jason, Briggs asked you to kill Benton, is that what you said?"

Linkletter said, "Any more questions of my client are in your dreams, Detective. This interview is over, over, over. I need to talk to my client in private." They accommodated her and after twenty minutes she left, and Edwards was taken back to his cell.

As Hawk and Ricci walked back to their desks, they were met by Perez and Holliday. "That was interesting," Perez said. "He has a short fuse, that's for sure. Good job in sizing him up. Evidently, insulting his boss, put him over the edge. Very strange fellow, he is."

Mortimer said, "Hawk, I see that you used my tactic in throwing the lawyer off her game a little bit. It doesn't usually work, but I think the strategy helped me once in a while in Tampa."

Hawk answered. "Didn't intend on doing it, but she sat there so smug that I wanted to wipe some of that arrogance off her. And, I think she understood that by her representing the New York killers and Jason Edwards that it would tie them all to Simon Briggs. She should've at least had an associate represent Edwards in that room."

Perez said, "Well anyway, I'll have Salazar and Ling bring Briggs in. But whether his people actually killed Amanda Ellis—" he looked at Hawk and Ricci, "I want you two to put all your efforts in finding out who murdered the poor woman."

Mortimer said, "What about me? I assume I'm with them, right?"

"All right, I'll let you work with Hawk and Nora, at least for this afternoon. Then we'll see where we can use you."

Mortimer returned to his desk and Hawk grabbed Nora's arm as they headed for theirs. "Nora, did you change your mind about lunch? I'll miss you."

Nora really wanted to go. But she was determined and with her heart aching, she said, "Sorry, Clint. Not today." She turned abruptly and scurried to her desk, but she liked what he said about missing her.

As Hawk walked past Mortimer's desk, he thought, *what the hell, I'll ask him to lunch. He's always good for laughs.* "Do you want to have lunch together today?"

"Oh, no, better not. Josephine will expect me. Today, she said that she found a recipe for an edamame hummus wrap and will try to prepare it for lunch, or was it dinner?"

"Sounds delicious."

"Not really. Josephine is not the best cook. But she tries."

"Well, maybe next time then. The treat's on me."

"Oh, then. Let me call Josephine and tell her again that I have to work through lunch. I don't think she'll mind. It'll save her some money."

Hawk chuckled to himself. *If I'm paying, he's game. Interesting.* "We still have a half hour till noon. I'll work on a witness statement, and we can go around twelve."

"Oh, all right. You know I don't have much to do. I finished the reports on Nellie Pyle and Roger Benton. I'm pretty fast. I don't believe in a lot of words that say nothing or repeat the same thing."

"Good. If you're bored, why don't you write up what you heard in our interrogation of Edwards?"

"Oh, I'll do what I can." Then Mortimer sneezed with the sound of a shotgun going off and his nose began to run.

Thirty minutes later, Nora watched as Hawk and Holliday went off to lunch without her. Hawk had once again asked her to go, but she resisted. A few minutes after they left, she decided to drive home, skip eating and just lay down on her couch. As she was about to leave, Lieutenant Perez showed up at her desk. "You decided not to eat today?" Before she answered, he went on, "You wouldn't believe this, but one of your suspects, Nellie Pyle, was found dead in her garage."

"What?! Say that again."

"Nellie Pyle is dead. District 4 is on the scene, but Captain MacGregor is trying to get our detectives to work this case since she thinks it might be related to our case here. If she'll talk them into it, we'll want you and Hawk out there this afternoon."

"Yes, sure. We'll do it."

"Fine. Is Hawk out to lunch?"

"Yes, he and Mortimer went out together."

"That's surprising."

"What is? That they eat?"

"No." Perez chuckled. "That you're not with them."

"Oh, I had other plans for lunch."

"Well, go do them. We won't know if we're allowed to help or to investigate Pyle's death until later anyway."

At that moment, MacGregor joined them at Nora's desk. "Find Hawk, I want you out to the scene, pronto."

CHAPTER TWENTY-SEVEN

HAWK AND Mortimer were on their way to lunch at Park Tavern. Hawk liked the place as he liked the staff and knew several of the regular patrons. Mortimer seemed to be agitated. He could not make himself comfortable on the bucket seat to sit. He squirmed from one side to the other and when he sat back in the center, he let out an ear-shattering sneeze, followed by two quieter ones. Hawk opined that Mortimer sneezed when he became nervous or maybe he was in pain. "What's bothering you, Mortimer? Hemorrhoids?"

"Oh, no. I just feel guilty for not going home for lunch and joining Josephine. When I called her that I couldn't, she didn't seem to believe me. Her attitude was rather cold, I thought. But I do have hemorrhoids, but they don't bother me today."

Hawk fought an urge to laugh because Mortimer was so serious. "Well, my friend, women are hard to figure at times. Josephine may be having a bad day, that's all."

"But I don't like lying to her. I'll have to bring her something."

"Like flowers?"

"Oh, no. She'd be mad at me for that. She thinks flowers are a frivolous expense since they die so quickly. No, I think after work I'll stop at the India Bazaar grocery store and get her some chutney. She loves the stuff. Personally, it gives me gas."

Hawk rolled his eyes as his passenger started to sneeze again. As soon as Mortimer stopped, Hawk heard *Bad to the Bone*. He fished the phone out of his left pant pocket and saw that it was Nora. "Did you change your mind about lunch, I hope?"

"No. How far are you from the station?" Her voice formal.

"We're almost at Park Tavern, why?"

"Sorry to tell you this, but you'll have to turn around and pick me up. MacGregor wants us to investigate the death of Nellie Pyle."

"What?! Where? How?"

"I'll tell you what I know after we're in the car." She hung up.

Hawk shook his head in bewilderment. Not only that Nellie was dead but also, even more so, as to why Nora was suddenly acting so differently towards him. "As I said, Mortimer, women are hard to figure out. I wish they'd tell you what's on their minds rather than you have to guess at it."

"Oh." Mortimer remained silent, mulling over what Hawk said. "You're right, Clint. Take Josephine, for instance." *I don't want to take her.* "She has these moods where I learned it's better not to talk to her. Then she gets mad at me because I didn't talk to her. Or there're times when she gets mad at me and for the life of me, I have no clue as to why."

"Yup, that's the truth. By the way, if you're still worried about having to lie to Josephine, don't worry about it." Mortimer squirmed again as he moved over to the right side of the seat and then looked at Hawk.

Hawk continued, "I don't know if you noticed, but we're turning around going back to the station. We need to pick up Nora and investigate the death of Nellie Pyle."

"Okay." Then it suddenly hit Mortimer as to the significance of what Hawk just said. "Really! That's certainly unexpected. She was my number one suspect for the murder of Ellis. Now I'll have to think some more about all that."

Nora waited for them at the entrance of the station. As Hawk drove up the drive, she stepped off the curb and waited for him to stop. When he did, she jumped into the back seat, behind Mortimer. "Took you long enough."

"We were almost at Park Tavern," Hawk said. "What can you tell us about Nellie?"

"Evidently, she was shot in her garage. District 4 cops are on the scene and MacGregor arranged for us to work with their detective in the investigation."

"I hate when we have to go into another district. Everyone is so protective of their turf."

They drove in silence for several minutes. On Colfax Avenue, they passed the Cathedral Basilica of the Immaculate Conception, the State Capitol with its shiny gold dome and the Civic Center. All were on the left. While on the right, downtown high-rises stood touching the sky. They traveled over the Platte River and I-25 onto the west side of Denver. On Federal Boulevard, Hawk turned left and headed toward Kentucky Street. He noticed Nora being unusually quiet. It bothered him to no end. He extended his hand to the back, toward her hoping that she would take it. He kept it there for half a minute before she took his hand and squeezed it. Hawk glanced back and he could see an amused look in her blue eyes, her sensuous lips breaking out in the beginning of a smile. He smiled back, feeling so much better.

Mortimer suddenly said, "Aren't we going to stop and get something to eat? My stomach is letting me know that I need nourishment. I really can't function all day long on that lumpy oatmeal and soymilk that Josephine fixes for breakfast every day."

Nora finally laughed, that infectious laugh that Hawk loved to hear. Chuckling, he said, "Okay, Mortimer, we probably don't have the time, but I see a taco stand up ahead. We'll stop for you."

"You said you'd buy, right?" Hawk paid for the four beef tacos and a large Coke that Mortimer ordered. He gobbled them down almost before Hawk left the driveway. Nora sat in the back chuckling to herself over the incident.

At the intersection of Kentucky and Federal, he turned left and not far away saw the sign for Decatur Street. They viewed a marked Ford Interceptor and a Chevrolet Tahoe with their lights ablaze standing in front of the small gray clapboard house with peeling white trim. The attached garage was converted to living quarters as so many others in the neighborhood. "Where's the garage?" Mortimer asked. "I thought you said that she was found in the garage, just like Amanda."

"It's in the back, from the alley," Hawk said. "The buzz is back there."

They walked through a side gate to the backyard. That is where they spotted Dr. Janeel Thompson, the Medical Examiner, her rotund body standing at the open garage door. The garage's side wall stood adjacent to the alley forcing a car to enter the one-car garage by way of a badly cracked driveway that took up a large chunk of the weed-infested yard. Another marked police car and an unmarked one blocked the alley from any traffic. As always, a crowd with their cell phones held high for photos gathered behind the yellow crime tape.

As the three detectives from District Six approached the garage, Janeel gave them a toothy smile. "It's you folks again. How come every murder I investigate lately has you showing up?"

"Just lucky, I guess," Hawk said, smiling.

Alongside Janeel stood a slim woman about five-foot-five. She was dressed in beige khaki pants and a violet-purple shirt wearing brown leather sneaks with thick white soles. Her brownish-black hair fell over her thin shoulders. A genuinely friendly smile lit up her oval, olive-toned face. Janeel introduced her to the three as Detective Jessica Flores. "I'm so pleased to meet you as I heard so much about Detectives Hawk and Ricci," she said, looking mostly at Hawk. "I was pleased when my lieutenant told me to work with you."

"What do we have here, Detective?" Nora said in a not-so-subtle attempt to get her attention off Clint.

"The victim is Nellie Pyle. Her grandmother, Susanna Devlin, found her this morning in the garage. Said she went looking for her because Nellie should've been home for their late breakfast. When she walked out into the yard, she noticed the wide-open garage door. She headed for the garage and said that she almost fainted when she saw her granddaughter lying on the floor with copious amounts of blood underneath her."

Janeel said, "It's pretty clear that she was shot in the chest as she exited her car. The bullet hit her heart. Strange, isn't it, that the last murder we saw also involved a woman being killed in her garage. Do you think they could be connected?"

"That's why we're here," Nora said, as Hawk and Holliday walked over to view the body. Nora joined them in a couple of seconds. "Poor woman, to be shot like that."

Mortimer said, "I'd say, the victim and the killer knew each other."

Nora said, "How do you know that?" She and Hawk exchanged glances.

"I can tell by her face."

"Really?" Hawk said with surprise. "All I see is fear, which is logical."

"No, I see a sign of recognition in her face."

"Okay…then," Nora said. "All I see is a dead woman who didn't deserve to be shot like that."

"I agree," joined in Jessica Flores. "I've been investigating gang slayings, but this one doesn't smell as one. I bet it's something personal, though."

Both women happened to glance at Mortimer. As if in a trance, he was looking up at the rafters of the garage, frozen in time. "What's he doing?" Jessica whispered to Nora.

"I don't know. He did the same at the last homicide. Maybe he's trying to get a vision of how it happened or who did it. Strange, isn't it?"

Hawk asked Janeel. "How far do you think the shooter was from the victim? And any idea what the caliber of the bullet was?"

"Hard to tell without me pulling it out. It left a big hole, like a forty-five. It could be a nine-caliber. It didn't go through her, so he must've been pretty far back. I'd say he stood by the garage door or beyond. But I'll let you know after the autopsy."

"Any idea what time she died?"

"Clint, don't pin me down on this, but judging from her body temperature, I'd say about twelve hours ago."

"It's almost twelve-thirty now. So that'll be around twelve or one this morning."

Hawk thanked her and went out of the garage, onto the gravel alley. At the back of the garage, he noted a narrow alcove of about thirty inches between the wall of the garage and the neighboring wooden fence. Dried tall weeds were matted down as though a person had laid or sat on them. He stooped down and lifted the weeds to get a look underneath, searching for any clue. In his mind, he had decided that the shooter waited for the victim to come home, drive into the garage, then rushed out of this secluded spot, round the corner into the garage and shoot.

"You having fun yet?" Nora asked, laughing. "You look like a squatting duck. You think you'll find anything?" Jessica and Mortimer joined Nora and all three watched Hawk pick through the dead weeds.

"Probably not, but it's worth a shot." He picked up another flattened weed and to his delight, spotted what he hoped could be a clue. "Well, what do you know? I found something." Suddenly, his lower back could not hold out anymore and an intense shooting pain almost brought him down. He hated that the effects of the accident were still with him. Particularly the nightmares, that still had not gone away, keeping him up at night. He tried to raise himself, but his back was as stiff as a board. He grabbed ahold of the fence to hoist himself up, but the excruciating pain gripped him. Nora saw his dilemma and quickly grabbed him underneath his right arm and helped him up.

Embarrassed at himself, acting so "uncool," so unmacho in front of the others, his face blushed as he grimaced from pain. Nora expressed deep concern and compassion. Hawk glanced at her, forcing a smile. "Thank you, Nora. I guess I was in that stooped position too long."

"Don't worry about it, it happens to the best of us." She looked down at the clutter of weeds. "What did you find?"

"I saw a wad of pink gum underneath one of the weeds. I know exactly where it is, I'll get it."

"Oh no, you don't. Point to it and I'll bag it."

Jessica said, "My goodness, that was lucky. You have quite an eagle eye, Clint. I looked through there and I didn't see a thing.

Although, I must admit that I didn't get down as low as you did. That would be quite a break if it was the killer's."

Mortimer took the plastic bag from Nora. He opened it a little and sniffed at it, then squeezed the gum through the bag. "I'd say it's not that old. It could very well be the perpetrator's. What's your theory then, Clint. Do you think that he hid in this spot and then ran over and killed Nellie as she was getting out?"

"That's exactly what I think."

"That's certainly possible." Mortimer nodded his long face up and down a few times, then raised his nose in the air, appearing proud that he understood why Hawk was searching in the weeds.

After the body was taken away, the four detectives scoured the garage for anything that might be helpful. Other than seeing some loose gravel, like the type in the alley, there was nothing of significance. "Which way would he or she, for that matter, make his escape?" Nora asked.

Mortimer replied, "He must've run down the alley to that street over there," pointing with his long index finger toward Tennessee Street. "Probably had a car stashed there, since it's the closest from the garage."

Jessica said, "He must've turned onto Federal. There're a lot of businesses on the corner and they may have a camera of the intersection. I'll contact them to view their footage for all the vehicles during the hours from twelve to two in the morning. Also, I've gone up and down the alley and noticed several cameras here. I and my team will contact the residents for that."

Nora said, "Great. With that, we'll leave you. Call us as soon as you get something."

"Since you had contact with Nellie Pyle, do you have any idea as to who might have killed her. I mean, I ask because if you do, it'll be easier to watch for their vehicle in the videos."

"The most logical one to me," Nora said, "would be Steven Ellis. He drives a big white Lexus SUV. But this death may not be related to anyone we're investigating. Nellie had a life separate and apart from her employer's. It could be anyone. A neighbor. A lover. Anyone."

The three detectives were back on the road, Hawk's back spasming. "Do you want me to drive?" Nora asked.

"I'll be all right. It won't take long."

"Well, you better get in shape for your coffee with Marcie."

Hawk laughed. "I almost forgot. I'm glad you heard our conversation."

"It's not like I intended to. You were pretty loud. Were you trying to make me jealous?"

Mortimer said, "Oh, Nora, you seem irritated. Maybe you're hungry. Neither one of you had lunch. Maybe we should stop and eat.

"Mortimer, you had four tacos less than two hours ago," Nora said.

"Well, if you stop, I could eat some more. I won't tell Josephine though."

Hawk said with a grin, "What's Josephine cooking up tonight?"

"Oh, let's see. Today is Thursday. Well, it'll be the hummus wrap I told you about that we were supposed to have for lunch. But usually on Thursday, that's one of the better days, she makes brown rice pasta sprinkled with sunflower seeds and vegan parmesan cheese."

Hawk asked, "How do they make cheese without using dairy?"

"I asked Josephine that once. I believe she told me it's made from cashews."

Hawk crunched his nose and said, "Sounds yummy. Better you than me."

"Oh, you don't think you'd like that?"

"Well since I never tried it, I shouldn't say. But I can see why you're so hungry all the time."

"That's why we should eat."

Nora said, "Sorry, Mortimer, I need to get back and besides Hawk has a date with Marcie."

"Oh, a date? I thought you two…"

Hawk said, "It's not a date, it's business."

"Oh sure," Nora said. "Business!"

Hawk shook his head in disgust. They sat silent the rest of the way. At the station, Hawk called Marcie and they agreed to meet in half an hour. They filled in Perez with what went on at the scene of Nellie's demise and shortly after that Hawk had to leave. He again asked Nora about dinner.

She declined. "I told you I want to be alone tonight. Tell Marcie 'Hi' from me." *That bitch.*

CHAPTER TWENTY-EIGHT

MARLENE LINKLETTER, Esquire, tried to work on a brief while waiting for her next appointment to show up. He was late and she hated that. As a matter of fact, she really did not want to see him as he proved to be a big pain in the ass. After fuming that he still was not there, she became even more convinced that she had to fire him as a client. The retainer he paid to represent him was great, but she did not need the money. She had plenty of other clients and was able to sock away a tidy sum in real estate investments.

Marlene knew what he was like, knew what he was capable of, and lately he made her extremely nervous. Not only was he forgetting things, but he was also acting erratic. Not the calm, calculating person she knew over the years, but one that made decisions at the spur of the moment without thinking anything through. He became vengeful, and unexpectedly violent, evidenced by bumping off people that posed a threat to him. She wondered if he became sick with some disease such as dementia or Alzheimer's. *I'll discuss this possibility with him if I find the appropriate moment.*

He admitted his guilt to her, and she could not morally continue to represent him, although, ethically, she was expected to give him the best defense possible or, at least, help him work out a plea agreement with the DA. What she really wanted to do was to turn him in to the police, but she was constrained by her oath and ethics to keep all communications to her as a lawyer confidential. Knowing how easy it became for him to try to silence whoever crossed him during the past year, made her realize that she might be in danger if he did not trust her to keep his confidence. And if he is sick, paranoia would place her in such a position because his mind no longer functioned properly. *Well, he better not try anything with me.*

Finally, she was notified that Simon Briggs was there to see her. "Show him in," she said in her typical commanding voice. Generally, her aggressive, superior tone was so resented by her staff that she had a constant turnover in her office. Due to her rough personality with little regard for her helpers, Linkletter found it difficult to recruit good attorneys and paralegals to the firm. Her reputation among the legal community as a true bitch and someone to stay away from was widespread.

She was born into a tough family, growing up in the roughest area of Bronx, New York. With four mean brothers and parents seldom home, she grew up mean and tough. Her father worked as a bouncer in a nightclub, came home beaten up more times than she could remember. Her mother sliced bacon and eggs in an all-night diner, frequently slapped on her butt, groped by drug dealers. Marlene was born smart and a hard worker, graduating at the top of her class in high school and college while working at McDonald's full time. She received a full ride scholarship to Cornell for her bachelor's in mathematics, then took out student loans to enable her to attend Boston University Law School to attain her Juris Doctor degree.

Simon walked in. She did not rise to greet him. "What's this about?" Simon said. "Couldn't you tell me over the phone. I don't have time for this nonsense."

"Simon, sit down and be quiet. You don't seem to realize how much trouble you're in."

"I'm not worried about it. I pay you a ton of money to keep me out of trouble."

"Money doesn't always buy peace of mind or your freedom."

"What's that supposed to mean?"

"I mean, they're building a good case against you for the attempted murder of Amanda Ellis and another one for the attempted murder of Roger Benton. And maybe, just maybe, if they prove that your boy, Jason, killed Amanda Ellis…"

"That's bullcrap! Jason didn't kill Ellis. At least I don't think that I ordered him to do it. Sometimes, he takes matters in his own hands thinking that he's protecting me."

"All right, then. That's one defense that we can go with. But the attempted murder charges would be hard to beat."

"They've got nothing on me. Let them try to prove something."

"Simon, what fantasy world do you live in. I thoroughly reviewed the police reports. I had a hard time getting them since the investigation is fresh, but a little bullying with the right people always seem to get me results."

"That's why you're my lawyer. I expect you to be a bulldog, take no prisoners, that sort of thing. And I expect you to get me out of this. I'm certainly not going to worry about some keystone cops putting me away."

"Simon, you're not listening. Get your damn head out of the sand and pay attention. Your sweet killers from New York, the bumbling fools, already confessed to the fact that some rich businessman from Denver hired them to kill Amanda Ellis."

"They have no idea who hired them. It could've been anyone."

"Pay attention, Simon. They know that Jason flew out on your plane, your plane! to Brooklyn and paid them off with instructions on who and when to kill Amanda Ellis. They have videos of Jason going there and coming back. The clowns confessed that they were at the Ellis garage at the time instructed, but she was already dead."

"You called them 'fools,' 'clowns,' and if this ever goes to a jury with your skills, the jury will agree that they didn't know what they were doing and would not believe a word they say. Besides, it is you that are telling me that I hired these men, but I can't remember that I did."

"You're still in that fantasy world. Now get out of it. There's more."

"Motive. You had a powerful motive to kill Amanda Ellis and her friend Marcie Turner because they knew of the fraud that you perpetrate on your customers. They had a copy of the documents showing a substitution of inferior materials and you wanted them silenced. I bet that Amanda threatened to divulge this information to your Dubai friends. "Is that correct, Simon?" He looked out of the floor to ceiling window overlooking downtown Denver with the purple mountains in the background. "Well, answer me. I want no surprises."

"She might've mentioned it. But I truly can't remember it. And if she did, so what? I didn't believe her. Besides, she wouldn't have known who to contact."

"Simon, fantasy world again. She specifically took a photo of names of developers for the project."

"Dammit! You're supposed to be on my side. What's this with the third degree?"

"It would be much worse in court. But I want you to realize how much they have against you to charge you with. You better prepare some money for some hefty bail, if the judge doesn't decide that you are a flight risk."

"Maybe, that's what I should do."

"What."

"I can run my business from anyplace in the world. Just in case, give me a list of countries that don't extradite to the United States."

"I can't do that. I can't encourage you to run. That would be totally unethical. And whatever people think of me, no one can ever say that I'm unethical."

Simon laughed sarcastically. "Well then, counselor, you're fired. And how will I know that you'll keep what you know about me and my business secret?"

"You know damn well that communications made to a lawyer are protected. I can't divulge them."

"I don't trust anyone that knows anything about me, even a lawyer. You better watch your back."

"That exactly what you told Roger Benton as he left his office. At least that's what it says in police reports. Are you threatening me?"

"No, Marlene, dear, I'm just giving you some sound advice."

"Get out of my office. I'll send you a final bill. Now get out, get out!"

"I'm leaving, you bitch. You'll never see any more money out of me." At the door, Simon turned and whispered, "You won't need money because you won't be around much longer." His cold dark stare sent shivers up and down the hard woman's spine. At that instance, she believed that he meant to kill her.

Marlene was tough and used to threats from opposing parties, even from her own clients, but she brushed them off as mostly hot air. But Simon's threat was a serious matter. *That bastard, that man without a soul, wanted Ellis and Benton killed, and almost succeeded.* Breathing shallowly, she noticed for the first time in her fifty-three years that her hands trembled. The killer, Simon, really had gotten under her skin. She called out to her paralegal. "Priscilla, get hold of a bodyguard service and tell them that I want one here now. And call Detective Clint Hawk of the Denver P.D.!"

243

CHAPTER TWENTY-NINE

MARCIE HAD not yet arrived. They were to meet at the Starbucks by City Park. While Hawk waited, his empty stomach sent him signals that he needed food. He ordered a bagel with cream cheese and an Americana decaf coffee. As he munched away, for the first time in days, he thought of Marcie. Usually, she had been on his mind frequently, even when he was with Nora. But Nora now was the one. He liked Marcie from the moment he met her with that heart-melting smile together with her silky blond hair flowing over her shoulders like a gentle waterfall cascading down a mountain. *Nora has deep blue eyes, like sapphires, whereas Marcie's are lighter like topaz. Both beautiful, but Marcie's seem to just pull you in. What the hell am I saying. No, Nora is the one, although I must admit that there is an attraction with Marcie.*

He polished off the bagel, even scraped out the cream cheese container, but Marcie still had not come. Checking his watch, he noted that she was fifteen minutes late. *I'll give her another five minutes, then I'll call.* He took out his phone and looked over his messages and emails and as he looked up, there was Marcie standing over him. She placed her hand on his shoulder. "You didn't even see me come in, and you call yourself a detective." Marcie laughed.

"Yeah, I guess I'm slipping not noticing a beauty like you."

She blew him a kiss, "Oh, you're so sweet." She looked rested and happy. Wearing a low-cut sleeveless pink dress with a gold pendant and high heels, she slid into the chair opposite Clint's.

"Sorry for being late. I got held up by a terrible accident at Colorado and Ninth."

"No problem. What can I get you?"

"A strong coffee sounds great." Hawk went up to the counter and ordered while Marcie took a telephone call. She clicked off as soon as he returned.

After Hawk sat down, he asked, "So, how are you doing? I hope you had put that dreadful incident with those killers aside as just a bad nightmare."

"Actually, I have terrific nightmares. How are you doing with all the trauma you had? I mean, people shoot at you or threaten to kill you ever since I've known you. Although, it hadn't been that long, I feel that I've known you for a very long time."

"I, too, have awful nightmares. I haven't been getting much sleep, but I got to be truckin' on, as they say and so have you."

"Clint, Clint, please listen to me. You keep this up and you'll wind up dead. My offer still stands, run away with me to California and we'll have a fresh start. You don't have family here and it should be easy for you to leave. You are a psychologist and should get into that field. Why not open a practice and make some decent money?"

Here she goes again with that California thing. How many times do I have to tell her no? "Marcy, as I told you before, I just can't do it. I like what I do, 1 love Denver and the mountains and want to remain with the Police Department. Maybe, someday, I'll quit, but not anytime soon."

"It's really too bad." After a few seconds of silence, her face portraying her disappointment, she mumbled, "At least I tried again." She smiled, then leaned toward Hawk, her elbows on the table. At that instance, he smelled her perfume. He remembered Tina telling him that in Steven Ellis's office there lingered an odor of lavender perfume. He was not sure, but to him the odor was that of lavenders. *Oh, come on! It can't be? Marcie and Steven Ellis. No way!* Both remained silent. Marcie seemed to fall into deep thought. "I might stay in Denver a bit longer. Your stubborn decision helps me make up my mind."

"What do you mean by that?"

"Oh, it's something personal that I need to work out." She gazed deeply into his brown eyes. "Nothing for you to worry about. By the way, how are you and Nora getting along?"

"We're fine. Marcie, that's a very pleasant perfume you're wearing. Is it lavender by chance?"

"Oh, I get it, you're trying to change the subject. Don't worry, I'm not going to ask you to go to California again. And yes, you're good. It's my favorite. My mom got it for me as one of the gifts when I graduated from high school. I used it some, then I quit using any perfume until I rediscovered it a few months ago. Do you really like it?"

"Yes, as I said, it's very pleasant." After that, neither said a word while they sipped their coffees. Hawk suddenly felt awkward and did not know where to go with the conversation. Afraid that what he would discover would devastate him, he decided to avoid any more references to the perfume or Steven Ellis for now.

"Marcie, you said you have something important to talk to me about?"

"Well, don't you think it was important that I asked you to go with me. I mean, for me, it's a very big deal."

"I guess so."

Marcie laughed. "I knew what you'd say. Nora's got her hooks in you. But I wanted to talk to you because, I think that you should know that besides Tina Dionisio, Amanda told me that there was another woman that Steven had an affair with."

Oh man, I guess we'll be discussing Ellis anyway. "Oh, who was it?" *Was it you?*

"A receptionist at his office, Luanne Sue Adams. I met her at one of the Ellis's parties. She and Tina were arguing. I think both had too much to drink and almost came to blows.

"Do you know what the disagreement was about?"

"I don't, but Amanda told me later that they probably found out that Steven was two-timing them.'

"Didn't Amanda care? I mean she evidently knew of two women that her husband slept with while they were married."

"Sure, she cared, but she told me that she had to convince herself in not letting it bother her as long as she had the lifestyle that she wanted. After all, how do you think she became his wife? She took him away from his first wife the same way those women are trying to do now. And the fool lets them do it."

"Where do you fit into all of this drama?"

Marcie suddenly stiffened. "What do you mean by that question? I was Amanda's best friend."

"I mean, you're a knockout."

Marcie grinned. "Well thank you for that. Keep it up. What else?"

"Since you're so good-looking and sexy, didn't Steven Ellis go after you?" Hawk asked, hoping that she would deny it.

Marcie did not answer right away. Hawk could see that she was formulating the proper answer. *Oh no, there's something between them, after all.* "Well sure he tried. He's a womanizer after all."

"How did it make you feel? After all you were Amanda's friend."

"Clint, why all the questions? Of course, he flirted and tried to get me into a corner here and there. I'll admit that he is hard to resist, a handsome, powerful, wealthy man. But it certainly didn't go very far." Her answers were precise and calculated. Her long, thin fingers rolled into fists; her eyelashes fluttered. *Oh geez. I can't believe what I'm thinking. How far should I push this?* At that moment, Hawk's cell vibrated. He did not recognize the number and did not answer. He decided to continue with this line of questioning just to satisfy himself that Marcie didn't have an affair with her best friend's husband when the same number called again.

"Sorry, but maybe I better answer this."

"Sure, no problem. I need to go freshen up anyway."

Hawk answered the phone and was surprised to hear the abrasive voice of Marlene Linkletter. She minced no words to tell him that she feared for her life. Without Hawk having to say a word, she continued that Simon Briggs threatened her and she expects Hawk and his fellow detectives to take care of the problem. "Now, Detective!"

"We'll help how we can, counselor. Can you come down to the station?"

"No, you come here. I'm not leaving my office until I hire a bodyguard. So how long before you're here?"

"I'll send over some officers right away. Detective Ricci and I will see you in about an hour."

"All right. Hurry."

Marcie came back, still smiling, but her smile did not seem as bright. "Marcie, I'm sorry, I need to get back to work right away.

That's what that phone call was about. Can we do this another time?"

"Why not. We can still stay friends. Give me a call." They walked out together, and he walked her to her car. She grabbed his arm and gazed deeply into his eyes. Hawk could tell that she wanted to say something but refrained. Instead, she jumped into her car and hurriedly drove off. Hawk stood in the parking lot for a long second baffled with her. He could not get over the revelation that she might have been involved with Steven Ellis.

On the way back to the station, he called Lieutenant Perez and relayed the conversation he had with Linkletter. Perez agreed to send a couple of officers to her office. Next, Hawk called Nora.

In the meantime, Nora went home early. She felt guilty for leaving all the work she still had to do, but she felt her emotions strained. She did not know exactly why, but she knew she just had to get out. There was so much housework that she lately neglected and thought that if she immersed in cleaning the place, it would help her settle down. She knew that her emotional state was all related to Clint Hawk. She also knew that she was unreasonable in pushing Clint into a solid, steady relationship. She had talked to her mother about how she felt, and her mother told her to cool it and give him time to decide what he wants to do. If he decides, then her chances of a long relationship with him would be greater.

Nora tried to convince herself that it did not bother her that Clint met with Marcie, but it did. *What is it about Marcie that fascinates him so much? Or is it that she, that bitch, is pushing herself onto him. Well, it would be up to him to decide. And if he decides on Marcie, that's the way it should be.*

Nora was almost in tears as she stacked dirty dishes into the dishwasher. She sprayed clean the countertop and cleaned inside the microwave. She hit the bathroom next. The work was good for her.

She was starting to feel better. Clint and Marcie were out of her mind. Next, she changed sheets in her bedroom and for the first time since Marcie stayed with her, she went in the guest room to change the sheets. As she started to strip the bed, she noticed a book lying between the nightstand and the bed. *Marcie must've forgotten it.* She lifted it up and read the name, *No Return Home.* It looked interesting and Nora thumbed through it. Toward the end of the book, she spotted a photograph tucked between the pages.

She glanced at the photo and shouted out loud, "Oh my God! It can't be, can it? Wow!" She sat down on the bed, breathing hard, trying to soak in what the photo means to the case. *Hawk will be really surprised. No, he'll be totally shocked. I can't believe it! This is too much. I got to call him."*

Just as she reached for her phone, Hawk beat her to it. "Hi Nora, I received a call from Marlene Linkletter. Said her life was threatened by Briggs. I told her that you and I will come in and see her."

"Clint, I'm at home. Left early, but if its urgent, I'll come in."

"No, no. since you're home already, I'll go by myself, maybe take Nancy or Harry with me. Can't take Mortimer. She hates him."

"Clint, before you hang up…" Nora changed her mind from telling him what she found. She wanted to see his reaction the moment he looked at the photo. "Never mind, I'll be there in fifteen. Please wait for me."

CHAPTER THIRTY

DISGUSTED WITH himself, Simon Briggs growled at his staff and headed straight for his office. Slamming the door behind him, he fell into his soft leather chair. He leaned back and lifted his feet on to the desk and took some deep breaths to calm down. His arrogance with the usual accompanying temper once again got him in trouble. He even astonished himself when he threatened his attorney. He really had no intent to harm her, another incident where the mouth did not pay attention to the brain.

He was not old, in his early sixties, but these incidents where he didn't think things through carefully were becoming more and more prevalent. It was so unlike him as his mind had always been as sharp as a tack. That and his skill in diplomacy with future clients and calm demeanor got him to where he was today. He began to realize, though, that lately when he was overly stressed or placed under pressure, his proclivity to violent behavior surfaced. His mind no longer functioned as before. When Linkletter told him that the police have a strong case against him for hiring professional killers to kill Amanda Ellis, he did not remember doing that. When she told him that he threatened Roger Benton and then had Jason Edwards kill him, he did not remember that either. But he still remembered threatening his attorney, still fresh in his mind. *What's wrong with me? What in the hell came over me? I'll give her a call and apologize, promise to pay her more money, anything she wants.*

He punched in Linkletter's number. Her paralegal told Briggs that she was not taking any more calls. He had her private cell number and called. It went into voicemail. He tried the number again and then again. Finally, Marlene answered, "What in the hell do you want?"

"I want to apologize for what I said. I didn't mean it. I'm just used to getting my way. I'll make it up to you though. Name your price, you'll have it."

"Listen, you bastard. I've been threatened before, but your threat and the look on your face told me that you were dead serious. It's too late, I called the police and there're two police officers here protecting me, and I expect a couple detectives any minute. Your song is sung. Your ship has sailed, you bastard. And the worst part of it is that you no longer have the best defense attorney in Colorado defending you. Rot in Hell!" She clicked off abruptly.

Fury invaded Simon Briggs. Again, not thinking through what he was about to do or the consequences of the act, he grabbed a Cobra Patriot 9mm pistol out of his drawer, slid it into his jacket pocket and rushed out of his office. Engrossed with continuing rage, so strong that he trembled, he drove his Lincoln Navigator toward Linkletter's downtown office. *I'll take care of that bitch myself; I'll take care of her. I'll show her she can't talk to me like that. I'll show her.*

His mind fixated only on that thought. His driving was erratic, changing lanes, forcing cars over, speeding fast, running through red lights, cars dodging him along the way. So concentrated on his intent of shooting Linkletter, that he had not heard the siren or noticed the red and blue lights flashing behind him. Finally, he heard the officer on the loudspeaker behind him ordering him to pull over. He did not. Instead, he increased his speed along Cherry Creek Drive, traveling at sixty-seven miles per hour only to be halted three intersections later by a horrific collision with a Dodge Ram pickup. The impact rolling it over, the police cruiser barely able to stop behind him.

CHAPTER THIRTY-ONE

HAWK ENTERED the Homicide unit. Nora had not yet arrived. Mortimer stopped him as he walked past his desk, "You've been doing a lot of investigating on your own. I distinctly remember Lieutenant Perez say that I'm to work with you and Nora. Would you please include me?"

Hawk was surprised by Holliday's attitude. He seemed truly upset and Hawk did not blame him. So far, Perez had not given him anything substantial to do, other than follow Nora and he around. "Sorry, Mortimer. I didn't include you because it's been a rather strange day." Mortimer looked perplexed. "I mean by strange in that the first suspect of the day, Tina Dionisio specifically asked for me to come alone. I didn't like it, neither did Nora, but I thought if I complied, she'd give us more information. I'm just coming back from having coffee with Marcie. It was more a personal thing. You probably don't remember her, but I believe she was in the room when you first came in."

"Oh, I remember her all right. I also know that you're gaga over her."

"Now, where would you hear a thing like that?"

"While you're gone, this place is a gossip mill, particularly Orlinski and Nancy. That confused me because I thought that you and Nora have something going on. Just like me and Josephine."

"Not quite like you and Josephine. You two are engaged. We're not even close to anything like that."

"Oh well, that's your business. Where is Nora anyway? Is she interviewing someone, and shouldn't I be with her?"

"No, she took some time off this afternoon, but we need to go see Marlene Linkletter and she should be here anytime now."

"Good, I'll be ready to go with you then."

"Certainly, but don't you usually hurry home for dinner by this time?"

"I'll call Josephine and tell her I'll be late." He called and Hawk heard him say, "Josephine, I can't get away. We need to go see someone now...just put the cabbage and potatoes in the warmer… I should be home in about an hour."

"That's your meal today?"

"Yes, it's actually quite good. She fries the cabbage and some tofu, oh sorry, she'll get mad at me for saying 'fried.' She calls it 'sautéed.' Then she boils some potatoes to go along with it. Believe me, it's better than most meals she makes."

Hawk laughed and walked away. Nancy and Harry heard the conversation and were snickering when Hawk strode past them. Orlinski had been out sick the whole day. As Hawk passed the white board with the names of possible suspects, he stopped and gazed at it. *Don't tell me that I have to add Marcie to that list. Oh geez, I can't believe it. Marcie of all people. But I bet I'm wrong and it's just a coincidence that she uses that perfume and there's nothing going on between her and Ellis.*

As he stood deciding how far he should carry his suspicion, Nora rushed into the room. She had on a snug maroon knit dress that outlined her curvaceous body very nicely. A small, holstered weapon and the shield were attached to her black leather belt. Hawk's eyes almost flew out of the sockets at her sight. He liked looking at her with those gleaming dark blue eyes offset by her dark-brown hair that was tied back into a ponytail. He smiled broadly at her, she returning a sweet smile. Mortimer stood and asked Nora, "Are we ready to go now?"

"Oh, sure. But give me a minute. I have something to show Clint."

Hawk and Ricci went back to his desk. "Clint, I need to show you a photo I found this afternoon in a book Marcie was reading. She dug it out of her purse and gave it to him.

Hawk studied it carefully. Obviously, a selfie, it depicted a profile of Marcie and Steven Ellis as they sat on a boulder with Mt. Evans in the background. Ellis had his arm around her as she planted a kiss on his cheek. Nora's eyes scoured his face for his reaction. Hawk's face showed more anguish than Nora liked, but it was she that was surprised that the photo did not illicit a larger reaction. "You aren't astonished out of your mind with this photo?"

"Nora, pull your chair over." Nora rolled the chair toward Hawk's desk. "I guess I'm not surprised, just disappointed at Marcie. I thought that she had better morals."

"Why aren't you surprised? Did you suspect something?"

"Yes. Well, not until this afternoon. I almost listed her name on the whiteboard but decided to talk to you first to see what you thought." Nora's right eyebrow arched. "You see, during our coffee this afternoon, I detected a faint scent of lavender perfume. Remember, Tina told me that she was sure Ellis had an affair with some woman that wore lavender perfume?"

"Yes, you told me about that. And you put two and two together and determined that Marcie was the one, just like that."

"Well, think of it. She was Amanda's best friend. She probably hung around the house a lot. Steven was there flirting with her, maybe trying to seduce her. By the way, she admitted that Steven was interested in her. And basically, she also told me that he's hard to resist, at least that's the impression I got from her."

"Some best friend?" Nora said, shaking her head. "I hope I don't have best friends like that."

"Nora, you can only have one best friend."

Nora lightly slapped him on his arm, "You jerk, you know what I mean." Her smile deepened into laughter.

Suddenly, Mortimer stood over them, his lips taut. "Shouldn't we be going somewhere like to that attorney's office?"

"You're absolutely right, Mortimer. Let's go. Ready, Nora?"

Nora was ready. She sprung up from her chair, rolled it back and almost skipped out of the unit. She felt giddy, so relieved that Marcie may finally be out of the picture. *Clint must let go of her now. Especially, if she is the murderess of Amanda Ellis. All those reasons why I think that Tina is the one, apply to Marcie now. She has a motive to get rid of her so that she and Steven can live happily ever after in high society. Hah, best friend!*

As the three walked into the office of the Law Firm of Marlene Linkletter, they recognized the two officers assigned to protect the attorney standing within the old British-style reception room. Looking disgusted at their assignment, they said their 'hellos' and in a flat voice informed the detectives that Linkletter's staff had gone home and that she waited for them in her office.

In her office, Marlene had a finger pointed at the bodyguard that she hired, scolding him for wearing shorts and a T-shirt with the rock band of *Imagine Dragons* plastered on the chest. She was yelling into his face, "I want you to look professional, not like some hoodlum off the street."

She noticed the detectives enter. Her eyes immediately fell on Mortimer. "What's he doing here? I thought that just the two of you would be coming. I want him out of the office. He's a rude, creepy bastard." Mortimer stood straight and still. His face showing no emotion.

Nora said, "That's too insulting to our colleague and unbecoming for an officer of the court, I'm sure. He's with the Department and has been assigned to help us. He was just doing his job, and I'm sorry that he made you nervous." She gazed at Mortimer to see his reaction, but only noticed his head raised toward the ceiling. Suddenly, Mortimer filled the room with a roaring sneeze. And continued to sneeze, then cough for at least a minute.

Marlene appeared shocked, "Is he all right? I really apologize for my unwarranted behavior. I'm under so much stress over this incident with Simon Briggs." She turned toward Mortimer, "I'm sorry, sir. Please forgive me." Then she looked at the forlorn bodyguard and apologized to him for her aggressive conduct. Hearing her apologize, Mortimer stopped sneezing and wiped his running nose with some well-used handkerchief that he pulled out of his tweed jacket sporting leather patches on the elbows. *Another prized purchase from a thrift shop,* Nora thought.

Hawk said, "May we get on with it, counselor. We can see that you're very shaken up. Would you tell us what happened?"

Mortimer was still standing, and she asked him politely if he would sit down and join the others. She asked the bodyguard to leave the room. When the four of them were alone, she repeated the exact words that Simon Briggs used that convinced her that he would kill her. Because of the attorney-client confidentiality, she tried to be careful in not saying anything that would incriminate him for previous crimes.

Nora asked, "What makes you think that Mr. Brigg's threats were real?"

She gazed at Nora as though she could not believe she would ask such a question. "I saw it in his eyes. His anger boiling over."

"No other reason than that?"

"Look Miss Ricci, I've been around a while, and I know when I'm being seriously threatened and to take precautions."

Mortimer said, "Attorney Linkletter, you represented him for a while, I gather, do you believe that he's capable of carrying out his threat? Or is he blowing off steam?"

She peered at Holliday with antipathy. "Yes, I believe he is capable, otherwise, I wouldn't have called you folks or hired a bodyguard. That's a silly question. Shouldn't you go out and find him?"

Hawk said, "We will. We'll head out to his office immediately. The officers will follow you home and guard your house."

Both Nora's and Clint's cells dinged. A message from Nancy at the unit read, "Simon Briggs was in auto accident half an hour ago. He's in the ICU at Denver Health. Call me for more details."

Nora said, "Well, counselor, we know where Simon Briggs is at the moment. You needn't worry about him trying to kill you." She explained what the message from her colleague said.

"Well call this Nancy and I want to hear more details."

Hawk was already on the phone with her and received a more complete report. Addressing Marlene, he said, "I don't think you'll need to worry about Briggs for the time being. After driving erratically, possibly heading here, he crashed into a truck at the intersection of Cherry Creek and Clarkson. He was banged up pretty bad. He's in the intensive care unit. The docs don't know if he'll survive."

Linkletter said, "Well, that's a relief to me." The muscles in her face relaxed and she blew out a breath. Thinking for a moment, she looked at Hawk and Nora, ignoring Mortimer and said, "I feel embarrassed for being so frightened. We trial lawyers get our share of threats, but this one really screwed me up. I wish to thank you for sending someone so quickly to protect me and thank you for coming."

Nora said, "We're just doing our jobs. And we'll keep an eye on Briggs. He'll be arrested as soon as he is released, assuming of course, that he'll recover."

"Well, while he's there, perhaps they'll address his mental condition. He needs help. I truly believe that he's got a medical issue that should be looked into for his own safety and others." She thought for a minute than said. "I'll cancel that bodyguard, I thought he was incompetent anyway, too young, and you can have those rather unpleasant officers leave. Thank you, detectives. I feel foolish for panicking as I did. That's not me."

Walking towards their car, Nora, addressing Clint, asked, "Do you really think that Briggs was on his way to kill Linkletter when he got into that accident?"

"I understood from Nancy that there was a unit in pursuit of Briggs because of his reckless driving. I'd like to read the officers' report on that. From what I heard from Linkletter and then from Nancy that his driving was erratic, I'm beginning to think that perhaps there might, indeed, be a mental issue. I mean, his behavior just doesn't fit the profile of a successful businessman who must be in control of himself."

Nora said, "Clint, is that you as a psychologist talking or are you simply overanalyzing this. If he survives, it'll be up to the legal and medical people to determine that."

Mortimer said, "I agree with Nora. Our job is to arrest him and let others worry about it."

"Okay, okay. We'll keep it simple, but…"

Nora said, "But, what? You want to psychoanalyze him, hold his hand?"

"No. What I wanted to say is, if he has early stage of Dementia or Alzheimer's where he didn't know the difference between right and wrong, then he has a defense. Anyway, forget what I said. You're right. It's not my job."

Nora said, "Are we bringing Marcie in for questioning?"

Mortimer didn't expect that. He scratched his head. "I thought that Marcie was your friend. Is she now a suspect?"

Nora was not reluctant to explain to Mortimer why Marcie might be a suspect for the murder of Amanda Ellis. "And possibly also involved in the murder of Nellie Pyle."

As Hawk drove back to the station, a deep sense of sadness and a weird feeling of chest pain came over him as he listened to the conversation about Marcie. His heart ached at the thought of Marcie as a lover to that sleazy womanizer and maybe even a killer. At that moment, he wondered if he was fooling himself and that he might be in love with her. As a psychology major, he studied the extremely emotional event of broken hearts. He remembered something about stress hormones that surge causing temporary constriction of heart arteries. Numerous times, he heard about people suffering from broken hearts, but before now, he never realized the physical effect on a body. *It can't be that I have a broken heart over Marcie, can it? That's ridiculous. How can I possibly love her, especially now, that I know what she's like? I really know very little about her. The attraction is all physical. Who knows? Maybe she is capable of murder. Regardless, because of that photo, I'm over her.*

Nora noticed Clint's erratic breathing. She was going to ask him what is wrong, but then refrained. They were talking about Marcie, and Nora was a good enough detective to understand that Clint was in an emotional state over her. She felt sad for him and sad for herself. *I'm a second fiddle to Marcie. I know.* Suddenly, Hawk turned toward the back seat and glanced at her. She met his gaze. He smiled and winked. She smiled back and returned the wink.

CHAPTER THIRTY-TWO

REALIZING THAT she might have said too much to Hawk, Marcie had a bad feeling about their coffee date. She fought with herself whether to meet up with him. By all rational reason she knew that she should not, but some overwhelming force pushed her to call and make arrangements to meet. She wanted desperately to see him. Marcie prayed that he would take her up on her plea to run away together to California and start a happy new life. She admitted to herself that she loved him, but the fact that he was a cop with an average salary and more importantly her having a constant fear that he may not come home because some crackpot took a shot at him, kept her from accepting him as he was. Of course, she realized that so far, Clint had not shown any indication how he felt about her, and maybe her feelings were probably one-sided. But she knew there was something there and felt his attraction to her. She believed at first that with some strong encouragement, Hawk could be hers, even though Nora was in the picture.

Marcie also realized that sooner or later, her relationship with Steven Ellis would be discovered anyway. She wanted to love him for himself, not for his wealthy lifestyle which Marcie was no stranger to. She grew up in it. Her parents owned one of the largest engineering firms in California and she lived the life of luxury. She was spoiled, always getting everything that she wanted. Her father, though, made sure that she studied hard and propelled her into the engineering field. She had an older brother that was also forced to become an engineer as it was her parents' plan that both would take over the business. Her brother, however, turned out to be irresponsible, a screw-off, a playboy that showed no interest in the family business. As a result, her father shifted his attention to Marcie as the last hope for the continuation of the family enterprise.

Marcie's father wanted her to go to his alma mater, California Polytechnic, but she rebelled and chose the School of Mines in Golden, Colorado. While a student and working out at a gym, Marcie befriended Amanda Escondido, a regular at the fitness center. They went out for lunches, dinners, drinks and before long they became inseparable friends, confiding in each other about every little thing. Then Amanda met Steven Ellis but hid their relationship from Marcie because he was married and wanted her to keep it confidential. It was a shock to Marcie when Amanda told her that she was "engaged to a great guy that Marcie would like," and she flashed an engagement ring with an enormous diamond. She bragged how rich he was and the great lifestyle that she will now live in.

"Well, what about his wife?" Marcie remembered asking.

"Oh, she had a terrible auto accident and died. Steven is free to marry me now."

Amanda asked Marcie to be the maid of honor and even though she saw photographs of the fiancé, she did not get to meet Ellis until the night of the rehearsal dinner. He was much older than Amanda, but he was tall, dark, and extremely handsome, full of charisma and charm. For some strange reason, when he spoke to Marcie, she was drawn to him. It was magnetism of some sort. He bestowed much attention on her, but she imagined he was that way with everyone. That was his personality and the reason for his success.

After the couple married and Amanda moved into Ellis's enormous house, Marcie came to visit, usually on weekends. Steven was never there, and she did not have any contact with him until the first big backyard bash where at least two hundred people were invited. Amanda was helping their housekeeper, Nellie Pyle, in the gourmet kitchen and Marcie offered to help them. Amanda and Nellie went out to the yard to serve the food, while Marcie stayed behind to fix up another tray of escargot. Steven Ellis walked in and immediately sidled up to Marcie. He wrapped his arm around her shoulders and squeezed her closer to him. Surprising herself, she did not back away.

"You look terrific in this kitchen."

"Thank you. Amanda loves the place."

"Ah, yes, Amanda. A little hyper sometimes, don't you think?"

"Oh, I didn't think so."

"Well, you're not married to her." He glared at Marcie with his warm, sympathetic eyes. She could not help gazing back at him. Their eyes met for at least ten seconds without either saying a word.

Marcie finally broke the silence, "Well, I better take this tray out to the party. I'm sure your guests are ready for more."

That's how it all started with Steven, Marcie thought. He called her the next day. From that time, their attraction for each other continued. They took drives to the mountains. Stayed in resort hotels, met in his office, particularly on his couch, and before long, Ellis talked about eventually getting rid of Amanda so that they could marry. Marcie knew all along that he was incorrigible as a womanizer, not really husband material for long, but the attraction to him was so strong that it overcame her deep guilt of betraying her friend. It ended abruptly when she discovered that he was not only two-timing Amanda but also her by an affair with his office assistant, Tina Dionisio. Amanda seemed to know and complained to Marcie about Tina Dionisio. But when Marcie asked what she is going to do about it, Amanda was not going to do anything because she did not want to lose her status in the community and seemed to let it go. Marcie, though, would not stand for it and dumped him.

Marcie dived deeper into her studies and upon graduation, her father expected her to work at the engineering company. She loathed the idea of working as an engineer the rest of her life and have her father as a boss. She loved computers, was good at it, and talked her father in waiting for her return so that she could explore life as a computer tech. She was persuasive and he reluctantly agreed for her to dabble in it for a year, then return home.

Prior to her graduation, Steven Ellis contacted her and asked her out. She refused. He called her again, apologizing for his behavior and promised never to do it again. He assured her that she was the love of his life, soulmates, and as soon as he was no longer married to Amanda, he wanted Marcia to be his wife. That did it. She agreed to see him and had been seeing him as much as they were able to under the circumstances of him still being married. Marcie resented Amanda and wanted her out of the way.

After obtaining her father's reluctant blessing, Marcie began her job at the Denver Police Department, Homicide and Robbery units. In this work, she described herself as a civilian computer geek. And that's when Clint Hawk walked into the unit. It was magical. Steven Ellis began to fade from her mind. She found excuses for not being available to him. She started to fantasize a life with Clint, but she could not see herself married to a cop, living that kind of life constantly worried about his safety. She had to try to change him and move him away from Colorado, away from Steven Ellis.

Since the coffee meeting with Hawk, she sat in an overstuffed chair in the corner of the apartment that her father paid for thinking about her life in Denver thus far. She finally concluded that it would not work out with Clint, no matter how hard she tried. He would not change. A detective's job was thought-provoking, and Clint thrived on the challenge. Now, tears began to flow with the stark reality that she must forget him and rekindle her relationship with Ellis. After all, she thought that she loved him, that is, until Clint came along. But that is okay, she would convince herself that there is no other man but Steven Ellis.

The cell phone played Marcie's uplift ringtone. She let it ring, did not check to see who called and did not pick up. A few minutes later, the phone rang out again. She picked it up this time. "Hello Marcie. This is Orlinski from the Homicide unit. Would you be available to meet with us tomorrow morning at nine?"

"What's this about?"

"Just some questions we have for you. It won't take long."

A long hesitation, then she finally answered, "Okay, I'll be there."

CHAPTER THIRTY-THREE

THE THREE detectives returned to the station to drop off the police vehicle and retrieve their personal cars. Mortimer shot out of the passenger side, mumbled something about Josephine would be mad, and scurried to his 1989 Oldsmobile 88, still sporting Florida plates. Nora looked at Hawk, blew him a kiss and started to get out of the vehicle. Hawk said, "Hold up. What's your hurry? Let's find a great, quiet place to eat."

"Sorry, Clint. As I told you, I want to be alone tonight."

"Are you mad at me or something?"

Yes, you idiot, I want more out of you than just a convenient companion. "I just want to go home, lay down on the couch and get some rest. Perhaps that fight with the New York killers took a toll on me, after all. Clint, I almost died. Actually, I don't know how you're holding up. I've seen how your back's giving you fits. You should do the same. Go home and get some rest."

"What about that massage you promised me?"

"I can't do it tonight. Maybe later sometime."

"Spose, I come by later tonight after you had rested up. I'll bring a pizza."

"Boy, you're persistent, like a mosquito. But what part of 'no' do you not understand? The N or the O?" Then Nora laughed because Clint looked so disappointed, like a little boy.

"I don't know what's so funny about that." He thought for a second of something that that he could say that would change her mind. He could not think of anything. And he did feel beat. He felt his back would go out on the way home. "Okay, you win. I'll see you tomorrow."

Nora began walking back to her Ford regretting that she took such a stubborn attitude. She would not mind being with him tonight, but she sincerely thought that if she distances herself just a little bit, Clint may begin to appreciate her more. She also had this fear that she was taking a chance. He might just give up on her and start going out with someone else. Clint watched as her butt wiggled to her car. She knew it, and half-turned toward him.

"Maybe tomorrow I'll give you a massage."

Clint smiled. "You better. It's a date."

Both were smiling as they slid into their cars. Before heading home, Hawk decided to take a drive over to Roger Benton's house and tell him about Briggs. A few minutes later, the modern-style house was visible. The police car with officers that supposed to be guarding him was gone. The Range Rover with its windows repaired stood in the driveway. The double garage door was open, and Hawk spotted an older black Dodge Durango SUV sitting in the garage.

Roger came out of the house through the garage and made his way to the Range Rover when Hawk pulled up behind it. Benton appeared startled to see Hawk. As Hawk exited his vehicle, Roger came up to him. "Detective, I didn't expect you. What can I do for you?"

"I notice the police officers are gone."

"Yes, I sent them away. I felt sorry for them, sitting in the car for hours. Anyway, they said they'll keep an eye on the place through frequent patrols."

"Really? You're no longer frightened of Briggs?"

"Well, yes. Of course, I am. But I decided that it's cowardly to lock myself in the house. I'm a big boy and should take care of myself. I'll be careful."

"I'm sorry, Mr. Benton, but with your garage wide open and for me to sneak up on you as I did, that is not being careful."

"It's an oversight, I agree. Promise to do better."

"I'm sure you know how to be careful with certain things as example when your blood sugar is too high or too low, but this is deadly business with Briggs." Benton looked at Hawk with startled eyes.

Hawk hoped that he would show a reaction, surprise perhaps, that Hawk knew of his use of insulin. And maybe he would tie together his use of the insulin with the murder of Amanda Ellis, but Roger was as cool as could be when he answered with a friendly smile, "You must've seen my insulin when you got those drinks out of the fridge. Unfortunately, I've been a diabetic for years, and, yes, I do have to watch my sugar and I promise to be very watchful of Briggs."

"Did anyone ever tell you how Mrs. Ellis was murdered?"

"No, I assumed she was shot." Hawk detected a light quiver on his lips, but not enough other body movements to determine whether he was lying or not. He did not suspect Roger of the murder, but, as a long shot, he thought he would ask those questions in case he could detect something in his answers.

"Well, Roger, the reason I'm here is to let you know that you should be safe now, at least for a while."

"Oh, how's that? You arrested Briggs?"

"No, not yet. He got into a bad auto accident and is in intensive care, fighting for his life."

"I don't know how to feel about that. I worked with him all these years and liked him up until a few months ago when his personality did a one-eighty."

"What do you mean by that?"

"He became a different person. Cruel. Angry. Forgetful. Vengeful. Don't get me wrong, I always thought that he was a little on the crooked side, but lately, he became more warped and irrational. Like trying to kill me, for instance. Why?"

"Maybe, you know too much." Roger did not answer.

The sun perched itself for a few seconds on the tall peaks of the Rockies. *Another fantastic orange and blue sunset*, Hawk thought as he made his way home. He did not feel like preparing a meal, so as he approached Park Tavern, he stopped for a burger and beer. Janice, as always, greeted him with a warm hug. He smiled and sat down at the bar. "How's the case going?"

"What case?"

"Hell if I know. Don't you detectives always have a case you're working on? And why aren't you with that pretty brunette. Nora's her name, right?"

"Janice, you're good with names. Nora's decided that she's too tired today?"

"Well, you two make a good couple. She's a keeper, Clint. Don't lose her." Janice laughed out loud as though she said something extra funny.

As Hawk ate his burger and watched a Rockies game on one of the numerous TVs, a woman in her forties sat down next to him. He glanced her way and smiled. She smiled back and ordered two Coors Lights, one for her and one for Hawk. She must have been a good-looking woman at one time, but now she reeked with cigarette smoke and had quite a bit of mileage on her tanned face with numerous creases and wrinkles. Her black hair was shoulder-length and thick, her dress was skimpy with a fair amount of cleavage visible. "You're a detective, right? I saw your badge on your belt."

"Yes, I am."

"My name's Bobbie, what's yours?"

"Clint Hawk, ma'am."

"Oh, honey, don't call me ma'am. That sounds so old. How old do you think I am?"

"Bobbie, I learned a long time ago not to guess women's ages."

"Oh, you're a smart one. And so good-looking?" Janice brought Clint and the woman the beer. *Oh man, I got to get out of here.* "Listen, sweetie, I'm glad you're a cop. Do you by any chance know anythin' of the Nellie Pyle murder off Federal last night?"

Hawk's ears perked up. Bobbie took a big swig of the beer and burped. "Yes, I know about it? How did you hear about it?"

"I'm sorta a neighbor, honey. I live at the corner of Tennessee and the alley where Nellie was killed. Oh, poor Nellie. I'm gonna miss her so."

"You're kinda far from home here, aren't you?"

"I just dropped off my kid to my no-good-for-nothing ex-husband. He lives a block from here."

"Did you know Nellie well?"

"Yeah. We were buds. We hung around together. I've been real sad over this. I was gonna call the police and tell'em what I saw. But since you're the police, I'll tell you. I saw a person run down the alley like a gazelle at about midnight. Happened to be on my back porch, couldn't sleep and I thought a puff or two of weed might make me drowsy. I saw this person fly down the alley toward an old black SUV, jump in and high tail it out of there."

Wow, this is more than I expected. "Was it a man or a woman?"

"Couldn't tell. A fast runner. Long legs. That's all I know."

"Didn't happen to see the face, clothing, shoes, anything?"

"Nope." When Bobbie said the word, spittle flew out of her mouth onto Hawk' face.

Hawk wiped it off and asked, "Was the person wearing a hood?"

"Yeah, that's it. I do remember a slim figure. Mighta been a woman, come to think of it. Oh, now I remember. The shoes had some kina florescent strip on them at the heel. And actually, on the side of the shoe. You see, sweetie, the streetlight made the shoes glow."

"Did you notice the stripes on the shoes, were they slanted, up and down or sideways?'

Bobbie thought about it for a while. "No, I think it was like an arrowhead on the side."

"Now what about the vehicle? You said it was old and black?"

"Well, it mighta been dark blue. A pretty big one. Oh yeah, I think it had the left taillight out. But, honey, don't hold me to it. I was feeling pretty good about that time." See poked Hawk in the ribs with her elbow and laughed, portraying lower misaligned yellowish teeth. "You know what I mean, don't you?" She continued to laugh.

"Did you get a glimpse of the license plate?" She shook her head. "Anything else that you can tell me?"

"Yeah, what if we go over to your place for some fun."

"Sorry, Bobbie. I got a ton of work to do tonight, but I'll buy the beers. Do you want another?"

"Oh yeah, you betcha. The more the better."

"Let me write down your name, address, and phone number. There may be other detectives that contact you."

She gave him the information then said, "So, what about that beer, better yet how 'bout a whiskey?"

"No problem."

"Now, honey, you have my phone number. You can call me anytime."

"Sorry, Bobbie, I have a girlfriend and unless it's official business, she'll be pretty angry."

"Damn. Okay."

Before Hawk left, he thought to ask her about Nellie.

"What was Nellie like as a friend?"

"Oh, she was a great friend. We used to hang around together until somehow, she got into money. Then she changed. Became a different woman, all fancy, trying to act so sophisticated. It was all an act and then she died. I bet it had somethin' to do with the money why she got killed."

"When did she get the money?"

"Just a few days ago. Said she hit the gravy train."

"What do you think she meant by that?"

"I asked her, and she wouldn't tell me. Said she earned it and there'll be more to come. 'Earned it,' that was bunch of BS and I told her so."

"Thanks for your information," Hawk said, "but I got to take off."

She grabbed his arm and said, "Don't go. Have a whiskey with me."

As politely as he could, he freed himself from her grasp, paid the snickering Janice who looked like she enjoyed the encounter, thanked Bobbie for the information and left in a hurry. He laughed, shaking his head, as he made it to his Jeep. *Damn, that was unusual as hell. Who would've thought a stop for a hamburger would lead to more evidence? Nora will be flabbergasted. Now, we have to look for a black SUV with a taillight out. A runner, hah. Tina is a runner. Interesting.*

CHAPTER THIRTY-FOUR

HAWK COULDN'T wait to call Nora and tell her about the encounter with Bobbie. She answered on the third ring. "You just can't live without me, can you?" She laughed.

Hawk was relieved to hear her joke around and laugh as opposed to the cool way she acted earlier in the day. He still couldn't figure out, for the life of him, what her problem could be. "I'm glad that you're in a good mood. What bothered you today?"

Nora suddenly sounded sullen. "Nothing. I told you I wanted to be alone, that's all. What's up, anyway?"

"You won't believe what happened to me at Park Tavern a few minutes ago."

"You were in Park Tavern? Partying without me?" She chuckled to show that it didn't bother her, but it did.

"Yeah, I just stopped by to get a hamburger. Didn't feel like cooking tonight."

"Okay, so what happened?"

"This woman by the name of Bobbie sat down next to me at the bar and ordered a beer for me and…"

"What! What did she want, as though I don't know?"

"She saw my badge and wanted to tell me what she witnessed regarding Nellie Pyle's murder."

"Shut up! You're kidding, right?"

Hawk described Bobbie in not too flattering terms and Nora felt better about some strange woman in a bar trying to hustle him.

Nora remained silent, and Hawk continued, "She actually saw Nellie Pyle's murderer run down the alley and take off in a black SUV."

Nora had a million questions and Clint answered what he could. After listening to his details of the incident, she asked, "So where do we go from here?"

"Let's see, a dinner and that promised massage tomorrow, then…"

"Clint, don't be so silly, I mean with the case."

"I'll call Detective Jessica Flores tomorrow and tell her of the conversation. See if she can help with finding that SUV. I need to check with her anyway to see if the videos in the area did any good. We also need to call Chet Watkins at the crime lab to see if he's making progress on those syringes and the gum we found."

"You found, not 'we.' Anyway, it sounds like a plan, stan. And don't forget to fill in Mortimer otherwise, he'll have a conniption."

"Yeah, I know. Good ole Mortimer. He's a character all right. So have you rested up."

"I guess so."

"You know, I kind of missed you tonight."

"Really. I thought you'd not even notice that I wasn't there."

"Oh, come on, kiddo, I like being with you."

Nora had a wide smile as she listened to his words. She suddenly felt that maybe there is a future with Clint. "I missed you too, actually."

"Good. I'll see you tomorrow. Sleep tight, don't let the bed bugs bite."

Nora laughed and said, "Good night."

But Hawk did not have a good night. He had a reoccurrence of his auto collision and the gun pointed at him. In his nightmare, the weapon grew in size. He slithered to it, like a cobra, then entered the barrel which was large enough to hold him. Suddenly, the gun exploded, and he shot out in pieces of flesh. Toward morning, he finally fell asleep. He had another dream. Not a violent nightmare this time but turned out to be of concern to him. In the dream, he and Marcie stood with her arms around him, kissing him on his neck and on his lips when suddenly, two police officers barge in and begin to pull her away from him. He is desperate to keep hold of her, but it is of no use as the officers overpower him and snatch her away. She is screaming for him to help, but he is powerless as one of them holds him back and the other cuffs Marcie before escorting her out of the room.

Relieved that it was only a dream, Hawk abruptly sat up in bed wondering what the dream meant. Did it mean that he loves her and does not want to lose her, or did it foretell that Marcie is the guilty one and would be arrested for the murders? *Oh, that's just plain silly of me to make anything out of that dream. Dreams don't mean anything. And why am I even dreaming about Marcie, anyway?*

It was still too early to get up out of bed, so he tried to fall back to sleep, but could not. Turning on the Today show, he listened to the news a bit, then showered, put on his dark gray suit, blue shirt, and a multi-colored tie. After eating a bowl of raisin bran, he took off for the station, the dream about Marcie still on his mind.

Surprised to see Orlinski already there at such an early hour, Hawk walked up to him and after exchanging a brief greeting, he asked him if he would do him a favor.

"Sure, but you'll owe me a lunch."

"Orlinski, you don't even know what the favor is."

"Doesn't matter. I told you before that we need to get together for lunch sometime. We really don't know much about each other."

"You're absolutely right. Let's do it next week. How 'bout Thursday, if we're both available?"

"Sure. Now what do you need, my friend?"

"Any way you can get financial records on Nellie Pyle, like recent bank statements? And could you also check on money withdrawn within the last week from Tina Dionisio's account, Luanne Sue Adams's account, Steven Ellis, and Roger Benton's account?"

"Man, that's a lot of favor. It'll take me a while. More than lunch worth. More like a fifth of good Polish vodka."

"You got it. I'll even help you drink the vodka."

"You're on. Why do you need all this info? Do you think Nellie was blackmailing one of those people?"

"I think so."

"Well, shouldn't you include Marcie in that?"

"I really can't believe she would do anything like that. Let's wait to see first what you come up with on the others."

"You know, Marcie is coming in at nine-thirty for interrogation. You'll see her there."

Hawk did not want to see her, not like that anyway. Perez came in and Hawk asked to see him. He followed him into his office and said, "Lieutenant, I understand that Marcie Turner will be in for interrogation later this morning. I'd rather not do it. I kind of dated her a few times and I don't think I can be unbiased."

"No problem. Orlinski told me about how you feel about her. Nora and Mortimer can take care of it. What are your plans then?"

Hawk could not believe how much of a gossip Orlinski was. *What does he know of how I feel about Marcie?* "Hawk, I asked you a question."

"Sorry, after making a couple of calls, I thought I'd go back to the scene of the Ellis crime and look around some more. Maybe talk to the neighbors. I know that Nancy and Harry did some of it, but maybe I'll run across some other people that might have seen something."

"Okay, go for it. Give me a report once you get back."

Hawk called Chet Watkins at the crime lab. Chet answered his cell on the first ring. "Yeah, Clint, you're calling so much lately that I have you in my contacts. What can I do for you?"

"Any progress on those syringes?"

"Didn't think we'd find anything. They must've used gloves. But on closer scrutiny, we found a partial fingerprint, right at the side of the barrel flange. I figure that whoever took it out of the packaging had to take the gloves off to yank out the syringe from a sticky piece of cellophane, or they simply didn't do a good job of cleaning the barrel off and a partial fingerprint was left. There's not much there, but we're running it on the FBI database to see if there are enough points to make a match. Hopefully, we'll get one sometime by late morning."

"That's terrific. What about the DNA on the gum I found near the scene of the Pyle murder?"

"Yeah, Detective Flores, gave me the gum as we processed the scene. We haven't found any hits on that. Nothing in our database."

"A long shot, but did you run an analysis on the hair that I sent you to analyze?"

"No, not yet, Hawk. We're slammed here and I know you and Nora always want it yesterday. We'll try to get to it later today."

Hawk thanked him and next called Jessica Flores. The call went into voice mail, but a minute later, she called back. "Hello Clint. I was about to call. I've been going through videos from several sources around the neighborhood and there's just too many vehicles for me to pinpoint any in particular."

"Jessica, I have something that might help you. Look for a black SUV at Tennessee and Federal at around midnight the morning of the murder."

"That makes it a hell of a lot easier. I have the best video of that area running right now. Let me check." Hawk waited as he heard Jessica humming an Abba tune while she searched. "Clint, I see it!"

"Do you have a view of the back to see if a taillight is out?"

"Hang on. Let me rewind it."

"Yes, yes. How did you know about it?"

Hawk explained how he got the information from a woman that just happened to sit down next to him. He gave her the woman's name of Bobbie Carpenter, her address and telephone number. "You might want to follow up with her, maybe she'll remember some more details."

Jessica said she will do it early afternoon and Hawk thanked her and asked her to forward the video of the SUV to his phone. Once he clicked off, Nora came in dressed in a maroon suit, gray shirt, her long hair flowing over her shoulders, looking fresh and smiling. She came up to his desk and asked Hawk if he was ready for Marcie. Disappointed that Hawk would not be doing the interview, she joked that he was scared to face her.

"I'd rather not, Nora. I'm sure you understand. I'm off the to the Ellis crime scene and dig around a bit. It'll be you and Mortimer in there. Have fun."

"Sure, I understand. It'll be rather awkward, won't it?"

"Yeah. I think so."

"Hope you find something out there, Clint. Good luck, but then you're Mr. lucky."

Hawk walked out of the door, down the hall and down the stairs. At the bottom of the stairs, he ran into Mortimer who looked better than usual. He wore a white shirt with a wide-lapeled dark blue suit accessorized by bright red suspenders and a matching bow tie. "Morning, Mortimer, you look sharp today."

"Thanks. Josephine said that she found this suit in my size at some consignment store. Said it cost her a whopping thirty-five dollars, but she thinks the way I look in it, that it was worth it. Are we going somewhere right now?"

"No, not we. I'm heading out to check the crime scene a little more, and you and Nora will be interrogating Marcie Turner."

"Oh. I get it. It'll be hard on you since you love her."

Hawk was thrown by that statement. "No, I don't love her. But I do know her and, yes, I'd rather not be there."

"Oh, okay, if that's what you say."

Hawk left just a few minutes before Marcie arrived at the station. Her breathing was shallow and rapid as she slowly lumbered up the stairs. She did not want to be there. She was not sure why they wanted to see her, but she knew it was not good.

She walked into the Homicide unit, no usual smile on her face this time. Instantly gazing at Hawk's desk, disappointed that he was not there. Nora saw her, waved, and immediately rose to greet her. After an exchange of a morning greeting, Nora showed her into Interview Room Number One. She asked her to sit down and told her that she would be right back.

Marcie sat waiting, her temples throbbing. *What is this all about? Do they think I did something wrong? And why isn't Clint there?* She fidgeted in her hard wooden chair, a big see-through mirror directly in front of her. She thought that the Lieutenant would probably be behind the glass watching. She wondered if Hawk was back there. A moment later, Nora came back in with Mortimer accompanying her.

Marcie forced a weak smile, "Hello Mort, nice to see you."

"It's Mortimer or Detective Holliday, please. I despise being called Mort, always have."

"Oh sorry, Mortimer. I won't do it again."

Nora sat down across from Marcie, but Mortimer remained standing, hovering over the women. "Mortimer," Nora said. "Would you sit down and join us?"

"Oh, okay. If that's what you want."

Nora looked at Marcie and said, "Marcie, we need to advise you of your constitutional rights since you are a person of interest in this case?" Marcie's eyebrows shot up to almost her hairline. She was going to protest, when Nora held up her index finger, indicating for her to hold off. She read her the Miranda rights and then said, "Marcie Turner do you understand what I just read off to you?" Marcie was barely able to muster an affirmative answer. "And do you understand that this interview is being recorded?" Again, she barely was able to acknowledge it.

"Now, Marcie, you wanted to say something before I read you your rights."

Marcie was breathing hard. The veins in her temples protruded as beads of sweat formed on her forehead. She looked pleadingly at both Nora and Mortimer. "I don't understand how I could possibly be a person of interest in what, the murder of my friend. Is it because I told Clint that I had an affair with Steven Ellis? That was several years ago when I was a college student at Mines."

Nora said, "Not so much what you told Clint, but it's the photo of you and Ellis that I found in a book that you left in my guest room." Nora pulled out the photo from out of a file and slid it over to her.

"Oh, that. I just have used it as a bookmark from one book to another. Yes, we were together at that time the picture was taken, but then I broke it off when I found out he was cheating on me with another woman."

"As you and he were cheating on his wife, your best friend."

Marcie broke out into tears. Mortimer's usually stoic face seemed to have a strand of sympathy for Marcie as he reached over at the edge of the table and shoved a tissue box her way. "You can't imagine how badly I've felt about that. Yes, Amanda was my friend, and I knew that I shouldn't have been mesmerized by Steven, but no matter how I tried to avoid his advances, I couldn't help myself. Even the deep, deep gut-wrenching guilt that I felt could not make me run away from him. He is an amazing man in looks, charm, charisma and he pulled me in to him. For some reason, I could not resist him. He convinced me that his marriage to Amanda was over with. That he didn't love her, nor did she love him. The marriage was a big mistake. Money, a great lifestyle, status in the community kept her married to him. He told me twice that once she is out of the picture, he'd marry me. And I, as the biggest fool in the world believed him. But listen, I would never kill Amanda. I couldn't kill anyone. I'm a big coward."

Mortimer said, "Ms. Turner, you said that Ellis mesmerized you and that you couldn't resist. He then convinced you or mesmerized you, as in your own words. to kill Mrs. Ellis."

"No, no. He would never ask me to do anything as vicious as that. That, I am sure I could have resisted."

Nora said, "You're seeing him now, aren't you?"

"Yes, after Amanda's death, he called me out of the blue and we got together for dinner."

"That's all that happened, dinner?"

"Well, afterwards, we went to his house." Marcie hesitated as she wiped some tears from underneath her eyes. "He shocked me when he asked me to marry him."

Mortimer said, "What!? I thought that you and Clint Hawk had something going on." Nora was startled by that question.

"No, we never really did. Just a meal together. Some coffee together." She looked away at the bare pale green wall to the side. Remaining for a long minute while Nora and Mortimer patiently waited, she looked directly at Nora and spoke, "You know, don't you, that I'm infatuated with Clint. I would like nothing more than to be with him, but he has turned me down more than once." She remained silent again for a few seconds, then said, "I'm not as enamored with Steven as I was years ago, but there is still something there, I must admit. I might take him up on his proposal."

Now Nora sat silent trying to digest what Marcie said about Clint. Mortimer looked at both women that were staring at each other and scratched his head trying to figure out what was going on between them. Then he sneezed so loudly out of the blue that both women jumped in their seats. "Mortimer you scared me," Nora said. "I thought a bomb went off. But bless you."

"Oh, sorry."

Nora once again turned her attention to Marcie. "I must compliment you on how clever your narrative has been to us. You're trying to show that you would not have a motive for killing Amanda because you broke up with Ellis years ago and now that you've reconnected after her death, you really aren't sure if you want to marry Ellis or not. To me, that's just covering yourself by trying to eliminate any motive that you could have."

"Nora, I told you the truth. I had no reason to kill Amanda. Remember, it was Steven that called me after her death."

Nora asked, "Besides you, who was the woman that Ellis had an affair with?"

"I don't know exactly. Amanda suspected it to be Tina Dionisio, his assistant."

"Had you ever met her?"

"Just at a party or two at the Ellis house."

Nora asked, "Okay, Marcie, if you didn't do it as you say, who could have killed Amanda?"

"Look, Nora, I have no idea."

Mortimer said, "But you suspect it was her husband, Steven Ellis, don't you?"

Marcie displayed a shocked look. "No, I don't suspect him at all. He wouldn't do such an awful thing. He really is a kind, gentle man that I think was abused in the relationship with Amanda."

Nora said, "What do you mean by abused?"

"Well, after I got to know Amanda better, I saw another side to her. Hate to speak of the dead, but she really was a mean, vicious person who belittled and yelled at people. I think that Steven was a recipient of that kind of tongue-lashing from her on a regular basis." She thought for a moment, then said, "Actually, I still can't forget how she lost her temper when I came fifteen minutes late for a luncheon. She lashed out at me with such terrible language that the manager of the restaurant asked us to leave. Then as we were out the door, she apologized and said something to the effect that she always had trouble controlling her temper."

Mortimer said. "Oh, from what I hear you say, Amanda was mean to Steven and to you and you both resented it. Perhaps resented it so much that you two conspired to kill her."

"Oh my God, no. Neither one of us could do a horrible thing like that."

Nora asked, "Could Tina Dionisio commit such a crime?"

"I have no idea. I saw her arguing with another woman at a party, and both seemed to have quite a temper. But that's all I know."

"Who was that other woman?"

"I think Amanda introduced her as Luanne."

Nora asked, "Now, did Steven Ellis ever mention the word, divorce, in connection to his wife?"

"I don't think he specifically said 'divorce,' but that was the intent, obviously, when he stated that when she was out of the picture, he'd marry me."

"You don't think he meant, that after she was dead, he'd marry you?"

"No. I don't believe that at all."

Nora could not think of anything else to ask. Marcie tried to sound sincere in her answers, maybe too sincere and rehearsed. Her face was flushed, moisture swelled in the eyes, her hands trembled, and Nora suddenly felt a little sympathy for her. "Detective Holliday, do you have any more questions of Ms. Turner?"

"Mortimer cleared his throat twice, then looked up at the ceiling as if a question would be written up there, then gazed at Marcie. "No, I don't have anything else."

Nora concluded the interview by shutting off the recorder. "Marcie, I know this was hard for you, but we had to talk to you about it to cover all bases. Sorry for the inconvenience. You may go now."

"Am I in trouble, Nora?"

"I wish you had told us about your relationship with Ellis before."

"Well, it's something that I'm not proud of."

"I understand."

"Do you?"

Mortimer left before Nora and Marcie walked out. "Nora, I'm really scared. I didn't do it. Should I get a lawyer now?"

"Marcie, I don't know what to tell you. The case is still being investigated." Then in a low tone so no one could overhear, "But if I were you, I wouldn't worry about it." *Or should you?*

CHAPTER THIRTY-FIVE

HAWK WONDERED how Marcie's interview would go as he drove toward the Cheesman Park area. He hoped that she would be cleared as a suspect after it. He could not imagine her killing someone. He had been fooled by her already when she he realized that she had an affair with her best friend's husband. But an affair is not murder. There was no comparison and just because Marcie had that affair, it did not mean that she could take someone's life. *No, Marcie didn't do it. It's just not in her character.*

He drove up to the Ellis house and luckily found a parking spot halfway down the block. He saw Steven Ellis in the grassy strip next to the sidewalk picking up dog poop. He did not look happy about the chore. Ellis saw Hawk approach and exhibited a friendly smile.

"Hello Detective. What brings you out here today?"

"Hello, Mr. Ellis. I'd like to walk around a bit and question some of the neighbors. Perhaps they saw something that would help."

"How's the case going? Any suspects?"

"That's the problem. There are too many suspects. Each that we zeroed in on has a motive."

"Oh. I hope you eliminated me as one."

"We haven't eliminated anyone at this time, but I feel we're close to an arrest."

"Would you like to come in and fill me in?"

"Not at this time, sir. We need a little more proof before we can discuss it." Both men remained silent for a moment, then Hawk thought that this would be a good time to question him on his affairs. "Perhaps, I'll take you up on your invitation to discuss the case inside."

"Sure, sure. Come on in. Excuse how the place looks, with Nellie not being around and Amanda gone, I'm doing a bad job of keeping it tidy."

Hawk followed him to the sitting room and they, as before, sat across from each other. "I didn't plan on running in on you today, but since we're here I'd like to talk to you about a rather sensitive matter. Could you be frank with me regarding the several affairs you had that we uncovered in our investigation."

Ellis took a deep breath, pressed his lips together, closed his eyes and took another breath. "Detective, I had been very unhappy in my marriage to Amanda. She wasn't a warm, cuddly type of person after we were married." He took another breath. "I mean, she was wonderful, full of life, happy person when we dated and probably the first year of our marriage. Then she changed. She was sharp with me, critical, nagging, yelling to the point where for my own sanity I had to escape from the house just to get away from her. I didn't want to be around her. The marriage made me so unhappy that, I admit, I sought the companionship of other women."

"Why didn't you divorce her?"

"I should have. But I was afraid that a divorce would scare away some of my big clients that might've thought that if I failed in my marriage, I would've failed them. I believe my clients are funny that way. But that might be only an excuse because I love this house and after talking to a divorce attorney, I'd most likely lose it in a sale to split assets. I have been lucky in my career and have a good net worth and I just couldn't bear giving half or more to that woman that made me so miserable."

"That was very important to you?"

"Yes, it was at that time. Important enough that I decided that I'd let her yell and scream at me, but I'll hang in there, see other women, and maybe she'll be the one that'll ask for the divorce. For some reason, I thought that if she filed for the divorce, I would feel better about it. But, Detective, I was close to filing shortly before she died. We even had the papers prepared and the lawyer was waiting for my go ahead, which I gave him, and the papers should've been served on Amanda the afternoon of her death."

"Why didn't you tell us that when we first saw you?"

"I don't know. I guess since Amanda was gone, it didn't matter. It's hard to discuss your dirty laundry in front of others." Ellis hesitated. He looked at Hawk trying to resolve in his mind whether to confess to something else. Hawk seemed easy to talk to and for some reason, he trusted him. "I finally decided to go through with the divorce because I found someone that I wanted to live my life with. You can say that I was going to choose love over money. For this wonderful woman, I would give up most of my wealth."

"That's a powerful statement. I'm pleased that you found someone like that. Who is she?"

"Please, I don't want to tell you until she agrees to my marriage proposal. For some reason, she is hesitant. You see, we haven't seen each other for a long time, but I could never get her out of my mind. Then, a month or so ago, we reconnected, and I'm still head over heels for her. I believe she's the one that will return to me a joy for living."

Hawk knew who Ellis was talking about. It had to be Marcie. "Mr. Ellis, you said that you reconnected with this woman before Amanda's death, correct?"

"Yes. Why?"

"And did you ask her to marry you before Amanda's death?

"Yes. Detective what are you insinuating?"

"Before I answer that, I need to know whether you told her that you planned to divorce Amanda."

"I don't remember. I don't think so at the time."

Hawk was disappointed to hear that timeline. "I hope it doesn't mean that your girlfriend had a motive to harm your wife."

Ellis shot up from the couch, his voice raised, "Detective Hawk, I resent that, that's a bunch of bull. That woman is such a gentle soul. She would never, she could never even think of harming Amanda. You should throw such trash out of your mind."

Hawk rose also to meet Ellis's eyes. "I'm sorry, Mr. Ellis. It's my job to follow all leads and put pieces of puzzles together, even though most lead to a dead end. I certainly do not wish to malign your future fiancé. I'll get off this subject, but I do have a few questions about your housekeeper, Nellie Pyle."

Ellis sat back down and so did Hawk. "What about her? I haven't seen her since yesterday."

"She was murdered in her garage, just like your wife."

"What?! Hawk watched Ellis closely to see any mannerisms that portray a deception. Ellis, though, seemed sincere in his surprise of her death. Hawk explained how they found her but gave no details of the murder weapon. "Do you know who did it?"

"No, not yet."

"Was she also killed by an overdose of insulin?"

"I'm not in liberty to disclose that at this time, but had you noticed a change in Nellie in the last two or three days?"

"Yes, she started looking completely different in her appearance. She fixed her hair, got new clothing, just looked better.

When I commented on her new appearance, she said that she came into some money, but didn't say from where." Ellis hesitated, "Actually, I believe she was coming on to me and it made me nervous. I planned to fire her. She wasn't the person that Amanda had hired any longer."

"Mr. Ellis, thank you so much for your candid discussion. It makes my job so much easier." Ellis nodded, his face morose. Hawk understood that he probably thought that he blabbed too much. Hawk also realized that Ellis deeply regretted that he mentioned his girlfriend at all, placing her in the spotlight like that.

Ellis walked him to the door. No friendly smile this time; nevertheless, the two men shook hands and Hawk began to cross the street wondering if the residents there had seen anything that might be helpful the morning of Amanda's murder. As he slowly ambled, he tried to digest what he heard about Marcie. It really disturbed him. He didn't know whether he was upset that she wasn't forthright in her relationship with Ellis or whether she was going to marry him. At any rate, he was at the doorstep and rang the bell, hoping someone would answer.

Waiting for half a minute, he pushed on the doorbell again. Again, the inside chimes rang out. Ready to knock on the magnificent carved walnut door, it opened and a friendly-looking blonde woman in her early forties, wearing sweats and a colorful headband asked him what he wanted. Hawk pointed to his badge and asked if he could have a word with her regarding the neighbor's death. She giggled and said, "Well you caught me on the treadmill. I know, it's strange that I live next to the park where I could run and yet exercise on a machine inside. but I prefer it that way." She let out another giggle. "Actually, I'm glad you're here as last night we were debating whether to call you people. You'll need to talk to our son, Noah. Please come in."

Receiving a much better reception than he anticipated, he walked into the huge house with the foyer that seemed a football field long and at the end, a wide staircase leading up two more floors. He could see the colorful stained-glass skylight way up high. The bubbly woman led him into a spacious gourmet kitchen, obviously updated from the original. Double ovens, a Sub-Zero refrigerator with a glass door, custom mahogany cabinets and light granite countertops graced the rectangular room with large sliding glass doors that led onto an expansive brick patio surrounded by exquisitely manicured landscaping. She asked him to sit at the kitchen island and poured him a cup of coffee without him even asking for it. "Now let me call my son down." She went out to the foyer and shouted out in an ear-splitting yell for him to come down. Hawk raised his eyebrows when he heard her bellow. He could not believe that a short, thin woman could produce such a sound, enough to raise the dead, *no wonder the ghosts are restless in the park,* he chuckled to himself.

They waited a few minutes and still no sign of Noah. "He didn't hear me. I'll give him a call." Hawk must have shown his astonishment at that, especially, how anyone could not hear her because she said, "This house is too big. He's on the third floor and if he has his door closed, playing his favorite video game, Fortnite, he can't hear a thing of what's going on in the house. We wind up using the phone to communicate." She used her phone to call him and in two minutes he was down. He was short and pudgy. His long hair looked scraggly. His mother introduced him to Hawk, then said, "Tell the Detective what you told us at dinner last night concerning Mrs. Ellis."

"Ah, ah. I used my birthday money to buy a video camera and, ah, hooked it up to my computer."

His mother chimed in, giggling, "Yes, he's fifteen now and suddenly discovered girls."

"Mom! That's not why I bought it. I want to just mess around with the camera."

"That's okay, Noah," Hawk said. "Please go on with your story."

"Ah, ah. Before dinner, I looked to see what the camera captured in the last few days."

"Where did you place the camera, Noah?" Hawk asked.

"Ah, right outside my window overlooking part of the park and, ah, I guess it was wide enough to capture a shot of the neighbor's house."

"Okay, very good. So, what was on the camera."

"The morning that the neighbor died, the video showed someone in a black hoodie run in from the park into the garage, then back into the park."

"You still have the video?"

"Yeah, It's on my phone." He found it and send it to Hawk. Hawk studied it, zoomed in on the profile of the face. Even with the hoodie and dark glasses, he immediately recognized who it was. Upon further scrutiny, he noticed that the killer looked back suddenly, the face a little more visible, and on the far side of video frame, he thought he recognized Nellie standing on the sidewalk, gazing at the killer.

"Wow, Noah. You're a hero in my book. I think you helped solve the case."

"I did? Cool. See mom, that camera came in handy. Can I go now?"

"Sure. Thanks so much for your help." Hawk finished his coffee, chatted a little with the mother, wrote down her name and address and headed back to the station. He was elated. That was exactly who he was coming around to suspecting.

295

CHAPTER THIRTY-SIX

ORLINSKI STOPPED Hawk as he strode into the unit. With a dry smile, he handed Hawk a report that he prepared and said, "Nellie Pyle had deposited ten-thousand dollars on the day after Amanda's murder, and another ten thousand the next day. At the same timeframe, the same equal amount of money was withdrawn from the account that I marked in red. Based on that, I think I know who Pyle's killer is."

"Just as I thought," Hawk said. "Good work. Thank's."

"Did you expect it?" Hawk nodded in the affirmative. Orlinski continued, "I would've never guessed. Anyway, MacGregor wants us all in her office for an extensive update as soon as Nora comes back. I think she went to the ladies' room. She was pretty happy after she got a report from Chet at the crime lab. She let out a whoop and holler and as she left, she said, "We now know who the killer is."

"So do I. I think the brass will be happy with our work."

Nora came back, happy as a cat that swallowed the canary. "Clint, we got the killer."

"I also know who it is. It'll confirm what you got?"

"How do you know what I got?"

"Oh, I know who it is."

"Clint, you're full of it again," Nora said, laughing.

As they stood next to Orlinski's desk, Mortimer walked in, again wearing the suit from the 1980's. After Marcie's interrogation, he arranged for a couple hours off to see a dentist and had not had a chance to discuss the case further with the other detectives. "Good morning, everyone. You both look happy with yourselves," Mortimer said, addressing Hawk and Nora.

"Oh, we are, Mortimer," Nora said. "We'll have to fill you in."

But before they were able to tell Mortimer about the evidence they received and who had done it, Lieutenant Perez came out of his office, "Come on, people, let's go. Captain's waiting for us and we better have something good. She needs to give the mayor an update."

MacGregor sat behind her desk drumming her fingers on it. She appeared annoyed. "Is everyone here, finally? Ling and Salazar are missing." She looked at Perez. "Where are they, didn't they get my memo of the meeting?"

"Captain, they were out all morning on a Dreamyland Motel death and didn't get the memo. But if we're to discuss the Ellis and the Pyle murders, Hawk, Ricci and Holliday are the ones that would know best what's going on."

MacGregor's scowl turned into a faint smile. "Okay then, what do you have?" She looked directly at Nora and why are you smiling like that? Don't tell me you know who the murderer is."

Nora said, "Yes, I think so. I reviewed the report from the crime lab. We have a fifty percent fingerprint match to one of our suspects in the Ellis murder. We also have a DNA match to the gum found at the Pyle scene."

"Okay, is that enough to convict? Pretty weak if you ask me. A good defense lawyer would say that a fifty percent means that someone else has fifty percent as well. And the gum, the lawyer will argue that someone walking by just dropped it."

"But, Captain, why would our suspect be walking down the alley behind Pyle's house unless he was there to kill her? And who else other than one of the suspects on our list would have that high of a percentage on the murder weapon, the syringe? The lab also confirmed through DNA that those syringes were used to kill Amanda Ellis."

"Good points," MacGregor said. "Just testing you. Okay, then, who is it?"

Before Nora could answer, Mortimer spoke out, hoping to steal the thunder out of Nora as he was so certain that he was right. Becoming increasingly envious of the work that Hawk and Ricci were doing, mostly conveniently without him, he decided to follow Josephine's advice and become more assertive. "I think, for the record, that I believe, after meditating on the subject, that there was a conspiracy to kill Amanda Ellis. That the husband, in cahoots with his lover, Marcie Turner, did it. Who else, but Steven Ellis had a better motive? Marcie said in her interrogation that once Amanda was no longer in the picture, that they'd get married. I'm seldom wrong. And my fiancé, Josephine, after I explained everyone's motive, also came to the same conclusion." Surprise filled the room. His reference to Josephine agreeing with him almost brought out a burst of laughter, although Perez couldn't help but have a snicker escape. *Boy, that Josephine, she just knows everything,* Nora thought, barely holding her laugh.

MacGregor chuckled. "Detective, there is no record here. But I'm curious why did you come to that conclusion?"

"Simple. As I said, the husband had the strongest motive to kill his wife. He had all these affairs and had to get rid of his wife, but didn't want to divorce her. At first, I thought that he plotted together with Tina Dionisio, but after listening to Marcie Turner this morning I firmly believe that it was she that he conspired with. I think that she is a very good liar and can pull the wool over anyone's eyes." Mortimer then started to sneeze, but avoided eye contact with Hawk.

Nora said, "Mortimer, you at first thought it was Roger Benton. Why did you change your mind?"

"I know. Those are the first vibes that I had. But upon further consideration, I don't believe he had…" Mortimer sneezed again and pulled out a well-used handkerchief from his pocket to wipe his nose, the same one that Nora was sure he used the day before. "Roger didn't have a strong enough motive to kill Amanda Ellis. You really believe he'd kill someone so not to be embarrassed by touching someone's rear? I, nor Josephine, buy it."

MacGregor's annoyed expression returned. In a raised tone to her voice, she asked, "Detective Holliday, are you making light of sexual harassment?"

Holliday began to sneeze again. "Ah, oh, not at all. We just thought it wasn't grave enough motive to kill someone."

MacGregor shook her head and blew out a breath. "Say anything like that again, and I'm sending you to sensitivity classes. Do you understand?"

"Sorry, Captain. I see…" Mortimer sneezed again. "I see that I was wrong about making that comment."

"Okay, Nora hold off on who is the murderer and I want to hear from you, Detective Hawk who you think did it and why?"

Hawk was pleased to surprise everyone with the great find he had earlier. But first he needed to dig into Mortimer somewhat. It really bothered him that Marcie was painted as a murderer, a conspirator, or a liar. He turned toward Holliday and said, "Well, Mortimer, you're flat-out wrong about everything." He looked at MacGregor, then Perez and said, "Roger Benton is the one, and we have a strong case against him."

"Yes," Nora said. "He's the one."

"What was that?" Mortimer said, followed by a coughing fit. After he finished, he said, why wasn't I told before now?"

Hawk said, "Didn't have a chance to tell you, Mortimer. All this information came in this morning while you were out."

Mortimer was about to answer when Macgregor said, "All right, detectives, I want to know what's your strong case against, to me, this unlikely suspect?"

Hawk looked at Nora and winked. She returned a sarcastic grin. She had no idea what he came up with but knew with Hawk's smug expression that it would be good.

Hawk said, "This morning I struck gold when I interviewed the neighboring fifteen-year-old kid. He just happened to install a video camera, with his own money, by the way, out of his third-floor bedroom window overlooking part of the park and part of the Ellis house. The camera just happened to catch a fairly decent view of Roger Benton going into the Ellis's garage and coming out of the garage, throwing the syringes into the opening of the cinderblock wall." Hawk saw his superiors raise their eyebrows, Nora whispered a "wow" and heard a faint whistle from Orlinski.

"Interestingly, it also showed Nellie Pyle in one of the frames gazing straight at Benton as he exited the garage. Orlinski gave me a report this morning that showed Nellie depositing substantial money into her account the next two days after Amanda's murder. And an equal amount was taken out from Benton's bank account on the same days. To me, it's obvious that she was blackmailing him to keep her quiet. But that probably wasn't enough for her, so she hit up Benton for more money. That's probably when Benton decided to take care of her. After all, he killed Amanda, killing another person probably wouldn't be as difficult for him."

MacGregor said, "I'm impressed. Anything else?"

Hawk said, "Speaking of Pyle, we have information that the killer was a runner, and his get-away vehicle was an older black SUV with a broken taillight. I noticed such a vehicle in Benton's garage. Don't know if the taillight is out, but I bet you a dozen donuts that was the vehicle he used that night. And I noticed the numerous tennis trophies in Benton's office. You have to be fast and in shape to win those."

Nora's mouth remained open from Hawk's find. "You lucky devil," she said. "I always told you that you're just a lucky guy."

MacGregor had a big smile on her face, as did Perez. Perez said, "Good work, but Nora, you didn't explain what was the DNA match to the gum found outside Pyle's garage?

"Oh, yes, I forgot, the match was to the fibers of hair that Clint picked up from Benton's bathroom rug."

"Okay. Sounds good to me. Go pick the bastard up, all three of you."

"Shouldn't we have backup?" Mortimer asked.

Perez said, "I think the three of you can handle it, Mortimer."

Mortimer stood up, looked at the ceiling, took a deep breath and said, "Sorry people. I admit I was wrong. It happens to me occasionally, but Josephine will really be upset."

Except for Mortimer, they were laughing as they left the Captain in her office. Nora noted that she still had not seen him smile or laugh since she met him. As they walked out of the building and onto the lot to arrest Benton, Nora said, "I'll drive," she laughed as she wrapped her arm around Hawk's.

CHAPTER THIRTY-SEVEN

ROGER BENTON had a bad feeling in his gut after Hawk left the day before. He noticed the long glance by that nosy Detective at his old Dodge Durango that he kept around for years using it mostly for fishing and hauling bulky items around. He speculated whether the vehicle was seen when he drove off after killing Pyle since Hawk displayed a special interest in it. Also, the questions about his use of insulin made him nervous. He began to dwell on whether because of Hawk's interest and the way he phrased the question, that he suspected him of the murder of Amanda Ellis.

A nervous, suspicious man by nature, Benton decided that now was the time to flee Colorado, go somewhere far away. He had a secret bank account in the Cayman Islands where he stowed away his share of the income that Briggs and he received in cash from foreign sources. He would take as much as he could, then make arrangements at the bank to transfer the balance to a Swiss account that he would set up once he was there. He'd travel to France under forged documents that he would obtain in the Caymans, then take a train to Zurich, do the banking that he needed, then settle down on a chateau overlooking Lake Lucerne.

He did not have to worry about his wife and kids. The wife left him six months ago, rented a house in St. Paul, next to her parents, and already enrolled the children in school. His calls to her had gone unanswered anyway, so why should he worry about her any longer. But he would miss his children even though their mother had poisoned them against him. Perhaps when they are older, he would be able to reconnect.

Benton had not been able to sleep well since Amanda accused him of sexual harassment and threatened to expose the company for fraud. He worried that with the lack of sleep perhaps his mind was not as sharp as it should be, and he shouldn't be making rash decisions. But he knew that he needed to act now and escape since it was not just Briggs alone that participated in substituting inferior materials, so did he. He was as much responsible as the vice president and the chief architect in the crime.

He regretted having to kill Amanda, but at the time he convinced himself that he had no choice. The embarrassment of the publicity of sexual harassment, the loss of his career, the distinct possibility of going to jail for fraud were too much for him to handle. Then there was that blood-sucking Nellie Pyle who would have bled him dry and then in the end would have exposed him as the murderer if he couldn't pay anymore. She had to be silenced.

Jail, a trial, a penitentiary would not be an option. He would rather be dead than face any of that. He thought about taking his life. He came close to it by almost taking a double dose of insulin. It sounded like a solution to all his problems. But the thought of escape prevented him from that extra injection. So, after Hawk left, an hour of stewing over what he should do, he booked a flight to the Caymans through Miami. He withdrew most of the cash in his Denver bank accounts and made arrangements with his realtor friend, giving him a power of attorney, to sell the house, furniture and the Range Rover with it. He would take his Durango and abandon it at the airport. He spent that evening and the next morning packing up two large suitcases and a backpack, making sure to throw in a few photos of his estranged wife and children.

Now, three hours before his scheduled flight out of Denver International Airport, he looked out of the window to make sure the police unit assigned to protect him was gone. He loaded his luggage in the back of the Durango and backed out.

As they left the station to bring Benton in, Nora and Clint were in a joyful mood after solving the Ellis and Pyle cases. They sat in the front while Mortimer fidgeted in the back. It was obvious that he struggled to tell them something. He cleared his throat several times, would say "ah-er," then stop, then do it again. "Is something bothering you?" Nora asked. "What's wrong?"

"I don't know how to say it. I'm not much at apologizing. My father always used to tell us boys that that's a sign of weakness, but I feel that I need to say something to you both."

"Oh, what's that," Nora asked, her eyes shooting toward Hawk as she drove.

"It's just that…" Mortimer scratched the top of his head and grimaced. "Ah, I feel so stupid for what I said at that meeting with MacGregor. Not only that but when I said it. I was so sure that Ellis and Marcie did it and I thought that's what you two would also think, that I wanted to bring it out first as though I solved the cases." Hawk and Nora exchanged glances again, not expecting Mortimer to admit to anything.

"Once or twice, or maybe more, Josephine told me that I'm a fool. And I guess she's right. I shouldn't have left the Tampa Police Department. I seemed to do better there. And I don't know how much longer I'll be with you because it's obvious to me that MacGregor doesn't like me much. I'm sure my reviews by her and probably by Perez will be crap. Then what do I do with Josephine?"

Hawk turned toward him and said, "Listen, buddy, everything went fine. That's your job to come up with an analysis and you did. It made sense at the time. We're not up for review for months yet, so anything may happen. Don't fret over it."

"Oh, okay then I won't. But I'm sorry what I said about Marcie. I know how much you like her."

Nora turned her head briefly toward Hawk. "See, everyone knows about you and Marcie." Her voice was sharp.

Hawk laughed. There is absolutely nothing between Marcie and me. I like her, like I like a lot of people. She's going to marry someone she loves, and it doesn't bother me at all. I wish her the best of luck."

Nora felt a little better after hearing Hawk's words. She thought his tone was sincere and decided not to comment or joke about it.

As they rounded the corner, a block from Benton's house, they saw his Durango pull out of the driveway, enter the street, and proceed down the road. Nora followed him for couple of blocks until it appeared that he would turn on University Boulevard, a busy street. She switched on her lights and did a sequence of short sirens for him to stop. Benton had finally noticed the police car behind him. In a panic, he gunned the engine, went a block until he realized that he had no place to run. He slammed on the brakes, grabbed a .357 S&W Magnum revolver from underneath the seat and flew out of the vehicle shooting at the detectives' vehicle. Nora pounced on the brakes as well and all three slid down closer to the floor as a barrage of slugs rocketed through the windshield, some striking the radiator and engine block. When the shooting stopped, three heads popped up, two from underneath the dash and one from the back seat as he saw Roger Benton with the gun pointing toward them slowly approaching their vehicle, walking in the middle of the street.

"What's he doing?" Nora said, her voice high-pitched as she was breathing hard and fast.

Hawk said. "Suicide by cop. That's what he wants. Don't shoot."

"Hell with that," Mortimer said. "If we don't bring him down now, he'll shoot one or all of us. I'm going after him." He opened the rear passenger door, shut it, and crept around the car to the right fender. He pointed his pistol at Benton, his index finger curled around the trigger.

Hawk jumped out and shouted, "Don't shoot, Mortimer. He wants you to kill him."

"That's why I'll get him before he gets us."

Hawk shouted again, "Hold off Mortimer. He's out of bullets. I counted six shots from his revolver." Both Nora and Hawk joined Mortimer in a position behind the police SUV. All three had their weapons aimed at Benson when he shouted out, "What are you waiting for. Shoot me. That's what I deserve. Shoot me, you bastards!" He waved his gun at them and pulled the trigger. The hammer activated, but there were no bullets. He threw his weapon at them and ran like a wild man toward them, but Nora ran out to meet him and with a quick kick to his chest, he fell back and hit his head hard against the asphalt. He lay on the ground, his eyes squinted and mumbled, "Why didn't you shoot me? I can't go to jail. I just can't."

"Sorry, Roger," Nora said, "but that's where you belong, taking the life away from two women."

Benson began to sob. "I'm so sorry." Then in a rapid, unpredictable move, he pulled out a syringe from his pocket, threw off the cap and stabbed himself in the muscle of his arm before anyone could stop him. Screaming from the pain, he eventually passed out.

He was dead by the time the ambulance arrived.

EPILOGUE

ONCE AGAIN Hawk asked Nora to dine with him that evening. This time she was more than ready after the long, traumatic day. Still shaken up by bullets flying over her head and a shower of fragments of glass raining down, her mood was not festive. Although, she thanked God that once again they escaped a near death, an occurrence that lately had happened just too often. She loved her job, but a sense of sadness billowed over her that the career of her choice put her and the person she loved, Clint, in such peril. She hoped that her parents and grandparents in Pueblo never heard.

That evening, Nora needed to be with Hawk and dinner sounded terrific. She needed to vent her frustrations to someone, knowing that he would understand and had a knack of making things look not quite so bleak. She would love to be with him every second of the day, but she couldn't figure out his true intentions of whether he wanted a marriage and a family; nevertheless, unless he expressed that he loved her, she'll still try to keep a distance between them socially, at least for a while, to protect herself and hopefully for him to realize that he couldn't live without her. It was a gamble, she knew, but one that in her mind she had to take.

Nora appreciated that Hawk was more upbeat, reminding her that this was an unusual case and chances of it happening again in their careers would be very slim. Those words comforted her and gradually, especially after sipping on a rum and coke, her charming, sparkling personality floated up from the depths of the blues. Fully visible was her merriment as she laughed, joked and giggled as they dined over shrimp and jumbo crabs at the Pappadeaux Seafood Kitchen in Greenwood Village.

After dinner Hawk reminded her of the massage for his sore back that she promised. She laughed, "Okay, but are you sure you can handle it? I'm pretty rough."

"Ooo, the rougher, the better. Kinky!"

"Don't get your hopes up, buddy. All you're going to get is a massage."

The next morning, Nora prepared a delicious breakfast of French toast, Italian sausage patties and an assortment of fruit that Hawk and she enjoyed over a steaming cup of French roast coffee. "You know, Nora, it feels so good and right to be here with you." Nora smiled but thought, *don't get used to it, Clint, you have to say you love me first and mean it before we do this again.* As she cleared the dishes off the table, she leaned down and kissed him.

They were the last to enter the Homicide unit. Word of the shooting by Benton and his taking his own life spread throughout the Division and most likely throughout the Police Department. Orlinski shook his head as they passed by his desk, "There you two go again, attracting bullets your way. Anyway, I'm glad you're safe. We'd miss you at least for a few moments around here if you got killed." He laughed as though he said something very clever.

Hawk chuckled, "You're just full of crap, Orlinski. You wouldn't miss us for a second."

They laughed, then Orlinski glanced at Mortimer with a scheming smile, "Yeah, Mortimer told me that he almost died. His Josephine wasn't too happy about it and told him not to do it again. Isn't that what you said, Mortimer?" He laughed again, Nora and Clint smiled.

Mortimer stood and said in an aggravated voice, "Is that a joke? I really don't get it. Of course, my fiancé is concerned for me. When she heard how dangerous it was and that I survived she was so happy that she even kissed me on the forehead and to celebrate she took out a really delicious apple cake from IKEA from the freezer that she saved for a special occasion. I think you people are making fun of me."

Nora said, "No Mortimer, we're not making fun of you, but trying to lighten up what we went through yesterday. We all love you, but we all joke around here. It makes our job easier."

Mortimer sat back down but seemed upset when they made it to their desks to start on the numerous reports that they had to type up and present to Perez. After an hour, Hawk left for the restroom, but left his phone on his desk. Nora heard a text being sent. Being curious, she rolled over to his desk and her heart dropped as she read the message from Marcie, "*Hello Clint, I'm not going to marry Ellis. I can't trust a man that has a roving eye. I'm going back to California. You have my number. I still beg you to reconsider and come with me. Call when you can, Marcie.*"

Nora quickly rolled her chair back before Hawk returned. She shoved the keyboard away from her, placed her elbows on the table, her hands cupping her head. *Marcie is still trying to take Clint away from me. What am I to do? I guess it's all up to him, but it's hard to live this way.*

Hawk returned and saw Nora leaning over her desk. "Tired?"

"Yeah, I guess so. You kept me awake most of the night." She tried to make a joke of it but could not muster a smile.

Noticing that he missed a message, Hawk sat down, grabbed his phone, and read it. Nora watched carefully for his reaction. She could not immediately tell what his thoughts were as he sat seemingly indifferent. Finally, she felt a little relief that he pursed his lips and shook his head back and forth, then swiped his right hand in the air. She took it as though he has done with Marcie, at least she hoped.

Perez walked to them. "Forget the reports for now. I want both of you to go investigate a death in the Country Club area. By the way, the captain sends her congratulations on a job well done on the Ellis and Pyle murders."

THE COUNTRY CLUB MURDER

The author invites you to take a SNEAK PEAK of part of the first chapter of the second book of the Clint Hawk and Nora Ricci murder mystery series:

CHAPTER 1

Present day, Denver, Colorado.

THE BUTLER, Jarvis Benson, was busy setting up the massive dining table for an unusual event that his employer, William Hollister, had planned. Told not to make the affair formal, he used everyday china, tableware, and glasses. He was further instructed not to serve alcohol, only tap water. Consuela Rivera, the housekeeper and cook brought in an elongated flower centerpiece made of white daisies and pink carnations. It was a casual arrangement and not the usual elaborate bouquet that she usually arranged for a dinner party. Hollister told her not to prepare appetizers or salads and only serve a pot roast with potatoes and carrots. For dessert, the guests would only receive green Jell-O.

Both Benson and Consuela knew that the dinner was of great importance to their boss. Being privy to the purpose of the dinner, because of their close relationship with Mr. Hollister, they gossiped between themselves how unpleasant the evening would be and braced themselves for terribly angry outbursts from the guests. After twenty years for Benson and thirteen for Consuela, they knew their employer well and sympathized with his plight. He treated them well with deserved respect, and they reciprocated. The employees knew their places and acted accordingly. They also knew who the expected guests were and how difficult and bitter the dinner would be for their employer.

The scheduled time for arrival was 7:00 p.m. and Mr. Hollister gave Benson specific instructions on what to do with the guests once they arrived. The first invitees came about ten minutes early.

It was the eldest son, George, and his wife, Rhonda. "Hello, Benson, you're still looking good," George said. "How long has it been since last we saw you? Must have been at least a few months ago. Oh yeah, we saw you when you came by and delivered a gift from the old man."

"I believe that's right, sir. Would you please take a seat in the parlor?"

"What's this all about?" Rhonda asked, her face stern. "Coming here tonight is certainly very inconvenient. We had to drive all the way from Cherry Hills Village in this horrible traffic."

"Sorry madam. But it was important that you come."

The chimes of the doorbell rang out and the second eldest son, James, and his spouse, Kay, arrived. They gave warm and friendly smiles to Benson. Kay gave him a quick hug and James asked, "How's Dad feeling today? Is he okay?"

"Yes, sir, he's fine. Would you please join your brother and his wife?"

As the couple entered the sitting room, George and Rhonda stiffly nodded to them. Neither couple exchanged further words. Sitting opposite, both couples felt and acted uncomfortable. Finally, after a few minutes ticked by George gruffly blurted out, "So what's this dinner all about?"

"I don't have the foggiest," James uttered.

George stood up and approached Benson. "Now Benson, I demand to know why we're here?"

Benson shrugged, "Sorry sir, I'm not at liberty to say. You'll know in a few minutes."

At exactly 7:00 p.m., the eldest daughter, Cynthia Maxwell and her husband, Samuel arrived. "Why are we here exactly, Benson?

You said it was very important. I had to cancel my book club meeting over this, and we had to drive down here all the way from Vail. Is something wrong with father?"

"Mr. Hollister desired to see you all."

"Well, he could have made it more convenient for us. He's all right, isn't he?" Benson didn't say a word, just nodded.

"Benson, I asked you a direct question. Is my father all right?"

"You will soon find out."

At 7:07 p.m., the youngest son, Darren, arrived, bringing a woman with him. He appeared a little tipsy as he said, "Hello there, old man. I'd like you to meet my new girlfriend, Tina Dionisio. Isn't she hot?" He pulled her closer to him and planted a kiss on her cheek. "I think we need a drink. Get us a couple martinis, would you, Benson? I think Tina would like at least a couple of olives in it."

"Sorry, sir, but no drinks will be served tonight."

"Aah, you gotta be kiddin' old man. I thought this would be a party. Why are we here anyway? Tina and I had great plans until you called and insisted that we come. Of course, when you said that if we came, we'd get a great gift, then I'm all for it. What is it? I hope it's a yacht." He exploded into a hearty laugh. Still laughing, he placed his arm around Benson's shoulder. "Go get us some drinks."

"I have instructions against that, sir. Please join the others in the parlor."

"Aw, come on, Tina, this place sucks, as always." He had almost walked out of the door when George came up and grabbed him by the arm and pulled him into the parlor.

"We need to talk," George said. "Something is going on here. I've got a bad feeling about it. When's the last time you saw Dad? Did he say anything to you?"

"Listen, bro. I try to talk to him as little as possible. He's always on my back about something or other. He doesn't like my lifestyle. He thinks I drink too much, and chase too many women, but I just like to have fun. After all, what's life all about? He probably won't like Tina, here." As he said that, he leaned over his girlfriend and nuzzled her neck. Embarrassed by his action, she pushed him away.

Rhonda said, her voice raspy, "You clown, Darren. Get serious for once in your life. Something is going on here and I don't think it's going to be pleasant."

Darren laughed, "You get serious if you want. I vote to enjoy life." He looked at Tina and smiled. "I want to enjoy life with you." Tina blushed. She subconsciously glanced back at the front door. *This is awful. I want out of here. Why did I ever come along with him? He's obnoxious when he drinks.*

Benson waited until seven-fifteen for the youngest daughter, Ashley Hollister, to arrive. She still had not, but, nevertheless, he invited the guests to be seated at the dining table. After they took their seats, Benson notified William Hollister. The assembled sat in subdued conversation as they waited. After about five minutes, the old man shuffled in appearing grave, troubled, worn-out, grayer, and thinner than most of them remembered. He immediately noticed the empty chair. He also noticed a strange woman at the table. His children stood, tried to embrace him, but he briskly waved them away and told them to sit down. After they took their seats, at least a long minute passed before Cynthia spoke out sarcastically, "Well, hello to you as well. How long are we supposed to wait? We must get back home soon."

He glared at each of them. No one else said a word until finally, Darren broke the silence, "Dad, it's great to see you, but why are we here? What's this all about?" Then he laughed, "No wine, only water? Ha, you gotta be kidding."

William curtly answered, "Yes, only water. You had enough to drink." The severe answer left everyone silent, squirming and fidgeting on the Duncan Phyfe chairs. Suddenly the stillness was interrupted by the loud chimes of the doorbell. Ashley had finally arrived.

She came in laughing and as the baby of the family tried to act cutesy, "Hi Daddy, I'm so sorry for being late." Her hands flayed, theatrically. "I simply couldn't make up my mind what dress to wear. It was such a problem not knowing the occasion. Benson should've been more specific." Her smile faded abruptly after she noticed the somber crowd, her dark eyebrows raised as she asked, "What's wrong? Did someone die or something?"

"You're late. But then, I wouldn't have expected anything else from you." William's voice boomed. "Sit down!" He then gave Tina a pointed look and asked, "Darren, who is this woman?"

"Oh Dad, she's my good friend, Tina Dionisio. She's an investment banker and isn't she just gorgeous? I hope it's all right that I brought her. We both like to party, and I wanted her to see the house."

Sitting next to his father, George noticed William's lips quiver and his veined hands tremble. Placing a hand on his father's arm, he asked, "Why are you so riled up? You'll get a stroke. Just relax and tell us why we're here."

William pulled his arm away. He didn't answer George, instead, he turned to Benson and asked him to start serving supper. Now anxious, Ashley slipped into the chair at the end of the table looking to the others for an answer as to what was going on.

After Benson and Mrs. Rivera finished serving everyone, no one was in the mood to eat. The father barely touched his fork. He remained silent glaring at his children. The children were reluctant to talk and break the silence. All felt awkward.

After it appeared that they were through with their food, most of it uneaten, Benson brought out the green Jell-O topped with a dab of whipped cream. At that moment, William cleared his throat and began to speak, "After I say what I have to say, Benson will bring out envelopes for each of you, children, containing a gift of one-hundred-thousand dollars. Except for one of you, it is quite obvious that money is more important than love."

Objections from the group were immediate. Denials were swift. Breathing hard and heavy, Cynthia stood and screamed that they all loved their father. With tears in her eyes, Ashley cried out, "How can you say such an awful thing? We love you so much."

"Unfortunately," William continued, "Words are cheap. It's actions that count. And after all the years of watching you as adults, I know in my heart who genuinely loves me and who couldn't care less. I know most of you wouldn't have come unless you'd thought that you would get something out of it. That's why my invitation mentioned that there'd be a substantial gift. Even then, Benson had to text or call you to make sure you'd come. That's how uncertain we were."

"But Daddy," Ashley wailed. "I came over to see you a couple of days after Christmas. I brought you a tie, remember?"

"Yes, Ashley, I certainly remember. And it brought me great joy when you came. But you stayed only a few minutes, not asking how I was feeling or whether I was happy. Then, you begged me for money. I gave you a check and you grabbed it out of my hand, threw me one of your dramatic air kisses, said the perfunctory, 'Love you, Merry Christmas' and took off. Frankly, my little baby, you left me so saddened." Rivers of tears began flowing from Ashley. "Daddy, that's not fair."

"You all say you love me, but I've decided that for most of you, it's my money that you love. I admit that I would receive the obligatory call from you occasionally. But did we ever have a real conversation? No. Just, 'Hi Dad, how you doing? That's great. Have to run, call you later.' And those calls have become even more infrequent. Only one of you had invited me for Thanksgiving and Christmas. When is the last time that the rest of you invited me or came over and spent an evening with me? I can't remember when you'd just pop in to visit or invite me to a BBQ."

"William, it's not our fault," Rhonda protested. "We have busy lives wrapped up in our children. Don't be so doggone sensitive."

He stared hard at her, then at the rest. Taking a deep breath, he said, "I am extremely bitter. Very, very disappointed in you. I gave you everything you needed. I gave you security. And in that, I made a big mistake. And by your selfish actions, you plunged a dagger into my heart when I came to realize that I was just a money machine, an ATM, for you."

George began to object, but William demanded that everyone be quiet until he finished. "My hot-shot, social-society, children are too busy for their father. You can't understand how disappointed I am when I call and get a message that you're unavailable or too busy and will call me later. Later, most times, never came. I barely know my grandchildren. Now that they're grown, I never get a call from them because you never encouraged it."

Hollister paused as he took in some deep breaths, his voice shaky. "Only one couple here knows how precarious my health is right now. I asked them not to tell you as I wanted to tell you in person. Well, for your information, I have stage four prostate cancer. I'm fighting it, but the prognosis is very poor, and I don't know how much longer I'll live. The doctor says that maybe six months or maybe a little longer. But I don't want to give up."

"Oh Dad, you should've told me," Darren said. "I would've come right over."

Samuel Maxwell said, "That was awfully selfish of you to hold that information from us. You didn't give us a chance to support you."

Hollister looked hard at him. "Shouldn't you and my daughter have contacted me to inquire what I'm doing, how I'm feeling, and what my concerns are?" He looked around the table, "Except for one child, the rest of you didn't bother or think about me here all alone. No, too busy with your country clubs, parties, whatever, to bother to even think about me. If on rare occasions the bank failed to send the Trust check to you on time, then I certainly heard from you and sometimes the tone was such that I had better do something about it fast."

A loud murmur from the group elicited Hollister to shout, "Shut up! Let me continue. Cherish the money you'll receive today. Invest it wisely because except for one of you, it represents one-third of the money of the total that you'll receive after I die. Also, after sixty days, you will no longer receive your monthly trust payments."

"What! No, Dad, you can't do that! What's going to become of us!" Similar shouts were heard over and over. James had to restrain George whose fingers were balled into a fist from lunging at his father. Except for one child and his wife, all stood and yelled insults and swear words at their father, venom sprouting from angry eyes. Amid all the clamor he heard the voice of his eldest daughter, Cynthia, scream out that they will do whatever was necessary to stop him.

"Sit down and listen or no checks will be handed out tonight. Now sit! You need to know this so that you can make arrangements.

You're all adults and it's about time that you stand on your own two feet and not have me carry you around like babies." They sat, all breathing heavily. "Darren just yelled out that I couldn't cut you off the trust. Well, I can. I set it up years ago as a revocable trust. That means it can be changed or terminated at my will. It was always my intent that you each had enough money for your education and some help to get on your feet. That's been accomplished. Now you're on your own." The group listened carefully, their heads bowed waiting for more drastic news, or, so to speak, the other shoe to drop.

"So, next week, I'm going to meet with my attorney. As I said, trust payments will terminate in two months. As far as heirs to my estate, only one of you had been loyal and concerned about me, not just my money. That one family came by almost daily to see how I'm doing and asked what they could do to help. They even offered to take me to their home to live so that I wouldn't be alone without a family." Everyone looked around the table to see who that would be. They suspected James was the one.

"In gratitude, I'm giving that child the bulk of my estate. As I said, your share will be an additional two hundred thousand. Some of the money will go to the Cancer Society, and an amount each to my faithful servants, Benson, and Consuela. Except for that one child, you're a bunch of miserable spoiled people and I guess I must take blame for that because your mother and I spoiled you. Maybe she might have even poisoned you against me after our bitter divorce. But you all should have at least the decency to know that I exist and need your companionship, comfort, and support." Every mouth hung wide open, too stunned to say anything.

"Now, I've also decided to sell this house while the market is red hot in Denver. Houses are selling like hotcakes, and I already had made other arrangements. I want you now to go up to the rooms you grew up in and take out whatever you might want. A lot of your high school and college stuff is still there. Benson left an empty box in each room for you to use. In the meantime, I'm going to go to my downstairs office. I want no one to come around to moan, complain, plead, cry, threaten me, or anything else. The door will be locked so don't bother me." He continued to glare at them for a long minute. Tears filled his eyes. Shoving his chair back, he stood with effort and shuffled out of the room. Benson informed everyone that they can go upstairs now. Tina was reluctant to go, but Darren insisted, and they followed the others upstairs.

ABOUT THE AUTHOR

Victor Moss has been an attorney engaged in private practice of law since 1974 in both Pueblo and Denver, Colorado. Prior to that time, he had been an assistant attorney general for the State of New Mexico and assistant city attorney for Pueblo, Colorado. His prior books are Beware the Wolves: A Soviet WWII Love Story, No Return Home, The Soul Named Samantha, and Coffee House Murders. He lives with his wife in Highlands Ranch, Colorado.